Forgotten Storm

Storm Series, Volume 1

A.R. Vagnetti

Published by Wicked Storm Publishing, 2020.

This is a work of fiction. Similarities to real people, places, or events are entirely coincidental.

FORGOTTEN STORM

First edition. November 19, 2020.

Copyright © 2020 A.R. Vagnetti.

Written by A.R. Vagnetti.

Also by A.R. Vagnetti

Storm Series
Forgotten Storm

Watch for more at https://www.arvagnetti.com.

This book is dedicated to Jason Mamoa. Thank you for being my inspiration for Logan and the numerous titillating scenes your masculine beauty evoked.

Chapter 1

Nicole

Pain sparks through my cheekbone like a firecracker as my opponent's gloved fist connects with my jaw. A murmur ripples through the crowd sitting in the seats surrounding the sparring mat. How long has the match lasted? Two seconds, two minutes? My heart thunders in my ears. Sweat drenches my body, and it's an effort to keep my bruised arms up and moving. Hell, every muscle and joint are on fire. If I don't finish this in the next few seconds, he will end me. I've fought too hard over the last three years to let this jerk snatch the title within my grasp.

Nathan charges, attempting to wrap me up in a hold. I spin and punch left, missing his nose by a hair. Duck his roundhouse kick. Punch right, connecting with his temple. I barely evade his huge glove aimed for my jaw and throw my weight into a quick, solid left jab to his midsection. He grunts and folds forward.

With the last bit of oomph, I grab his arm and leap into the air, wrap my legs around his head, and drive my body forward. My weight forces him backward. I drive a solid right punch into the side of his temple as we fall. A sharp burst radiates through my fist and down my wrist, but I don't register the pain, only relief, as he hits the mat with a satisfying smack; my feet land on either side of his head.

Game, set, match, motherfucker.

I plant my knee in the middle of his chest. Sweat drips off my chin onto the bare, glistening chest of my opponent. Perspiration saturates my black spandex shorts and tank top. Long wispy strands of hair escape my ponytail, and ruffle with each heavy pant of breath as I scrutinize every twitch of meathead's bulging muscles.

Agony creases his brow, but it's the rage in his hazel eyes that stirs the aggressive nature I strive to control daily. He wants violence. I can oblige. I no longer care about the pain. I want blood as badly as he does.

I breathe in and force the bloodlust into a deep, dark hole and do what's expected, what I'm trained to do: ease back and observe my opponent.

When a full minute passes and he makes no counter move, the head krav maga instructor, Kurtis, strides onto the mat.

Every muscle prickles with aches and pains as I step back to my corner and await the verdict. Deep inhale in through my swollen nose, out through my busted lip. I transfer my weight on the balls of my feet and shake out my burning arms and shoulders. The enormous sparring room overflows with soft, matted flooring. But when your ass hits those mats, they are anything but soft.

A hush settles over the crowd as Kurtis kneels next to my opponent, Nathan Connor. He speaks to him in a quiet whisper. I can't hear what's being said, only the low, sexy rumble of his voice. I don't need to hear the words. I've been the one with my back on the mat more times than I care to admit over the last three years, so I know exactly what he's asking.

"Are you all right? Do you require a doctor? Can you get up? Blah blah blah," babbles through your ears. You just nod and pray the torture's ended.

By the time Kurtis helps Nathan to his feet, my breathing is under control. Pain, my oldest and dearest playmate, has already begun a slow burn throughout my body, with my forearms and midsection taking the brunt. Nathan wasn't my only opponent today. I took down three others in various stages of combat. This ache will intensify in the next couple of hours if I don't soak in an ice bath, ay-sap.

The watching crowd offers polite applause as the men walk to the center of the mat. Kurtis's lips twitch, trying not to smile, but the proud twinkle in his vibrant blue eyes gives him away. Nathan, on the other hand, is holding his midriff with one arm, his red face twisted with resentment.

Aww, poor baby had his ass handed to him by a girl.

When Kurtis motions for me to join them, I offer Nathan a quick wink. He's an arrogant, egotistical jerk, hitting on anything with a pair of breasts. With this defeat, I've checked off a box on my bucket list of things that bring me joy.

With a deep inhale, I take my place next to Kurtis. His size never ceases to amaze me. At six-foot-eight and two hundred eighty pounds of pure muscle, he makes my respectable five-foot-six look like a munchkin from lollypop land. The top of my head doesn't even reach his broad shoulders.

Kurtis reminds me of Thor in the Marvel movies, except taller, with a more serious disposition. He has the same short blond hair, piercing blue eyes, and a sexy smile with lush, full lips surrounded by a perfectly trimmed scruff. If my tastes didn't run toward the dark-haired, green-eyed variety, I'd consider dipping my toes into those waters.

During training, Kurtis strives for professionalism, but a spark exists between us. It's in the way he stares into my eyes longer than necessary, the low gruff tone he uses when he's pinned me to the mat, or how his focus wanders to my lips like they're candy.

Okay, it's not all one sided. Kurtis's strength, size, and looks make my girly-bits tingle. If I were any other woman, I'd explore this attraction with him, 'cause damn. But his friendship means more. Yet, I will admit, his interest makes me purr.

What I require from Kurtis involves the unique way he drives my body and mind to the brink of my limits. Correction... I need it. Crave it. The pain and exhaustion center me, giving me a minor reset or reboot. Without it... A tremble of unease shifts within me. Down that path lies guilt and shame. Best to keep those things buried.

If I'm honest, I must admit that every guy I've found compelling gets compared to the man in my dreams. Logan. My delicious fantasy man. The one with the most beautiful green eyes, magic fingers, and talented tongue. No living, breathing dude could measure up. Logan's an illusion, and every *sane* woman knows that fiction always trumps reality. But there's something fucked up about my obsession with him, and the fact the only way I can get off lives in my dreams.

But the dreams stopped two years ago, and so did my outlet for my aggressive nature—also mind-boggling orgasms. The apprehension and fear clawing at my insides over Logan's absence irritates the shit out of me.

The longer he's MIA, the more my illicit needs take control. What I lovingly refer to as *the itch* builds until fire ants start having a party on my skin. It requires a road trip to a specific club where membership involves a background check and a clean bill of health. The few friends I allow close to me don't know about the itch or the depths I sink to manage it. And they never will. It's not something I'm proud of. In fact, I'm ashamed I even require it.

In my day-to-day life, I demand complete control. Like most people, I'm under the delusion I live my life on my terms. Nobody tells me what I can or cannot do. Well, except Kurtis during training, and this one fucked up need I can't let go. Like a junkie, I tell myself it's the last time. It's never the case. I surrender myself to another person. Someone who provides what my soul cries out for; pain, not sex, just pain.

It calms the itch, which keeps me... sane. But the longer Logan is absent, the further my mind and body break down, and aggression surges forward unrestrained. Agony flares through every joint and sinew. The ever-present fear I'll hurt someone bubbles below the surface, producing nightmares to torment my sleep.

But after a club session, everything eases. I'm... better. Focused. Calm. The unrelenting itch subsides, and my body tingles and resonates with awakening. Aggression recedes, and the painful, physical episodes decrease. I move on to another day, another week.

So, sue me. What's a girl to do?

"Excellent match. Nicki, you have passed your brown belt final exam with flying colors. Congratulations." Kurtis raises my gloved hand in victory.

God bless him for not jerking my arm up, but son of a bitch, the pain that radiates through my shoulder makes me want to scream. I keep my expression passive—I hope.

The room erupts in applause, hollers, and whistles from men and women from my class, all the different levels of programs, and even newcomers here to learn more about krav maga.

Out of the corner of my eye, I notice Nathan stomp off the mats toward the lockers. I dismiss him and smile. I did it. After three long years of definite blood and sweat, I am a now a brown belt in krav maga.

And a total fucking badass.

Kurtis releases me and raises a large palm to quiet the room. "Not only has she mastered all stages of hand-to-hand combat required for this certification, Nicki Graves excelled at all weapons training, earning the highest marksmanship scores of any student in the history of this dojo."

I press my lips together, embarrassed by the praise, but pleasure floods through me, nonetheless.

"We are proud of all that Nicki's accomplished since joining Red Dawn. We hope... I hope, she will proceed on to the black belt levels, as I desire a worthy opponent to continue to hone my skills," he concludes with a sexy, lopsided smirk.

His smile obtains the desired effect amongst the women who eye him like a T-bone steak: they cheer. Yep, he'll have them signing up to get the shit knocked out of them in no time.

Chapter 2

After Kurtis removes my gloves, I receive many pats on the back and congrats before the group disperses. Kurtis leans close and murmurs in a low voice, "I'm proud of you, Nicki. You defeated your opponent with a calculated swiftness. Impressive."

Kurtis's husky voice washes over me, and I'm reminded of another deep sexy voice. Fuck. Why do I miss him so much? I clench my fists and bite down on the inside of my lip until I taste blood. Predictable as ever, the pain centers me. A deep inhale and I force my fingers to relax. My visceral response to the mere thought of my erotic dream man surprises me every time.

Are my dreams of Logan preventing me from being more attracted to Kurtis? I've asked myself that a thousand times. I could be missing out on a real relationship because I can't let go of a fantasy man.

"Thinking of moving on to the black belt training?" Kurtis asks.

"Yes, of course." I place a palm on his warm, bulging bicep. "But I need some time off before I continue." With a tired smile, I peer into the pretty blue depths.

"Agreed." His eyes zero in on my abused mouth. "Give your body time to recover, then we'll get back at it." Kurtis watches me, his tenor low and seductive as he continues, "But don't wait too long."

His need stretches into the space between us so swiftly it startles me. The muscles under my hand twitch and I pull away. To cover, I do a quick analysis of my nails. Nibble on one. Do a visual inspection of the mats. Adjust my sports bra.

Kurtis laughs. "Are you singing, or working tonight at the LeLoo?"

He studies me, his blue gaze shimmering underneath his impossibly long lashes. His large warm hand lands on my shoulder and desire blasts into my bones causing a tremor in my gut. Fuck. I hate how a mere touch intensifies a person's emotions. Unlike my ability to control my need for violence, this damn talent has only worsened over the years. Another added benefit to my sessions at the club—it lessens the severity of my strange abilities.

This emotion-sensing thing does aid me in reading my opponents during training, which could be construed as cheating. But come on, it's not my fault they're instinctually-challenged.

With nonchalance, I retreat a step from Kurtis. My gaze focuses in on his chin. "I'm singing tonight. You planning on coming by?"

My heart picks up speed. The LeLoo Blues Bar allows me to perform one of the other passions in my life, singing. Singing keeps me... real. It's an outlet for the turmoil buried within me. And bonus, I get paid for it. Having Kurtis there would make my night. He stares for a long moment, and I envision him sitting in the audience, then walking me to my truck after the set. He's a big man, but Riddick's back seat is spacious. We could make it work.

I shake off the notion. Passion has never been my strong suit. Sex is just sex with no strings. No way I'll embroil Kurtis in my issues. Besides, I'll likely tend bar afterwards. The club is often a bartender short. Between the singing and bartending, I make a decent living, so I can't complain.

Like most women, I have several passions: krav maga, boots, my Glock, a.k.a., Annie. And of course, the sustenance of life: coffee.

"Of course, I'll be there." Kurtis says.

His desire rolls into me in scalding waves and I grit my teeth even as my nipples pebble in response.

"Nicki, I..."

"Holy shitballs, girlfriend, you were amazing!" My best friend Alexandria slides in between us. She gives Kurtis a stern look over her shoulder before squeezing me in a crushing embrace.

Oooowww.

"You looked like you needed rescuing," she whispers in my ear.

Alexandria Svaldana: my best friend and roommate. With an inward smile, I recall the day, not long after I started, she came waltzing into the bar seeking a job.

She took one look at me and announced, "Girlfriend, you look like shit. Trust me when I say, you're in desperate need of someone like me in your life."

I'd raised an irritated eyebrow at her, frowning, taking in her wild red hair, humor-filled blue eyes and perfect makeup. On anyone else, the crazy mane would've looked like they'd stuck their finger in a light socket, but on her it was... sexy. She carried that just-fucked appearance to perfection.

"God, I love that face." she laughs. "But we will turn your frown upside down, sista. Trust me."

From that moment on, we were inseparable. She even wormed her way into becoming my roommate when I bought my house last year. But we are complete opposites. She oozes energy. Falls in love at the drop of a hat. Grew up in a loving family, with caring parents, an older brother who sizzles with intensity but dotes on her to a sickening degree, and a younger sister.

I can't even remember if I have a family, let alone one who might have spoiled me, and nobody would accuse me of being outgoing or boisterous. My dry, sick sense of humor I keep to myself, unless I've been drinking. I keep to my one personal rule: never fall in love. Love makes you weak.

"We have to party tonight, to celebrate." Her big smile bounces me to the present. At five feet, perhaps an inch, she's height challenged—her phrase, not mine—with a slim athletic body, and the cutest pointed ears. It's the one feature she hates with a passion. Good thing all her hair keeps them hidden.

"Like you need a reason to party." I snort as I extract myself from her painful grip on my shoulders. If there's one thing my roomy excels at, it's partying.

Alex bobs on the balls of her feet, clapping like a two-year-old. "True. But this is a real reason. Your elevation from warrior princess to warrior queen."

I stare, appalled. "Warrior princess? I've never been a damn *princess* of anything in my entire life." That I know of. "Warrior... yes. Princess... *no*."

I nod to Kurtis, then head for the locker room as images of girly girls in pink pom-pom dresses, wearing tiaras and gobs of makeup flashes through my mind. In the background, I hear Kurtis's taunting, sexy laugh.

UGH.

"Okay, okay, maybe princess wasn't the right word." Alex jogs to keep up with my long strides. "But you get what I mean. We must celebrate your brown belt victory. By the way," she continues, oblivious to the fact I'm trying to ignore her, "you were sooo damn impressive out there. I don't lean that direction, but you turned me on."

"Oh my God." I roll my eyes. Why am I still shocked by the things that spew out of Alex's mouth? The filter between her brain and lips is absent. And yippee, she's telling the truth because hey, no brain freeze.

"No. I'm singing tonight." With purposeful strides, I head straight for the big, stainless-steel tub of torture next to the lockers. I so wish I could slip into the sauna instead. Breathe in the heat and steam and relax. But it will have to wait. Cold first, then heat.

"After, then," she counters, hands on her hips.

Seriously?

"Tomorrow. Right now, I'm dragging this sore, aching body into an ice bath, a sauna, and a shower. I'm taking massive amounts of ibuprofen, doing my damn set at the bar, after which I will pass out in my bed."

"Buzzkill." She pouts. "Okay, okay. Tomorrow. No excuses. Just because you've achieved warrior queen status, doesn't mean I won't drag your ass out of the house to have fun." She wags one perfect, manicured finger back and forth in front of my face.

I inhale a slow breath and pray for patience. The adrenaline dissipates, replaced by so many aches and pains I want to curl into a ball on the cold floor.

"Fine. Now get your skinny ass out of here so I can torture myself in peace."

Oblivious to my irritation, Alex skips over, her short floral skirt swishes against her tan legs, and blue eyes sparkle with glee. She plants a triumphant kiss on my cheek. "I knew you'd see it my way." She whispers.

I snort. "Don't I always." When she steps back, her demeanor changes. Lids lower over blue eyes looking everywhere but at me.

"Don't wait up for me." My instincts tingle. "I, ah, met someone last night, and since you refuse to go out, I'm gonna get my freak on."

Lie.

Pain pierces my temples as shock numbs my brain. Why is she lying? Underneath Alex's fun-loving attitude lurks something dark and mysterious. Throughout our three-year friendship, I've sensed it on several occasions. Like now. In the forced smile, the effort to appear innocent. What is Alex hiding? And why lie?

I shake my head and don't pry. Though my instinct whispers I should, my body's screams to ease its suffering wins out. Besides, we all have secrets better left hidden. Hell, some of mine hide so well I can't remember them.

"Have fun in the bath, sista." Alex waves over her shoulder, then she hurries to the exit, her long red hair bouncing with every step.

She pauses at the doors and wiggles her eyebrows, her voice low and sultry. "Should I send in Master Kurtis to rub your aching muscles?" When I flip her the bird, she laughs, then makes a quick escape.

"Bitch." I mean it in the most affectionate way.

My worry for Alex disappears as I contemplate the shining torture device before me. After I twist the cold tap on full, I reach into the standing freezer next to it and pull out several bags of ice. It's time to start the process of inflicting more pain on my already battered and bruised body.

And not even bruised in a satisfying way.

Chapter 3

Logan
New Orleans

To live as a vampire in a human-dominated world where humans have no clue we exist, is challenge enough; add being King Dimitri's Guardian to the mix, and the demands get more complicated. Tonight is a prime example.

The last three hours, Sebastian and I have stood in the mayor's office, concealed by darkness, listening for anything that might inform us the mayor's allegiances to Dimitri changed. This is the third official we have monitored this evening.

Dimitri's clandestine integration with human politics sickens me. Every new alliance, whether through mind control or greed, takes him one step closer to his desire to control the fragile race.

'Tell me again, Logan, why we are here watching this idiot?' Sebastian telepaths.

His frustrated snort mirrors my mental sigh, but I say in an even voice, *'Feel free to leave and tell Dimitri why you disobeyed his command.'*

Bastian shoots me a sour look, but remains motionless, as I knew he would.

I do not blame him for his frustration, but a man does not ignore the orders of the most powerful vampire in existence. Dimitri Tobias Giordano, the last true ancient one, with his life spanning over a thousand years, is not a vampire to be trifled with.

My chest tightens. There was a time I loved and admired my King. We fought side by side in many wars, bled and pursued pleasure together. In those days, his leadership had been severe, but fair.

His causes just. But that changed two hundred years ago when Dimitri's one true mate died in childbirth. The infant passed not long after, and a furious, power-hungry evil seized Dimitri. Though I knew the child's death hadn't grieved Dimitri one wit.

Three hundred years prior, his first child had died under mysterious circumstances days before his coronation as king. The timing had been too convenient for my taste. Others, as well.

Now another heir exists: Nicole.

I rub at the chronic ache in my chest, recalling the Council of Unity meeting twelve years ago when our Oracle, Icarus, shocked us with the prophecy.

"IF THERE IS NO NEW business, might we adjourn?" Syn Grayflame, King of the Dark Fae requested. His silver eyes glowered at the leaders around the table with irritation. Large, pointy ears twitched between the strands of his long white hair.

King Grayflame. What an evil son of a bitch, one of three on this council I would not trust for a second. At six-foot-five, his height rivaled my own, but with a leaner build. His twelve-foot, blinding white wingspan set him apart from most species. When retracted, they laid along his back, and moved and undulated with him like a cape.

"I second the motion," announced Jilaya Oresha, the succubus queen. She leaned forward and her thick, red hair brushed her red-tipped fingersnails.

She was the second one I did not trust. Her divine beauty was both breathtaking and alluring, yet deadly. Her shapely body drew you in while the intense light blue of her eyes held you captive. She also boasted wings. Unlike Grayflame, however, hers retracted all the way into her body, by way of thin slots on her back. They were small and delicate with glistening obsidian feathers. But like her beauty, they too deceived. They were wings designed for fight only, not flight. Deadly blades hid along the edges, ready to pierce your heart in a blink.

Icarus stood. "I have an announcement."

His words froze Jilaya halfway out of her seat. Her startled gaze swung to the eerie blue depths of the High Priest Oracle. In fact, every supernatural being around the table, and lining the room, stared at Icarus with widened eyes.

"What have you seen, Priest?" the werewolf king demanded of the Oracle.

The whites of the creepy little priest's eyes vanished, and the more in-depth blue of his strange irises leaked out. Dark blue tribal tattoos encompassing his body pulsed with light, their radiant glow showed through the white fabric of his toga-like robe. The air sparked with electricity, and I winced as pain rippled along my skin at his display of power.

"It is two-fold, my Lord," he answered in a monotone voice.

Every king, queen, and bodyguard in the room stared transfixed at Icarus. A few with curiosity, others with trepidation.

"My vision revealed an ancient prophecy, which has already begun." Icarus proclaimed.

At the collective gasps around the table, he reached into his robe and pulled out a yellowed, ancient-looking scroll the size of a rolling pin. Every gaze zeroed in on it, eyeing the thing like it's a snake about to strike. With slow, careful movements, he unrolled the scroll.

"Please read the prophecy out loud, Icarus," Cipher, the shapeshifter king, instructed.

He was the deadliest-looking royal at the table. With tanned skin and a tall, muscular build, his black-as-night hair fell to his collarbone in long, tight waves. A thin, black goatee and intense blue eyes gave him the look of evil incarnate. But in this case, looks were deceiving. Cipher ruled with fairness and honesty, and his people loved and respected him.

Without looking at the scroll, Icarus quoted the prophecy in a soft, ethereal voice. His glowing blue eyes moved and swirled like a turbulent ocean.

"9 August The Year of Our Lord 1482. During the reign of King Dimitri Tobias Giordano, a female Halfling will be born of his seed. Half human—half vampire. The first and last to ever exist."

I tensed. An heir? Is it possible? I snapped my gaze to Dimitri. His face was etched with shock. My heart ached. *Oh, my King, what means will you use to try to murder this child as you did your firstborn?*

Dimitri's widened eyes never left Icarus as the Oracle continued.

"During transition, the halfling will require blood. But only the blood of her one true mate will save her. After her transition, she will gain King Dimitri's powers while maintaining her human capabilities: immunity to the sun's deadly rays, the ability to eat and digest regular food.

As the first vampire queen, she, her one true mate, and The Council of Unity will destroy those who oppose peace.

She will bring unity to the other species and give birth to the first vampire king with the ability to walk in the sunlight, thus ending the vampire curse of eternal darkness.

Should the halfling become with child before her transition into immortality, her change will not occur, and she will live an average human lifespan, ensuring King Giordano's reign for another three hundred years.

"Under his rule, war will continue among the Others."

I glimpsed the tightening of Dimitri's fist at his side.

"The Council of Unity will cease to exist," Icarus continues. *"King Dimitri will lead the vampire race into open conflict with the humans. A catastrophic, hundred-year war will begin. Hundreds of thousands of*

humans and Others will perish, some species to the point of extinction. Devastation will ravage the planet.

Beware. The halfling's life essence is linked to King Dimitri. If one dies, the other dies."

Icarus stopped and focused his gaze on the members of the council. The blue receded back to normal, and the pulse of his tattoos diminished. He resumed his seat and placed the scroll in front of him as he awaited the council's response.

There was complete and utter silence.

This child ... this Halfling, will mean the end of Dimitri's nine-hundred-year reign. That was a cause worth fighting for. Whatever the cost.

"You declared your vision two-fold," King Scott reminded us, looking a little shell-shocked himself. "What's the second part, Icarus?"

"The child has already been born, my Lord."

"What?" Dimitri leapt to his feet. His floor-length black robe billowed out around him. The ice-blue of his eyes darkened, foreshadowing a coming rage. The occupants around the table tensed, and the security detail lining the wall reached for their weapons but held steady.

"When?"

"Thirteen years ago," Icarus answered with his usual calm serenity even though everyone else stilled.

"Thirteen years?" Dimitri's eyes narrowed on the priest. "Are you certain?"

"Yes, my Lord."

The leaders erupted in chaos, but I ignored everyone but my King. Dimitri's demeaner changed. It was subtle, and if you did not know him, you would not even have noticed the slight darkening of his eyes, or the subtle lift his lips.

He already knew who the child is. I would have bet my life on it.

Dimitri slammed his fist onto the table. His long braid swung out in a wide arc. The blonde highlights danced under the bright lights as it whipped over his shoulder before settling against his chest. His seven-foot frame towered over the rulers around the table. "Enough." He bellowed. "She is a female with no right to the throne. Per law, only a male heir can take my seat. Vampires will never align with a female, let alone one that is half human. And since I have a fondness for my own life, I demand we find her and keep her protected. I have many enemies."

"Dimitri," King Scott snapped. "Do not pretend an interest in any heir of yours, male or female. Don't insult our intelligence by pretending you wouldn't take every precaution to ensure she never reaches her transition."

A prime example of why King Scott and I remained friends. The wolf exuded intelligence, boldness, and a fearless disposition.

"Be careful, Scott," Dimitri warned in a low whisper. His eyes darkened further, and his blackened claws extended.

"Put your claws away, Dimitri," King Scott responded. "I have an idea to ensure her safety. Per protocol and law, the council will vote."

My breath froze in my lungs as my King's gaze narrowed.

Surprisingly, he offered a slow nod and resumed his seat. Long slim fingers caressed his braid. "By all means, Scott. I cannot wait to hear it."

The werewolf put forth a proposal that King Cipher, Queen Arra, and he would put together a protection detail of their choosing to watch over the child and keep her, not only safe, but hidden until her transition.

The fate of the world rested on a vote from these seven powerful beings. But no matter the outcome, I would do everything in my power to find this child and keep her away from Dimitri's deadly clutches until her transition.

After that fateful council meeting, the king and I traced back to the castle. He ordered not to be disturbed and locked himself away in his private office.

The second the door slammed, Icarus materialized next to me. His blue eyes swirled with a vision.

"I suspect the king knows who this child is, Icarus."

"Indeed."

"Can you help me find her?"

"Yes. She is safe from Dimitri for now. The prophecy prevents him from killing her."

Icarus gave me the coordinates to a small redbrick home in the burbs of Louisville, Kentucky. The second my gaze fell on the beautiful young girl sound asleep; I fell to my knees. She was my one true mate. Our bond seared my heart like a hot branding iron and linked my soul to hers in an instant. No force in this universe would stop me from protecting this child. I would lie, cheat, kill, and sacrifice my own life to ensure her safety.

A VAMPIRE COULD LIVE out their entire existence, hundreds of years, and never discover their true mate. Before Nicole, I despaired of ever finding mine.

Now, it eats away at me we cannot be together until her transition. The day I became commander of the Guardians, nearly five centuries ago, a binding spell physically linked the king and I. It gives us the power to find one another anywhere in the world in a matter of minutes. It is an ancient ritual done for the king's protection in times of war. It affectively sealed my ability to be with Nicole in the physical realm.

I rub at the constant ache in my chest. So much rides on her survival, but damn it, I miss her. Two years I have denied myself from entering her dreams, and it has stretched my control. With the deadline for Nicole's transition fast approaching, Dimitri redoubled his mental invasions against all the Guardians, no doubt in a desperate attempt to find her location. The meditative process it requires to enter her dreams weakens my mental shields. Fear for Nicole forced me to end our dream world.

'An exotic new sub waits for me at my club,' Sebastian mutters.

I cut off my wayward daydreaming and scrutinize the soft-around-the-middle mayor in his suit, seated at his desk. *'You have a different submissive every week, brother,'* I say, but I can't see any reason to stay. *I've learned all I require. The mayor's loyalties remain with the king.'*

"Steve. I'm in need of your P.I. skills to locate a woman." The mayor speaks into the phone with a hushed intensity that raises the hairs on the back of my neck.

'Oh shit,' Bastian mutters.

"Her legal name is Nicole Tiana Giordano, but she uses various aliases. Her last known whereabouts was three years ago in a small town in Wyoming called Powell."

'Fuck,' Bastian breathes.

"She works as a bartender or singer," the mayor goes on. "Based on my intel, she's on the west coast somewhere. Northern California or Oregon."

"Not enough to go on, Mayor. Do you have her age or a picture?" the voice on the other end asks, irritation evident in his tone.

"Twenty-five, about five-foot—seven, dark auburn hair and light gray eyes. A real looker. I'll email you some photos, although they're not recent. I'm sorry, it's not much, Steve, but this girl's essential to a powerful... um... man. He's authorized double your normal fee."

Fangs punch through my gums, the mayor's words sparking a protective instinct. I want to rip his heart out and devour it while he watches.

'Take it easy, Logan,' Sebastian whispers in my head.

'Fuck. We have allowed her to stay in one spot too long.' I grit my teeth, never taking my focus from the mayor.

'What now, brother?'

'Alter his memories, Bastian. Send him down the wrong path some-where in Michigan. It is far enough away to ease my mind, yet not so far it will raise suspicion. Find out about Steve and do the same.' My voice is icy and controlled, like the fury rushing through my veins. *'If their memories cannot be altered, kill them both. Wipe all emails and hard drives. If hard copies exist, burn them.'*

'You got it.'

'The mayor is another human pawn in Dimitri's attempts to locate Nicole.'

'What are you going to do?' Bastian asks, his voice laced with con-cern.

A red haze of unbridled rage clouds my vision. My single obsessive thought: get to Nicole. Extracting my phone from my pocket, I shoot an urgent text before responding to Bastian. *'I will require Icarus's help, but I believe it is time for a face to face encounter with my female.'*

'Shit.' Bastian blinks. *'You might want to calm down first.'* He cuts me a glance as we materialize in front of the mayor, our need for cam-ouflage at an end.

"You take care of your end. I will take care of what is mine."

"Exactly what I am afraid of," Bastian mutters to my slowly di-minishing form before swinging his intense blue stare on the stunned mayor. As the office begins to blur, a menacing smile lift the corners of my brother's lips, exposing his deadly, white fangs.

Chapter 4

Nicole

I forced myself to endure the ice bath until my lips turned blue and tremors shook my frame so much that water sloshed over the tub, then relaxed in the sauna until my eyes refused to remain open.

After a brisk shower where I scrubbed my skin pink, I slathered lavender lotion all over using slow, massaging motions to loosen the strained muscles even further.

I blow-dried my hair into a shining mass of deep auburn before smoothing on mauve lipstick, and lining my eyes with kohl liner.

But instead of the usual on-stage attire of a dress or skirt, instinct demanded comfort. I squeezed into a pair of my favorite skinny blue jeans, with a purple, long-sleeve button down, loose enough to cover my gun, Annie, at the small of my back, and of course, I slip on black biker boots. Boots are my one and only girly fetish. Every woman needs to own at least ten pairs.

Strolling out of the dojo, my body hums with renewal. Why couldn't my boss, Jimmy, have given me the night off? Plopping my butt on my comfy couch with a glass, or two of wine and a decent movie sounds damn appealing.

With a sigh of regret, I head across the darkened parking area to my black-as-night Ford Raptor, a.k.a., Riddick. A cool breeze whips around my legs and I hug the soft leather jacket tighter while hoisting the gym bag higher on my shoulder as I dodge and weave around a surprising number of vehicles still in the lot.

The chirp of the alarm disengaging fills the night air just as my boot crunches over something on the asphalt. Glass fragments lay scattered along the ground. My body stills as awareness sweeps over me.

I'm no longer alone.

I glance up at the smashed parking light. How could I not notice that? Someone wanted the shroud of darkness. Reaching for my gun, I pause when that *someone* saunters around the corner of a van parked in front of Riddick.

Well, well, well. Nathan Connor. Dickwad extraordinaire. And he's not alone. The jackass needed backup.

The other two men flanking him I recognize from class. I've taken down all three idiots at one point or another throughout training. I guess they need one more ass whooping.

"Hey assholes." I drop the gym bag at my feet. "You're so sweet. You didn't have to escort me to my truck." I suppress the rising anger as they advance.

Nathan's jaw clenches in the moonlight. "Oh, we're gonna escort you all right, bitch. But it will be far from safe."

Dumb and Dumber span out, but I keep my focus on Nathan. Two inches taller than me, his body is bulky with muscle. Too much muscle. He looks like a tick on steroids.

"Geez, Nathan. You must be a real glutton for punishment." I let out a melodramatic sigh in the dwindling space between us and angle my back to the truck bed, denying the douchebags the chance to move behind me.

Nathan snickers and spits on the ground at my feet. The dim glow from other light poles reveals the deep-seated hazel eyes blazing with cruel intent. Large meaty fists clench and unclench in fury. Nathan's hatred for me consumes him. It stabs into me like knives.

He edges closer. "Oh, I'm gonna enjoy shutting your pretty mouth. But not before you scream for mercy as I fuck you in the ass."

Discomfort prickles over my skin; my brain recoils at the image.

Sudden movement behind Nathan catches my eye. I chuckle and try not to stare over his shoulder at the menacing figure approaching our little group. But I can't miss the powerful gait gobbling the distance like a panther. Every move full of purpose, every motion performed with the deadly grace of a predator.

As much as I'd love to wipe the asphalt with this idiot and his friends, I don't have the energy. I've got better things to do. I'm content to hand them off to someone who can do it in half the time.

"I wish I could say it's been nice knowing you, Nathan," I wink as a giant palm slams down on Nathan's shoulder, knocking him to his knees with little effort. His companions next to him take a stride back.

"Is there a problem here, Mr. Connor?" Kurtis's low, menacing pitch sends chills up my spine even though his words aren't directed at me.

"No, Mr. Ruse," Nathan whimpers. "We were just… um… walking Nicki to her car."

I narrow my eyes. Fucking twit couldn't come up with his own line. And after his threat, does he honestly believe I'd cover for him? Fat chance.

"Not what it sounded like." Kurtis sinks his fingers harder into Nathan's shoulder, provoking a cry of pain. "It sounded like you planned to rape her." A low growl full of menace rumbles from his chest.

A loud crunching fills the air, accompanied by Nathan's bellow. I recoil. Oh my God. Kurtis just pulverized his collarbone. I gape as the big man wraps his hands around Nathan's head. Readying to snap his neck?

"Kurtis," I whisper. Swallowing back the shock, I ease to his side, and slide my fingers around his powerful wrist. I'm aware the other two have taken off, but my sole focus remains on Kurtis. "I'm fine."

His blazing gaze snaps to mine. Icy and calculating. I gulp as a tingle of awareness ripples through me. This man will kill to protect me. Wow. Just... wow.

Powerful fingers flex along Nathan's jaw. "They meant to hurt you," he states with dangerous calm. "They must pay."

I glide my palm up the tense muscles of Kurtis's massive arm. The power emanating from him astounds me. It tingles along the surface of my skin. Unexpected emotions burst through me and I swallow, cupping his cheek. My face softens when he leans his cheek into the caress, his piercing stare darkens. I'm stunned. I understand Kurtis was a Navy SEAL but this is a side of him I've never seen. This cold, menacing killer is... sexy.

What's wrong with me?

"Please, Nicki." Sucking up is so unmanly. As were the tears and snot flowing down Nathan's face. "I'm sorry. I... I didn't mean it."

"Your call, Nicki," Kurtis whispers.

The deep-seated darkness I struggle every moment of every day to keep hidden bubbles to the surface. It thirsts for Nathan's death. His blood.

A gentle wind swirls around our little trio as I peer into the cerulean depths of Kurtis's piercing gaze. Part of me wants the evil darkness to engulf me, have its way. The other part, the rational, boring side, shivers with unease by my desire to kill.

"Please, Nicki. Don't... don't let him kill me." Pain and fear etch in every muscle of Nathan's face.

I slip my palm from Kurtis's cheek, lean down to Nathan, and stare into the hazel eyes filled with agony. "It won't be Kurtis who kills you, Nathan. It will be me."

With a mental push, I project my rage and aggression into him, visualizing it as little daggers stabbing into his flesh. His body gives a violent shudder, his eyes squeeze shut against the onslaught. I straighten in shock.

Hmmm. That's new. I've never been able to thrust emotions on others before, only forced to endure theirs.

"What are you?" Fear and pain fill his eyes.

I wonder if, 'Your worst nightmare,' would sound cliché?

"You ever come near me again, I will not hesitate to take you out." With a fierce growl, I slam my hand on his broken collarbone. "Are we clear?"

"Yes!" he shrieks.

The second Kurtis and I let go, Nathan staggers to his feet, and grips the shattered collarbone.

"You and your friends are no longer welcome at Red Dawn, Mr. Connor. Never set foot in my building again." Kurtis steps to my side. "Stay away from Nicki, or I will rip your goddamn head from your body," Kurtis threatens with a low snarl that vibrates down my spine.

Nathan nods, features contorted in agony and fear. But as he turns to leave, his glower meets mine. Hazel eyes dilate as he pins me with a murderous stare. Rage and humiliation pounds into me like a spike into a railroad tie.

My gaze narrows on his retreating form, and I'm second guessing the use of mercy. Instinct tells me it's not the last I'll see of Nathan. Someday, I'll have to kill him.

I've only postponed the inevitable.

Chapter 5

A calm invades my body in response to the sensory onslaught of the LeLoo. My fingers ache to skim along the long, scarred, wooden surface of the bar as I pass. The ancient behemoth runs from the front doors to the stage at the rear, with an office door dividing it in two. Lit up from beneath, scads of liquor bottles of every shape and size line the wall behind it. The hardwood floors creak and groan under my weight, the sound adding to my sense of peace.

Soft blues music envelops the place from concealed speakers throughout. And like a silent beacon, the raised stage at the back calls to my soul. Leaving this place would be like cutting off a limb; the phantom pain would pursue me forever.

The LeLoo, the Chinook Indian name for wolf according to my boss, Jimmy, is rather large for a blues bar, with high-beamed ceilings, dark walls, and low lighting. Patrons unwind on cozy couches and plush leather armchairs near the stage, complete with coffee tables and end tables with lamps. It gives the sense of a private living room, but with a live band performing.

Booths and high-top tables occupy the rest of the space, with a small dance floor front and center right below the stage. Two dozen or more wooden barstools with low backs and cushioned, leather seats line the bar.

Relief flows through me I'm not bartending. First, there's a damn butt in every barstool, and second, the emotional dump I receive from customers could send me spiraling over the brink.

It perplexes me why people blurt out all their troubles and sins to a bartender. Like I'm a freaking priest or therapist. But over the years,

I've mastered the art of presenting my best fake smile and throwing the occasional "mm hm" or "uh huh" when needed. But inside I'm shouting at them— "Life is shit, suck it up, buttercup and stop making stupid decisions." —which I foresee being my response this evening. Not too sure how my boss, or the patrons would appreciate it.

Speaking of bosses, my eyes narrow on Jimmy Dickerson, owner of the LeLoo Blues Bar, striding toward me.

I slow mt roll with a frown. Is it too much to ask to just get my set over with, say farewell to my imaginary wet fantasy man, to my forgotten past, and go the fuck home?

Tonight, saying goodbye to Logan, to letting go of the fantasy of him, pounds in my heart. My subconscious has grown up. My conscious needs to catch the fuck up.

Despite the exhaustion that hounds my every step, a tender glow fills my chest. Jimmy is the father I never had. Or I should say, have no clue I ever had.

He's the one man my instincts guide me to trust. And the last person on the planet I'd wish to disappoint. In my heart, and the vacant black spot I claim as my brain, he's the only father figure I've ever experienced.

"I need a minute," he announces, guiding me toward his office behind the bar.

Oh boy... this is gonna suck ass.

"OOOH, someone's in trouble," Liam mocks with a smirk as he serves up pretty frou-frou drinks to the women itching to get a bite of him.

Huffing with all the drama queen I can muster, I throw him the evil stink eye and I flip him the bird. Liam chuckles. "Anytime, anywhere, sweetheart." This wins me several glares from the ladies vying for his attention.

"Been there, done that, and I've had better." I dig back.

Liam's scowl resembles his father, Jimmy, and I smirk as the ladies come-fuck-me vibes drop down a notch or two. At over six foot, Liam's built like a damn semi—if a semi had eight pack abs and bulging biceps for tires—with dark, wavy hair and dark eyes. When he's working the bar, most of the patrons are women.

Our interactions energize my brain. The back and forth is our way of showing we care without having to say the words. His work schedule always coincides with when I'm on stage, and his handsome face, with those dark, mischievous but compassionate eyes, gives me a boost of courage. Like any big brother, Liam holds a special place in my heart. But I'd never reveal that. His head would explode.

I follow Jimmy through the office door when he suddenly turns and grasps my shoulders in a determined grip. Caution flags flutter in my vision.

"What's up, Jimmy?" Pinpricks of worry light up my skin where he touches me.

"I would prefer it if you didn't go on tonight." He towers over me, his deep, graveled pitch steady. Natural. Like he's not requesting anything out the ordinary. But it's a forced nonchalance. The tenseness of his jaw gives him away. Discomfort prickles over my skin, and my instincts rear their ugly heads.

"Why?" His tension seeps deep into my bones like acid. What the hell's going on here?

He shrugs. "Just short staffed, and Liam needs help behind the bar, that's all."

Lie.

Sharp pain shoots through my head like an ice pick pierced my temple. I bite the inside of my lip to keep from revealing a reaction. Thank God I only experience pain when someone lies to me directly. I'd have a permanent facial twitch if every lie affected me.

Why lie? Jimmy's never lied to me before.

"Bullshit. What's going on, Jimmy?" The pain drills deeper into my temple.

Through the crimson haze of discomfort, panic tries to claw its way to the surface. Jimmy's unease freaks me out. Nothing rattles him. He's my rock. The calm in my life. He's fifty-six, with a firmly muscled body, not buff like Liam or Kurtis, but solid with broad shoulders. A sturdy chest always encased in a t-shirt showcasing some band from the 60s, and faded blue jeans that hug lean hips.

The dusting of gray at the temples of his thick brown hair hints at his age, accentuating his masculinity. And like Liam, it's his eyes I'm drawn to. That I count on. They're the color of dark chocolate, warm and inviting. They project the battle-worn fierceness of a seasoned veteran. I know Jimmy would have my back if I were ever in trouble. But tonight? He's... unsettled, his eyes haunted with an inner anxiety.

Which in turn freaks me the fuck out.

He inhales a deep breath, holds it for a brief second before freeing it on a quiet sigh. The grip on my shoulders lifts and he steps back, grimacing at his hands. It's like he's aware touching me makes the pain and the assault of emotions more acute. But that's impossible. I've told no one about my little curse.

"It's a hunch." Leaning against his desk, he grips the edge. "Call it instinct."

Loki, Jimmy's gigantic malamute, trots through the office door, then drops his butt at my feet. Correction—on my feet. His big furry body leans against my legs and I stumble as his weight almost knocks me over.

"You know how I listen to my instincts." Jimmy gives the dog a brief nod.

Funny he should phrase it that way. I survive by mine.

When I don't offer a remark, his brow furrows. "Strange people have been in and out of the LeLoo today. More than normal. A few caused the damn hairs on the back of my neck to rise at attention, and when that happens, kid… I take notice. You should too. Stay behind the bar. Or better yet, go home. You are too vulnerable on stage."

Half-truth. Part of what he's claiming exudes truth, part a lie. But which part is the lie?

The knowledge Jimmy's hiding something produces a small crack, fissuring the wall around my heart. I observe the tension in his shoulders, his neck, and his palms as they clutch the edge of his desk. I force my expression into a blank mask and press the hurt to the background.

I fled Wyoming three years ago. I set my internet alerts to warn me if anyone searches for my actual name or any aliases I've used in the past. Nothing. Not a damn thing.

What the hell did I miss? Could Jimmy just be paranoid? Or does a real threat exist? I've grown weak and soft, unable to read the clues, anticipate the impending danger living in this pretend world of butterflies and flowers, and lost sight of the realism of my existence. I ignored the two most important rules. Trust no one, and safety is an illusion.

Round and around my thoughts course through my brain, like the Indie 500. To his credit, Jimmy doesn't move a muscle. Allows me the chance to absorb his remarks.

A flare of anger ignites in my gut with a jolt and I grit my teeth. No, goddamnit. I refuse to run again. I always maintained that one day I'd deal with whatever pursues me. Well, the moment's arrived.

I attempt to separate myself from Loki's mammoth weight, but it's as if he senses my fury and anxiousness and moves with me, keeping his 200-pound body pressed against my leg and hip. Loki is the biggest malamute I've ever encountered. More wild predator then pet, coming and going as he pleases, never leashed or locked up.

"Jimmy, did anyone ask you about me?" My low voice vibrates through the office. The angrier I become, the more the rigid control I've held over my facial expressions begins to slip. But underneath the rage and frustration there's a smidgen of fear. Fear I won't be able to handle what's coming. If my recurring nightmares foreshadow what's trailing me, it must come straight from the gates of hell.

Loki growls low in protest, inching even tighter. For the moment, I give up on trying to move away from the hairy beast. Instead, I peer into his intense, penetrating gaze at my chest. They say dogs can discern and react to our emotions. I suppose I agree. Loki's response to my anger and worry is human-like.

I've never experienced a dog stare into my eyes with such concentration before, except when they wanted to rip my head off. Loki's mammoth size, deadly canines, and predatory brown eyes should scare me. His head alone larger than a basketball, and those tusks must be two inches long. For whatever reason, Loki doesn't frighten me. His presence calms me. No one dared mess with me when this frightening creature was by my side.

Even with all the concerns running unchecked through my mind, I sink my fingers into the thick, gray-and-white coat of his enormous head, seeking to calm his unease, while my other hand moves behind me to the small of my back where Annie rests. I stroke her cool exterior. Her presence reassures me the way my touch soothes Loki.

Jimmy's eyes narrow on me with worry. "No," he finally responds. "But in my experience, it's better to be safe than sorry, kid."

Who is pursuing me? And why the fuck hasn't Logan warned me? He always alerts me in my dreams when the time to move has come. What is blocking me from remembering my past? Life before my seventeenth birthday is an utter void. I retained the essentials. I can read, write, and do math, but I have no memory of a childhood.

Parents. Friends. Now my stupid mind betrayed me again, refusing to conjure up Logan in my dreams.

How long will I continue to allow this to be my life? Always on the run. Never knowing why.

I'm done. I refuse to run again. Irritation and anxiety pinball around in my skull. For the first time, I've discovered a place I call home, with people who I think care about me. I don't want to leave, dammit. The prospect of setting up all over again somewhere else...exhausts me.

"I'm not running again, Jimmy." Decision made. I'm proud of my even, calm manner. With a last sensual caress, I release the reassuring grip on Annie's butt.

Jimmy is the one person I've confided in. He's aware I've been hiding from something or someone. But not the reason. Hell, I'd love it if anyone clued me in on the reason.

"I'm not suggesting you need to run, girl. In fact, I don't want you going anywhere. Not until..." He hesitates, gritting his teeth before continuing. "All I'm asking is don't go on stage." His eyes plead with me as he fishes his vibrating cell phone out of his front pocket.

"No. I need to sing tonight. You're here. Liam's working the bar, and I'm more than capable of dealing with whatever comes my way." Running my fingers through my hair, I sigh. "Look, I appreciate your concern, Jimmy, I do. But I'm finished with this debate."

Loki huffs and I scratch behind his ears once more before extracting myself from his enormous weight. I exit the office to Jimmy's flowery curses and fast-texting fingers.

I've lost my mind. I've never once ignored the warnings or my instincts, which scream to get the hell out of town. Run.

No. I refuse to spend the rest of my damn life hiding from God-knows-what. It's past time to take a stand. And if whatever I've been fleeing from catches up with me... so be it.

Chapter 6

Logan

Shrouded in the blanket of darkness that camouflages my presence, I stand in the corner of The LeLoo club. Amongst the odors of booze, perfumes, colognes and... blood. Her scent fills my nostrils. *Nicole.* She smells of spring with a faint scent of lavender. My fangs throb inside my gums as I discern the thrum of her warm blood in the instant before she emerges from a hallway at the far end of the club. My heart swells with pride. She moves with the lithe grace only our kind possess.

As I watch her progress across the room, need courses through me. Despite my efforts at control, my cock begins to lift. It has been so long since I have been this close to her.

Our dream time together diluted the blood lust. Or, the two years of abstaining from my mate's presence enhanced it tenfold. Whatever the reason, the need for her overwhelms me.

Want and desire swirls within me and I fear I cannot take another breath without her. Every waking thought revolves around Nicole. The distance forced upon us these past two years has been hell, eating away at my insides every minute of every night. Does she feel the same? Has she imagined me over the years? I frown with uncertainty.

Her eyes glitter like gray diamonds, fringed by long, black lashes. Thick, dark auburn hair frames her oval face. Silky tendrils curl to caress delicate shoulders and full breasts. Dark blue jeans hug a delectable ass and long, shapely legs.

My cock swells in my leathers, to the point of pain. A fierce possessiveness uncoils in my gut, manifesting a driving need to be inside

Nicole. To devour those full lips, the rich, sweet blood. To hold her naked and submissive beneath me, moaning my name and begging for more. Live. Not in the dreamscape.

Too long without blood and the hunger becomes irresistible, but the need for Nicole devastates me. Must take her. Draw from her vein. Glut myself on the sweet blood calling to the vampire within while pounding into her tight, wet heat.

Fuck. Calm down, Logan.

Nicole cannot deal with my true self... yet. I must be gentle. Restrain the inner beast salivating at her presence. An overwhelming need to materialize by her side, to mark her as mine, consumes me and my muscles tense. But another woman on the stage carrying a guitar asks Nicole how she is feeling, and I hesitate. I crave the answer to that question more than I wish to draw my next breath.

Nicole's body is... tense as she pauses. The sorrow, the anguish in her facial expression quenches my lust.

"Sad," she responds without emotion. A complete contrast to what her beautiful, expressive eyes shout.

Sad?

The word sits heavy on my chest. Why is my mate sad? We protected her. Made certain Dimitri never got near her. What developed during the two years I have been forced away? Could the reason for Nicole's unhappiness lay at my feet?

Does my mate miss me? A growl of satisfaction builds in my chest.

"Oookay," the woman responds with a frown. "What's up first?"

"'*Gravity*' by Sara Bareilles," she says after a quick hesitation. A sudden fierceness enters her gray eyes. The other woman is taken aback by her request.

When she strides across the stage to the grand piano, moving with graceful, predatory confidence, my eyes follow her like a starving man staring at his last meal.

Her eyes skim the room, alert. The slight bulge at her low back when she sits at the piano surprises me. Nicole came packing.

When Bastian materializes beside me I don't even glance in his direction. *'Everything taken care of, brother?'*

'Yes. The mayor's mind was strong, but the new memories should hold. The P.I. and any evidence of your mate was dealt with as well.' Bastian's low rumble skims through my mind. He watches my mate. His future queen. *'Nicole has become a fierce warrior, brother. Taken to her combat training like a fish to water.'*

I exhale in frustration. *'I missed so much of her life, Bastian. Nicole is my mate, my responsibility, mine to care for. It is my duty to watch over her, make certain she wants for nothing. And I have done a piss poor job of it so far.'*

'You did what needed to be done to keep her safe, Logan," Bastian responds with a comforting hand on my shoulder. *'From Dimitri, from his allies, even from yourself.'*

He speaks truth, but this double life takes a toll, only allowing me to pop in and out of her dreams every so often. But there remained no alternative.

Every dawn before rest, I poured over all the reports of Nicole from the other council members and my team. I coveted every sentence, every word. But the reports did not prepare me for the remarkable woman on stage.

The room dims, a spotlight shines on her and the piano. I hold the perfect spot. When she glances up from the keys, Nicole's gaze will be on me, even though she will not be aware of it.

'Enjoy, brother. Your mate's talent is amazing.' And with that Bastian disappears.

A stillness settles over the crowd in anticipation. Nicole has gained a definite following. Heart rates of many in the crowd accelerate with whispered murmurs of excitement. All eyes shift to Nicole as the haunting notes of the piano ring out, and I find myself as anxious as they are as she begins to sing.

Her deep, husky voice fills the bar and slips into my soul, but the heart-breaking, despondent tone catches my breath. So many emotions reveal themselves in her outward expressions, and the inflections of her delivery. Her voice and the words of the song reveal grief and sorrow.

I stand transfixed, my chest rising and falling with every panting breath. My baby... aches. She dealt with all this pain alone. Anger for failing my mate pulses with every beat of my heart.

When Nicole's eyes connect with a big man in the front row, my focus zeroes in on him and my insides freeze. My nostrils flare, scenting the air, but too many odors camouflage his scent. With a slight push, I probe this man's mind and my fists clench even tighter at what I discover. This man desires Nicole.

I look at my mate to discern if affection exists for him, but her gaze has already shifted away. She stares over the piano in my direction. A riot of fear hits like a punch to the gut. The risk she might meet someone else during my absence lived as a perpetual, nagging fear. Until Nicole's transition, the mate-bond remains strictly one-sided.

The need to identify if she harbors any feelings for the bastard overrides any restraints against invading her privacy as I give a slight telepathic nudge. In a split second, my push hits a wall. Nicole's psychological barriers coil around her like a fortress. Formidable.

Smart girl.

The words of the song, and their significance, finally penetrate my chaotic brain, and my smile fades. Nicole's suffering absorbs into my skin as if my own. Could the lyrics be about us? This song is about falling in love—with a forbidden lover. She sings about loving so passionately that love takes over her ability to walk away. She wants to leave; to do the right thing; but the moment she thinks she is strong, the feelings are undeniable, with no options but to turn back. In the end, she begs *me* to turn and walk away. The passion, pain, and grief of her broken heart cuts me to the bone.

Guilt and sorrow punch through me like a battering ram, and I lose the concentration on my shadow form for a brief second as her emotions jab into me like tiny daggers, ripping at my soul, consuming it.

The second those gorgeous eyes land on mine, her heart skips a beat, and they widen, pinpointing my position. They never deviate, even after I recover control and am nothing but a simple shadow once again.

The burden of guilt hits like a sledgehammer, and I gulp the bile threatening the back of my throat. I hurt Nicole deeply. She needed me, but the binding spell combined with Dimitri's mental attacks forced me to stay away. It is only because of the High Priest Oracle I am even here tonight. Icarus finally concocted a temporary shield around my mind. It's taken him eight years to perfect it so Dimitri wouldn't sense when the binding spell was blocked.

It will allow me the time I need with my mate without Dimitri sensing my whereabouts. But it lasts no more than an hour or two and has limited use. Icarus warned if used too often it will cause permanent damage to the cerebral cortex. Even in a vampire.

What choice did I have but to stay away? Should I have thrown away the future of my people? Sacrificed her safety and the lives of everyone I cared about so I could be with her? I took a huge risk just invading her dreams.

Christ.

At the sound of her sorrowful but determined voice whispering goodbye to me, I lift a hand to my chest, rubbing at the throbbing ache in the center. No, goddammit. She is mine. No one will have her but me. Fate bound us the minute Nicole entered this world. In time, she will understand that.

The remembered prophecy and our intertwined destinies ease the sorrow. The tension and fear recede. Patience. I must remember Nicole does not know I am a vampire, or I even exist outside her dreams. No awareness of the monster living inside me, one I battle to contain daily.

My mate has endured much in her brief life. Forced to move from town to town. I do not wish to add to her distress. Gentleness is the requirement here. The dominant, vampire side must be pushed deep down, and allow her to feel secure, to trust me. For centuries I have waited for my female—to caress her, to breathe her in, to savor every inch.

Lids close as I visualize her naked and writhing beneath me. My cock stiffens once again, lust the driving force within in a split second. How in God's name will I ever obtain the fortitude to abstain from plunging into her wet heat the second I'm alone with her? The overpowering desire for my mate clouds my judgment. I must remember the prophecy and the repercussions of my actions. Another reason I insisted on only having contact in her dreams. But she needed more. She needed me.

I continue to hover in the darkness and bask in her presence. Soothed by her voice, I prepare a strategy for our face-to-face encounter. Worry creeps up the back of my neck, but I take a deep, steadying breath, and will it away.

She needs to understand her destiny and what lies ahead. Her transition is approaching. Tonight, my mate will understand vampires exist, that her dream lover is real, and that she belongs to me.

Chapter 7

Nicole

I'm drained. My body aches, my head throbs, and my mind lives in mush. I crave my soft welcoming bed for the next eight uninterrupted hours. The mere idea of the thirty-minute drive home fills my stomach with dread. For the first time, it's a real temptation to slip back into Jimmy's office and crash on his couch.

One foot in front of the other, Nicole.

Exhaustion follows my every step as I shuffle my ass across the parking lot to my truck. I tilt my head from side to side, stretching the aching muscles in my neck. Last night's dream flashes through my brain. Not a dream. Dreams are pleasant and full of Logan. No, a nightmare. The same nightmare I've had for the last eight years.

Something tracks me through the woods. A massive, scary creature. Hot, putrid breath scorches my neck as I fall and stumble through the misty, dense forest. But like most nightmares, everything slows to a crawl. My lungs blister with fire. The muscles of my thighs quiver and burn from slogging through deep quicksand. Each step agony.

Lightning streaks across the sky, barely discernible through the denseness of the trees. Bone jarring claps of thunder shake the ground. Angry storms occur in every nightmare. Could the storms of the past be what haunts me? Or the beast pursuing me with the stinging bite of claws piercing my back? My mouth gapes wide to scream in pain and terror.

Piercing cries wake me, the sheets drenched in sweat. The erratic beat of my heart deafening.

When Alex first moved in—before she became intimately aware of my night terrors—she shot through my bedroom door at a dead run, her frantic blue eyes scanning for threats. When none appeared, her gaze swung to mine in confusion. The residual terror in my eyes, and the shakes and tremors of my body curled up against the headboard—clued her in.

"Are you alright, Nicki?" she asked.

I could do nothing but shake my head. Frightened to open my mouth for fear I'd bawl my eyes out. Alex hopped into bed, taking me in her arms. We laid there with my head cushioned on her shoulder as I listened to her soothing voice yakking about frivolous things—gossip at the bar, her ridiculous love life, her eccentric family. Bit by bit the sweat on my body cooled, my raged breath evened out, and my heart rate slowed.

Tonight, with exhaustion weighing down every step, a nightmare would take on a whole other level of terror. If I woke shrieking my damn head off in Jimmy's office, he'd scramble down the steps from his apartment above the bar, shotgun in hand, braced for battle. An explanation I'd rather not give.

Why the hell I offered to help close was stupid on my part. It's two in the morning and the only two trucks left in the acre-sized lot—Jimmy's and my Riddick—are parked clear in the back, near the tree line. At least Riddick's under a light pole. A mellow glow shines down on him like a welcoming beacon. A beacon that looks a thousand miles away at the moment.

What I wouldn't give to teleport like vampires do in the movies. A soft giggle escapes. That train of logic is living proof I'm dead on my feet, as I never giggle. Ever. Unless I'm drunk.

With a shake of my head, I add further to the illusion. I imagine standing in the comfort of my home with the snap of my fingers. My warm, cozy bed steps away, or enjoying a hot bath before my body slides beneath soft sheets and....

Tingles of unease skid along the surface of my skin and I put an immediate kibosh on the stupid daydreaming. I'm being watched

My steps never falter as I focus on my surroundings. The eerie shifting and swaying of the tree line, the vicinity around Riddick, and the darkened corners around the bar. Nothing. Visually there's nothing, but every instinct, not to mention the goosebumps covering my arms, warns something studies my progress.

I ease along the back of the cab, slide my hand under my leather jacket, and grip the butt of Annie. A quick glance inside the vehicle reveals it's empty. Relief courses through my nerves.

Trees sway back and forth with the wind, their dark, ghostly shapes making it challenging to detect who could be hiding among them. Adrenaline surges. Could this be the threat Jimmy dreaded?

Pinpricks of fear race along my spine, but I ignore them. Instead I open my senses to the night for any slight noise or scent out of place—a snap of a twig, the crunch of gravel, the panting of breath. Nothing. The only noise is the eerie whistling of the wind through the trees. Moist earth, pine and cedar fill my nostrils, but no foreign colognes, perfumes or body odors.

These heightened senses are another talent that have been slowly increasing over the last six months, which sucks when you're in a room full of sweaty bodies at the dojo. It's enough to cause me to gag sometimes.

Cool, salty air swirls my hair around my face in a frenzy. I surrender the security of Annie and reach into my pocket to disengage the alarm. The second my fingers grasp the cool mental of the door handle, I hesitate. Everything within me knows there's someone or something out there. The goosebumps multiply and the tiny hairs at my nape stand at attention.

It's like when you're standing in line at the grocery store and you perceive someone come up behind you, without even having to turn around. Tonight, it isn't the haggard looking mother with three rebellious kids in tow. It is more the spine tingle of Charles Manson.

A fresh wave of sensation tiptoes along my skin like tiny spiders, and the safety of Annie's butt is in my palm once more.

"Nicki." Jimmy barks from the back door. My body jerks in surprise and my heart nearly explodes out of my chest.

"Shit."

"You okay, kid?"

I twist in his direction, ready to... what? Tell him there's a boogie man in the forest? Really? Paranoid much?

"Nicki?" Jimmy's tension evident in his shout.

I open my mouth to respond I'm fine when a flash of white leaps from the surrounding forest, and lands with a soft thud in front of Riddick. I gulp back a girly scream and falter back a step. Annie is in my hand in an instant.

What the hell was that?

When an enormous, gray and white head with piercing eyes and pointy ears ambles around the hood, relief eases the tension in my muscles. I exhale and grin into the brown gaze of Loki.

"I'm fine, Jimmy. Loki just scared the crap out of me." I offer with a slight wave, proud at how calm my voice sounds. The lovable beast head-butts my waist as I holster Annie.

"What were you doing out there you big, hairy monster? Chasing poor little squirrels?" Loki sits on his haunches, allowing me to inspect the smattering of red staining the sides of his muzzle. "Or were you watching out for me, big guy?"

His warm intelligent eyes stare back as he offers a huffing sound in response. Something about Loki's intense, penetrating stare and body language give me pause, like the dog's responding in the affirmative.

I grin and kiss the top of his furry head, dismissing the theory as the ravings of an exhausted woman. I turn and wave to Jimmy once more.

"Get home, kid," he orders before whistling for Loki.

I couldn't agree more.

Chapter 8

Nicole

Although I dreaded the drive home, it provides me the time I need to wind down, to let the adrenaline ebb from my veins, and analyze the crap out of the events of the day.

The delicate aroma of pine and ocean fills the inside of the cab. I love this town. The way it's nestled between the coast mountains, the Pacific Ocean, and the picturesque Yaquina Bay.

I could never explain it in meteorological terms, but with weather in Newport, the one constant is change. Over the course of a day, we may enjoy sun and clear skies, followed by rain and wind. Or a foggy morning could give way to an unseasonably warm, sunny afternoon.

The winters bring big waves and significant weather, but also a surprising number of crisp, clear days perfect for long beach walks. But the summers remain the ultimate—with dry, sunny days and mild, perfect nights. Like tonight, or I should say this morning, since its after two a.m.

The thing I find so fascinating: Newport separates into two distinct areas of town. The Historical Bayfront, where the LeLoo Blues Bar resides, and Nye Beach.

Nye Beach is a popular haven for the arts, with unique galleries, bookstores, eateries, shopping, and lodging. I try to avoid that area of town as much as possible. Tourists flock there in the summer and traffic can be a bitch.

Bayfront, being the economic backbone of Newport, is where the locals hang out. It houses one of the largest commercial fishing fleets on the west coast, but it still maintains a small-town charm, while close enough to the bigger cities of Portland, Salem, and Eugene to offer me the options I require.

Home. The first true home I've ever had, that I remember. A place where the continual worry of looking over my shoulder doesn't exist. Tension eases between my shoulders with each mile. It's safe. Hidden.

For how much longer? This is the longest I've stayed in one place.

With a sigh, I rub my throbbing forehead as constant questions bombard me. They torment my aching brain. Why can't I remember my childhood? What caused me to forget? Something so powerful it haunts me with terrifying nightmares. Severe enough it forced me to live like a fugitive, always changing identities, drifting from town to town.

My brow furrows as I recall the small town in Wyoming. I was secure there for all of six months. The time before? Three months. And the time before? Shit, I've lost count of how many times I've run before settling in Newport.

Five years ago, I unexpectedly received a notice in the mail from a bank, notifying me my mother died in an automobile accident, and she willed me her entire estate. It freaked me out. I'd been on the run for two years, using various aliases along the way. Either a package with my new identity would mysteriously show up wherever I was, or I'd just lie to the next employer and tell them I lost my ID. So how the hell had they found me? Even more baffling, they deposited the money into a bank account opened in the very first alias I remember using. Overnight, I'd turned into a wealthy woman.

At first, my heart filled with elation. At last, a tie to my past. My mother. The letter revealed her name was Bridget Stallings. When I Googled her at the library, nothing turned up. I mean nada. Next, I called information, but they had no record of her name either.

Despondent, I tried calling the bank, but received a disconnected recording. So, I Googled the bank, but the only location happened to be a municipality in Switzerland, for God's sake. Every avenue detoured to a dead end. I was consumed by frustration. Not seeing what else to do—without revealing who or where I was—I had no choice but to let it go.

I didn't want the damn money. I preferred to discover more about my mother. More about me. Where was she before she died? Did she abandon me? Or did I runaway? She left me a shit load of money, but every instinct shouted she wasn't a decent woman, let alone a proper mother.

Could she be who I'm running from? Was the money a ruse to locate me? Fear and suspicion rode my back, and I did everything not to touch the damn money. Withdrawing it produced a paper trail and relocation.

But on several occasions, I had no alternative but to dip into the account. Every time I did, I seized my bug-out bag and disappeared to a new city. I've traveled across this great country, bartending and singing along the way but I never stayed in one spot for more than a year. The second my instincts urged me to run, I ran. When Logan urged me to move on in my dreams, I ran.

Until Newport. A year ago, I withdrew the down payment to purchase my home. Everything's been great. Right up until Jimmy's warning this evening.

If I'd been wiser, I never would've bought the house, but one glimpse at the place and I'd fallen in love. Maybe my subconscious drew a line in the sand and deemed Newport my final resting place.

The house sits on eighty glorious acres of dense woodland. It's a charming two-bedroom, two-bath cottage built in the early 1900s. The previous owners had undertaken extensive remodeling before they sold, modernizing the kitchen with high-end appliances, adding a huge master suite with an ensuite, complete with a copper claw-foot tub and a considerable stand-alone glassed-in shower.

The detached two-car garage I've converted into my studio. Every Sunday the band drives out and we rehearse for the coming week.

The cottage sits far back from the main road, down a mile and a half-long dirt drive with no sign marking the turnoff. No mailbox to indicate there's a home back there. If you weren't watching for it, you wouldn't even notice it.

"Home," I whisper to no one, my smile returning as I head down the drive. The stress and anxiety lodged like a rock between my shoulder blades eases at the sight of it. It's nothing big or luxurious, but it carries loads of character. From the pale gray exterior and black shutters, to the impressive wrap-around porch with redwood rocking chairs and red metal roof. It cozies up to the giant grand firs surrounding it, who appear to defend it from the outside world.

Inside, the original, scarred wood floors prove they've experienced life. The antique wood stove squatting in the great room adds warmth.

It's all mine.

After parking to the right of the house, I snatch the gym bag off the passenger seat, and clamber down. Before my boots even touch the dark earth, my instincts rear their ugly heads with a vengeance.

The impression of being observed is back in maximum force. Fear plows through my veins like a football player on steroids.

Loki isn't lurking around the truck this time.

I drop the gym bag and withdraw Annie in one fluid move. With my gun in a two-handed grip at my chest, legs braced, I scan the area around the house, and keep cover behind the open truck door.

Nothing.

The dim lights from the porch cast a yellow glow that barely pierces the forest beyond. I squint into the gloom. If someone lies in wait among the timbers, can I make it from Riddick to the front door?

I'm in a fight-or-flight situation here. Do I dive back into Riddick and haul ass in reverse down the mile drive and hope to God whoever's out there isn't armed, and I don't get struck by zinging bullets? Or do I make a stand?

I could be overreacting. It wouldn't be the first time.

The bitch in the equation is that I don't know who's out there or how many. One or two individuals and I like my odds, but if its multiple armed assailants, I'm fucked.

"Show yourselves, you fucking cowards!" I yell at the surrounding redwoods. Decision made. Good or bad? T.B.D. I must identify what I'm up against to determine my odds of winning. Or losing.

Within a second, I get my answer. My anxiety spikes as three enormous men, clad in black leather pants and black, tight-fitting t-shirts, stride from the forest edge. Chills sprint up my spine. None of them appear armed, but I keep the truck door between me and the three amigos just in case.

Great God almighty. They're the most gorgeous men I've ever encountered. And big. Damn, they are Kurtis-big. Their bulging muscles are on stark display under skin-tight shirts.

"Nicole Tiana Giordano?" the dark-skinned giant in the middle asks. His accented speech a deep, grating rumble.

Oh, shit. I'm screwed. He used my real name. Damnit. What was I thinking staying in one place for so long?

This is not good... not good. I have only one course of action here: kill or be killed. I refuse to go down without a fight and my instincts scream not to let them capture me. I'm a proficient fighter with years of training for this scenario.

I must get inside the house. There's an arsenal at the ready in there. Right now, it's a fully loaded Annie, one extra magazine, and my bare hands.

I've got this.

"Sorry. She moved to Alaska, assholes." I shout and open fire.

Chapter 9

Nicole

The loud clap of my nine-millimeter has my ears ringing. I squeeze off several rounds at the three menacing figures sauntering across the drive, and haul ass to the other side of Riddick. Their response scares me. They act like they couldn't care less as bullets rain down on them. Granted, the initial rounds aren't meant to be on target, just a momentary distraction to take cover, but still... they don't duck or attempt to protect themselves. Nor do they draw any weapons.

I drop to one knee behind the back tire, and draw a deep steadying breath before I leap up and brace my arms on the bed of Riddick. As soon as I'm focused on my sights, my nerves calm. Three years of training kick in, and I discharge the magazine with lethal precision. This is what I excel at: pinpoint accuracy.

I'm so good, I shock myself with my badassery.

The self-boasting dies a quick death. Every bullet strikes my targets center mass. Repeatedly. Their bodies jerk with each hit, but they just keep moving across the drive.

"What the fuck?" I squat to reload and my insides quiver. "Should've picked the flight option, Nicole." I push the threatening panic deep down, eject the empty magazine, and slap in the spare from the holster at my back.

Just as I'm about to pop back up, a deafening roar pierces the surrounding darkness. My thighs freeze mid-squat. *What the hell was that?* Annie trembles in my sweaty palms. I wipe each one down my jeans and take a better grip; the fear continues its sprint along my skin. Did a lion just enter the battle? 'Cause that's what it sounded like: an enraged lion.

Focus on remaining alive, Nicole. Thrust the fear away like Kurtis taught you.

Hunched over, I shuffle to Riddick's front tire. *Okay girl, this is it. Do or die.* After three deep inhales, I snap back up to let the goons have it once more.

Gone. They're fucking gone.

If it weren't for the spent casings around the truck, I'd suspect hallucination as the correct diagnosis. Tingles snake up my arms as I search for movement. Around the house, Riddick, the tree line, the dirt drive. Nothing. Where the hell did they go? If they're dead, there should be bodies in the driveway, blood at least.

With slow cautious movements, I move around the front of my truck, Annie still drawn and at the ready. I tighten my fingers around her butt to stop the shaking and gaze around in bewilderment. There's not a single drop of blood anywhere. No footprints but my own. Not a goddamn sign anywhere that they'd even been here.

What just transpired? No way I imagined them. Did I? I lower Annie and spin in a stiff circle. Confusion mixed with a large amount of alarm churns through my muddled mind.

I stumble in a daze over to the gym bag still lying on the ground and try not to freak the fuck out. The last couple of minutes replay over and over again.

When no resolution magically presents itself, I snatch the bag and slam the truck door. The sound echoes all around the house.

Thank God I don't live in a sub-division where my neighbors are within a handshake distance. I could have injured or killed an innocent bystander.

The image causes my knees to wobble as I attempt to mount the front steps of the porch. The second I comprehend a face plant on the wood planks is a sure bet, I turn and plop my butt on the top step. The gym bag drops at my feet.

The powerful outpour of adrenaline ebbs, and exhaustion overwhelms me. My elbows drop on quivering thighs, and my hands swing between spread knees. Even the weight of my head is too much, so I let it slump forward, grateful when my hair shrouds my face like a protective veil.

In a stupor, I follow the motion of Annie swinging between my thighs. My brain shuts down one synapse at a time. Annie is the only thing I can comprehend. I watch her in a trance as she swings back and forth. Back and forth.

From somewhere, an inner voice urges me to get up, holster the gun, and go inside the damn house. But I can't muster the strength. My brain stopped corresponding with the rest of my body, and no matter how many times I chant, '*Get up Nicole, get up Nicole,*' I don't.

"Nicole."

I glower at Annie. Was that my inner voice? It sure sounded low and sexy.

"Nicole."

Nope, not my voice.

A strong, masculine hand enters my line of sight. Mesmerized, I follow its gradual progress as it reaches through my veil of hair. Rough fingers grip my chin and raise my head. My gaze follows.

A tan, muscular forearm. A powerful, well-built bicep, with a sexy vein running down the center. Black t-shirt stretched across an expanse of a well-defined, sculpted chest. Strong throat with skin so smooth I have a sudden urge to lean in and lick it. A closely-trimmed dark goatee, sinister and provocative, wraps around lush, generous lips.

A warm tingling spreads through my fingers, begging me to reach out and run my fingers along their smooth surface, but my stupid body still refuses to cooperate, so I continue to eye what's being exposed, inch by glorious inch. A straight masculine nose with slightly flaring nostrils. And lastly, the magnificent light green eyes that have invaded my dreams for years.

I stare into those incandescent orbs, adorned with lush black lashes, and a sharp ache crawls up the back of my throat. My eyes sting. I tuck my lips between my teeth and bite down to hold the tears at bay. If I opened those floodgates, the flow would be hopeless to dam up.

Besides, warriors don't cry.

With my mind still obscured in a fog, I struggle to evaluate this potent being. He's not pretty, far too masculine, but he's the whole package: intense green eyes and muscular body. The sexy scar slashing through the middle of his left eyebrow gives him a sinister look. He has dark wavy hair that sweeps from his forehead to settle in loose waves to his collarbone. It all falls together to provide him the face of a deadly, but panty-wetting pirate. Even through the haze in my brain, my insides clench at the sight of him.

"Baby, are you hurt?" The beautiful man asks.

"Yes." The strong jaw clenches, and the luscious lips compress.

"Where, Nicole? Where are you hurt?" Green eyes scan my body.

"My mind." *Duh*. "I'm losing my mind."

The soft lips curve into a half smile, the hottest thing I've ever witnessed. A painful knot forms beneath my ribs, making it hard to breathe. I frown and blink several times.

"Why are you here? I already said goodbye to you tonight." My brain struggles to clear the fog. Next to the cool breeze on my face the long masculine fingers capturing my chin sizzle with warmth.

"There is no goodbye between us, Nicole."

The low timber dances down my spine as if he traced every vertebra. Certainty penetrates my senses and my head rears back. His fingers slip from my chin. The reality of my situation sinks into my overstimulated brain like a lead weight. Shock stalls the breath in my lungs, and I scurry back across the deck on my butt, away from the dream standing over me. Annie digs into my palm. *Oh yeah, shit. Gun, stupid.* With a fumble, I jerk the muzzle to point at the man's heart.

What a picture I must be. Here I sit—legs spread for stability, my back leaning against the screen door, arms stretched out between my knees, and Annie positioned at her mark. Not the finest of positions, but hey, a crazy girl's gotta work with what she's got.

"What the—where—who?" *Oh yeah, who, good one, stick with who.* "Who the fuck are you?" With each pant of my accelerating breaths, the gun trembles in response.

"You know who I am." Brow furrowed; he uncoils to his full height.

A sense of déjà vu flashes through my brain. We've had this debate before. Haven't we?

"No. No—no, I don't." End with the stuttering already. "You're —not real." I shout, my eyes wide with fear. My voice quivers with confusion and distrust. This gorgeous man doesn't appear imaginary, he looks pretty fucking real. I swivel my legs under me and rise to one knee, adjusting my aim on his chest.

"I am as real as you, Nicole." Ever so slowly he lifts his hands in the air, and withdraws a step, as if to say, 'Hey calm down. You're safe with me.'

What the hell? I just need a goddamn minute to sort this shit out and I...I can't do it with the dark-haired pirate staring at me with those penetrating green eyes.

In an ungraceful move, I rise to my feet, making sure Annie never veers from her target. "Turn around. Lace your fingers behind your head."

The sexy pirate stares back at me, eyes narrowed, head tilted to the side. Does he think I'm bluffing? Am I? I'm not so sure myself.

"Which part of 'turn around' didn't you understand?"

When he acquiesces, I let out a quiet sigh of relief. Now that those extraordinary jade orbs no longer drill into me, maybe my brain will kick into high gear and figure shit out.

This new position highlights his bulging shoulders and thick biceps. The vast muscular expanse of his back narrows to a trim waistline and rather yummy, well-defined ass, encased in leather.

Seriously? Who wears leather pants?

"Did you see three men in my driveway?" When he hesitates, I interject, "Lie and I will not hesitate to shoot you in the back of your goddamn head." Not really. Maybe a leg or something.

"Yes. There were three males in your drive."

Males? What a peculiar way to phrase it, but hey, at least he's speaking the truth. So far so good. I wasn't the only one who'd seen them.

"What happened to them?"

He shrugs. "They are dead."

"Did I kill them?" I whisper, more to myself than to him.

"No."

Truth.

"No?" I echo in confusion and step closer. Even though I'm on the porch and he's standing three steps below, his head is almost level with mine. Fuck he's tall. "Then how did they die? Where the fuck did the bodies go, Logan?" The ring of his name escaping my lips sends a jolt of electricity coursing down my spine straight to my core. His body stiffens in response.

"At last, you acknowledge who I am." The smug satisfaction in his manner causes irritation to ignite in my gut.

"Answer the damn question, *Logan*." The emphasis I place on his name isn't meant to be endearing, and his shoulders bunch, and I take a second to ponder if they are as solid as they appear.

"It does not matter. They can never threaten you again," he says in a low growl and turns to face me; his hands stay locked behind his head.

Sweet baby Jesus. He's impressive. My focus moves over his seductive body. The way the black leather pants hug lean hips and powerful thighs. How the defined muscles of his chest flex through his shirt with every shift. Below the edge of the sleeve on his right arm a complex, black tattoo curves around his bicep. Logan was built for sin, every inch of him tight and bulky with corded muscle. A killer.

It hits me again; Logan stands before me. A man I've been in lust with for eight years. A man who radiates sensuality like other people radiate insecurity.

His head tips, eyeing me. The green eyes sparkle in the low light from the porch. Unease ripples through me and I squirm. I never squirm.

"You will forget they were ever here, Nicole." His deep, husky voice fills the space between us. "Do you understand?"

A warm tingle nudges my brain and pressure builds behind my forehead. The power of Logan's voice is extraordinary. I'm compelled to respond yes. In fact, I open my mouth to answer yes, to tell him whatever he demands to hear.

But a split second before doing something stupid, like obey, my mouth and mental shields slam down so hard and swift my head spins and my teeth rattle. Logan's forehead creases with concentration. He's deeply surprised—mildly annoyed—by my resistance.

"Is that so?" Sarcasm wraps around me like a bulletproof vest and I throw off whatever magnetic pull he was trying to exert over my mind. "It looks like I'm the one with the upper hand here, so you need to answer my question. What happened to the bodies, Logan?"

"We have more urgent things to discuss," he evades with a low growl.

Before I can stop it, a snort escapes. "More critical than three missing dead bodies? Oh... goody."

This situation is surreal and numerous questions swirl around in my brain. And not just about tonight. I open my mouth to propose a question but snap it closed, unsure what I want to ask first. Logan's existence blows my mind. The man looks even hotter than he did in my dreams. The dreams were murky, muted in color. Now he's... incredible. Vibrant. Alive. It's like switching from a small black-and-white TV with wavy lines and static, to a 75-inch HDTV flat screen with cable. There's no comparison.

"I'm not certain what to ask you first." I swallow my fear and confusion.

"Baby," Jesus, I seriously hate when he calls me that. It makes me crave to jump his bones. "I will answer whatever questions you wish but let us do so inside the safety of your home," he implores. "You are vulnerable in the open."

"No shit." Again with the sarcasm. I can't help it where he's concerned. Maybe because I still don't trust he's real? That I'm standing on my front porch talking to myself after having a total *Call of Duty* moment in my front yard?

His eyes narrow and he looks down at Annie for a long moment. A muscle flexes in his jaw. I almost hear his mind whirling with what options lay before him.

Then he's in front of me. His formidable body towers over me, and I'm... gun-less.

Son of a bitch. How the hell did that happen?

Not taking the time to figure it out, my training kicks in, and my fist slams into Logan's granite jaw with a hard-right hook.

Holy fuck that hurt.

His head jerks to the side, and he stumbles back a step. More from shock than from the impact of my punch I suspect, but still.

Yay me.

I drop into a crouch and swing a leg out, knocking his feet out from under him. For a split second, I watch the big man tumble backward off the porch. His massive body lands with a resounding thud, and dirt poofs around him like in a cartoon.

Not waiting around to determine if he's injured, I spin, fling open the screen door, and reach in my pocket for my keys. Up close, I'm no match for his strength and size. I had the element of surprise, but now it's gone.

With hands steadier than my heart rate, I shove the key into the lock. But before I even twist it, a solid body slams me into the door. A hand winds in my hair, the other wraps around my midriff like a steel band, pinning my arms to my side. His breath at my temple smells of cinnamon and the hard planes of his body press into my backside like a second skin.

And just like that, my body bursts into flame. The current arcing through us becomes stronger with each breath, each heartbeat. The wood door rubs against the hard points of my nipples through my shirt and I'm suddenly glad I didn't wear a bra.

My mind screams to sink back into him and experience his hands on my body. I envision them reaching for my breasts. Pinching my aching nipples, sending bolts of electricity to my core. My stomach quivers as I imagine them sliding down the waistband of my jeans into my slick heat. He'd whisper all the dirty things he wishes to do, and I would shatter in ecstasy around his fingers.

Holy shit. I'm about to explode right here if I don't get my carnal thoughts under control, and he hasn't even touched me. Well, except for the steel band wrapped around my waist and arms restraining me.

It hits me like a jolt of electricity. The reason my body explodes with fiery need. The man I've ached and yearned for my whole life, or as far back as I recall anyway, restrains me. It set off all these delicious fantasies in my head.

"I smell your desire, Nicole," he whispers in a low groan.

Oh God, he smells me? My heart rate shoots into overdrive.

"Feel what you do to me."

His lower body presses tighter into me, and his hard erection pushes into my lower back and the top of my ass. Wow. He's big everywhere.

The stubble of his goatee scratches my neck, and I need more of the light scraping. The slight sting proves he's here. This is real. My insides clench at nothing, begging to be filled. By him. I arch back into his hard cock, demanding more of him.

"Nicole." Logan growls low, undulating his hips into me. "I want to fuck you until the sun rises." Hot breath fills my ear, his voice a low rumble at my back that does things to the very essence of me. "Bury my face in your sweet pussy and savor you until I have my fill."

Hooolly shiiiiit.

I love that he says such dirty, wanton things to me. My whole-body flushes with heat, need, and a hunger so fierce it threatens to devour me. It craves his like a drug it's long been denied, and I could shatter into a million pieces, right here on my front porch.

Oh yeah. We're still standing on my porch. I sober as the reminder penetrates the lust-filled fog. My all-consuming reaction to him scares the crap out of me.

"Logan,"

"No," he growls. "Do not push me away."

The tingle of my scalp eases as his fingers disengage from my hair and I want to moan in protest. In a haze of longing, I watch his hand as it moves into my line of sight. With my forehead pressed into the wood, my eyes track the movements. He turns the key in the deadbolt with a determined click and swings the door wide. His hold tightens as my support gives way.

"Invite me in, Nicole."

What? Now he wants to be polite? Requesting an invitation after he's slammed me into the door?

"Are you kidding me?" I say, my eyes rolling in irritation. Fine, I can play. "Do come in, Logan."

Never letting go of his hold on me, he walks us both into the entryway. The sound of the door slamming is a cannon explosion in my brain, and my whole body jerks in response. The haze of lust morphs into panic, and every muscle tenses in reaction.

I'm alone in the house, in the middle of nowhere, with a powerful and deadly man. One who could easily subdue me if he chose to, no matter how much training I've had. The last residual pull of lust squelches beneath my rapidly growing fear.

What the hell did you let into your house, Nicole?

Chapter 10

Nicole

The heat from Logan's chest buffets my back. It surrounds me. Overwhelms me. His presence sucks all the oxygen from the room, and my head spins with his clean, masculine scent.

"Let me go, Logan."

His response? A low, feral growl. "No."

Unease fights with lust. My body tight and hot. Tingles race along my nerve endings as Logan's need shoots through me like a nuclear blast. "Damn it, let me go."

Again, "No."

Tonight steamrolled into an episode of The Twilight Zone. Bullets flying into men's bodies, but they don't die and then vanish altogether. And the icing on the cake? The man I assumed a product of my imagination, encountered only in dreams, presses so close behind me I can't tell where he ends and I begin. There's a part of my brain craving nothing more than to twist in his embrace and let him have his wicked way with me.

Fuck, yeah. Yup, that part.

But it's warring with the rational side. The one telling me to resist, to get control of this situation and obtain answers. It's unfortunate when the logical trait prevails.

"Logan—" but before I even complete the sentence, he spins me around, locking both wrists behind my back with one powerful hand. My erect nipples rub against rock-hard abs with every panting breath. I bite my lip to keep a moan from escaping, wanting nothing more than to stroke against him like a damn cat in heat.

My gaze lifts. Bright emerald eyes bore into mine with intensity. The beauty of them leaves me dazed. As vibrant and emerald green as the rainforest, with the longest lashes I've ever seen on a man.

For several heartbeats, I'm still not positive Logan's real. Did I trip and fall, knocking my head on the porch while coming into the house? Am I hallucinating?

A lazy, tantalizing smile spreads across his mouth. So wicked. My lower abdomen tightens, fingernails cutting into my palms. Holy. Shit. I'm in trouble.

The thick lashes drop, and he presses that sexy mouth against mine. The blistering heat from the kiss sears my lips as his tongue separates them, diving inside. He tastes dark and dangerous. My insides clench, the grip on my wrists tightens, holding me with ease against his rock-hard body as he devours me. I kiss him back, loving his possessiveness, his dominance and control over my body. Logan's aware I want him, and takes complete advantage of the fact.

Sexy.

My skin ignites with tiny flares as his other hand slides along my neck, burying itself in my hair. Taking a handful of my tresses, he yanks my head back, allowing him better access to my mouth.

Fuck. I've been kissed before. Logan doesn't just kiss, he consumes. His talented tongue slides past my lips and he explores my mouth as if every crevice is his and his alone. No one's ever kissed me like this before. It shouts possession. Demands submission.

When I press closer, he lifts his lips, letting out an inhuman growl of satisfaction, his vivid green eyes snap to mine. The ownership in them makes my insides burn hotter, drenching my panties. I close my eyes against the intensity.

"Mine."

The low, sexy rumble vibrates my nipples. The hard pressure of his cock against my stomach makes me purr, and I press even closer, the ache between my legs unbearable.

"Been craving your taste for eight goddamn years."

My eyes snap open, and in a split second, I'm back to reality. It's like a bucket of cold water was thrown in my face. Eight years. Yes. Where the hell has he been? More remarkable, how is he here? Alive and real? I need answers.

Right the fuck now.

Logan notices the shift in me. His body stiffens, and he straightens, never letting go of the control on my wrists.

"Take your fucking hands off me," I pant, uncertain I want them gone.

A low growl erupts from his throat, and before I blink, I'm on my back. The unforgiving hardwood knocking the breath from my lungs. He pins my wrists above my head with one hand. The other plants on the floor by my rib cage, holding most of his weight.

Even through the red haze of anger, I acknowledge the sexy way his biceps ripple and flex, the heaviness of his hips cradled between my thighs, and the enormous erection grinding against my aching core as I struggle in his hold.

This is a situation I've maneuvered out of many times in training. It's a classic dominant position. So why can't I move? Logan's not as bulky as Kurtis.

The power in Logan's grip, in his body, ignites a past fear I can't contain. Even though I perceive no evil intent from Logan, visions of another face take residence in my head. My breathing jacks, and I squeeze my eyes shut, willing myself not to panic. Terror takes hold, and my pulse whooshes in my ears. I shake my head to try and clear the images. Logan won't harm me. He would never hurt me. But fear seizes my lungs when I open my eyes and...

Dimitri.

The black cloud enshrouding my childhood lifts with a savage jerk. Pain lances through my skull and *his* leering face emerges above me. My mind seizes as memory after memory assaults me with the rapid fire of a machine gun. I'm sucked back into the past where my innocence was stolen with brutal force.

With a transparency I don't want, all the nights Dimitri visited my room flash behind my closed lids. The horrors endured at his hands, the contempt of my mother, Bridget. Every threat. All the suffering and humiliation. Oh, God. No wonder my mind blocked it out. It was too much. It's too much now, but there's no stopping the onslaught.

The weight of Logan's body above mine jolts me back to the present. But instead of Logan, the past and present fuse and my skin crawls as Dimitri's putrid breath rushes across my face. The hissing of his voice fills my head.

"Relax my sweet, sweet girl. I will enjoy this."

The firm, bitterness of his lips fills my mouth again. I gag. Pinned. Powerless. Afraid. I'm a young girl again. My body trembles as I cry out.

"No! Please stop!"

"Nicole?"

In an instant, the weight disappears. The punishing grip on my wrists lift and I roll to the side, wrapping my arms around my middle in a protective gesture. With every muscle quaking, I draw my knees up to a fetal position, rocking back and forth. My brain doesn't possess the capacity for more.

My world tilts, and I'm lifted into powerful arms. Cradled against a warm and inviting chest. I tense in protest but the pulsing throb in my head overrides the need to struggle.

"Nicole. It is me. Logan. I am... so sorry. Just hold on, baby. I have you." He declares in a broken whisper near my ear. The tone laced with... regret. Pain.

I lift lead-filled lids and stare at him, too depleted to sense much emotion. Logan blurs before me. I blink, but my vision slides out of focus again.

"Logan?" I whimper.

"Yes, baby. You are safe."

We're moving, but I'm uncertain to where, until I descend into the willowy softness of my bed. I don't even try to resist, just roll onto my side and bury my face in the pillow. The need to bawl my eyes out, to saturate it with my tears threatens, but not a single one falls. I'm beyond exhaustion. The damn house could burn down around me, and I wouldn't move from this spot. I want to slip into a deep sleep and forget this day ever happened. Forget the hideous memories.

Why, oh why, did I remember? The nightmares make sense now. My subconscious tried to prepare me. Desensitize me for the coming reality. But nothing could've prepared me for the flood of images, and the pain and terror they'd bring.

Dimitri's who I've been running from. My own stepfather. Why didn't he just kill me as a teenager? There'd been plenty of opportunities.

Ten of them.

The laces of my boots loosen, before slipping from my feet, hitting the floor with a soft thud. I don't stir. I'm conscious of my surroundings, but it's like my brain turned out the closed sign. Not open for business. Under construction.

My body lifts again, and the sheets and comforter slide out from underneath and spread over my still form. I don't speak or help. I shiver as the icy tundra seeps deep into my bones.

Logan's weight presses on the bed behind me. Glorious heat sinks into my back through the blanket. I ease into it, my body pursuing the warmth. But it's not enough, every muscle and tendon tremble out of control. A powerful arm reaches around me, and draws me closer. Warmth surrounds me and I want nothing more than to turn into his embrace. Could his heat invade my chest and thaw my frozen heart? I breathe in his familiar scent of cinnamon and spice.

"Sleep, Nicole," Logan whispers into my hair. "You are safe tonight. Even from me."

The rasp of his voice penetrates my brain. "I'm not safe from anyone or anything, Logan. Especially you." The words escape on barely a whisper, but his body tenses. The fist at my heart clenches, although Logan says nothing. The deepening silence and his presence eases the trembling from my limbs. Darkness invades.

With a last sigh, I embrace the oblivion and slide away into the dark, welcoming abyss of sleep.

Chapter 11

Logan

It warms my heart to watch my mate sleep, but something in me still reels from the look she gave me earlier. In all our dream time together, I have witnessed every emotion flicker through her pretty grey eyes, but the terror tonight threatened to bring me to my knees.

In the split second the barriers around her mind slipped, the overwhelming emotions simmering below the surface tore into me. Nicole ceased to be in the room and I no longer existed. To her, I become someone else.

But who? And when? Anger and fear gnaw at my insides. The notion of anyone hurting my mate seizes my lungs. I reflect on our dream encounters over the years. Not once did Nicole ever hint at anything troubling her. How could she not disclose something so traumatic?

A fucking team member guarded her. Always. Where had her damn protection detail been? King Scott and I will have words at the first opportunity.

My fists clench remembering the sound of her frantic plea. It pierced through my lust-filled haze like a knife through my heart. I would sooner face the sun than cause her pain. Nicole fell apart into tiny, fragmented pieces, and the agony in my chest almost took me with her.

Dammit. Tonight's debacle falls at my feet. My control vanished. The demand for my mate overrode all the vows I made earlier. The ones to be gentle, go easy. The second those Guardians challenged her, something snapped. I ripped into them with my bare hands in a matter of seconds. The beast within took over. It demanded I protect what belonged to me, to take out the threat to my mate.

Once the danger was neutralized, I sought Nicole. She sat on the porch steps looking defeated, and the violence vanished as rapidly as it arrived. I immediately believed she befell injury and my heart almost exploded in my chest.

Not for the first time, I reflect on how easy it would be for the king's enemies to execute her. Immortals, humans, a goddamn human virus or disease. When her eyes found mine, vulnerability and softness reflected in the beautiful gray depths and my arms throbbed with the need to wrap Nicole in my embrace.

The reports indicated she took self-defense classes, but her fighting prowess shocked the hell out of me. It also... aroused. The primal need to conquer overrode my common sense. Her gray eyes sparked with anger. Her skin flushed. My cock swelled. Thank God she hadn't run. The predator within would have hunted her down and taken her like an animal.

No matter how much she worked to fight it, Nicole was not immune to our attraction either. The sweet, musky perfume of her desire filled my senses, and her body relaxed, responding to my touch. Need, thirst, and lust drove me to delirium. If my fingers had slid down her jeans, they would have come away wet.

The mere notion of tasting my mate has my cock once again straining against my leathers. My fangs throb to sink into the flesh of her neck and drink my fill.

Nicole stirs. A husky moan escapes, as if she senses my hunger and her body responds to it even in slumber. When she twists, curving her luscious little body into mine, I draw her closer, wrapping myself around her slight form.

My eyes close in ecstasy as I inhale the aroma designed perfectly for me. I clench my fists and wage war with my vampire. It urges me to remove the blankets and ravage her breasts with my teeth and tongue. Lick every inch of her stomach, and the sweet spot between her thighs. Fierce, shaking lust steels my breath, leaving me hard and aching.

Mine. The beast whispers.

I freeze in place and pray for her to do the same. If one muscle moves, if those gray eyes open, if she pushes into me one more inch, all will be lost. It is the concept of Nicole peering at me with betrayal and mistrust that keeps the beast in check.

These years of being without my mate were worth the misery. Worth the risk of hiding her. Worth the risk of the king's wrath. There is nothing I would not sacrifice, including my life, for hers. Nicole is my everything. My mate.

"Tomorrow night we will start anew, little one," I whisper into her ear. "I pledge to be gentle, to allow you time and the answers you seek."

The pull of the coming dawn claws at my skin. I ignore it, requiring as much time with Nicole as feasible. I do not wish is to take off without explaining matters, but she is in no condition for an in-depth discussion. Tomorrow night will be soon enough to hash everything out. Tomorrow night, Nicole will come to terms with who and what I am. Who and what *she* is. And what she means to me.

Once those things get settled, we will flee this town and locate a new sanctuary. A home on the stunning beaches of southern Mexico, or a cabin in the thick woodlands of the Ozarks. Wherever we decide, I will make certain she stays protected.

Frustration runs through my veins as I recall the money sitting in the account I opened for her. Such a minuscule sum she has withdrawn over the years. Why? Sebastian set the account up so she would never struggle with finances. It gives her the freedom to never work again if she prefers not to. He opened it under the guise of her mother, the name as fictitious as the bank. Dimitri could never tie it back to her or me. But Nicole hardly touched it.

The emerging differences in her body waft through my senses. Her transition is close. More than ever it is imperative she remain hidden and protected. If Nicole is safe, it will allow me to focus on the final placement of our army to fulfill my end of the prophecy. She will require support to thwart the rebellions from those loyal to Dimitri. An army at her back will ensure the safety and survival of the human and vampire races and enable her to bring peace.

Dammit. So much rides on Nicole's survival. Our biggest challenge being how to defeat Dimitri without killing him.

Easing from the bed, I balance on the edge of the mattress and watch my mate in fascination as she sleeps. The fates granted me an exquisite female. Lush, deep auburn hair lays around her face and shoulders in thick waves. A body toned and athletic with full breasts. Olive skin so velvety soft, keeping my hand off it is nigh impossible. She is breathtaking.

I breathe in her scent one more time before planting a tender kiss on her forehead. The first rays of morning kiss the horizon, and pinpricks of pain intensify along my skin, but I endure it, coveting every second.

When the pain becomes unbearable, I ease from the bed. The mere belief of being with her again tomorrow eases my inner anguish. I take a second to glide my fingers along her cheek, pushing strands of her soft hair from her face before letting them skim over her sweet, full lips. A groan escapes, reliving the feel of them against mine.

"Until tomorrow, baby," I whisper before disappearing from the room.

Chapter 12

Nicole

Life is unpleasant. Life is unfriendly. It provides you sips of joy when you're thirsty, then brutally yanks it away. My childhood was cruel, leaving not even a bitterness in my mouth. Instead, it left a burning acid that consumes me.

I'm on the verge of losing it. Who am I kidding? I've already lost it. Apparent in the shootout with leather-clad thugs in my front drive, who may or may not have been there. Or in the erotic groping session in my foyer with a man from my dreams. And the best part of the evening; my past slamming into my brain with the force of a hurricane, followed by a complete and total blackout.

Yup, I've lost it. I chew my bottom lip and stare out into the sunlit forest, not sure how long I've stood on the porch, zoning out.

The minute my eyes snapped open this morning, I'd flipped the blankets back and sprang from bed. Not my everyday custom for waking. Most mornings, I have to drag my ass out of bed with eyes closed, shuffle straight to the kitchen, and flip on my little custodian of morning joy: java. The one sure thing to perk me right up. Well, after about two cups anyway.

But not today. I'd dashed outside, still in my clothes from last night, sans my boots, scouting the area for clues I wasn't a complete lunatic. Hysteria bubbled when the sole evidence confirming a complete meltdown glittered in the morning sun: the spent shell casings still scattered on the ground. The only footprints in the dirt, mine. No blood. No bodies. No Logan.

I could chalk it up to another nightmare if it weren't for the bullet casings. And let's not overlook the fantastic comeback tour of memories from my horrific past. They flash through my mind like a stuttering slide projector show.

I hug my midriff and wander back inside the house with the energy of a zombie. In the foyer, I gaze at the spot on the floor where I imagined Logan over me. Then later it wasn't Logan. My past intruded, spoiling a most erotic and enjoyable romp in the hay.

I squeeze my eyes shut, inhale a deep breath, before beelining it to the coffee pot; the demand for my morning fix an all-consuming force.

After my first cup, I sag against the kitchen counter and peer out the bay windows, not really noticing the birds and critters flitting about among the lush firs. What the fuck is wrong with me?

It takes two cups of ecstasy before I'm stable enough to call Alex. Where the hell is she? If I don't get a distraction soon, I'll do something drastic. Like crawl under the table, curl into a fetal position, and bawl my eyes out. I swipe my cell phone charging on the counter—uncertain how it got there—as it buzzes. Alex's name pops on the screen.

"Where are you?"

"Good morning to you too, sunshine. You have coffee yet?" Her groggy voice on the other end is a welcome relief.

"Yup. Two cups." Irritated at the wobble in my voice, I draw in a steadying breath, and work to push all the shit from the previous twenty-four hours from my mind.

"Are you alright, Nicki?" Alex asks in a hushed voice.

"I'm fine," I lie, finding it impossible to assimilate everything and act normal at the same time. "Just worried about you."

Alex hesitates. I'm lying. And if she forces the issue, I could crack. Not gonna happen.

Whispering into the phone, she changes the subject. "I think I'm in love."

"Oh my. Again? I'm shocked." My eyes roll even though she can't see me, but I'm secretly thankful her love life is such a distraction.

Alex falls madly in love with every man she has sex with. How she moves through life with the endless hurt and disillusionment is beyond me. Every single one of them bruised or crushed her heart in some way.

"Where are you, Alex, and why are you whispering?"

"You know, I don't appreciate your sarcasm." The hurt in her voice makes me grimace.

"You have often needed protection from your own vagina. Just saying."

"You use sarcasm to push people away, Nicki."

"And yet, you're still here." I counter.

Guilt radiates through me at Alex's deep sigh. "I'm whispering because I'm in his bathroom," she continues as if the last ten seconds never happened. Relief courses through me. Sometimes I want to duct tape my own mouth. "I don't want him to overhear me. I'm not certain when I'll be home today. It'll depend on how things go once he wakes up, but Nicki..." she hesitates, "if you need me, I'm so there. You know that, right? Chicks before dicks."

I smile at her juvenile comment. The temptation to take her up on her offer pushes to the forefront, and I want to blurt out, 'Yes, come home.' Instead, I grit my teeth, and hold the words in. I'm a warrior. This should be a walk in the park... right? My gut burns and frustration lodges like a lump of coal in my abdomen. Or maybe it's too much caffeine. *Impossible*. I shudder at the traitorous thought. Only one thing will help me deal with the shit life hurls at me.

The club.

Third cup of coffee in hand, I head to the shower. "Be careful, and text me his name and address."

"Hey." Alex blurts out as I'm about to hang up. "Remember your promise. We party tonight."

Oh crap. I forgot. The club is necessary, but maybe I can kill two birds with one stone. The club first, party later. "How about we hit a nightclub in Salem. I'm heading there earlier this evening, anyhow. I have some errands to run." Not a lie, just not the whole truth. "But I'll meet you afterward."

"Huh. One of these days you will trust me enough to tell me what you do when you sneak off to other towns."

I blink, frozen in the hallway with my palm on the bathroom door. "I'm not sneaking off," I lie. Thank God I don't experience the horrendous side effects when I lie.

Does Alex suspect? No way. And even if she did, it's not for the reasons she assumes. She'd never imagine the warrior queen she believes me to be is sneaking off to get spanked and flogged by strange men to ease her tormented mind.

At least, I hope to hell she doesn't.

"Hello? Nicki, you still there?" Her urgent whisper snaps me out of my paranoid musings. "I'm giving you shit."

"Just text me the info on where you want to meet. Say around ten?"

"You got it sista. Later." Alex blows me three quick kissing sounds before ending the call.

MY KNEES LOCK AS I stand under the scalding spray and scour the shit out of my skin like a madwoman. I'm hoping it will obliterate the remembered bite of Dimitri's hands off my body. What I need is a mind scrub. The images bouncing around keep pinging from one side of my cranium to the other, causing my head to throb. I try concentrating on a single memory rather than all of them at once, but I can't cease the images from spinning. My low growl fills the shower and I rub an aching hand over my wet hair. I try again, focusing on one picture. With the same damn results.

Head bent, the searing water pounds onto the back of my neck. Out of nowhere, my breathing jacks, becomes ragged. My pulse ramps into overdrive while every muscle and joint in my body ignites on fire. A moan of agony slips from my quivering lips as I crumple to my knees on the tiled floor. The scalding water continues to pound on my sensitive flesh.

With a ferociousness that takes my breath away, what I affectionately refer to as a *fucking episode*, digs its claws into me with brute force. The episodes started a year and a half ago, and have since increased in frequency and intensity.

Hyperventilating, I suck air, the noise loud and high-pitched to my ears. Eyes slam shut when the pounding in my skull intensifies, like there's an acid rock band performing in there. My gums ignite with fire, pulsing with sharp jolts of pain in cadence with the pounding in my head. Squinting my eyeballs joins the fun, surging with a blinding light.

My fists pound the tiles to distract myself from the agony all over my quivering frame. Image after sickening image from my teenage years flash through my mind with the momentum of a jackhammer to my skull. A low animal growl vibrates through my chest as I attempt to bring them into focus once more through the crimson haze of pain.

I slap the wet floor in rage and torment, my back arches, and an inhuman cry blankets the glass enclosure. I rear back when Dimitri's face blazes with crystal clarity before me. It's like he's crouched on the tile floor right in front of me, his black-as-night eyes boring into my soul. A snarling a hiss emerges as his image brings forth all the horror endured at his hands.

Dimitri had taken his time with his little games, hoping to break me, getting off on my pain. I wouldn't be broken then, and I refuse to be broken now. I need to work out a way to get over the unbearable agony of my past. The bitterness and humiliation eat away at my insides like a colony of termites. The resurrection of memories steam-rolled this episode.

There's one way to ease your mind and body, Nicole.

For once, I've gotta agree with my inner bitch. Pressure builds in my chest and I gasp for air, wrapping my arms around my waist. I'm out of control. Understatement of the fuckin' century. The mental barriers I've worked so hard to erect threaten to crumble down around me, and fortifying them back up needs to happen, ay-sap. Only one way to fix me. Granted it's a temporary fix, but it's better than nothing.

Oh God. If Alex had been home last night, I could've shot her. Killed her. The theory has me plopping my butt on the shower floor and leaning against the wall. I hug knees to my chest, squeezing my eyes against the visuals. The violent tremors escalate. If Alex got hurt because of me, I couldn't live with myself. It would be the straw breaking this camel's back.

Even with the scalding water beating down and the steam swirling around the enclosure, a wave of cold washes over me, heightening the racking pain in my body.

This is why having friends is messy. They're a liability. I put them in jeopardy, and it's obvious now, not only from who's chasing me; they're in danger from me.

It's been a year since the last club visit. New shudders rack my frame as I relive that complete cluster fuck. I'd sought a new place in Portland. One I'd researched, as I always do before stepping foot into a new club. But I'd waited too long. My body and emotions were in complete meltdown mode, and my instincts failed me. I paired up with a real winner.

I'd gone in search of pain as a release. Not sex. Never sex in those places. But I'd gotten way more than I bargained for. Locked in this idiot's private playroom, I'd screamed my safe word over and over again until my voice turned ragged, and my throat burned with fire.

I threatened to tear him limb from limb and eat his entrails while he watched. But it hadn't stopped him. He became more frenzied. The red belt striking harder and harder against the flesh of my torso and hips.

When you're tied up and restrained, there's not much you can do but grit your teeth and bear it. Even with the tight security and cameras, I was a mess by the time someone came in and rescued me.

The second the last restraint left my ankle, I'd lost it, overpowering the guards and launching my naked self at the jackass, slamming my fists into his face until a loud, satisfying crunch of bone filled the air. I shattered his nose and jaw before they could tear me off him. A deep-seated yearning to kill overrode everything. An overpowering need to sink my teeth into his neck and rip his throat out sought to devour me. So powerful, my gums ached with the prospect of it.

It took the bouncers ten minutes to subdue and calm me enough so I could communicate like a rational person. The owner demanded to call the police, have him arrested. But I'd refused.

Police meant paperwork. Paperwork meant a link to finding me. And even though my fake IDs are top notch, I don't want some nosy detective testing just how legit they are.

So, all the club owner could do was ban the asshole from his club and put the word out in the BDSM community to refuse future memberships from him. I swore to never set foot in his establishment again.

They need to work on screening their Doms properly.

Two days later, they discovered the asshole brutally murdered in an alley behind a run-down, seedy BDSM club in Portland. Irony? Karma?

Whatever it was, I was pleased as punch the fucker found a horrible end. It took two days to recuperate. I lied to everyone, stating I had the stomach flu. Remained locked in my room, cursing my stupidity. And although they've faded, like the scars from my past, I still bear the evidence of his brutality under my breasts and across my hips from that prick.

When the piercing pain and trembling finally ease, my thoughts bounce to a club I'm a member of outside of Salem. I've been there several times with great success and it's past time to pay them another visit. If I don't get my shit together, I'm liable to harm someone I care about. I can't let that happen.

Chapter 13

Instead of materializing in the grand dining hall, I take form in the spacious courtyard. I need to wander through the gardens. Take time to shake thoughts and concerns of Nicole from my mind. It requires extreme fortitude to withstand Dimitri's mental probes, and after last night's fiasco, those barriers better be solid steel.

A peace invades my blood as I finger the gentle softness of a rose petal. The sweet fragrance of hundreds of flowers fills my senses. Ten square towers dominate the skyline of this colossal fortress, all connected by high, impenetrable walls made of golden stone. Where narrow, rough openings used to be, now full picture-windows are scattered here and there in an asymmetric pattern. During the day they are protected with either heavy drapes or automatic metal shutters that close at dawn.

In the warmth of summer, the courtyard flourishes with the abundance of a grand Italian garden. It also houses the outdoor training facility for the Guardians. Beyond the massive walls, acres and acres of isolated Canadian wilderness stretch out from horizon to horizon.

A deep inhale allows the perfume of exotic flowers, and the comforting presence of my home to soothe the chaos within my heart and mind. But instincts intrude. They roar for me to hunt down Bastian and find out if the king discovered anything. Were those Guardians able to get a message out to him before I slew them? My insides freeze at the prospect and I clench my fists. I'm holding on to the raging beast within by a mere thread.

All of a sudden, the tranquility and stillness of the castle no longer calms, it is replaced by the demand to protect what is mine. From Dimitri. Myself. Our enemies. My lungs refuse to inflate as I recall the expression on Nicole's face last night. I caused it. Not Dimitri. Not her mother. Me. All because I could not control myself.

Son of a bitch.

When I arrived to observe her taking on three powerful Guardians, my heart almost burst through my chest in fear. Nicole did not perceive how vulnerable and fragile she had been in that moment. The bullets were no match for a vampire, even though her aim had been true.

Shock stole my breath when she knocked me on my ass, but pride surged at her fierceness. In her fighting skills, even as the ground slammed into my back. The knowledge she can defend herself during the daylight hours soothes me. So many goddamn hours I am powerless to protect her. Yes, others watch over and guard Nicole, but the concept does nothing to ease my torment.

With deep, even breaths, I force my muscles to unwind and approach the long wooden table in the great dining hall. I am the last to arrive. Ninety-seven high ranking Guardians relax around the giant table. The three vacant chairs serve as a fierce reminder of last night.

I dig deep for strength and snap the barricades tighter around my mind. If I allowed the king a second inside, he would discover the commander of his Guardians conspires with the council to keep Nicole from him. Dimitri must never doubt my devotion, or we are all dead.

"My King." Tired to the bone, I lower into the chair at his right. Sebastian's seated across the table to the left of him. "Brother," I nod.

'*Any news?*' I inquire with a quiet telepathic push.

'*Nothing unusual.*' Sebastian throws me a shrewd glance. '*Why?*'

'*The three Guardians missing from this table are dead.*'

'*The three you texted me about?*'

'*The same.*'

"Gentlemen," Dimitri bellows as he rises. His manner low and menacing. All chatter around the table ceases, and focus goes to their king. "It appears we have three fallen Guardians," he indicates, pointing to the vacant chairs. "Logan?" Dimitri's piercing blue regard shifts, zeroing in on mine.

My obligations as commander of the Guardians, is to each one of the males. So, it is not surprising for the king to question me about their loss. With ease I stand, my outward expression giving nothing away. My heart rate normal.

It has taken me years to master the art of camouflaging emotions to such an extent that even the king himself cannot invade my barriers. This ability served me well over the last twenty-five years.

"Derek, Mikhale, and Peter were all slain by an organized gang of rogues outside of Pisa, Italy." I know full well this is where I appointed them, so the lie is plausible. "I apologize for being late, my King, but I needed to make certain their bodies found the sun this morning." With deference, I bow to him and await his response.

An expected hush settles over the table. The room is silent as death, awaiting Dimitri's response. The steady heartbeats of my most devoted warriors fill my ears. They give nothing away. A testament to their discipline. The king is a powerful empath, will he uncover our lies today? Could this be the moment Dimitri confronts me with my scheming? Our secret rebellion might end this dawn with our executions.

The utter quiet fills the room, and I sense Dimitri's gaze boring into the top of my skull, but I do not move. Will not. Any slight movement will give me away. The future of these warriors' lives rest in my hands. The fate of humanity. Even more significant—the destiny of Nicole's precious existence. If Dimitri doubted for even a second, all would be lost, and Nicole would be within his vile grasp.

"A tragic time when you lose the ones you *trust*." Dimitri's voice silky smooth, emphasizing the word trust, and my insides freeze. "Would you not concur, Alaric Logan Moretti?"

"Yes, my Lord." Dimitri's usage of my complete name is a hint of his state of mind. He is angry.

After several long, tense moments, he continues. "A death rite for them tomorrow at pre-dawn meal." The king's voice booms throughout the room and it takes everything not to slump with relief.

"Yes, my Lord. It will be done." I give the proper response, obediently waiting with head bent for him to sit first before I lower to my seat.

'*Organize a meeting before dusk,*' I order Sebastian telepathically. '*It is time to escalate our preparations.*'

'*Yes, my Lord. It will be done.*' Sebastian's mocking tone irritates my nerves. '*How did things go?*'

The impulse to snort out loud at the reminder of last night's cluster fuck tickles at the base of my throat just as a delicate hand settles on my shoulder. Dinner.

"I am here for you, my Lord. To appease your thirst."

Her thin, high voice causes my jaw to clench. With an exhale of dissatisfaction, I glare at the vein in the wrist she offers. Her blood is not what I crave with every molecule of my being. This young woman smells nothing like Nicole—sweet, with lavender and ocean breeze. The human reeks of perfume. So much it scorches my nostrils.

"Will you not drink from me?"

She does not bother to disguise her disappointment. Her emotions rush at me, unguarded and unwanted, driving me to wince. She's assuming I will welcome her to my chamber and fuck her while satisfy my thirst. Her desire stinks of desperation, and I swallow back the bile in my throat. But my thirst rages, demanding to be quenched. The king's piercing glare evaluates my reactions, scrutinizing every move.

"Yes. Thank you for your generosity." I grab hold of her wrist and pierce her tender flesh without preamble. I ignore her sharp intake of breath at the pain. She is not what I desire. Need. Crave. She is a miserable substitute.

Even as I choke down the bitterness of the girl's blood, it replenishes my strength. My inner contemplation shifts to Nicole's exquisite features. She is what I thirst for. The fullness of her breasts, her sweet juices coating my fingers, her intoxicating blood flowing down my throat. My cock hardens at the images flash behind closed lids.

Dammit. Focus Logan. Remember where you are.

I withdraw abruptly. The girl staggers, and grabs hold of the back of the chair for balance. Her blood curdles in my stomach at the prospect of licking her wrist to close the wounds. Instead, I pierce my thumb with a fang and dash my blood over the puncture wounds. They heal in an instant.

"Thank you." I drop her arm. The girl forgotten the second I peer into the cold black eyes of Dimitri.

The king slams a fist on the solid surface of the table. Every vampire and human servant jerk their focus to him. It creaks and groans under the assault. This solid oak entertained many kings over the centuries, human and vampire. Overseen hundreds of wars, festivals, and death ceremonies. Yet it still stands. Sturdy as a rock.

With his glower fixated on mine, Dimitri bellows. "Where the fuck is she, Logan?"

A full-on rage bubbles below the surface. His eyes pitch-black. Does he suspect it is me keeping Nicole hidden? Or is the king fishing?

"I do not know, my King." I project a calm authority, hoping to ease his rage.

"How is it possible a mere human child could elude us for so long? Someone in this compound is helping her and the council." His hands clench tight; the blackened nails draw blood, dripping under his fists, oozing into the wooden surface unnoticed.

"The council has been meticulous, my Lord."

On the night Icarus revealed Nicole's birth, the werewolf, King Scott, set forth a plan to safeguard her survival, passing a law which prohibited Dimitri from contacting his offspring. In fact, for her safety, her whereabouts were kept concealed from him, and two others on the council who were loyal to him.

"Bullshit. Those fuck-wits could not circumvent us for so long without help. I demand every Guardian's room ransacked. I will tear this goddamn castle apart until I turn up the traitor responsible for her keeping her from me." The crazed expression on his face intensifies. "I sent those three Guardians to investigate her last known whereabouts, Logan. On the west coast of the United States. Now you're informing me rogue vampires killed them? In Italy?" Leaning into me, his vile breath fans across my face. "Someone is lying?"

Christ.

"My King, I assure you, every Guardian at this table is trustworthy. Loyal to you." A lie. "I assigned those three to Italy, which is where I found them. Dead. I had received several urgent texts they were in trouble." Thank Christ Bastian is an I.T. guru. He placed the text messages on my phone so there would be verification; it is standard protocol that my phone is monitored.

"I have no idea where they were before. If you sent them on a special mission, perhaps nothing came of their inquiry. Besides, we raided the Guardian's quarters last week per your order. Found no evidence anyone betrayed you," I assure him, keeping my voice steady and composed.

"Mayhap it is you, Alaric Logan Moretti." Spittle drips from an enormous fang as they descend past his lips. He leans closer, his ridged features mere inches from mine. I hold perfectly still. Not a muscle twitches as I view the evil darkness swirling in the depths of his eyes. The putridity of his breath fans my face. It smells of stale blood and death. Out of the corner of my eye, my brother's fist clenches around the hilt of his sword, ready to strike to defend me.

"Is that what you believe, Dimitri?" I forgo the formality, and seek the friend I once knew behind the swirling madness. I must slow this rage, or this will be a very long day. "After all these centuries? The many wars we have fought side by side? The countless women we have fucked together? You still doubt my allegiance?" My tone projects an edge of indignation. Fear emanates from my brother at my recklessness, but it produces the desired effect.

Dimitri eases back in his armchair, sniffing. One crucial fact I understand about our king—he craves loyalty and devotion above all else. In his mind, Nicole's disappearance was the gravest sin she could have committed against him. He will spend the rest of his life searching for a way to either stop her from becoming a powerful immortal, or since he can't kill her, finding a way to make her suffer. His ultimate goal being to secure his continued reign. If he ever gets her in his evil clutches, he will break her, and laugh with delight while doing so.

Never going to happen.

"You are right, my friend." Dimitri nods. He trails his long braid over his shoulder and strokes it. His eyes still churn with ink. "You have been my most trusted confidant and ally. But," his maddened, wicked leer pins me to my chair even as a powerful mental push tries to pass through my shields. "Know this. She can run, but she will never escape. There is no escape. When I find her, and I will find her, I will make her beg for death. She will cry and she will plead, and she will offer me everything."

Fuck.

"Yes, my King. We will locate her."

"Ah, but time runs out, Logan. Her transition could be upon her at any moment. I demand all the Guardians team up in pairs. No one searches alone. Sedric will accompany you, Logan. He is to be your constant companion, there to help you in any way possible."

Goddammit. Sedric is Dimitri's lap dog. How the hell can I get back to Nicole with a damn shadow?

"Are we clear, Alaric?" Dimitri's regard settles on the human blood slave at his feet. "No one goes anywhere alone." With a flick of his wrist, he orders her onto his lap. The fear radiating from the poor girl is nauseating.

The human blood donors at the castle came here willingly, with the hope of being turned. But the promise is a lie. It is against Council Law to turn a human, for any reason. It happens, but the majority of the newly turned go rogue, unable to control their bloodlust. One of the main reasons the Guardians exist—to protect the humans by putting down the newly turned.

"I so tire of my current food choices," Dimitri whines, shredding the front of the girl's blouse, exposing her ample breasts to everyone at the table. He plunges his enormous fangs into the soft flesh of her nipple; she cries out in agony.

"Yes, my Lord. We are clear." Even though I crave nothing more than to smash his pretty face into the table until it bursts open and his brains soak into the wood, I give nothing away. With extreme fortitude of centuries of training, I resist the sleep struggling to claim me.

'*Start the process, Bastian. We need to talk before the sleep.*'

'*Yes, my Lord. It will be done.*' Sebastian nods somberly and rises to take his leave.

Chapter 14

Nicole

The sun submerged deep below the horizon by the time I enter the Black/White Club, and by the looks of it, not much has changed. Music pulses out of concealed speakers, the bass thumping with a sexual vibe. Various stations command attention along all four walls of the enormous playroom, for those who enjoy an audience. The area is dim, the lighting subdued.

In the center of the chamber a large round bar offers seating where men and women mix and mingle. A few already obtained their submissive or dominant for the evening but relax before initiating their... play. A two-drink limit exists at this bar. Booze and BDSM do not mix. For the Dom, it's imperative he always stays in control.

My eyes scour the room, analyzing every potential Dom, searching for clues to indicate they can offer me what I crave. Absolution, and the need to do more than just survive. My history has long arms and sharp claws, holding on tight, requiring these drastic methods.

Exhibitionism is not my style, and each Dom who is a member of this business rents a private playroom. One loaded with their various tools and toys of preference. It's what I require—privacy. Although, after what transpired last time, having the security of people around would be a wise choice. But I could never stomach putting my shame and humiliation on display for all to witness. The ones out here get off on it.

I'd spent most the day working to talk myself out of coming here. In my studio, I drove the band hard during rehearsal, until the drummer, Jessica spoke up. She ordered an end to the grueling three-hour session. Exhausted and hoarse, I agreed.

After the band fled, I took off for a ten-mile tromp through the woods, pushing myself until my legs quivered like Jell-O. Nothing worked. If anything, the emotions amped higher, and my mind kept replaying last night over and over again, convinced more than ever I imagined the whole damn thing.

On the long drive here, every muscle along my spine tensed with uncertainty. The butterflies in my stomach multiplied with each mile. Several times I'd wanted to turn around. I even pulled over to the side of the highway twice when the tingles of anxiety morphed into trembling. I drew deep, steadying breaths until the quaking subsided, and I contained the anxiety and tension in my shoulders. Riddick's poor steering wheel became my outlet, creaking and groaning under the assault of my clutching fingers.

Once calm, I put the truck in drive and continued to the club. Buried deep in my soul, this release burns through me. It's what's necessary. For me and for everyone around me, even more so since the past, and my stepfather, came forward. The need for this had never been more urgent, or more crucial.

The second I'd entered the club, relief flowed through me that common sense won out, and refused to let me turn around. In the darkest parts of me lives fear. Fear I won't be able to function without this. Every molecule yearns for the tingle and burn of pain. The demand to subdue the madness lurking beneath the surface.

My eyes zero in on him, and my muscles tense with awareness. He's what I crave tonight: an Alpha male. He's by far the most dominant man in the place. The confidence and authority in his stance speak volumes, and it fuels my instinct. No weak, touchy-feely vibes coming from this man. No evil, angry darkness lurks inside either.

Perfect.

My heart pounds with excitement and fear, and adrenaline spikes the tremors again. I'm so jacked I could light up a city with the energy inside me. These sensations raging under my skin stem from last night, from my yearning for it to be real. One, I don't want to accept I'm so screwed up I imagined the whole scenario, and two, it would mean Logan existed. He'd saved me from those men. Killed them.

Why is that so provocative?

Even after the vigorous scrubbing in the shower this morning, my wrists still burn with his remembered restraint while he devoured my mouth. His huge cock pressed against my belly. The slight sting on my scalp as his fist clenched in my hair, tugging my head back. He'd dominated my body.

Christ.

I force the erotic images of Logan to the back of my mind and concentrate on the Dom in the center of the playroom. He's good looking, always a plus.

Check.

Well built. Check, Check. Not big and cut like Logan, but more like a swimmer's body. Lean and strong.

Strong. Good. Check, check, check.

Muscled arms cross over his chest as he leans against the bar. I can't tell what color his eyes are from this distance, but they skim the room, scrutinize submissive after submissive with a bored expression. On the surface he's relaxed. Biding his time until he encounters what he desires. What will he observe when he glances at me? A challenge. A woman who needs to submit, be brought to heel.

"You'll work for it, buddy," I mutter as a wave of heat rises through my body. I will not lower my gaze, nor will I kneel for him. I am not *his* submissive. Once he provides me what I require, I'll walk away and not give him a second thought.

Every single day I live a lie, pretending to be someone I'm not. We are all broken. Everyone deals with the broken pieces of themselves in various ways. I just possess more broken pieces than most. Now, I remember every single piece.

Soon my haunted dreams, and the terrors of my past will float away with the sting of pain. The episodes will lessen, and I'll be free. At least until it all builds back up and I require this again. It's the only way.

The instant he spots me, I tense. His back stiffens and his regard narrows. With his head tilted he assesses me. Gauges my worthiness. A dark eyebrow lifts when I refuse to lower my gaze. After several long minutes of scrutinizing each other, he smirks with sexy confidence, and motions me over with a crook of his finger.

Yes.

After a quick mental fist pump, I saunter over with a sauciness unbecoming a sub. Chin up and shoulders back. Excitement bubbles in my gut when his golden eyes gleam with ruthless determination. This man wants my submission. The thrill of the challenge I present evident in his bulging pants and the humor curving the edges of his full lips.

Once introductions are out of the way, Dominic—not sure it's his real name—gets right to the point. "What is it you seek tonight, beautiful?" he purrs, his pitch rich and gruff. "Pleasure? Pain? Or both?"

"Pain. My pleasure is my own." The sexy half smile sends shivers up my spine. His powerful hand grips the back of my neck as he guides me out of the colossal playroom. The minute we enter his private domain, the tremors inside me calm and my heart rate slows.

Peace.

He backs me up to a low leather padded bench, which strikes me right below the curve of my ass. I acknowledge nothing about the room; my sole focus is on the man in front of me. With a defiant lift of my chin, I raise the hem of my skirt to reveal that I hadn't bothered with panties. Yeah, big fat no-no for a submissive. His golden gaze falls to my smooth-shaven pussy. His brows furrow in displeasure.

"I didn't give you permission for that." The deep, calmness of his low tone sends shivers up my spine.

Oh boy.

A flutter of fear slithers through me. Could things get out of control again? I shiver, but then recall the horrors of my past. Nothing could go as far.

I gulp and grant my fear free rein. It adds to the experience and my need for this release is a demanding bitch wanting its due. This itchy, uncomfortable feeling clenches me like a vise. I don't respond, but the resolve in my glower speaks for me.

"Disobedience requires punishment."

He spins me around, slamming my chest onto the cushioned bench with such force it knocks the breath from my lungs. Bare ass in the air, he binds my wrists to the leather shackles already in place on the underside of the bench. I'm hugging it like a giant pillow. My insides quiver, but my breath remains steady.

Come on fucker, get to it.

He spreads my legs, and plants my feet on the outside of the bench legs before snapping metal handcuffs around each ankle. With a few loud clicks he cinches them tight. Slow and methodical, he takes his time. Strolls around the bench, testing each restraint to make certain I'm secure.

I'm spread open to his scrutiny. Powerless to protect myself from whatever this man chooses to do. My lust rages, wetting my opening. Electricity shoots from my bound wrists to coil between my legs.

He strides around behind me, and my thighs tense. A resounding slap fills the room as his big palm connects with my ass cheek. *Fuck.* My insides clench at the pain, but the slow burn spreads from my cheek right to my clit. He smacks me again on the other cheek. Hard.

The burn of pain makes me crave to rub my pelvis against the bench, but I don't move.

"Your pleasure belongs to me. Your pain belongs to me," he declares in a deep, demanding voice.

No. Not to you.

"What is your safe word, little sub?"

Oh yeah. Shit. Glad one of us is responsible. "Guardian," I murmur.

Ironic I know. He is my safe word. It draws him into the room with me and allows me to imagine Logan is performing these dark, wicked things. Logan owns my pleasure and pain. My insides clench in agreement.

The image of Logan escalates my desire, sending me into a euphoric state. He dominates my mind and body's responses. The man standing behind me will heighten my pain, ensure I forget the anguish of the past. Tonight, they war with each other. Pleasure verses pain.

"Guardian," he repeats. Like he might forget? "Interesting."

My cheek rests on the padded leather, and the heat on my ass fades. My gaze follows Dominic's every step as he saunters over to the wall on my right. Along the surface, his tools of torture are clearly on display: crops, floggers, whips, belts, and canes. On a long, velvet-lined counter beneath it lay all his tools of pleasure: dildos, vibrators of every size and color, butt plugs, nipple clamps, and so much more. Shit. This guy is a career dominant. Some items on his counter look like a cross between a medieval torture device and a really dedicated back scrubber.

I never let the Doms pleasure me, bring me to orgasm. Not with their bodies or toys. I make it clear right up front; I'm not searching for pleasure when I come here. Although the burn of pain gets my juices flowing—and if I allowed them to stroke me, I'd come apart—it's not what this is about. Not with them. This is about managing and controlling my physical responses to my fears, to the past I now remember. This allows me to take back the visceral and psychological control it possesses over me.

His hand hovers over the various floggers, but veers to the belt section. When he chooses a medium width, bright red belt, my insides congeal. How could he choose the one weapon on the wall that terrifies me the most? This is going to hurt.

Well. Suck it up buttercup.

Chapter 15

Nicole

Three days after what I've since dubbed, *The Incident*, I stare out the bay windows in the kitchen, and savor my first mug of sweet awakening. I honestly don't understand how people get through their day without four cups of java. They must be robots. Or aliens. Or Nazi's. That would explain Hitler's problem. Lack of caffeine. Just saying.

I inhale a deep meditative breath as my emotions drive through me like one drives through the gigantic trees at the National Park. Guilt. Pain. Rage. And their resolution? Acceptance. All the reasons the reboot needed to take place: to remind myself I'm strong, to let go of the weaknesses I loathe with a passion, and to remember who I've become, a badass warrior, so I can let go of who I was, a psychotic victim of her emotions.

After the satisfying club session—I will definitely use Dominic again since he remained professional throughout the whole thing and gave me exactly what I needed—Alex and I met at the dance club she suggested. With the new, tingling warmth in my body, I let loose. Consumed considerable amounts of alcohol and danced till sweat drenched my hair. Afterwards, we relaxed at a cozy all-night coffee shop, and drank cappuccinos until we both sobered up. Overall, a decent night.

I pour my second cup of joe just as Alex comes waltzing into the kitchen, dressed in dark-blue skinny jeans, low-heeled, tan, knee-high boots and a brown and white swirl tunic sweater. Her bright red hair curls around her face and shoulders, still damp from the shower.

I raise my eyebrow. "Going somewhere?"

"Yes." Alex heads for Joe, a.k.a., the coffee pot. "If you don't mind me tagging along, I would love to spend the day with you."

Both eyebrows raise. "Um… sure." I don't perceive a lie but there's something lurking under the surface. "Everything all right, Alex?"

She shrugs. "Can't I kill the day with my bestie?" She hides behind the steaming coffee cup now cradled in both hands.

"Of course." Emotions are troublesome for me, especially someone else's. Should I probe further? It's what friends do right? Hound each other until they spill their guts? "Alex… you know you can talk to me. I may not offer the best guidance, shit, I'll probably offer horrible guidance, but I promise to listen."

"I'm cool."

"I won't take no for an answer." I tease, hoping to ease whatever shit's going on in her head.

"How rapey of you."

I bark out a laugh at her response and her lips curl in a brief smile. For whatever reason, Alex's lips are sealed. Who am I to judge a person's need for secrecy? I'm the queen of secrets and being a queen of something is *sweet*. Now, if I could just get Alex to bow, all would be right with the world.

AFTER A HASTY SHOWER and an even quicker breakfast, we head out for rehearsal with the crew. And since it's only twenty paces to the garage, it doesn't require we travel far. I told Alex to hang at the house, but she insisted on sticking to my side like glue.

Something in the back of my brain nags at me about her behavior, but I let it go and devote the next two hours working on several newer rock songs for Friday nights. A couple of times Alex joined in as a backup singer or a duet with me. She has a soft sultry voice that compliments my deeper rasp.

When the band finally packs it up, my cell phone buzzes and Jimmy's name pops on-screen.

"Hey, Jimmy. The band and I just finished rehearsing. We've got some terrific new songs to include this week."

"Wonderful, kid, but I've got a touring band coming in, so you guys take a break." *Dammit.* "But I still need you at the bar for your regular shifts."

"Well, that sucks."

He chuckles. "You guys can get back at it next week."

The band was much happier about this little reprieve than me, and immediately started organizing a camping trip up north as they headed out the door. I glance over at Alex sitting in the corner, texting, and frown. She's been sitting there for the past half hour and it's obvious she's bored, so why insist on sticking around?

"Hey, Alex?" Blue eyes pop to mine in an instant.

"All done?"

"Yeah. I've gotta grab my gym gear and head to the dojo." I inform her as I proceed out the side door of the garage, just as the last vehicle from the band leaves the drive.

"Cool, let me grab my purse."

Once the door's locked, I face off with her. Arms crisscrossed over my chest, I narrow my gaze. "What the hell is going on?"

"I don't know what you mean." Innocence drips from Alex's attitude even as her blue eyes scan the area several times before landing on my irritated expression.

Lie.

I huff a frustrated breath, step into her space, and scowl down at her with my best death stare. "Why do I get the impression you're babysitting me?"

She blinks but says nothing. My heart rate hiccups. Why does she think I need protecting? I snort at the image of my five-foot shopping queen, with perfect manicure and hair, trying to protect me. What does she assume she's protecting me from?

"Alex—"

"Please, drop it."

The pleading in her eyes has my head slanting to the side and I scrutinize every feature. She carefully schools her expression into a blank shield of indifference. A clear indication she will refuse to divulge anything.

"Fine." Doing an about face, I march up the steps into the house in annoyance, Alex right on my tail.

Once on the road, my focus keeps bouncing to her in the passenger seat. She hasn't said a damn word for the past ten minutes. At any other time, I'd be praying for her to shut up. She's tense, her eyes hopping from the windshield to the side mirror, to the forest. Okay, she's freaking me out, 'cause I'm finding myself doing the same damn thing. What I'm searching for, I haven't a clue.

Alex's body stills at the same instant I spot a black SUV peel out of a drive we just passed. I tighten my grip around the steering wheel, eyes glued to the rearview mirror as I observe their approach.

Don't be paranoid, Nicole. It could be someone late for an appointment in town, but when I slow, Alex swings her gaze in my direction, dismay widening her eyes.

"What the hell are you doing?" Strain evident in her tone, her fingers race over her phone.

Who could she be texting right now? I throw her a brief sideways glance of pure innocence. "I don't know what you mean?" The time's come to fess up to whatever she's hiding.

"I suggest speeding up," Alex's demands in an urgent voice. "The SUV, which I know you noticed, is about thirty seconds away from striking."

What the hell? Striking? I swivel my gaze to the rearview again and notice the vehicle gaining fast.

"Why, Alex?" Infuriated, my foot hits the gas pedal. "What is going on? Why do you assume they're after you?"

"Not me. You." She reaches under her sweater, drawing out a silver-plated, Glock 19.

What the fuck? When did she start carrying a gun?

"What the hell, Alex? Do you even know how to use that?" I keep my eyes locked on the road speeding by and the mystery vehicle advancing.

"I've observed you enough times, I think I got it." When I gape at her in dismay, she snickers. "I'm kidding. Keep your eyes on the road, and I'll take care of the rest."

Sweet Mary and Joseph. I've plunged into an alternate universe.

"You should drive, and *I'll* handle the rest." I say, expressing serious doubts about her abilities. "Why do you think you're going to need that?"

"Better to have it and not need it, then need it and not have it." Alex's sarcastic attitude grates along my nerves as she quotes my favorite saying in a sing-song voice.

This is surreal. It's like we've switched roles and Alex is the badass warrior. And sitting in the driver's seat? The helpless female in distress. Do not like. At all.

"Mind telling me who's after me and why?" I demand, maneuvering a tight turn.

"Here they come," is her only response.

Sure enough, just as the road straightens, a chrome bumper comes into view on my left. The driver matches my ninety-mile-an-hour velocity.

"Roll down the window, Nicki." With a swift jab at the button, I obey. The SUV follows suit.

The second Nathan's leering face comes into view, rage hits hard. Son of a bitch. I should have killed that motherfucker when I had the chance. The second the first hint of a muzzle peeks out the window,

I slam Alex back into the seat with my right arm while stomping the brakes and gripping the wheel with my other. Letting off, I align Riddick's front bumper level with the SUV's back bumper. With calculated precision, Riddick kisses the corner panel and I gun it forward, throwing Riddick a mental apology and swearing to make it up to him.

The SUV spins across the pavement in front of us. I tap the brakes to avoid them but the second we're clear, I slam the gas pedal the floorboard once again. We fly past as they careen off into the forest, and smash head-first into a giant redwood. Nathan's body smashes through the windshield and slams into another tree.

Uh oh. Someone wasn't wearing a seatbelt.

"Holy shitballs, girlfriend," Alex hoots as I roll the window back up and slow our speed. "What a kick-ass move."

I ignore her praise, eyeing the wrecked vehicle in the rearview as it grows smaller and smaller. "Should we go back?"

"Only if you want to make certain they're dead. Like with a bullet between the eyes." She secures the gun back where it came from with a shit eating grin that would put the devil to shame.

"Who the fuck are you?"

THE REST OF THE DRIVE, I drilled Alex with questions over and over, but she'd locked up tighter than Fort Knox. I'd never seen this side of my roommate before and wrapping my brain around the whys and hows, not to mention the WTFs, made my head hurt.

As soon as we entered the dojo, I tried to persuade Alex to spar with one of the other trainers. Work off some of her aggression, but she shook her head, and headed for the bleachers to watch Kurtis and me.

"Goddammit, Nicki." Kurtis's growl jerks me from my reflections. "Pay attention. I almost took your damn head off."

We've been sparring for over an hour, and even though I'm wearing workout shorts and a tank top, I'm drenched in sweat. How can Kurtis not drip one sweat ball wearing dark cargo pants, black athletic shoes, and a blue t-shirt? It's sexy as hell but, come on.

He's right though. My head isn't in the game. He's driven me to the mat more times than I care to admit during this session.

"I'm sorry, Kurtis," I pant and drop my aching arms to my side. "I've got a lot on my mind."

"We're finished here. You're not giving me your best. I should have hooked you up with one of the other trainers if this is how you're going to spar." In disgust, he jerks his gloves off. His eyes smolder with anger as he towers over me. "I taught you to keep personal shit outside the dojo, Nicki. An attacker will not give a fuck if you've had a rough day."

Geez. What crawled up his butt and died?

"Yes, Kurtis." Teeth clenched, I lower my head. What I prefer to tell him is to go fuck himself. Except I can't. Not in here. Here, Kurtis is master, and I'm just the student. Which gets me going on a whole other level it shouldn't.

My respect for Kurtis stems back to when I first arrived. Lost to the unknown pain of my past, filled with anger and bitterness, strung out from being on the road, I was fortunate enough to find him. He forced me back from my pit of fear and despair and taught me how to survive. How to replace the anger with courage and discipline. The training brought out a tenacity I never knew existed and because of it, Kurtis will always occupy a place in the lump I call my heart.

He sighs with frustration, drawing me back from my musing, but I don't peer up. Not until I'm given permission or dismissed. As much as it galls me to allow a man talk to me that way, because it's Kurtis it also... excites me.

Sick, I know.

Normally, I wouldn't drop my gaze, but for some odd reason, something in my brain short circuits, and I poke the bear, and wait to see if Kurtis takes the bait. To play the submissive role outside the clubs, is a complete mindfuck. For me, but more so for whomever I'm messing with. Right now, I elect to test the waters with Kurtis and discover how far he will take the dominant role.

He's an Alpha male. You don't get to be a Navy SEAL and a third-degree black belt in krav maga without being an Alpha. But the challenge is whether Kurtis is dominant in the bedroom. Or does he allow the woman to control him? Could it be a give and take? I might be able to work with that.

"Look at me."

My insides clench at his order and I lift my head. My neck muscles stretch to peer into his eyes. The near feral look in those incredible orbs makes my breath catch. The blue gaze smolders with... desire. Curiosity? He wants me. And me playing the submissive is turning him on.

Interesting.

I open my senses to him further, and swallow at the raging hunger and need pulsing from him. Holy cow. But he's also gauging my reaction. Uncertainty lingers deep within on whether he should press this further.

Is there hope for us yet?

"Head to the lockers. Get cleaned up and meet back in my office," Kurtis orders, his heated regard never leaving mine.

"Yes, Kurtis." The huskiness of my voice is surprising, but I hold his gaze. Out of the corner of my eye, his hand clenches around the gloves. Like he's resisting the impulse to reach for me. A muscle pulses at his jaw.

What would it be like to experience those big calloused hands restraining me? Or the brief flare of pain, pursued by the slow burn of heat, as his massive palm connects with my ass. He's so tall and muscular. Could dominate me, bend me to his will without need for restraints? Damn him for being this provocative and seductively intriguing all of a sudden.

"Fuck. Now, Nicki," he growls. "Or I will throw you on this mat for a different reason."

My eyes widen at his bold words and the vision they imprint on my mind. Quick to obey, I walk at a brisk pace to the locker rooms. It takes everything in me, not to all-out sprint.

My gaze locks with Alex in the bleachers, and I give her the secret squirrel signal for her to join me. Which amounts to me pointing at her and then the directions of the locker room. She nods with eagerness, eyebrows lifted with bewilderment at the intense exchange.

A tilt-a-whirl of thoughts spins a mile a minute in my brain, and I struggle to process what the hell happened out there. I jerk my gloves off with my teeth and slam open my locker. My clothes are off and towel is wrapped around my body in record time. Sensitive nipples stiffen at attention at the rough treatment.

All the years I've been sparring with Kurtis, it's never once been anything but professional. Inside the dojo, he's said nothing openly sensual or forward. Never touched me in an improper way. So why is today different? What's happening inside to lead me to imagine Kurtis as my sexual dominant? Could I still be juiced from my reboot session?

Note to self; take more than a few days off before getting close to the opposite sex.

"What. The. Hell. Was. That?" Alex demands the minute she strides into the locker room. "There was so much heat out there, I'm amazed the mats didn't burst into flames."

"The heat was more from his end than mine." Not wishing her to witness the flush across my cheeks, I turn my back and seize my shampoo and conditioner. Which is a half-truth. I mean, I've always found Kurtis sexy. Hell, what red-blooded female with an active vagina wouldn't? He's like a god for Pete's sake.

But Logan still comes first in my mind. I've survived because of my tall, dark, and handsome wet dream. The sexy beast who's affected my slumber since the time I was old enough to remember them. Throughout the horrible Dimitri years, Logan stood strong, soothing me, drawing my mind away from my vile life.

I shake my head with confusion. Have I been hung up on Logan for so long I've overlooked the signs? Ignored my responses to Kurtis? His desire's been there, bubbling at a low simmer below the surface.

"Bullshit." Alex straddles the bench sitting between the lockers. "The fuck-me lasers definitely shot out your eyeballs, sista. Straight to his dick, by his response, eh." Giggles erupt from Alex's throat, her Canadian upbringing shining through. "And wow. The growl was enough to wet my panties clear in the bleachers."

"Zip it."

Alex holds her palms in the air. "I'm just saying you need to tap that. How can you resist?" A flabbergasted Alex makes me smile. "He's so damn yummy. Don't you want to scale him like a tree? God girl, if he wasn't so hung up on you... well, let's just say, Kurtis and I would do the bump and grind all damn night."

When she demonstrates by grinding her hips into the bench like she's fucking it, I'm out, hitting the showers.

Chapter 16

When I enter Kurtis's office, I'm once again overwhelmed by the masculinity of the space. It's not a typical office space you'd encounter in a dojo. There's no sterile metal desk or chairs. No trophies or awards covering the walls. The large wooden desk looks old and sturdy. It must be to accommodate his size. At the top of each leg, intricate, carved wolf heads stare out at me, following my every move around the room. Identical heads adorn the end of each arm on his massive seat. No leather, rolling office chair for this man.

Kurtis sits there like a king on his throne, elbows resting on the arms, fingers brushing the top of the wolf heads. The dark mahogany bookshelf behind him is crammed with a wide assortment of books, and yes, a few trophies. The beautiful oak floors showcase the room, as does the deep red Persian rug sitting under the desk. Two light tan wingback chairs face it. Like I said, the masculine effect overwhelms, but fits Kurtis to a tee.

"Sit."

His command causes butterfly wings to come alive in my stomach, but I refuse to sit. If I stand, I get to pretend I hold a measure of control over the situation. We are branching out into new territory here, and I'm not positive how to proceed, what to say or how to act. I've never attempted a relationship with anyone I've been friends with before. This is way out of my comfort zone.

Kurtis's observation intensifies and my teeth clamp down on the inside of my lip. "Sit down, Nicki."

Okay, yeah, possibly a prudent suggestion. Which I'm doing because I want to, not because he ordered it.

Once I'm seated, Kurtis leans back in his immense throne, pressing the tips of his fingers together in front of him. He watches me with a thoroughness that sends tingles to my nether regions. Two can play the staring game. I cock my head to the side and return the favor.

Kurtis is incredibly sexy and virile. His height sets him apart from most men. His broad shoulders corded with muscles put "The Rock" to shame. There is nothing sexier than a well-built man sporting a snug fitting t-shirt tucked into tactical cargo pants and combat boots.

Yum.

But what captures my attention is the fierceness in his expression as it devours me.

"Have dinner with me tonight."

Whoa. Not what I was expecting to come out of his mouth.

"Why?"

A dark blonde eyebrow arches. "Why?"

"Yes. Why do you want to have dinner with me?"

Kurtis grunts, a slight smile plays at the corner of his oh so kissable lips. "I'd like to have more than dinner with you, but let's start there."

I swallow.

Can I do this? This sensation I'm betraying Logan is ridiculous, but I can't help it.

There is no Logan, idiot. The bitch reminds me.

Right.

"But... what if I screw it up, Kurtis? Will you still train me? Will we still be friends?" The apprehension at those things ending sends panic spiraling down my neck. No point in disguising it. I'm a screwed up individual and it's a sure bet I'll mess this up. "I don't do relationships, Kurtis. Never have."

"I'm aware." His comment surprises me. "But there's something between us. Something we both itch to explore." Kurtis leans forward, arms settling on top of the gleaming desk. His blue eyes bore into mine and I inhale with nervousness. "I've been content to sit back in the shadows and wait. But today, I glimpsed what you're hiding. I'm no longer content."

Oh boy.

Kurtis leans back into his throne. "I'll pick you up at seven."

"No." I require a shred of control here. "I'll meet you."

THE RESTAURANT KURTIS chose is one of the swankier places in town. And since I don't own a dress, I'm in borrowed apparel. Alex's. She insisted on helping me get ready. So, we wasted an ungodly amount of time "preparing me" for my first date.

Pathetic.

I'm reminded again why I don't wear dresses when I open my truck door. A blast of cool air sweeps under the skirt of my... what did Alex call it? Little black dress?

Brrr.

Although, I must admit the dress is exquisite, and it hugs and flows in all the right places. Thin, fragile spaghetti straps—that I worry will snap at any moment—grace my shoulders. Soft silk covers my bare ladies to perfection, emphasizing them with every move. I balked at going braless in this thing, but I have to admit the sensation is freeing.

The expensive material hugs the curves of my waist without being too tight, falling to about mid-thigh. Since my shoe collection consists of boots, tennis shoes and flip-flops, which Alex informed would be a fashion disaster, her red Jimmy Choo pumps encase my feet. I'd nearly chickened out when she'd admitted how much they cost and elected flip-flops the better option. The horror on Alex's face made me laugh, and she promised retribution if I dared.

I clamber down from Riddick, struggling not to expose my teeny, black lace thong to anyone in the parking lot. I pray I don't wrench my ankle and drop flat on my face before I even reach the damn door. After several tentative strides with no mishap, my confidence soars. I've got this, and bonus, they make my legs look sensational.

I could get used to these babies. Well, not these, because never in a million years, would I pay over a thousand dollars for a pair of shoes. Boots yes, but these ankle breakers, never.

A stunning hostess greets me right inside the door. She doesn't even inquire who I am, or if I'm here with anyone, just guides me through the restaurant to an intimate table at the back overlooking the cliffs and ocean below. Mesmerized by the view through the windows, I obediently follow the lanky blonde through the dining area.

The bottom fraction of the sun looks like it's striking the surface of the water, flowing and swaying with the waves. Little shimmering lights glitter across the vast expanse of the sea, like a moving blanket of diamonds. Its beauty is breathtaking.

Kurtis stands at my approach, and I peel my gaze from the enchanting view to gape at the beauty of the man before me. He's wearing black jeans that hug his lean hips, a blue and black striped dress shirt and a dark blazer which expertly encases his upper body. He must get his clothes tailor-made. No way he buys anything off the rack to fit his massive frame. I've never seen him dressed up and the transformation leaves me speechless.

"Beautiful," Kurtis murmurs before walking around me and pulling out my chair. His scrutiny devours every exposed inch of my skin. And in this dress, it's a lot of skin.

Wow. How chivalrous of him. I love it. A warrior I may be, but I'm still a woman, and I relish being treated with courteousness and respect.

"Thank you." I lower into the chair, careful not to flash my panties, and place my little black jeweled purse on the chair next to me. Another loan from Alex. "You look terrific as well. I've never seen you dressed up before."

"This old thing." Kurtis grins and takes his seat across from me.

I chuckle and the tension between my shoulder blades eases.

To say I'm apprehensive about this date is putting it mildly. When getting ready, Alex threatened to slip me a Valium if I didn't calm down. In retrospect, it wouldn't have been a bad idea.

"You're nervous. Don't be." Kurtis leans forward. "You know me. Tonight is about two people getting to know each other better. That's it."

That's literally what I dread the most. I'd rather have sex first, break the ice. Work the other shit out later. But, it's not what's expected. All I can do is answer honestly without giving too much away. The less he's aware of, the better. I don't want to put him in danger because I couldn't keep my stupid mouth shut.

This is a bad idea, my inner self warns. Again.

My apprehension grows with the warning, and I fidget in my seat. I start to express as much but the waiter interrupts to inform us of the specials for the night.

I don't hear a word, too caught up in the turmoil of my mind. This nagging worry in the pit of my stomach insists I'm betraying Logan by being here. Why should I be guilty? For deciding to find happiness? With someone real? Logan doesn't exist. The sooner I accept it, the sooner I can carry on with my life. The whole point of my goodbye the other night.

"Nicki? Nicki?"

"Ah, I'm sorry. What did you say?" *Get your head in the game, dumbass.*

Kurtis tilts his head, analyzing me. "Would you like me to order dinner?"

A relieved sigh escapes. "Yes, please." His eyes darken at my response.

While he rattles off our order, I take a moment to peer around the room. I've never been to this restaurant before. It's way out of my price range. It's warm and inviting. The atmosphere is intimate with subdued lighting; delicate crystal chandeliers hang throughout the room with candles flickering at every table. White tablecloths, black linen, and gleaming silverware cover every surface. And if the food tastes as wonderful as it smells... bonus.

After the waiter leaves, I direct my full attention to Kurtis. Maybe if I keep him chatting about himself, he won't inquire about me. "So, I don't think you've ever told me where you are from?"

He scowls. I'm finding his expression hard to read. I wrestle with the urge to open my senses to him, but I made a promise to myself: tonight will be about experiencing this date like every other woman in the world. No cheating by reading him.

"Here's how this will play out," he offers with a harsh sigh. "I get what you're trying to do, Nicki. I read you better than you think. Tonight, will not be all about me. We are going to play a little game. It's called Tit for Tat. You reveal something about yourself, and I will return the favor."

The command in his voice annoys me. I'm all about being the submissive in the bedroom—or in my case the club—but I'm not a passive by nature. I refuse to allow a man to tell me what to do outside the bedroom... or dojo.

"Kurtis, let me be clear. I..." The words strangle in my throat as I catch something out the corner of my eye that stalls my heart. My head whips around, and my shocked gaze clashes with the piercing green of... Logan's.

"What the..." I hiss. Disbelief strangles the words in my throat.

Chapter 17

Nicole

My jaw drops. My full gaze is riveted by the wet dream walking with casual grace across the room. The vivid jade stare, zeroed in on mine, penetrates to my soul. Striking is the word coming to my mind when I gawk at this man. And lethal. The dark hair shifts with every step. His massive body swathed in a black pinstriped suit fits him to perfection. A blinding white dress shirt and narrow black tie finish the sexy-as-hell outfit.

This man dominates the room and everyone in it. All eyes shift, following the masculine prowl across the plush carpet. The women practically swoon as he passes. The men don't make eye contact, but secretly watch his progress, greedy to discover who he's with.

Logan is extraordinary, with the sculpted jaw and perfect cheekbones of a god. But there is also an old-world presence about him that matches his confident and fearless expression. My body reacts to him on a molecular level: my breathing speeds up, fists clench in my lap, nails digging into my palms, and nipples tighten anticipating his caress.

Christ, I'm hallucinating again. In the middle of a restaurant. My eyes squeeze shut for a split second before I snap them back open. Nope, still there.

"Nicki, do you know him?" Kurtis asks.

My head whips back to him in shock. "You see him?"

"Of course." Kurtis frowns, blinking in confusion.

What the hell. How is this possible? Every synapse in my brain is shrieking: not real, not real, yet everybody in this room is gawking in his direction, drawn in by his imposing presence.

"Good evening, Nicole," the deep voice rumbles.

With hands clenched, I lower my head and stare at my white knuckles. My mouth opens to respond, then clamps down on my lower lip instead. I got nothing.

This can't be real. This can't be real.

Kurtis stands, but I don't peer up, too caught up in remembering how to breathe, before I embarrass myself and pass out on the plate.

"Kurtis Ruse, and you are?"

Silence. I perceive Logan's stare boring into the back of my head.

"Ruse?" Logan finally muses. "Thought your scent was familiar."

What the hell does that mean? He smells familiar? This shit gets weirder and weirder. The other night—which I can now confirm happened since Logan's standing right next to me—he said he smelled my desire. Does this man possess extrasensory capabilities? Can he sense others' unique fragrances like people see auras?

"Is that so?" Kurtis sneers, accepting Logan's weird comment. "Who the fuck are you?"

"Alaric Logan Moretti."

Logan's first name is Alaric? Why didn't I know that?

"Goddammit." The curse startles me, as does the clenching of Kurtis's fists.

"Exactly. You have taken your duties too far, young Ruse."

The deep authority in Logan's pitch is dangerous and I glance up, puzzled. Wait a minute. Do they know each other? How the hell is that possible? Until this minute, Logan lived only in my mind. But the hostility between the two men balloons through the restaurant. The ripple effect puts everyone on edge, fidgeting in their seats, including me.

"You've no idea," Kurtis taunts between clenched teeth.

Oh, shit.

A low, threatening growl emanates from the depths of Logan's chest, causing every head to swing in our direction. His knuckles pop in protest at the force of his hands clenching. The beautiful face a sinister mask of fury. The green eyes take on an odd light.

"Careful, boy." Logan's voice drips with menace and fear races up my spine for Kurtis. "If I find out you have touched her, it will not matter who your father is. I will rip your goddamn throat out."

Logan's leg brushes mine and his fury sinks into my skin like sharp daggers; my teeth grit against the strength of it. The cuff link at his wrist blinks with the clenching and unclenching of his fist. Logan's scent reaches my nostrils, and I inhale a deep breath, filling my senses with the familiarity of his aroma. Flutters of comforting warmth spread through my chaotic brain cells.

I peer back at Kurtis—it's like following a tennis match, my gaze swinging back and forth between these two mountains of men—you don't need to possess instincts to see he's livid. The hard jaw clenches so tight I worry for his teeth. The full lips compress. Cold blue eyes loaded with hatred glower at Logan. Kurtis's raging emotions gush at me like tiny shards of glass. But the power of his anger is nothing compared to Logan's.

Kurtis isn't just angry, he's frustrated, disappointed and... suspicious. His nostrils flare as if scenting an enemy. His massive body tenses, at the ready. Like the badass soldier he is.

Several moments pass as the men size each other up. I'm not certain who I would put my money on. Logan's combat skills are a complete enigma. Although, he killed all three men the other night with crazy-fast efficiency. But I'm more intimate with Kurtis's fighting techniques, having experienced them up close.

When the staring contest continues, neither man prepared to back down, my eyes roll in exasperation. "I'm so lucky I get to bask in the glow of such testosterone. Please let me know when the standoff is over." I grit out in agitation.

"Kurtis, ask me to join you."

The overpowering command in Logan's voice startles me. I inhale a quiet gasp of air mingled with Logan's addictive scent, but it no longer calms. I glance at the masculine profile. Damn, he's gorgeous. The tremor of my taut muscles deepens with each passing moment. I clutch the table, frightened I'll vibrate right out of the chair.

A sideways glance over at Kurtis, and I'm astonished to discover his emotions altered to a drastic extent. The hatred and suspicion weaker, replaced by uncertainty. Like he longs to obey but isn't certain why.

I gape when the rage drains from Kurtis altogether. The tension in the massive shoulders relax, and he nods in agreement.

"Please, join us." Kurtis's speech sounds flat, like all his boiling emotions just died an abrupt death. What the hell? I stare open-mouthed. Baffled. Kurtis is backing down?

The power in Logan's voice is strong. It stimulates you to do anything he asks. It draws forth an overpowering urge to please, and Kurtis falls under the spell. Responds in such a way it reminds me of how my mother responded to Dimitri. Disappointment crushes me.

When Kurtis sits, his eyes lift to mine. I struggle to interpret his expression. Nothing. It's like he's a complete void.

Logan eases around the table, takes the seat on my right with his back to the window. Strategically, it's a good move. Since the restaurant is perched on a cliff, no one can attack from below. His complete attention is on the room and the entrance. Smart.

"Hello, baby." The low, silky voice floats over me, and need vibrates through me. Immediately my focus shifts to him. "We have unfinished business."

The moonlight pouring through the windows reveals the left side of Logan's face. There's such an intensity, a hunger in those orbs staring back. The urge to crawl over the dinner table, straddle his hips and feed on those lush lips seizes every muscle. My aching, wet core tingles, longing to rub against his hardness till I explode.

For God's sake, Nicole. You're in a damn restaurant with Kurtis sitting right across the table. Get a grip

Like a lightning bolt, it hits me right between the eyes. *This* is what's missing between Kurtis and I—this all-consuming desire to devour and be devoured. To lick and suck every inch of skin. To experience the hardness of his flesh against mine as he pounds into me. Or his mouth sucking, licking, and biting between my legs.

Good Lord, I'm wet already, and he hasn't even laid a finger on me.

Logan's nostrils flare and his lids grow heavy. Panic surges, worrying he'll detect my desire, scent my desperation to be with him. This all-consuming need for Logan scares the shit out of me. I don't want to need anyone.

My stare bounces to Kurtis, and I attempt to determine his reaction, to my reaction, to Logan. His face is still a complete blank, and it cools my desire about ten degrees.

Logan peels his smoldering gaze from mine and turns to Kurtis. "You were just leaving," Logan commands. "You enjoyed a wonderful meal, by yourself. Now you are going home. Alone."

In astonishment, I watch Kurtis as he nods, and rises to leave. A frown forms between his eyes even as he reaches into his pocket and peels off two one-hundred-dollar bills before flinging them on the table.

"Kurtis, what... wait."

Ignoring my stuttering attempts to stop him, he turns to leave.

"What the..." In stunned disbelief, my widened stare follows Kurtis as he strides across the room and out the front door without even a backward glance.

"Let him go, Nicole. There are matters we need to discuss."

My head whips back to Logan and I glare at him. "How did you do that?"

"It is not important. Nor is he." Logan's eyes harden in irritation.

"Maybe he is." Annoyance overrides my common sense. It does that from time to time. But the piercing intensity of Logan's scrutiny pins me to my seat. The deep, brilliant green pulls me in.

"Be careful, Nicole. You will find I am extremely possessive of what is mine." The restrained delivery scares me, and I swallow.

By all appearances, Logan is not a man to be messed with. Poking the lion when he's already pissed, probably not one of my better ideas. Besides, the sexy beast couldn't be more right. We indeed have matters to discuss. A butt-load of them. But I will not let him control me the same way he controlled Kurtis. Nor do I want this conversation, or the inevitable meltdown bound to happen, in the middle of the restaurant. All eyes are zeroed in on us already, thanks to the gorgeous, dark-haired devil sitting next to me.

"You are magnificent," he smiles. The deep voice causes me to jump, and I concentrate on him once again. "But when you are angry, it is such a... turn on." The green gaze devours every inch of me.

I ignore the sparks Logan's words ignite between my legs. "Let's get one fact straight." I lean in, my voice husky with lust as I stare into those brilliant green eyes devouring my face like he's marking his territory. "Kurtis is important. I don't know how you know him, and right now I don't care, but don't you dare hurt him."

Logan's eyes narrow, his jaw clenches. "Important to you in what way, Nicole?"

"He's my friend. My trainer. And Kurtis was there when...when you weren't."

There, I said it.

Logan's head rears back as if I slapped him. Guilt pricks at my insides. Why? I'm not the one who's been hiding behind the security of dreams. Logan is real. So, where has he been all this time? And how the hell did the man invade my dreams to begin with?

"You're right about one thing, Logan. There is unfinished business between us, and I have loads of questions. But I'm not doing this here." Tension and anxiety edge every syllable. Do I want the answers to my questions? How and why is Logan here? Why hasn't he aged in all this time? Did the other night happen?

I can't fathom how he will spin this. How he'll explain away the need to haunt my dreams for years? Why he didn't come forward before tonight... or I guess I should say the other night. And the most important goddamn question of them all: was Logan aware of what Dimitri had done?

What if I don't like the answers?

Chapter 18

Logan

My throat tightens, and a wave of lust sweeps through me, making my skin feverishly hot. The scent of Nicole's desire and blood overwhelms. The accelerated pounding of her heartbeat syncs with the pounding in my cock. Fangs pulse in my gums, demanding the sweet flesh of her neck.

We need to get the hell out of here before I lose control and sweep the contents of this table to the floor, bend her over it, and sink my throbbing cock deep into her wet heat. Right here for all to witness.

I clench my teeth at the image and stand abruptly. "Shall we?" My gaze zeros in on her exquisitely shaped ass as she moves, hips swaying back and forth with every step.

When I entered the restaurant tonight, Nicole's beauty almost stopped me cold. The smooth perfection of her skin exposed in the little dress caused the blood to drain straight into my groin. Those red fuck-me pumps kindled a whole host of fantasies. Delicious things I could do with her wearing those and nothing else

Then my gaze scrutinized the male at her table. The same big man from the bar, and my fangs pulsed for an entirely different reason. I examined his mind, and the things he envisioned doing to Nicole had the mated beast within rising to the surface in the middle of a restaurant full of mortals.

I knew his scent was familiar the other night, but with all the bodies in the bar, it was hard to siphon out his aroma.

The man is King Cipher Ruse's son, and a shapeshifter. One of the many assigned to Nicole's security detail. It does not matter who he is, or who his father is, this giant of a man and I will come to blows. The dominant vampire in me cannot tolerate anyone—human, vampire, or other—to imagine such thoughts about my mate and live.

As we approach her truck, I place my hand on the small of her back, gently ushering her to the passenger side. She halts, spinning to face me.

"What are you doing?" Fuck, she's adorable.

"I am being the gentleman and driving you home."

"Don't you have a vehicle? How did you get here?" Nicole questions, scanning the lot trying to determine which one is mine.

"I did not come by car." I hold out my hand to her. "Give me the key, Nicole." I attempt to bend her will to mine, even knowing it is futile. Her ire bubbles below the surface. It wars with her desires, but her mental shields stay securely in place.

I move in and she retreats until her spine hits the door. Her glorious scent fills my nostrils. The musky fragrance of passion, the soft lavender wafting from her skin and hair. The tantalizing aroma of her blood, sweet and rich. "You have nothing to fear from me, Nicole."

A lie?

"I fear no one, Logan." The bite in her words is softened by the huskiness, exposing the desire. There is a half-truth in what she claims. Nicole is not afraid of me, but of herself. Her emotional response to me.

Tread with care, Logan. No desire to repeat last time.

"Let me drive you home. Then we talk." With a small step back, I give her space, allowing Nicole to choose. It goes against everything not to dominate the situation, to control her. I desire to throw her delectable body over my shoulder like a cave man and materialize at her house with swift efficiency. I must keep reminding myself, Nicole is unaware of what I am. Everything will be exposed before the coming of dawn. No more secrets between us.

Nicole heaves a tremendous sigh. Her gray eyes assess me. I don't move. Allow her the time to make the right decision. It frustrates the hell out of me I cannot read her emotions. Her facial features give nothing away. Will she trust me? Or will I need to force the issue and reveal my vampire side too soon?

Never taking her eyes from mine, she reaches into the little bag and pulls out the key fob, passing it over. Relief flows through me. I want to pull her close, but I refrain. Instead, I press the button to release the locks and open the door.

When Nicole steps up into the seat, it is just about my undoing. Her dress hikes as she moves, exposing smooth, muscular thighs that ignite my bloodlust. The urgency to latch onto her inner thigh and sink my fangs into her vein wars with the need to lay her back on the seat and ravage her pussy with my mouth.

Christ.

Once the seatbelt clicks into place, I close the door and stroll at a snail's pace around the back of the truck, needing a few moments to adjust my throbbing cock to a more comfortable position, and mentally will it to behave. My visceral reaction to Nicole is overpowering. The last thing I wish to do is frighten her again with my demanding need.

When she was young, my driving force was to protect. To love and cherish her. To instruct her how to safeguard her mind, and control her emerging abilities.

As she grew older, our dream meetings... changed. Desire added to the mix. Our encounters took an erotic turn, always leaving me craving more. Dream sex will never come close to the real thing. It pales to physical touch, taste, and smell. Things muted in the dreamscape.

At the house the other night, the lust for my mate raged out of control and things became too raw, terrifying her. The dominance and physical control over her brought something from her past be-tween us, and there is no way I will allow that to happen again.

The fear, panic, and her cries of alarm crushed me. I will do everything in my power never to trigger that reaction again. If build-ing trust means fighting my true nature every step of the way, then so be it. If I wish Nicole to submit willingly, she must trust first. Trust is paramount. And it will take time to cultivate it, earn it.

I obtain distinct goals for our future, but the first step is honesty and answering her questions. The next step, getting Nicole out of Newport.

Once I pull out of the parking lot, I am once again in control of my raging desire. I glance at Nicole with curiosity. She must have a million questions whirling around in her mind, and I am more than ready to give her the answers. How will she react? Apprehen-sion pounds at my temples.

Nicole is strong, but humans cannot always process the concept that they are not at the top of the food chain, that other species more powerful in every way exist. To find out they are a food source for another species can fracture their minds. For Nicole, it will be even more unreal.

The discovery of vampires is one thing, but to find out she is half vampire, could send her over the edge. Not to mention the burden of her destiny. Panic seizes my lungs at the mere prospect of losing her in any way. The risk of what I reveal tonight could shatter her mind, and it scares me to death.

"Were you at my house the other night?" Nicole asks, voice de-void of emotion as she stares straight ahead.

"Yes." Her body sags. Her eyes close.

"I thought... I thought I'd hallucinated the whole thing."

"No, baby," I assure. "It was all real."

"And you're real." Not a question. The accusation more than evi-dent in her voice.

This is where things could get interesting. "Yes." My tense fingers grip the steering wheel.

"Yes? How is that possible, Logan?" Nicole demands, her voice rising. Her delicate hands clamp around the purse in her lap, and she glares in anger. "How have you not aged? Why did you take off the other night, making me think I was psychotic? And the most crucial goddamn question of all, how could you stand by and do nothing while I suffered?"

Christ.

My jaw clenches at her allegations. Nicole's resentment and betrayal wash over me like acid. Suffered? Is she referring to whatever trauma she experienced which caused her to fall apart? Anger burns in my gut at the mere belief of her thinking I knew about whatever happened and did nothing.

I lock my jaw. This argument should not take place driving eighty miles an hour. Unless my head were cut off, I would survive an accident. Nicole would not.

"I will not discuss this until we arrive at your home, Nicole." I war with my inner beast to keep the pulsing glow from my eyes, my wrath in check.

An angry, accusing glare bores into the side of my head. Out of the corner of my eye I notice her mouth open and snap close several times. The death grip on the purse causes her knuckles to whiten.

"Obey me in this, Nicole."

"Fine," she concedes after several tense minutes. She faces the front and crosses her arms over her chest in a defiant gesture.

How did things get to this point? Someone hurt or terrified her. When I contacted King Scott yesterday, he was as bewildered and furious as I.

The conclusion, no matter how improbable: Dimitri. He got to her. Scared the shit out of her. Rage builds in my chest. What did he do?

I must keep reminding myself of the prophecy. Nicole is alive. And with her transition fast approaching, her safety is paramount. That has always been and will forever be my priority. I could not go on in a world where she did not exist. Life would hold no meaning without her. Nicole is my everything.

No matter the outcome of tonight, whether she accepts what I tell her or she spits in my face and tells me to fuck off, the plans move forward. I will do everything in my power to ensure the fulfillment of the prophecy and help her unseat Dimitri. Nothing will change that.

Not even Nicole.

Chapter 19

Nicole

As soon as Logan opens the front door, I stalk past him, and bee-line it to the kitchen. Alcohol is needed to settle my chaotic nerves. So many questions ping-pong around in my head, I'm not even certain where to start. Thank God Alex isn't here. She's aware of my dreams of Logan. How would I explain he's come to life like Pinocchio?

I reach into the wine cooler and jerk out a bottle of red, not even bothering to glance at my choice. I yank open the upper cabinet and grab a wine glass, tightening my grip when it slips in my shaking fingers.

Heat penetrates the thin dress, sinking into my back. It soothes the quivers threatening to overtake me. A strong, masculine hand reaches around, taking hold of the bottle of wine, loosening it from my death grip. The silver cuff links wink with every move and my insides clench as Logan's fingers wrap around the neck of the bottle and I imagine them wrapping around my throat.

"Opener?"

The gruff voice spreads straight to my aching nipples, and I fumble to the right, searching for the drawer handle. I yank it open and reveal the wine opener. The soft silk of Logan's shirt slides across my exposed back as he bends and plucks the opener from the drawer. Heat ignites. Every muscle inside clenches at Logan's closeness. The skin around each wrist tingles, remembering those hands restraining mine, and my breath accelerates with growing hunger.

The need to forgo the stupid Q&A and twist in his embrace, to experience those strong hands against my bare flesh, rushes to the forefront. An erotic image flashes through my mind of Logan lifting me on the counter and plunging deep while still wearing his suit. I bite back a moan.

"Christ. You test my control," Logan whispers above me.

For a brief minute, he lays his forehead on top of my head before stepping away. The loss of heat causes my knees to buckle, and I grab onto the counter for support.

He prowls into the living room with the wine bottle and opener. The way he moves with such confidence, dominating the room and me, is so damn sexy. I bite my lip and savor the view of his backside, the ripple and flex of powerful leg muscles as they gobble up the floor with long strides. Even through the fabric of the dress pants the strength of those thighs is more than apparent. Unfortunately, the suit jacket covers his ass, which is a damn shame.

With the wine glass clutched in my hand, I follow Logan like a junkie craving her next fix. The power and control he commands over my raging hormones is disconcerting. If Logan turned and demanded I kneel and suck his cock, at this point, I wouldn't hesitate. The prospect of tasting his hard silkiness makes my mouth water.

What the fuck is wrong with you? My inner bitch rears her ugly head. *This man's lied to you for years, practically your whole life, and you want to submit to him and suck his dick?*

Well, when she presents it like that.... "Sit down, Nicole."

Logan rips the foil off the bottle and opens it with quick efficiency. Maybe sitting would be a good idea before I fall flat on my face, but my innate stubbornness wins. I refuse to be dictated to, and need to take control of this situation and my stupid, raging hormones. So instead, I walk straight up to him, chin lifted and hold out the wine glass.

The corners of his lips twitch as his stare roams over my defiant face. But he says nothing, just pours a generous glass of wine. I swallow two huge mouthfuls, needing the fortification of the alcohol to steady my hectic nerves. My gaze never deviates from his.

Logan's eyebrow arches when I hold out the glass once again. When he hesitates, I give him my best stink eye.

He snorts, shakes his head, but pours more wine into the glass before setting the half-empty bottle and the opener on the coffee table.

I step over to the baby grand nestled in the bay windows, needing a moment to collect my scattered thoughts. I slide my palm along the cool, gleaming surface of the closed lid. I'm not sure if it's the piano or the wine taking the edge off, but in case it's the wine, I take another healthy swig before facing Logan.

He sits in my large recliner, one ankle resting on the opposite knee, forearms relaxed on the cushioned arms. He looks out of place in my living room, but at the same time, like he belongs. The missing piece finally home.

His piercing green eyes roam the length of my body. They pulse with an inner light the higher they go. Everywhere the blazing gaze travels, my skin tingles, like a physical caress.

Too much. Logan's presence is too overwhelming. Confusion bites at my insides. I don't know whether to jump his bones or yell at him. Instead, I turn my back and peer out the windows over the length of the piano, into the dark night beyond.

The heat of his regard penetrates my backside and I'm not sure this position is any better. Gulping down one more calming swig of wine, I set the glass on the piano, and flatten my palms along the smooth black surface. I throw my first question.

"Do you know Dimitri Giordano?" My question is met with a lengthy silence.

"Look at me, Nicole."

I shake my head.

"Look. At. Me."

Unable to deny the low command, I swallow the lump building in my throat and spin to peer into his eyes.

"Do you?"

"Yes," he grates out between clenched teeth, brow furrowed.

Yes? *Holy fuck.* I stare at him for a whole minute, my mouth hanging open and eyes wide with disbelief. Even though my subconscious knew the answer, it still shocks the shit out of me he admits it.

"What the fuck, Logan?" My eyes never surrender his. The trembling begins anew. There isn't enough alcohol in the world to dull these emotions. "Did you watch?" I shout, hands clenched so tight the tips of my nails pierce flesh. The slight pain centers me.

Logan's jaw clenches even tighter, fingers grip the arms of the chair. "What are you talking about?" He growls low. "Watch what?"

The rage and bitterness scorch through me, like a forest fire burning rapidly from the inside out, igniting with a sudden rush.

"Did you watch while Dimitri made me suffer?" My fists squeeze harder at the words. "Enjoy every sickening touch? Every painful invasion? Did you get off on my cries from the burn as his nails pierced my skin? The sounds of my screams as my bones broke?" Guttural and low, my voice projects the shame and pain suffered. I'm not even aware I'm crying until a tear splashes on my fists clenched in front of me.

"No!" Shock and horror stamp his face as he leaps to his feet. "That is not possible. You were safeguarded. Protected. I pulled you out of there before he found you. You should not even know who he is." The despair in Logan's expression gives me pause.

"What are you talking about, Logan?" I unclench my fingers and swipe the humiliating tears away.

Logan steps toward me with the fluidity of a lion. But it's his emotions that seize my lungs, and I inhale a sharp breath to inflate them. So much pain and anguish. My chest rises and falls with every harsh and erratic breath in response.

Two feet from me, he halts, head bowed, eyes on the floor in front of him. Like he can't bear to meet mine. What the hell is going on here? What did Logan mean I was protected? That certainly wasn't the case. And he didn't get me out of there. I did.

"Nicole. I... I am unsure what to say. Words cannot express how deeply I failed you." The broken whisper pierces the barriers around my heart. "I thought... assumed, I made it to you in time. Please. I beg you. Forgive me."

Truth.

Logan's pain and torment ring loud and clear, and I falter. My anger eases somewhat at his obvious suffering. His sorrow slices through me like a dagger and I'm baffled. What is happening?

After several tense minutes, Logan's gaze lifts, the blinding light within them startling. What the hell? The glow pulses with the raging emotions warring within him, flaring and subsiding in time with the clenching and unclenching of fists. Every muscle is tense, ready to snap.

"You are my mate. It was my responsibility to protect you. To keep you safe." The agony in his voice generates an answering ache in my chest. I want to wrap my arms around him, reassure him everything is fine. That I'm fine.

But, I'm not fine. I'm broken. Damaged. Beyond repair, I think. So, I say nothing. Stare at him with an expression utterly barren of emotion. At this moment, I have nothing to offer him. Everything inside is gutted, and it's all I can do to remain standing. To not collapse in a sobbing heap at his feet.

Logan steps closer, bends on one knee, and bows his head. Shock penetrates the void, and I swallow. But it's the words which stall the breath in my lungs.

"My life is yours, Nicole. Even though I do not deserve it, I beg for your forgiveness, and I vow to never let anything, or anyone hurt you again."

My world falls apart, my heart breaks, and my insides splinter. This magnificent, dominant and vibrant man is subjugating himself before me. My eyes close, and I inhale his masculine scent of cinnamon and spice into my lungs. I choke back the sobs threatening to engulf me because Logan's words ring true.

Where is my armor, my strength? Where's the warrior I claim to be? It's as if Logan punched his fist right through my heart and tore it from my body, leaving me raw and bleeding on the carpet. But my beautiful Guardian is also raw and bleeding. Suffering and in torment. This man was under the assumption he'd protected me from Dimitri. Why or how he imagined that was true, I can't comprehend.

The muscles in my chest constrict with the knowledge Logan had no idea what was happening. In all our dream time together, I never once alluded to what I was going through. I kept that hell separate. Now, my guardian angel, my white knight, kneels before me, and begs for forgiveness.

I wipe at the tears still drenching my cheeks and rest a trembling hand on Logan's bent head. This man is real. And real will always—always—be better than imagined, and I've imagined him a lot.

Every minute we've been apart, I've imagined his scent with each breath. The flavor of him. His caress. The deep rumble of his voice. My imagination, my dreams, can't compare to this. As much as it terrifies me to accept, I need him.

Falling to my knees, I grab his face in my hands, and draw his eyes level with mine. The beauty of this man takes my breath away. But it's the suffering in the green depths that gives me the courage to speak.

"What am I to you, Logan?"

"What are you to me?" His voice coils around me in a velvet caress. "Nicole. You are my mate. My everything."

I have no idea what being a mate means, but no one's ever needed me. I scarcely know him, yet Logan's comments mean more than anything. The honesty of them vibrates through every molecule. How is it conceivable to experience such a powerful connection to a man I hardly know?

"Logan." It takes everything to swallow the uncertainty and let go of the terrible images from my past. "I don't understand how or why you're here. Or what did or didn't transpire in the past. And I certainly don't understand our connection." I falter as emotions threaten to spill over once again. Logan doesn't reach for me. His palms grip his thigh, but a spark of hope flickers in his gaze.

"We have a shitload of things to hash out, but right now... all I want is you," I whisper. His quick inhale warms my ears, his nostrils flare, and the pulse brightens with his passion.

"Baby," he moans. In the next instant, I'm crushed against his powerful chest, and his mouth is devouring mine.

This kiss differs from before. Before, Logan lost control, dominating the kiss with lost abandonment. Now, his embrace, while still all-consuming, is gentle, slow. Like he's taking his time to explore every inch of my mouth.

I melt into him, hands sliding into the silky softness of his hair, gripping the strands, holding on for dear life. The world slips away and the concept that I'm drowning in him makes my clit pulse with excruciating intensity.

Something sharp pierces my lower lip, and the tang of copper sears my tongue. The acute pain causes a moan to escape, and the kiss changes. No longer is Logan gentle and exploring. He is sucking and licking my lip with fervent urgency.

His hands drift down my body, gripping my ass to drag me even tighter against his large erection. I whimper, and rub my aching clit against the hardness, demanding the release only this man can deliver.

Tearing his mouth from mine, Logan runs his lips along my jaw and down my neck. I'm desperate for his skin. His body. To run my hands over the hard muscles, to savor every inch of it. He holds me tight against him and I can't move, so I throw my head back to offer him better access as I shamelessly grind against his hardness.

With my body on fire, consumed by my need for this man, a realization hits—dream sex paled compared to this. This desperate need to crave skin against skin. A growl of frustration rips out, and my fingers tug on his hair, lifting the sucking lips from my neck.

For a moment, the blinding intensity of Logan's regard distracts me from the fire between my thighs, and I gape in astonishment at the lovely green light radiating from the sockets. How can his eyes do that? Where is the light coming from?

With a suddenness that takes my breath and tears me from my wonderings, Logan stands. Arms still crush me to his powerful torso, my feet dangling around his shins. I flip off Alex's pumps and wrap my legs around his waist.

Expecting the cool leather of the couch, I'm astonished when he lowers me to my bed. How the hell? As quick as the notion arrives, it flees when Logan's firm hands grip my ankles and haul me to the end of the bed, my butt right on the edge. The dress hikes, bunching around my waist.

"Logan. Please..." I am trembling so much, I fear I will shake apart.

"I have to taste you, Nicole."

Logan kneels at the end of the bed, pushing my ankles to my ass. This position exposes my core. The only obstacle is the tiny lace... A slight rip and the material of the thong is torn away. Yep, now I'm completely bared to him, and I love it. I lean up on my elbows to watch his face. The green pulses with lust as he stares with rapture at my core.

"God, you smell incredible." Hot breath hits my pussy and my insides clench. I moan, arching, head falling back. "So fucking wet," he groans as if in anguish. His hands squeeze my ankles, and a ripple of sensation shoots straight to my clit. "Do not move, Nicole. Keep your legs where they are until I say otherwise."

"Logan." I'm fixed to combust at the combination of his firm restraint on my ankles and his commanding voice. At the first swipe of his tongue across my clit, I cry out. "Oh God. Logan." My head lifts, and my eyes lock with green fire.

His finger finds my clit, rotating the tight bundle of nerves. "You are mine, Nicole. My mate." The intensity of his expression both frightens and thrills me. "No man but I will ever touch you, taste you, or enjoy the pleasure of your body." He taps his finger over my clit, and I cry out once again. My insides quivering, wanting to explode. "Say the words, Nicole. Tell me you are mine."

Speak? I can scarcely form a coherent thought, let alone speak. A desperate whimper leaves my lips and my hips thrust up. Logan draws away, squatting back on his haunches. The strength of his stare bores into mine, and I'm powerless to refuse this man anything.

"I've always been yours, Logan." The words push past swollen lips with little effort.

A possessive, feral grin spreads his luscious lips, exposing two deadly... fangs.

Chapter 20

Logan

The sight of Nicole's bare, glistening pussy makes my fangs punch through my gums and my cock pulse against the zipper. The brief sip of her blood when I pierced her lip was my undoing. Sweet and addictive, I craved to sink my fangs into her throat and appease this demanding thirst. It had taken every ounce of restraint I possessed to hold back the powerful yearning.

My reward? My mate laid out before me like a gourmet meal. The first sample of her wet pussy made my eyes roll back in my head in ecstasy, wanting to dive in and feed on her juices. Sink a fang into her clit and lap at both nectars.

My inherent need to dominate, to force her submission, won out. Nicole's body was so damn responsive to every word and caress, but I desired her beautiful mind to surrender. She is mine. No one will ever have her but me.

When my strong, proud mate submitted, conceding to my demands with ease, I could not help the victorious smile. I recognized my mistake the second her eyes landed on my fangs. Shock and fear clouded her desire.

I hesitate a brief second before leaning forward and latching onto her pussy with the ferocity of an animal. *Oh, fuck.* The sweet savor of her explodes in my mouth. Soft lavender fills my nostrils, the smooth silk of the skin around her ankles heats my palms. Nirvana. Bliss. Home.

Nicole falls back onto the bed, and she is mine. The sight of my fangs erased from her brain as I devour her sweetness. Every pulse and tremor of her pussy vibrates through my lips, and I delve my tongue into her essence, wanting to stroke and bite every inch of her.

"Logan."

The sound of my name on her lips eggs me on. Nicole is close already. Right on the cusp. I continue to lick and suck on her clitoris and her hips buck. Delicate hands bury in my hair and tug me closer.

Fuck, she's perfect.

I let go of one ankle, and slip a finger into her wet, clenching core. Nicole's body is begging to explode, but still she does not go over the threshold. The reason why slaps me between the eyes.

I did not give her permission.

"Come, baby," I command. "Explode into my mouth."

Nicole erupts, obeying the command. I delve two fingers into her sweet pussy, and the muscles clench around them. So tight. With lips and tongue locked on her clit, I pierce it with a fang while exercising more pressure to her ankle.

"Fuck, Logan!" Nicole's scream erupts around the room as she shatters a second time. The honey of her orgasm, combined with her blood, triggers an impulse to come in my pants, like a youngling vamp. I could spend all night licking and suckling this pussy, the flavor a hundred times better than imagined.

The apprehension of having a replay of last time spears through me. If I crawl up her body and drive my cock into her quivering heat, will a flashback intrude? Nicole needs to control the next step. How can I suppress the raging desires to dominate this encounter and be tender, when tenderness is the farthest thing from what I crave?

What I need is to fuck her hard and rough. Watch the beautiful backside pinken from the heat of my palm, hold her wrists together behind her back with the other, and pound into her pussy from behind. Then flip her over, pin her wrists above her head and plunge into the tight heat as I sink my fangs into her neck, and enjoy her coming apart around my cock, helpless to move.

That is my true nature. One that would terrify her and cause the nightmares from her past to rise again. I will not allow Dimitri to come between us.

When the quivering in her pussy eases, I rise. I slide my hands along her shaking thighs, and gaze at the beauty of my mate, half naked, body trembling with the aftershocks of her orgasms.

Nicole's eyes flutter open, her gaze settling on mine. I hold out a hand. When she places the small delicate palm in mine, I ease her into a sitting position with her legs dangling off the end of the bed. The silk of the dress settles around her hips.

I slowly step back and remove my suit jacket before tossing it onto the back of the chair behind me. The tie follows as an idea develops. If I am correct, this is the best way to proceed with Nicole while still granting me a measure of control. Another step back and I ease into the chair, relaxing back, and spreading my knees.

Nicole swallows and her focus falls to my crotch. Her tongue sneaks out and licks her lips like she already tastes me. My jaw clenches to keep a moan from escaping.

"Stand, Nicole." Her eyes whip back to mine and she hesitates. I open my senses to gauge what she is thinking, but the barriers remain in place. No clue if she is okay with this or not.

"Obey me." With risk, I deliver the command. Her throat works as she swallows again, but her expression gives nothing away. When she sets her feet on the floor and stands, the dress falls back into place around smooth thighs.

The small act of obedience speaks volumes. My mate is proud, independent, and a fierce warrior. Her submission also acknowledges a yearning to give up control. I glory in the small measure of faith placed at my feet.

Yes. This is what I need. Her breasts in my hands, her wetness coating my fingers, her blood on my tongue, but most of all I need her submission.

"Remove your dress." Voice thick, my pulse races as she obeys. My gaze travels the length of her body. Beautiful. Strong with lean shoulders and arms. The round perfection of her breasts, with pink nipples puckering in tight little points. The quivering tightness of her belly. The slight flare of her hips tapering to shapely thighs and calves. Nicole is impressive to look upon.

"Mine," I growl and her breath hitches. "Come to me, Nicole." This time there is no indecision. She steps between my spread knees with lithe grace. "Kneel."

My mate settles between my thighs, and I trail my fingertips along the velvety smoothness of her cheek. Leaning forward, my lips slide across her swollen lips to her ear.

"Thank you for trusting me. Now I will trust you." I lean back and stare into her beautiful gray eyes. "Tonight is about you. From this point on, you retain complete control." When her eyes widen in surprise, I continue before I back out, push her to the floor, and fuck her mindless. "I am yours, Nicole. Do with me what you will."

A small, feral smile lifts the corners of her generous lips, the thrill of having made the correct decision tonight causes my cock to pulse with delight. Nicole glances at the bulge in my slacks, and it twitches at the scrutiny. She licks her lips and the visual causes my hips to buck.

Nicole places her palms on my knees, sliding them along the length of my thighs, and I moan deep, wanting to throw my head back and surrender myself in this moment. The desire to watch Nicole pleasure me wins out, and I clutch the seat of the chair tighter.

"Don't move, Logan." Nicole mimics my previous command with a fierce whisper.

Enthralled I watch her. In all my hundreds of years, never have I allowed a woman to dominate me. But the notion of obeying Nicole now sends a sudden thrill through my body, straight to my cock.

I analyze her expression before providing a slight nod I will obey. I stated I was hers and immense curiosity impales me to the seat, dying to discover how this plays out.

When her hands reach my groin, she runs her fingertips along the length of my cock, and I inhale. My grip on the cushion causes the fabric to groan in protest, but it is the only thing holding my hips in the chair. Nicole glances at my death grip with a small, seductive smile. Her warm palm on my cock gives a hard squeeze through the fabric.

"Fuck, baby." A groan bursts from my throat. My fangs pulse against aching gums, but I hold them in place. Nothing will interrupt what is about to develop here.

Nicole unbuckles my belt, pulling it through the loops one by one, freeing it from my slacks. Instead of flinging it on the floor, she runs her palms along the flat leather surface before lifting it over her head and letting it dangle from her neck. The leather skims her nipples, and they pucker and harden in response. She closes her eyes and moans low in her throat at the contact.

Christ.

The sight of my belt against her breasts sends jolts of electricity straight to my dick. The desire to seize the belt and bind her wrists behind her back while she sucks me off flashes through the lust-filled haze clouding my brain.

Her fingers undo the button of my slacks and slowly lower the zipper. "You like your belt against my skin?" Overwhelmed by Nicole's throaty whisper and my raging lust for her, I cannot speak. "Answer me, Logan."

"Fuck. Yes."

"I like it too, but I'm gonna love it brushing my nipples as I swallow every inch of you, even more."

Christ. My heart is ready to burst from my chest. Loud, harsh breathing fills the room. Mine. I cannot control my responses to her words. Her fingers slip beneath my boxer briefs and grip my throbbing cock before hauling it out. My gaze remains transfixed upon the absolute beauty of my mate.

Nicole wiggles even deeper between my spread thighs and lowers her lips. The warm wetness of her tongue running along my engorged head lifts my hips from the seat. My fingers twitch to seize her by the hair and fuck her mouth, but I resist. Instead, I clutch the cushion of the chair even tighter, and relax my hips back onto the seat.

She moans around the head of my cock as she tastes and explores for the first time outside our dream world. When she takes me deep into her throat, the moist heat of her mouth engulfs me. My stomach muscles clench with lust, and a low rumble emanates from my chest.

The sound spurs her on, and she devours me as if starved. Slow, deep pulls followed by quick, shallow sucks on the head. One hand grips the base while the other reaches in further and cradles my tight, aching balls. Nicole's head bobs up and down, the movement sways the belt. It taps the puckered nipples. Back and forth.

She comes up for air and stares directly into my eyes; hers darken with need. She darts a quick look at my hand and again back to my face. "Guide me, Logan. Show me what you like."

"Nicole, are you sure?"

"Yes," she breathes.

Setting my palm on the back of her head, I grip the thick strands at her nape and guide those luscious lips back to my engorged erection. I set the depth and pace. Nicole responds to it all. Her moans of pleasure vibrate along the head and shaft, and I nearly lose it. I do not want to come this way. I prefer to do so buried deep in the glorious constrictor of her sex.

Not wanting to stop, I continue to fuck her mouth, gritting my teeth against the pleasure. When one of her hands sneaks down to her pussy, rubbing it in small frantic circles, I hold back no longer.

"Nicole!" I shout in a hoarse bellow, and shoot my seed down her throat. She takes it all, devouring every drop and sucking for more.

After several minutes, my vision clears and I gently extract her suckling mouth from my cock, even though it has already begun to swell anew. One of the many significant benefits of being vampire: stamina.

I lift Nicole into my arms and lay her in the center of the bed. With frustratingly slow human movements, I shed the rest of my clothes, and ease on my side next to her. Elbow bent, my head resting on my palm, I run the pads of my fingers along the silky smoothness of her abdomen. Fascinated, I watch the muscles twitch and tremble under the contact. Her hands clench with desire.

"Are you on birth control, Nicole?" The repercussions of the prophecy plow through the haze of passion. When she nods, a sigh of relief courses through me. Condoms are not something a vampire worries about.

"You are still in control." My focus trails to her pretty gray eyes. "Tell me what you desire."

A slight frown forms between her brows. Is she pondering what to tell me, or could she be displeased? I hold my breath, awaiting her response.

If she would trust me enough to open her mind, I could sense what she needs. Sift through those expectations to determine what she craves, but the walls stand strong. My trepidation increases at her extended silence, and my fingers pause on her midriff. Dread itches along my gut. Have I screwed this up once again?

"Logan..." Gray eyes lift to mine.

"Yes. baby?"

"What are you?"

Chapter 21

I've never been so turned on or wet in my life, but afraid at the same time. Logan consumes my every thought. His alluring scent runs through my veins like a blast furnace, igniting every inch of my flesh. The addictive saltiness of his cum still lingers on my tongue, and I want more. The sensation of his enormous cock, both hard as steel and silky soft, drove me wild, and I couldn't stop my hand from relieving the fiery ache building between my thighs.

His impressive girth both intimidated and excited me. I had a difficult time adjusting my mouth around it at first. I've never been with someone so large, and my insides clenched in anticipation of the coming invasion. The pleasure-pain it will bring.

I'd devoured every inch of him as he removed the rest of his clothes, and all coherent thinking fled. I was surprised drool wasn't oozing out the corner of my lips. Logan's body is incredible. The sculpted muscles of his chest had me licking my lips to make sure I *hadn't* salivated all over myself.

His strange, black-inked tribal tattoo covered his right bicep. It snaked up over his bulky shoulder and across the full expanse of his right pectoral muscle. The beautiful, intricate swirls and slashes of ink extraordinary. I'd wanted to trace my fingers and tongue along every inch of it.

The image of his feral smile flashes through my mind. It sends my brain into overdrive. Were those fangs in his mouth? Did they draw blood earlier? Cause the flash of pain on my clit that spiraled me into ecstasy? And why do his eyes give off that strange light?

There's something unnatural about Logan and it frightens me. The way he moves, with such ease and confidence, with an other-worldly, animalistic grace. He picked me up as if I weighed nothing at all. And I can't forget the unnatural way he controlled Kurtis's mind.

As his fingers trailed over my stomach and under my breasts, desire threatened to overwhelm me once more. But he's asking me to take control, so I do. I push aside my raging lust and ask the one question playing repeatedly through my mind since the minute he walked into the restaurant.

"What are you?" He stills at my words, fingers pause, and the unusual green eyes shoot to mine. For a split second, the surprise is evident.

I examine every nuance of his face, but it's hard to read him. It's like a wall dropped over his emotions. The glow in his eyes dims to the incandescent green I remember so well.

Logan hesitates so long I fear he won't answer. Is he angry? Irritated? What if he gets up and leaves? My stomach somersaults at the notion. Tension causes me to chew on my bottom lip, wanting to take the question back as his eyes bore into mine.

"Nicole." With a sigh he leans over me and runs his hand through my hair at the nape of my neck. "I promise, I will answer every single question, but I have waited years to be with you. To taste you. And the only thing I can focus on is sinking my aching cock into your tight, wet heat."

Well, okay then. I moan low as the erotic images his words incite flash through my mind. The skin-on-skin contact spurs me past reason. I press against him and seize his mouth in a desperate kiss.

Screw the questions.

I thread my fingers through soft, thick hair, fisting the locks, holding him, kissing him as though I'm starved for his taste. Which I am. My mouth slants across his, and my kiss borders on the edge of violence. I've waited years too. My mouth punishes him for staying away so long.

He nicks my bottom lip again but jerks away. With a snarl, he rolls over on his back, pulling me on top of him. My aching core connects with his incredible hardness. Needing to combust again, I slide my wetness back and forth along his length. My thighs grip his hips as I try to relieve the pressure building.

The heat from Logan's hands envelop my breasts, and I lean into them, seeking more. His finger and thumb pinch and roll both nipples and my head falls back as pleasure shoot straight to my core. I grind faster against his erection.

"God, you are beautiful." One hand slides over my stomach and his fingers find my slick center. I buck against him. They slide through my swollen flesh, and he sinks two into my clenching core. "Christ. So tight," he groans.

"Logan, please," I whimper. "I need... I need..."

"Baby, I know what you desire, but you need to be ready."

"I'm ready. I'm ready." Who am I? I've never been this wanton and needy before. Ever. But all I can think about is having Logan buried deep inside me, stretching, relieving the emptiness.

I glance down and revel in the lust filling his gaze. The masculine smile on his lush lips. The sneak peek of a fang gets me wetter. What would it feel like if those sank into my neck while he fucked me?

Whoa. Where the hell did that come from? For a second, the control over the barriers around my mind slip, and Logan slides in.

"Yes, Nicole." His breathing accelerates and his eyes glow brighter as he slides a third finger inside, filling me to perfection. He works my swollen bundle of nerves with the pad of his thumb. Lean hips thrust in time with his fingers.

Tremble after tremble convulses through me and I grip Logan's shoulders until my nails bite into his skin. "Oh God, Logan." The shout tears through me as my sex constricts, squeezing tight around his fingers. The orgasm overtakes me, and I shatter into a million pieces.

Ragged breaths heave from my chest when Logan bolts upright. My knees grip his waist tighter. He tilts his head back and his nostrils flare as if sniffing the air. In the next second, I'm pinned to the headboard and his muscular back pressed against my chest. A low snarl erupts from his throat as his glowing gaze zeroes in on my bedroom door.

"Logan?" Tension leaches into my bones. I grip his strong shoulders and attempt to peek around his side to find out what the hell is happening. If there's going to be a battle, it sure would be great if I wasn't butt-ass naked.

When a tall, gorgeous man walks into my room, I freeze. *Note to self, install more damn locks.* He's dressed much the same way Logan was the night of "the incident," with a dark t-shirt stretched across muscular chest and flat abs, leather pants and black biker boots. A long leather duster falls from wide shoulders to brush the carpet. Handles stick above each shoulder. The handles of swords?

His black hair is short and thick. His lips ridiculously lush. A sexy cleft rests in the center of his strong chin. Like Superman. I snort as hysteria bubbles below the surface. And like my favorite superhero, the man's eyes are the most startling blue.

"What the fuck are you doing here, Bastian?" Logan snarls, keeping my body hidden from him.

"Please tell me you have not had sex with her?"

What the...?

"Not that it is any of your goddamn business, Sebastian, but no." Logan's infuriated, and I can't blame him. My insides still convulse with disappointment.

"Do not," the other man, Bastian, orders.

Who the hell is this guy? And why is he ordering Logan not to have sex with me? It's beginning to feel a lot like Alice in Wonderland in here. Did I drop down the rabbit hole? Where's the blue pill? I want the damn blue pill.

The men don't utter another word, just stare at each other. Logan's head rears back, and his body tenses. Bastian nods. It's like they're having a private conversation in their heads. Wait. Can they communicate like Logan did to me at the restaurant?

"Will someone please tell me what the fuck is going on here?" I shove at Logan's back, but it doesn't move. I might as well be pushing against a brick wall.

When my muscled warrior nods, the other man backs out, closing the door behind him.

Logan runs a hand through his hair in frustration and inhales a deep breath before moving away from me.

I want to move with him, missing the heat of his body, but I don't, sensing his mental withdrawal along with the physical. Whatever the other man said was significant enough to cause Logan to put distance between us.

"Get dressed, Nicole," Logan orders before leaving the bed and heading toward his clothes.

Oh my. His ass is the sculpted perfection of a statue. I stare, mesmerized as it flexes and moves with each stride. The sudden image of his fangs bounces back to the forefront with a vengeance. Fear and anger war with each other to decide who will win out.

With a shake of my head, I ignore his command. I shove the comforter from under my butt, and bring it to my heaving chest, clenching it like body armor. I watch Logan with unease as he dresses.

"I will ask you again, Logan, and you'd better tell me the truth." The warning in my low tone is clear. My eyes never leave his. I refuse to allow his gorgeous body to distract me. "What. The. Hell. Are. You?"

Logan heaves a resigned sigh and leans against the tall wooden bedpost in front of me, his dress pants and belt back in place. I watch in fascination as the muscles of his chest and arms move and flex as he shoves his hands into the pockets. I raise my gaze to the unnatural green, refusing to be side-tracked by his body, and await his reply.

"I think you already know, Nicole." His evasion pisses me off.

"Say it."

His jaw clenches at my command. "I am vampire." Announced like it's no big deal. Well, it is a big deal. A big fucking vampire deal.

"How is that even possible?" Disbelief runs through every muscle and tendon, but a small part of my brain realizes the truth. No mere human would have the ability to invade my dreams?

The sexy beast tilts his head to the side and examines me. The corner of his mouth lifts in a lopsided grin. A large, deadly looking fang peeks out.

"Are those real?" Without thinking, I blurt the first thing which pops into my brain and his smile spreads, showcasing them both.

Sweet baby Jesus. Why do those make me wet all over again? When the tip of his tongue slips around one, caressing it, I swallow as pinpricks of electricity shoot through my nipples.

"Yes, baby," he purrs. "They are real. As your clit can attest."

At his words, my insides shudder at the memory. The pleasure-pain they inflicted at the right moment was a-maz-ing. The urge to crawl across the bed into his arms so he'll do it all over again wars with my need for answers.

"You drank my blood." Not a question, but an accusation.

"Yes."

I expected an apology, or at least guilt. But no, there is no guilt or apology in Logan's manner. Just pure masculine arrogance.

Sexy motherfucker.

"You could have killed me." I lean forward and slap the comforter for emphasis with one hand while still clutching the material to my chest with the other. Logan gives me a strange look like he's angry. With me? What the hell?

"No, Nicole." Frown in place, he shakes his head. "You were never at risk of dying. I would do nothing to hurt you. Ever." His low growl rumbles across the mattress, and I swallow at his beautiful display of aggression. "Do you not get it?" When he leans toward me, the green of his eyes flicker. "The bond connected us the day of your first breath. I would lay down my life for you, Nicole."

His vow rings true. It rings right down to the heart of me.

"What do you mean by bond?" I ask.

"Vampires are given one true mate through their lifetime. You, Nicole, are mine."

I lean back against the headboard in shock. The stupid, emotional lump of muscle in my chest constricts at his words.

How? I don't know him. But as soon as the thought crosses my mind, the lie pierces my brain. I do know him. He's been with me since the day Dimitri came barreling into my life and stripped me of my innocence. My childhood.

The blood drains from my face and I freeze, eyes wide. That can't be a coincidence. Earlier Logan admitted he knows Dimitri. Assumed he'd protected me from him. *How* is he linked to him? My stomach churns with bile. How could the man I assumed my white knight be friends with such an evil son of bitch? Or befriend me, his buddy's sick obsession?

"Nicole?" The concern for me is clear in Logan's voice. "Talk to me, baby. What goes through your mind?"

"I need to get dressed before we finish this." To keep my fears and emotions at bay, I tuck them into a dark, dusty corner in my mind, where I keep all the crap I don't want to deal with. It's how I keep my shit together. This reveal session is too overwhelming, and I suspect a shit-ton more is coming that just might send me spiraling into crazy town.

I leap from the bed and dash into my closet. With the speed of light, I throw on a pair of sweats and a tank top and emerge one minute later to halt in my tracks. Logan's dressed. Tie and all. Right down to his shiny black dress shoes. My mouth gapes open, and I gawk at him. How the hell did he get dressed so quickly?

Vampire. Right. They must be super-fast just like in the movies. I wonder what else Hollywood got right?

I rush past, flicking him a cursory glance, and force myself not to dwell on the beauty of the man in his suit. When I reach the living room and turn around, Logan's already standing behind the couch, his intense gaze on me. I didn't even hear him follow me. The long masculine fingers that just brought me to heights of ecstasy rest on the cushions. The stillness in every muscle is eerie.

With agitated movements, I pace back and forth in front of the piano. I can't stop my hands from clenching and unclenching as I attempt to get control over my turbulent mind. If I opened my mouth right now, it would spew out as unintelligible gibberish.

Logan is a vampire. What the ever-living fuck? My mind is officially blown. My dream fantasy is a vampire. It doesn't matter how many times I say it; it sounds ridiculous. Vampires don't exist.

Wrong.

In the movies and books, vampires are like... old. I wonder how old Logan is?

Really? That's gonna be your first question? The bitch snorts.

No. Of course not. Just... curious. *Yeah, you know what curiosity did to the cat, Nicki.*

I need to clarify tonight's little revelation. "Since you drank my blood, will it turn me into a... vampire?" Panic shoots through me as the idea pops into my brain. No doubt from a movie I'd seen once, because I have no clue how this works in the real world.

Logan offers a lopsided, sexy grin, giving me another quick glimpse of one erotic-as-hell fang. Why do those turn me on? They should scare me. Should freak me out like any rational human being when confronted with a bigger, badder version of ourselves— and we're its food.

But nothing about Logan scares me. The sexy pirate vibe, the height and width of his rock-hard body, the intensity of his light green eyes, or the deep, sexy rumble of his voice. I could go on and on. All of it sends tendrils of desire slithering through my veins.

"No," he replies, and I let out a relieved breath.

"Who was that man? Is he a vampire too?"

"Yes, he is my brother."

"You needed an invitation into my house the other night. How did he get in here?"

Logan's smile disappears. His sexy throat moves as he swallows. "On paper, Sebastian owns the house under an assumed name."

What? No fucking way. "No. This is my home," I grate out, anger spiking through me.

"Yes, Nicole. This is your home. It does not matter what name the title holds. The money you submitted for your down payment and your monthly payments go right back into your account."

This can't be happening. The house is not mine? Disappointment and sadness weigh on my heart. Well, that just sucks balls.

"Nicole, I know you are upset, but it was done for your own safety."

Okay. I get that. I've spent my whole life living in the shadows. Under the radar. I let go of my disappointment and move on to the more terrifying questions. With a deep inhale, I lower my gaze, and stare at the swirls and patterns of the wood grain at my feet. I am hoping enlightenment will come up and smack me in the face.

Question after question about my past flashes through my over-stimulated brain. I attempt to sort them all out, one by one, and put them in order. But like in the shower, they're not cooperating.

"Nicole, sit before you fall down." Logan indicates with his hand to take a seat on the couch. "I want to explain everything, but it might be best if you were sitting."

The nagging sensation that I will not like what he's about to say skitters across my fevered skin as I ease onto the cushion in the corner of the couch. I face my piano and hope the sight of it will calm my erratic nerves, shift my feet under me, and clench my hands in my lap.

Never taking my gaze from the beautiful being before me, I track Logan's every move as he prowls around the couch before taking a seat on the opposite end. After a deep breath he throws one arm along the back of the sofa and faces me. He gives off the illusion he's at ease, but the tense readiness of his powerful body states otherwise. It's as if he's bracing for an impact. A dead giveaway to the turmoil beneath.

Well, hang on buddy 'cause it's about to get a lot worse. I swallow down the nervous tension and throw my first bomb.

"Are you connected to Dimitri?"

Chapter 22

How do I answer that question? Whatever I reveal will upset and infuriate her. It frustrates the hell out of me I cannot read her emotions. I have no clue what she is thinking or feeling, and it forces me off my game. I am used to reading others to anticipate their next step. With Nicole, I sense nothing, no matter how hard I struggle to penetrate her mind.

"Yes." Expecting outrage or shock at the least, I arch an eyebrow in amazement when there is no noticeable response to the confession. After a few seconds of brave indifference, a slight chink in her armor reveals itself. Nicole's lids close as if in pain. The creamy skin at her throat moves as she swallows.

"How?"

My tense thigh muscles twitch with the need to slide across this long couch and hold her, but any offer of comfort from me would be rejected, and it hurts more than I care to admit.

"Dimitri is... my king." Those piercing gray eyes pop open and gape at me with stunned disbelief. I say no more and provide her mind time to process.

"King?" Nicole chokes out. "King of fucking what?"

"The vampire race."

Her mouth drops open further before she snaps it closed. "Get the fuck out." The soft voice is a mere breath, but I hear it loud and clear. "So, you're telling me Dimitri is a... vampire?"

"What I am saying, Nicole, is your father is not only a vampire, but the king of all vampires." There needs to be no confusion.

"That bastard is not my father." Incensed, Nicole's voice rises, muscles straining.

"I am sorry, Nicole, but it is true. Dimitri is your father." I attempt to present it again as tenderly as possible, but gauging by the near-violent trembling of her body, and the white knuckles of her clenched fists, Nicole is about to lose it. Her anger is a remarkable sight. The gray eyes shimmer with fury, her jaw clenched tight.

Just when I assume to predict her emotions, my mate shocks me. The storm of fury drains in an instant, and her tense shoulders slump in defeat. Pain and anguish fill the gray eyes lifted to mine, and my heart freezes. The bonded mate within swells to the surface. Hold. Comfort. Protect. My cramped fingers clutch the back of the couch to contain the urge to draw my mate into my embrace.

I don't. Nicole would only cast off a display of compassion. The wrath would build again and eclipse all the other emotions. She needs to process everything disclosed tonight. Wrap her brain around it and push past it so I can pound her with even more.

Christ.

I inspect every twitch and move as anxiety slithers through my veins. Will her fragile mind be strong enough to handle the truth? Will Nicole's undoing be at my hands?

"Baby?" With slow, easy movements, I shift to the middle of the couch. The need to have her within arm's reach is too strong to ignore. "Talk to me. Tell me what you are thinking."

Tears of helplessness well up, and she stares right through me. Petal soft lips part, then clamp shut with a snap as Nicole struggles to gain control over her boiling emotions.

Most humans would be in hysterics after what I revealed, but Nicole is no mere human, mentally or physically. The emotional conflicts within are an animated transformation in both her expressions and body language.

I'm in awe of her strength when her defensive barriers fall back into place. The sparkle of her rage fades, replaced by cold steel. The pain or anguish of moments ago gone. Her tense shoulders relax, and her fingers unclench one by one in her lap.

"Tell me where he is, Logan."

Why the hell would she demand to know his location? "Not relevant. What is important, is your time in Newport has come to an end."

Nicole's head rears back, and her focus sharpens on mine.

"So, it is true. Dimitri's the one who's been tracking me."

"Yes. From the minute you fled Kentucky. Dimitri is obsessed with finding you." If I am going for all-out honesty, it might as well be all-out brutal honesty, so she grasps the danger she is in. "It is time to leave, Nicole," I repeat. "I need you to trust me. You have trusted me in so many ways throughout the years. Trust me in this." My chest is caving in. All I want is for her to be happy and protected, to never experience fear or sadness. Her life has been filled with it.

"Why, Logan? Did Dimitri send those three men who tried to kill me or the ones who attempted to run me and Alex off the road?"

"Yes." I acquired the report of the incident the second I woke this evening. Infuriated, I wanted to bellow to the rafters in a rage. It took all my strength not to materialize where she was and transport her some place secure. Willing or not. It still might come to that if she refuses to leave.

"Why is my... *father*," she hisses the term like its acid on her tongue, "trying to kill me? If he wants me dead, why didn't he just do it when I was a teenager instead of torturing and raping me?" Nicole's voice breaks with her emotion.

The simple utterance of what Dimitri did to my mate has my fangs throbbing. They crave to rip his throat out. My body shudders with the need for violence. To avenge my mate. The anguish builds and my claws lengthen with the need to rip my own heart out and offer it over to the mate I failed to protect.

"Nicole..."

"Did you give him my location?" Her tone is flat and guarded, but an underlying rage simmers below the surface.

My anger ignites. "Is that what you believe? I would betray you?" The flames of my temper flare in an instant. I close the distance between us and grip her upper arms. "You know me."

The heat of her hands sears my chest through the silk shirt as she braces them against me. Her nails dig in. My visceral response to Nicole is savage and passionate. My powerful instincts accelerate to the highest degree, driving me to possess and defend every inch of her delectable body. My cock swells at her scent. Her caress. My gaze sweeps over full luscious lips as they move. The pulse beating at the base of her neck. The vampire within demands its fangs deep in her flesh, to gulp her sweet nectar. It drowns out her response.

Fangs punch from my throbbing gums with a swiftness that astounds me. The raging beast within claims control. It craves to guzzle her glorious essence while slamming my cock deep into her heat over and over again. A low feral growl escapes as my head drops to her neck.

Bastian's threat from earlier pokes at the rising haze of lust. Icarus sent a warning. Even with protection—her on the pill and a condom—the risk of Nicole becoming pregnant by her mate is exceedingly high. Bastian cautioned me against having sex with Nicole until after the transition. A pregnancy would be devastating for all.

The beast calms and Nicole's comments permeate the bloodlust. I raise my head, and peer into the steel gray eyes laden with sadness and confusion. Before I can question her, she repeats the words that pierce my soul.

"No, Logan." Her anxious eyes roam my face. They stall on my fangs. "I have no idea who you are."

Chapter 23

Nicole

Holy Christ. He's magnificent. Those fangs make me want things that should disturb me, but don't. The pounding of his heart beneath my hands matches my own. Below the uncertainty, I'm desperate for Logan to lose control, to take me as savagely as the fiery stare promises.

I grit my teeth and clamp down on the raging desires that threaten to burn out of control like a massive wildfire. There are too many barriers between us. They spread out like an intricate obstacle course with no end in sight. The most significant barrier—Logan reports directly to my step... to my father.

How could the bastard be my father? Just saying it causes my skin to crawl. The fact he's my flesh and blood makes what transpired so much worse. It wasn't just sexual abuse on a minor. It was incest. Bile churns in my gut, and I swallow as it ascends and burns the back of my throat.

"Let go of me." Bitterness and shame squelch my desire like a bucket of cold water.

Logan eases away, and I draw a deep breath for the first time. I fill my lungs to capacity, before surrendering it on a heavy exhale.

A part of me is bereft from the loss of Logan's warmth as he rises with an unnatural grace. I clamp down on my tongue to keep from groaning. I drink him in as he turns to stand in front of the bay windows. The absence of his green gaze hits hard, and I want to call him back. I can't. Lust muddles my brain when he is near, and too many questions require answers that only Logan can provide.

How am I expected to handle this? Vampires exist. Logan is a vampire. My stepfather is my father and the king of all vampires. Not to mention the fact he's trying to kill me. And the icing on the cake—Logan works for Dimitri.

Damn it.

Wait... back the damn bus up. If Dimitri is my biological father, and a vampire... what in the hell does that make me?

Holy Mother of God. Am I a vampire?

No, that's stupid. I go out in the sunlight, eat normal food. My focus narrows with apprehension as my tongue swirls around my teeth. No fangs.

I do heal quicker than most though. I sense other people's emotions or when they lie. Are those the beginning? Will more abilities develop as I age? Speed and strength would be cool, but I'd miss food. The warmth of the sun. And what about my horrible episodes which have grown worse over the last year?

Christ almighty. This is a cluster.

It's too much. Sparks ignite in every nerve throughout my brain, shrieking to shut it down. I collapse forward on the cushion with my head in my hands, and grip handfuls of my hair. "Logan," I whisper. No matter how quiet my voice, I know he will hear it. "Am I a vampire?"

"A Halfling. Your mother, Bridget, was human."

Thank God.

"What is a Halfling?"

"It means you will always be able to walk in the sun. Eat food."

It's like Logan read my mind. Wait. Can he read my mind? Shit.

"You are human, with some unique abilities until your transformation, when you will become... immortal."

Immortal? Immortal. Hoolly shiiit. As in live forever? I jerk upright. "Will I need to drink blood and stay out of the sun once I'm I—immortal?"

Please God, say no.

"Yes." Logan turns and my heart plummets. "And no. You are the first Halfling to exist for our kind. What your full abilities will be is an enigma. Based on the prophecy, one we will go over later, as a Halfling you receive the benefits of both species. You will walk in the sun, eat normal food, but you must consume blood to stay alive. My blood." The grin lifting those heavenly lips proves he's pleased as punch about that.

Well, shit. Gross.

"Nicole." The smile slips, and a heavy sigh escapes before he drifts back over to the couch, and eases onto the coffee table. Resting his forearms on his thighs, he stares at his clasped fingers.

Uh oh. More bad shit is coming. I sit up straight and inspect the bunched muscles of his shoulders. I can't take too much more. I might pull my hair out and bang my damn head against a wall if he proceeds to thrust more mind-blowing crap at me. How much can a mere human take? No—correction: a Halfling.

Why does that sound awful? Halfling. I bet if you looked it up in an immortal dictionary, it would read: not adequate enough to be a full-fledged vampire and too fucked up to be a mere human.

Figures.

"How old are you, Logan?" I finally ask the one question that's been burning through my brain since the second he admitted he was a vampire.

"Six centuries."

"As in hundred? Six hundred?" I gape. "You've got to be kidding me?"

He chuckles. "Yes. I am six hundred years old, and that is how long I have been waiting for you."

"Oh, my God." My voice breaks in wonder.

"Now do you understand what you mean to me?"

No. I can't. I hear the words, but their meaning is beyond my comprehension. It's one thing to wait a decade or two for what most people refer to as a soul mate, but to wait six hundred years... blows my mind.

"You're like really old," I can't help but tease. "Rob the cradle much?"

He tilts his head to the side with a smile. "I hope you like older men."

"Not normally, but I might make the exception for you." His rich masculine laugh sends tingles down my spine, caressing every vertebra.

The teasing light in his eyes dims and his smile fades. "Nicole, do you recall the night you escaped Dimitri?" Logan's voice is a hushed fervor and his gaze returns to his hands.

"Escaped?" What the hell is he talking about? "I was seventeen, Logan, I walked out." Even as the words tumble past my lips, my mind rebels against them, and I grimace in confusion.

"Did you?" When he raises his head, the unnatural regard zeroes in on mine. I don't understand what to make of his expression. Those eyes transfix me and pin me to the couch.

"Yes, I... I left."

"How did you leave, Nicole?"

The tender glow penetrates straight through my skull into the chaos swirling through my brain. Hundreds of images flood my mind. A fierce need to close my eyes seizes my muscles, but the brilliant light prevents it, forcing me to keep my eyes on his.

A myriad of images in a discombobulated mess dart forward and back with no clear order. Dizziness attempts to engulf me as scene after scene from my past swirl in circles. Over and over. Round and round.

"Concentrate, Nicole." Logan's command is rough and strong. "Bring a single memory into focus."

Teeth clenched; I struggle not to throw up. My sweaty palms press against my throbbing temples, hoping to end the nauseating Tilt-A-Whirl ride going on inside my skull. "I can't."

"Yes, you can!" he roars, piercing me with his stare. "Narrow your focus. Find an image and separate it out." The blaze in his eyes intensifies several notches at his command. The powerful glow causes my eyes to water, but I can't look away. Instead, I deepen my concentration, and work to slow the roiling mass in my brain.

At last, an image of my childhood room peeks through. I snatch it from the tornado and force it to the forefront. I focus all my effort into that one single image. It swirls closer and closer until it becomes more distinctive, more detailed.

The longer I concentrate on the image, the more the swirling mess in the background coalesces into a more organized sequence. The pictures arrange themselves in a sort of slideshow, one behind the other. The nausea eases and my hands lower to my lap.

"Good girl. What do you see?"

"My room as a child. It—it's the night I took off." Surprise hits as the image clears with crystal clarity. It's like I've gone back in time, and I'm standing in the shadowy room, the flashes of lightning and booming thunder my only company.

"Exceptional," Logan praises. His warm fingers clasp my cold, trembling hands. "Nicole, you must remember, you are only an observer. You are not there. You are with me in the comfort of your home."

"I know," I snap. Although I needed the reminder because what's going on in my head feels damn real. Logan chuckles. The warm, appreciative sound sends a flutter of heat through me.

"Let the scene play out in your mind." The soft command forces me to fall back in time to what I assume must be a pivotal moment Logan needs me to remember.

Chapter 24

Nicole

2009...

Tonight, I murder my stepfather.

For the past four years I've lived in constant terror of him. His deep, grating voice, the sickly-sweet stink of his body, the smell of his putrid breath. But what I abhor the most is his painful, invading touch.

My saving grace, and the reason I'm still sane: the beautiful man from my dreams. This muscular giant of a man with his long, dark hair and piercing green eyes is my beacon, the light in the darkness. He soothes my terror and pain, taking my mind on fantastical journeys far away from my life. I don't know how I conjured him up, but our time together kept the insanity and suicidal thoughts at bay.

But nothing would have helped if Dimitri had lived with us. Thank God he only visited a couple of times a year. His appearances conveniently corresponded with my mother, Bridget, being out of town.

Tonight is such a night.

The minute she packed her bag, dread and acceptance battled within me. Scheming and plotting consumed me. I've spent the entire day—no, to be fair, the past four years—planning my revenge.

When the abuse began, I'd done what any thirteen-year-old would've done: rushed to my mom.

"Nicole." Her long auburn hair, several shades lighter than my own, had swayed around her shoulders. The lack of emotion in her hard, hazel eyes had hurt me as severely as her words. "Instead of sniveling, you should glory in the attention he offers you. Dimitri is a king."

Clearly, my mother's a psychotic bitch who took the whole "a man's home is his castle" thing way too far.

Fast forward two years. At fifteen, fear was my constant companion. My heart would plummet every time Mom walked down the hall with a stack of clothes, only to rise again when I'd discover she was just doing laundry, not packing.

I had attempted to run away. Once.

The plan had started out great, as my plans invariably do. No rain to slow me down, no lightning to illuminate my escape. I'd squirreled away a hundred bucks from tutoring other kids and borrowing from Bridget's wallet from time to time.

The idea would have worked. My bug-out bag had been ready, tucked under the bed. It wasn't a real bug-out bag, just an old backpack with a change of clothes, toothbrush, toothpaste, and a flashlight borrowed from a kid's locker. I liked to borrow things.

I'd slithered out the bedroom window into the night, and the sweet smell of freedom filled my lungs. Our modest, red-brick house sat on the corner lot, on a peaceful tree-lined cul-de-sac in the 'burbs of Louisville, Kentucky. Easy access to the main thoroughfare into town.

The plan? Hitch a ride to the first bus terminal and go anywhere my little heart desired. At fifteen, I could've passed for eighteen. Could've waited tables. Gotten a small apartment with a roommate. Excitement had filled my chest at the uprising of my dormant bravery.

But those meticulous plans had been crushed by Mister Tall, Dark, and Creepy around the next corner. He'd snatched me up by my neck. My feet dangled above the sidewalk as I'd struggled to scream, but the meaty fingers had squeezed harder, trapping my breath in my throat. Screaming had been a definite no-go.

Anger had radiated off this mountain of a man in waves, grating down my nerves like sandpaper. Scratching and clawing at the beefy fist, I'd dug my nails in, but Goliath ignored my pitiful attempts, drawing me closer.

"Your father's been informed of your escape attempt, little brat." The hand cutting off my air supply squeezed harder, shaking me like a rag doll. "Your punishment will be forthwith." The smile stretched across the grotesque face had been pure evil, causing my bladder to loosen, but the prospect of provoking this man further held the flow.

Dizziness had engulfed my brain, and the backdrop of the trees swaying against the night sky darkened around the edges. I was certain I was going to die.

In the next instant, I'd been back in my room, tossed on the bed with such force my neck cracked, and my brain sloshed around in my skull. I'd gulped for oxygen, frantic to catch my breath thanks to Sir Squeeze-a-Lot. My stomach sank in dread when I'd spied my stepfather, the much-needed oxygen frozen in my lungs.

Dimitri's anger had pulsed from him like a wave of pure electricity, penetrating my skin as the first streak of lightning reflected in his soulless black eyes. If a gun or a knife had been handy, I'd have ended my existence. What took place next was the worst suffering and degradation I'd ever endured.

I still have the scars to prove it.

Fast forward another two years. Tonight, is my seventeenth birthday. A storm rages outside my bedroom window, matching the turmoil within me. Blinding white streaks pierce the blackness of night, splitting across the sky. Deafening roars of thunder follow, vibrating the glass panes. Storms always warn of things to come. Horrible things.

Mom left an hour ago, after a hasty birthday wish. Since then, I've mulled over my next step. Tonight, there will be no escape attempt. Tonight, I murder Dimitri. Could I fail? Yes. Will I die? Probably. But I couldn't care less. That bastard will never lay a finger on me again.

I can't stop the quivering in my body. The heavy blackness of my room between the lightning strikes is freaking me out, but the shield of the bedroom door gives me a false sense of security. So, I wait. Resolved. Terrified doesn't even encompass the whirlwind of emotions seething within me. A shudder of fear ripples down my spine. My pulse pounds like a bass drum in my ears as I struggle not to hyperventilate.

"You can do this, Nicole. You can do this," I whisper to the kaleidoscope of light flickering through my room. The butcher knife clenched in my hand quivers, each lightning strike displaying in its shimmering, killing surface. No matter how terrified I am, I will not hesitate. I can't. Four years I've worked to build up the cajones for this moment and I will show that prick the same mercy he's shown me: none.

A huge, shadowy figure takes form by the window, and my panting breath stalls in my lungs as fear paralyzes my muscles. He lurks in silence, watching me. The eerie stillness unnatural. Like Dimitri's. A little voice in the back of my mind advises he's not Dimitri.

The pitch-blackness enveloping us shrouds the face, but where the eyes should be, emits a beautiful green light. The intense glow seeps into my soul and I struggle to inhale. Terror seizes me in a vise-like grip.

"Who are you?" I whisper.

In that instant, slashes of charged light streak across the sky, illuminating my bedroom. I squint against the brilliance, concentrating on the shadowy figure showcased in it. I gasp in astonishment at the handsome face from my dreams staring back at me.

This tall, beautiful man has invaded my sleep for years. He became my mental guard, permitting the fear to recede. Our time together released the anguish in my mind and provided an illusion of security and love that allowed me to evade the purgatory of my real world. These dreams were the one place Dimitri didn't exist. This man had become my lifeline. He sheltered me in slumber and shut my stepfather out.

With awe and fear, I'm absorbed by the sheer magnitude of his presence. His wicked appearance starkly contrasts with the pink lace curtains, pink comforter and white carpet.

How is this possible? I am not dreaming. My whole body is alive with quivers. Just in case, I pinch my arm. Yep, I'm awake.

He's not real, Nicole.

But, for the first time since this man captured my mind, my body awakens with awareness. Tingles shoot along my skin, electrifying every nerve ending. Whoa. I've never experienced this. Not even in the few groping sessions I'd endured with boys at school. Their clumsy attempts repulsed me, conjuring up images of Dimitri. Never will I enjoy the loving caress of a man. My stepfather destroyed that.

"You must come with me."

Shit. The deep rumble wasn't just inside my head. He sounds... alive. In the room. The low commanding voice vibrates down to the core of me. Am I so lost I can no longer tell real from imaginary, dream from reality?

My aching fingers clench the knife tighter. Anguish and uncertainty shift within me. Looking back, it dawns on me, this man had been with me every damn time Dimitri abused me. Not literally, but in my mind. Right? If this man is real, why hadn't he stopped him?

My breath hitches. Goose bumps scatter across my skin, and my stomach rolls with nausea. Had he been aware of what my stepfather was doing? Could the gentle, loving man I've clung to with desperation... be a lie?

"Who the fuck are you?" The urgent whisper mimics the crazed uncertainty within me.

"I am Logan, your Guardian. You know who I am." An edge of impatience creeps into his voice. "What are you going to do with the knife, Nicole?"

"Kill Dimitri." Anger battles with fear and I raise the blade. Lightning illuminates my intent.

Logan's eyes widen in shock. "How do you know of your father?"

"What?" The knife lowers at his odd question.

"It is not relevant." With a shake of his head, the intense stare focuses on mine once more. "His storm is approaching, and we do not have time for this. You cannot kill him, little one. You will die and I will not allow that to happen."

I blink several times. Confusion runs rampant through my mind. His speech is strange. Logan never contracts his words. Every can't is cannot, every won't is will not. Why did he call Dimitri my father? Sir Squeeze-a-Lot said the same thing.

"Listen here... Logan... my *Guardian*," I whisper with scorn. Fear escalates into anger with a swiftness that startles me. The constant lightning and thunder resonate in my soul. "This ends tonight. I won't let you stop me. All the nameless men who spied and kept me prisoner, will not stop me. No one will. So..." Eyebrow lifted, I leer at him with disdain, and project a bravado I'm far from feeling. "If you're not here to help me, crawl back into whatever dark, demented hole in my mind you came from, and leave me the fuck alone." My teeth clench as I fight to stay calm. Rage builds, escalating in intensity. My body hums with it.

Good. This is what I need. Anger. Rage. It will be easier to accomplish what I've set out to do with anger than fear.

So tired of fear ruling my life.

"Come, Nicole. I can take you from this place." His low, even tenor is mesmerizing. The sound of my name in that deep rumble sends shivers up my spine. The soft green glow from his eyes captivates me with its alluring pulse.

My breath escapes in a quick little whoosh, and I'm suddenly staring into those dazzling emeralds. One second, he was across the room and the next he's a mere two feet from me. My God, he's massive. He must be six and a half feet tall. I don't remember him being this tall in the dreams.

Stepping back, my head bangs against the wall behind me, jaw drops open, and my gaze transfixes on his. His eyes burn with something I can't identify, the intensity of his expression bordering on pain.

In a daze, I watch the magnificent muscles ripple and flex under his black t-shirt as he holds out his arms, beckoning me to him. How the supple black leather pants hug his perfect body. A body that, even at seventeen, and despite everything I've been through, I can't help but admire.

Logan's unlike any man I've ever encountered, live or on TV. He exudes an aura I'm unnaturally drawn to, and his eyes stare deep into my tortured soul. Before I even think about it, I've taken a small step in his direction, and lower the knife clutched in my fist.

Dizziness swamps me. What is happening? Isn't there something important I'm forgetting? But I can't remember what. Nor do I care. I must be with Logan, do what he demands. I need to experience those massive arms wrap around my body, his warmth engulfing me. I crave to feel protected and loved as only Logan can.

Another small step and the knife slips from my numb fingers to land with a soft thud on the carpet.

"Good, Nicole. Submit. You are mine," he says in a low growl.

Yes. The word rings true, echoing within me. I am his, and he is mine. His presence is seated deep in my soul. I close the distance, despite the uncertainties continuing to nag at my brain, until we are toe to toe, my nose even with the center of his massive chest.

A deep inhale and my lids close. Oh, my. He smells amazing. Earthy, spicy, and masculine. It does strange things to my body that I don't quite understand.

Massive arms encircle my waist. Soft lips kiss the top of my head. "I am sorry you discovered your father's plans for you, but I am here to protect you, Nicole. Always." His voice is a ragged, desperate growl in my ear. "I should have seen to this sooner."

To what?

Intense pain and dizziness swamp my body, dispelling the fog from my mind in an instant. Terror grips me, and I cry out in his embrace. Everything around me blackens. My room vanishes. I clutch the soft fabric of his shirt with desperation, trying to hold on for dear life. Fear pools hot in my stomach, the acid burning its way up my throat.

"What's happening?" My voice is a hoarse rasp as I struggle against him, but he holds me tight in an iron grip.

Am I dying? Could this beautiful man be the angel of death? Was this God's answer to all my prayers over the years? For me to die?

Perfect. My suffering is over, and I finally found my escape.

Chapter 25

My body shudders as I remember the agony of dematerializing from my childhood room with Logan. I believed I was dying. Then the heartache I suffered when he'd dropped me at the all-girls boarding school back east pierces my heart. Logan convinced the Head Mistress I belonged there, that I had in fact been attending since junior high. It went down pretty much the same as the encounter between Logan and Kurtis at the restaurant.

Then those extraordinary green orbs of fire stared deep into mine and informed me everything would be fine. Logan commanded me to forget everything up until that day. He reassured me he'd always be watching out for me and would return often to check in.

Confusion had washed over me. I remember thinking, why was he telling me all this bullshit? My insides froze. Hardened. Died. I just nodded, and watched him walked away.

With a snap, my mind plunges back into the present. My heavy lids lift to stare at the stunning man—ah, vampire—before me. Logan watches with intensity. His big hands clasped around mine as anxiety and worry swirl in the iridescent gaze. Is he afraid I will crack? God knows I've plenty of damn reasons to snap, and they all center around him.

"It is time to leave again, Nicole."

The sorrow in his whisper ignites my ire and I shake my head. "No. No more running, Logan. This is my home. I'm done tucking my tail between my legs and hiding out from the big bad vampire."

"Dimitri is close, Nicole." The unease is clear on his face. "I am not sure how much longer I can stall and deceive him if you remain in one spot."

My eyebrows raise as comprehension hits me like a thunderbolt. Logan hadn't spied for Dimitri. In fact, he'd done everything in his power to protect me from him.

I have no idea what the penalty for betraying a king is. Was it equivalent to treason? Life imprisonment or death? Christ. Logan risked it all whisking me away that night and hiding me from his king. My father.

Why do it? Why would he risk so much? It's clear Logan believed the mind control, or whatever it was at the school, had worked. It wasn't the mind control that caused me to forget. It was a multitude of things: the trauma of what Dimitri put me through, the joy of discovering Logan existed. His rescue. Only to abandon me the next minute with a promise to return. But he never did. What caused him to stay away for so long? Only one guess needed— Dimitri.

"Logan. I'm sorry."

Shocked by my whispered apology, Logan leans back. Warm fingers slip away, and I ache with the loss of their heat.

"Sorry? Sorry for what?" Confusion furrows his brow.

"I'm sorry you risked so much. For me." Anticipating the ever-present tears threatening again, I clench my teeth.

Logan is visibly dumbfounded. He stares at me for several long moments. "You amaze me. One day, you will be a great queen, mate, but you have no need to apologize to me."

What the... queen? What a peculiar thing to say. He must be delusional. "What are you talking about?"

When he doesn't crack a smile, anxiety flutters in my belly. Damnit, I knew there would be more bad stuff coming.

Without a word, Logan reaches into his suit jacket and drags out a folded piece of paper. I glare at it with panic and fear as his strong masculine fingers unfold it. Instincts roar. This nondescript document is about to alter everything. And not in a good way.

Without warning, Logan reaches for me and hoists me onto his lap with ease. Warm hands grip my thighs, opening them so I straddle his hips with my knees resting on the coffee table.

My cold, aching fingers clutch his wide shoulders, and I admire the tightening of muscles bunching beneath the suit. I peer into his intense gaze, and the all-consuming power of it takes my flight response into high gear. It urges me to run for the hills because that look... scares me. The scrap of paper still clutched in his hand scares me.

When did I become such a fucking scaredy cat?

"Nicole, I would walk into the sun for you." His breath whispers across my lips as he cradles my face. A roughened thumb caresses my cheek. "You are my mate, and no one, in this world or beyond, will ever change that. Not even a king."

Well, shit. Doesn't that just melt a girl's heart?

In a heated whisper, I demand. "Where have you been?" Instinct demands I put whatever is on that paper out of my mind and I obey. My stiff fingers thread through the silky hair at the base of his skull. God, I love him in my hands and between my thighs. The suit is seductive as hell, but I need him naked. Earlier, I was denied the chance to explore his body and I crave to trace and devour every inch of him. Run my tongue along every line of that impressive tattoo and every sculpted ridge and valley of his torso. It's a madness overpowering my senses.

The memory of his hard length—now pressing against my aching core—in my mouth, on my tongue, and down my throat bursts through my mind. I moan and rub my throbbing center against the impressive hardness.

The paper flutters to the coffee table, forgotten, as Logan grips my ass, pushing me harder against his length. With a deep groan, he buries his face in my neck. Soft but insistent lips suck at the vein with gentle pressure, and wetness floods my core.

"Fuck, baby." The growl vibrates against my feverish skin, sending waves of electricity down my neck and straight to aching nipples. "I want nothing more than to bury myself deep within you."

There's a *but* coming. Crucial things need to be discussed, no doubt. One of them is glaring at me right now. The whiteness of the paper blinds me with panic. At this moment, I don't give a shit. The silky hardness of Logan's cock filling the emptiness inside is all this girl can process.

"Nicole..."

He pulls back, but before he utters another word, my fingers grip his hair tighter, holding him still. I slam my lips to his, and ravage his mouth with lips, tongue, and teeth. Frantic for more, I let loose all my repressed desires—and yes, fears—into the kiss.

When his full attention is focused on me, I ease off, and let my tongue trace the line of his lower lip, making teasing forays into his mouth. Logan answers with ferocity, delving in. The world falls away, and my clit pulses with excruciating excitement.

"Baby." The lust roughening his voice sends electric tingles rippling across my flesh.

"Logan. Please...."

His eyes pulse with desire at my begging, and a deep growl rumbles from his chest. One hand grips the back of my head, and seizes control of the kiss, dominating it.

A soft whimper of need escapes me, and my hips grind against his hardness, back and forth. The soft fabric of my sweatpants rubs against my swollen nub, and a shudder ripples at the gratifying sensation. Need more. Want more. Visions flood my mind of all the dirty, naughty things I want Logan to do and it fuels my desire even further.

When the heat of his other hand yanks down the fabric of my tank top, so one breast pops out, I want to cry out in victory. The wet heat of his mouth leaves mine to cover one nipple, and I throw my head back with a moan and pull his head tighter, grinding faster and harder.

For a split second, I'm weightless, then the cool leather of the couch is at my back, all the while his mouth never leaves my breast. Logan's weight sinking between my thighs feels... right. Like this is where he belongs. Over me, in me, a part of me.

I've waited my whole life for this man. Never believing this would come true, or he was real. But Logan is real, and it's foolish to waste a single second of whatever time we enjoy together fighting over the future, or the past.

When sharp teeth bite down on an already sensitive nipple, I cry out, arching off the couch, needing more. With a swiftness that no longer surprises me, my sweatpants slide off my body, and the front of my tank top lays under both breasts, putting them on full display.

I gawk at the vampire kneeling between my thighs. The green fire gobbles my wet core. It's the most erotic thing to be half naked, helpless with need, while this beautiful being in an expensive suit worships my body.

Logan's eyes trail down my torso like it's something to devour. Cuff links twinkle in the light from the lamp as he runs a hand between my breasts and over a shoulder. He shoves his fingers under one strap, and lowers it down my arm, halting at my elbow before mirroring the action on the other side.

My chest heaving with desire, I ache to launch myself at him. As though he gathers my intentions, Logan shakes his head and commands in a quiet voice, "Do not move, Nicole."

I love it when he commands me. The way he gently dominates me. But I don't want gentle. I crave for Logan to lose the tight control over himself. The control evident in the clenching of his jaw, and the intense concentration in his green gaze.

With excruciating slowness, Logan's hand runs around the shape of my breast. He pauses when his fingers trace the line of small scars on the underside. A slight frown mars his forehead as he proceeds to examine the other one, encountering similar scars.

Panic bubbles in my chest when the questions and concern enter his expression. His hands continue their exploration, but it's not with desire. It's clinical as he searches for and discovers the deeper scars along my right hip.

The air charges with energy. It causes the hair on the back of my neck to stand. I swallow at the rage pulsing from the green fire of Logan's gaze.

A large palm slams on the cushion by my head, and his big body towers over me. Deadly fangs lengthen when his lips lift in a snarl. For the first time, real fear grips me and I freeze. A deep, animalistic growl emerges from Logan's throat.

"What the fuck, Nicole? Are these from Dimitri?"

Shit.

Chapter 26

Nicole

What the hell do I say to calm the vampire down? There is no way I'm telling him how I got the majority of those scars. Logan's already on the brink of losing it.

'Oh, those? Yeah, a Dom in a BDSM club went ballistic on me with a belt. No biggie.'

Yup, pretty confident it would shoot him right over the proverbial edge. He hasn't wrapped his mind around the fact my father abused me yet. Shit, I haven't wrapped my mind around it. How would Logan handle my dark side? Would it prompt him to walk away from me in disgust? Forever? Not certain I'd recover if he disappeared again.

There are so many unknowns between us. To suppose I understand this man... vampire—will I ever grow used to saying that?—would be ludicrous, but I suspect Logan keeps a tight rein on his emotions. Until me.

There's something about our connection that strips his control. It's in the intense expression, the furrowed brow, the unsettled glow of those penetrating green eyes, the sharpness of bunched muscles beneath the suit, and the elongating of his fangs.

How do I salvage the evening and calm the raging vampire between my thighs? My lips part as I warm up to impart some senseless words of wisdom when Alex bursts through the front door. Multiple shopping bags dangle from her arms. The second she spies Logan hovering over me, she stops dead in her tracks. Her blue eyes shift to a shimmering silver, and a blood-curdling scream pierces the room.

Holy crap. Did the living room windows shatter? 'Cause my eardrums sure did.

With speed and a fierceness that stuns us both, Alex launches onto Logan's back, and a tiny dagger presses against his jugular. The luminous green gaze swings back to mine, shifting from a full-on fury to shock, like he's not certain what to do with the wild creature clinging to his back. A bubble of laughter threatens to emerge at the vampire's expression.

"Easy, valkyrie."

Logan's angry growl vibrates the couch. What did he call Alex? Valkyrie? My frown deepens, and I gape at them both. That's not her name.

While Logan's distracted with extricating himself from Alex, I yank up my tank top and grab the sweats off the floor. He rises with Alex in tow. I slide out from underneath him and tug on my sweats. Before I can help, Logan swings her off his back with ease and dumps her onto the couch. No sooner does her jean-clad butt hit the cushions than she jumps back up, ready to launch at him again.

"Alex." With raised hands, I jump in front of Logan. "Stop."

"What the fuck, vampire? Did you have sex with her?" Alex screams at him. She completely ignores me, never taking those glistening eyes off Logan.

What the...?

Okay. Alex must have witnessed the unusual glow in Logan's eyes, or maybe the massive fangs on display during his anger. Because correct me if I'm wrong, but the knowledge of vampires isn't something you come across in your day-to-day life. And why is everybody insisting Logan and I don't have sex? Am I the only one out of the loop here?

I raise my eyebrow and glance back at Logan, pleading with him for guidance on what to tell the angry spitfire perched on the couch.

I'm somewhat comforted to discover his eyes back to their translucent green, and the fangs gone.

"Nothing happened, Alexandria. Calm down." He commands.

What in God's name is happening? First Logan's familiar with Kurtis, or his father at least, and now he addresses Alex by name? Like he knows her. How is that possible?

Someone should etch those remarks on my tombstone: 'How is that possible?' Because I've uttered them more in the last few weeks than in my entire existence.

Yup, no doubt about it, I've tumbled down the rabbit hole and swallowed the fucking red pill. I blink up at Alex, dagger in hand, ready to battle the vampire. What's up with her eyes? The blue transformed into a metallic silver.

I side-step from between the two and fling my arms wide. "Could someone please tell me what the fuck is going on?" The shout doesn't even snag their attention. "How do you two know each other, and how did you know who Kurtis was, Logan?" My ire spikes at being kept in the dark. "Someone better start talking or I'll..." *What Nicole? What the hell will you do?* "I'll walk out that door and disappear."

That gets their attention. Both heads snap in my direction. Alex lowers the blade and steps off the couch, her eyes fading back to the vivid blue.

"Nicki—"

"Nicole—"

When they both begin at the same time, Logan sighs with annoyance, and shoots a glower at Alex. "Let me handle this, valkyrie." Alex nods in agreement.

Logan captures my complete scrutiny and I scowl at him. My face is as hard as granite, but anxiety nibbles below the surface. "You better have a fucking good explanation because I'm so furious right now, I could spit bullets."

"Yes, I see that," he mutters, his face suddenly haggard with worry.

He plucks the forgotten paper off the coffee table and I freeze. Logan doesn't hand it over or read what it says. My fury diminishes at the sight of it. My heart rate spikes and I gulp in a deep breath. Based on Logan's expression, I work to prepare myself for more bad news.

"The day of your thirteenth year,"—just the beginning snags my full attention—"Icarus, our High Priest Oracle, foretold of a written prophecy, one that is now hundreds of years old. A prophecy about you, Nicole."

"Shut up." In dismay, my focus zeroes in on the piece of stationery gripped in Logan's fingers.

"It's true, Nicki." Alex comes over to settle next to Logan like they're a unified front.

Okay, I've tripped and crashed into crazy town. That must be it. I've lost my marbles. And the part blowing my mind—they believe what they're telling me.

"Icarus revealed the prophecy to the Council of Unity, a governing group for all the Other species." *Other species*? I gasp and Logan pauses. He contemplates my mouth hanging wide. "I understand your expression, Nicole, but let us leave that for now."

Logan steps closer and holds out the dreaded paper. I snap my mouth closed, and my muscles tense. I take a hesitant step back, needing distance from it.

"Icarus hid the original scroll, but I prepared a copy of it, understanding we would one day hold this discussion."

Dread seeps into my bones, and I keep my arms glued to my side. With a heavy exhale, I press my trembling lips together, and continue to gawk at the paper like it's a snake ready to sink its fangs into me.

Appropriate visual, considering.

"Who is the Council of Unity?"

Logan sighs. "There are seven members of the council. One leader from every clan of species who wished to come forward and take part. The vampire king, your father. The werewolf king,"—Christ. There are werewolves too? The rabbit hole can't go any deeper—"and the shapeshifter king... Kurtis's father."

Nope, I was incorrect. I've traveled so deep I've struck the core of the earth. What. The. Hell? Kurtis is a shapeshifter? If Logan reached out and slapped me across the face, I couldn't be more astonished. I part my lips, but nothing comes out except the breath I'd inhaled at his remarks.

Once again, Logan holds up his hand to stop the potential surge of questions. Yeah, don't worry, big guy, I couldn't compose a coherent sentence if I tried.

"And the valkyrie queen... Alexandria's mother."

I swing my widened stare to my BFF and she nods. Offers a gentle smile. I throw her a deadpan stare as betrayal sinks into my bones. Alex lowers her gaze and the smile evaporates.

No idea what a valkyrie is, but it sure as shit doesn't sound human. How could Alex not inform me? I assumed we were friends. Don't friends tell each other everything? Or at least the fact they're not even human.

'*You don't reveal all your secrets*,' the bitch reminds me.

Dread flutters in my gut. If I'm interpreting this right, my friends all conspired behind my back. Together. To what extent, and for what reason, I can't fathom. But if Kurtis and Alex are part of this, who else? Is everyone around me involved? The band? Jimmy? Liam?

"Who is the werewolf king?" A suspicion forms. Logan hesitates, and inhales a deep breath. A knowing glance passes between him and Alex, and it pisses me off. "Who, Logan?"

Logan runs his fingers through his hair with agitated movements. "King Scott is... Jimmy."

Fuck.

Even though he's who I suspected, just hearing the words makes my soul ache. Jimmy. Shit. The dread morphs into betrayal and a coldness snakes its way through my heart. Why does everyone I care about betray me? Jimmy was the one man I assumed I could trust above all others. My boss, the man I considered a father, is in on this little... whatever this is, and a fucking werewolf! No, not just any werewolf—the *king* of werewolves. How did I not see it? Why didn't my instincts clue me in?

"There are two members of the council we cannot trust," Logan continues. "The dark fae king, and the succubus queen. Both are in league with your father. And last, the Oracle High Priest, Icarus."

"Oh, is that all?" The sarcasm falls flat when it comes out as a constricted squeak.

"Nicole," Logan frowns. "After everything else revealed tonight, I appreciate this is a lot to take in, but time is running out. You need to get on board with what is coming."

Logan lifts the paper again. With a gulp, my arm reaches for it even though everything demands I fling it in the potbelly stove and burn it. Tingles race up my arm when I grasp it. Everything inside me screams that learning the words on this paper will alter my life in such a way that this mind-boggling reveal tonight will pale in comparison. It holds the future. Isn't that what prophecies do, foresee the future? People shouldn't have an insight into their fates. It's not natural.

With a bitter laugh, I turn my back on Logan and Alex's concerned expressions. Nothing about tonight—hell, nothing about my whole way of life—could be construed as natural.

In for a penny, in for a pound. I've heard the expression somewhere. Not certain what it means, but it seems suits this situation to a T. Maybe I'll Google it later.

Fear follows my every step to the kitchen table and plays through every nerve as my butt settles in the chair. My mind screams at me not to read the words that will fundamentally change everything about my world.

Chapter 27

Logan

I cannot justify my irrational fear any more than I control it. Sebastian assured me the three Guardians I took out in her driveway did not have time to report back to Dimitri. And since Sebastian took care of the mayor and the private investigator, that trail ended.

Whoever sought to drive her off the road still nags at me. Humans working for Dimitri? His numerous enemies eager to take him out via Nicole? Or some Other, working for Grayflame or Jilaya and therefore, Dimitri?

My gut clenches at the mere notion of her walking out the door and vanishing into the night. With effort, I tamp down the impulse to force Nicole to my will. I met the blackness in the depths of my mate's eyes, and my heart skipped with a tingle of fear.

Nicole possesses a sinister side. If provoked, it could cause her to do foolish things. To respond with reckless abandon, and let her temper control her. That could get her killed. She is still a fragile human, vulnerable to so many dangers. Fear twists my gut in knots.

A sigh of frustration rushes past my lips and I drag both hands through my hair. I regard Nicole with trepidation when she sits at the table to read the prophecy. There are so many issues to work through, one being where those scars came from. The first raging belief had been Dimitri, and the command over my vampire beast slipped. If it were not for Alexandria barging in when she did, I might have done something I regretted.

The image of him hurting her enough to leave scars breaks my heart and gets my temper rising to the surface. Earlier she spoke of his claws cutting, and bones breaking.

Christ.

If I could slay him, I would. A satisfying vision of flaying the skin from his body while he screams for mercy brings a sadistic smile to my lips. That bastard needs to suffer, the way he made Nicole suffer, only tenfold. As much as the bonded vampire within craves to avenge its mate, Dimitri's death can never be. He must be contained, and only Nicole can bring the prophecy to fruition. If she fails, King Dimitri bears the power to destroy us all.

Careful not to interrupt Nicole's concentration on the prophecy, I tamp down on my raging and chaotic emotions as I take my time walking to the table, Alexandria at my heels. We slide into chairs on either side of her.

While she reads, it gives me the opportunity to study her valkyrie guardian. Over the years, I have collected plenty of reports from this creature on Nicole's well-being, but this is the first moment we have met. Like all valkyrie, Alexandria Svaldana is small but beautiful, like Queen Arra but in an untamed, carefree manner.

Where Arra is an elegant blonde with grace and discipline, Alexandria's mane of crimson hair runs wild and free. Like her. Right now, anxiety and fear flicker across her face and she nibbles on her fingernails as she stares wide-eyed at Nicole.

I share the sentiment. Worry slithers through me with how much was hurled at Nicole tonight. Thus far, she is managing it reasonably well, and I marvel at the extraordinary woman my mate has become.

After several moments, Nicole lays the prophecy on the table in front of her. She spreads it with agitated movements, and anxiety gnaws at my insides. The desire to reach out and clasp her hands in mine causes the muscles in my arms to twitch. Instead, I clench my hands on the table.

What is she thinking? Is she angry? Hurt? Confused? Scared? With a delicate nudge, I probe her mind, looking for even a hint of what is transpiring in that intellect of hers. But like before, I hit a brick wall.

"Nicki?" Alexandria ventures where I dread. "Talk to us."

Nicole lifts her head and pins Alex, then me, with a frigid look of betrayal. My gut clenches.

"Everyone I foolishly assumed a friend, lied and slithered around behind my back for years."

My heart constricts at the bitterness in her voice. Gray eyes cold as steel. Hard. Void of emotion, and that alarms me more than anything. Okay, she is *not* taking this well.

I grip her icy hands between my own. "Nicole, we have done so to protect you. So much rides on your survival. On reaching your transition."

"Yes. So I read."

Fear claws through my center when she jerks her fists away.

"I understand my role. And yours."

Underneath the icy, tough exterior Nicole is angry, but also resigned. Is she accepting of her destiny? If so, why can she not look at me? Her gaze stays fastened to the table. Alarm spreads like a forest fire throughout my body. I dart a glance at Alexandria and her expression is anxious and filled with fear as well.

"Baby..."

"I accept my importance in the scheme of things, Logan, and I'm all too delighted to take down my father. It now makes perfect sense why he raped me instead of just killing me. He was attempting to get me pregnant."

Pain shoots through me and my teeth grind at the reminder of what she suffered, and my utter failure in protecting her.

Alex gasps at Nicole's revelation.

She stands. "And I get the need to safeguard me until the prophesied time, until my... transition is complete. Although where the protection was when I was a teenager is a... mystery I suppose." No sarcasm or resentment. No emotion at all. I want to shake her, bring back the fire in her eyes. "But let me make one point clear." Gray eyes bore into Alex's. "You will do so from a distance. We are no longer friends."

"Wait—Nicki—I" Alex stutters in shock and rises to her feet.

"I refuse to be friends with someone who's lied to me for years, whatever the reasons. By tomorrow morning I want you out of my home. How you proceed to do your duty to the council is your problem, not mine."

Tears shimmer in Alexandria's eyes, threatening to spill. So many emotions emanate from her. Guilt. Fear. Anger. Hurt. But she adds nothing in response, just bows her head to hide the tears rolling down pale cheeks.

"But you've lied to me as well," she whispers. Lifting her head, her shimmering blue gaze locks on Nicole.

Nicole's eyes widen, darting with apprehension in my direction. I glance between the two females with a frown. What are they hiding from me?

"Maybe," Nicole concedes. "But I never pretended to be your friend."

This situation has escalated out of control. What we did was for her protection. Her survival. The survival of thousands.

"Nicole..."

She holds up a hand in front of my face and anger clenches my jaw. "The same goes for you." Her expression is devoid of emotion. Her cool gaze pierces through the anxiety and dread building in my chest. "I don't know if this works or not, since I don't actually own the house, but I rescind your invitation to my home."

Resentment narrows my eyes. The energy in her words tingles along my spine, urging me to obey. Does Nicole think she can get rid of me with such ease?

I growl low and bare my fangs as I prowl around the table to tower over her. "So, you wish me to walk away? You can turn us off with such ease?" When she does not respond, I clutch her upper arms in a punishing grip. I want to shake her until she sees reason, or until the life comes back to her eyes.

"Keeping your distance should be simple for you, Logan. You've kept away from me for years."

The rising anger gets the better of me and I roar at her. "Dammit, Nicole. I had no choice. If Dimitri ever discovers where you are, this all blows up in our faces, and everyone you care about will be dead. But you will not. For you, it will be much worse." My breathing turns harsh, my eyes heat as fear fuses with rage, the earlier command to leave squelched by our fragile bond.

"Well, then I suppose I'm making it easier for you." The emotional paralysis spreads over her face. "Please leave and don't come back unless you have to for the prophecy. It's obvious to me how significant that is to you."

Before I can rail at her stupidity, Sebastian materializes next to us. One glimpse at his distraught expression and my stomach flip-flops, my heart plummets.

"Christ. He knows."

"I do not know, brother." Sebastian does a double take at Alexandria, inspecting her with a glower as his face drains of all color.

"Then why are you here, Bastian?"

Instead of answering he proceeds to gawk at the valkyrie with wide anxious eyes.

"Sebastian."

With a noticeable struggle, he pulls his contemplation away from Alexandria. "The king summoned us all for an announcement before the pre-dawn meal. I'm surprised you did not sense it."

I am shocked as well. No one is more connected to the king than I. Anytime Dimitri moves, I experience it like a shift in my body. He sent out a massive summons and I sensed nothing, too caught up in the turmoil with Nicole.

Bastian's blue eyes fixate on Alex. He inspects her up and down before transferring his regard to Nicole. "How is it going here?" A frown mars his perfect features as he notes the tension in the room, the steely grip of my fingers on Nicole's arms.

Bastian presents himself to Nicole with a bow. "I am Sebastian, Logan's brother." I relax my grip. "It is a great honor to meet you. With your clothes on," he adds with a smirk.

Nicole doesn't crack a smile. "Wish I could say the same."

When she struggles, I let her go. Bastian raises a brow in my direction, and I shake my head.

'*Things did not go well I take it?*' he asks reverting to telepathy.

'*Understatement.*'

'*Just give her time, brother. She needs to process everything thrown at her tonight.*'

"Nicki, please." With tears cascading down her face, Alexandria pleads with Nicole. "Don't push me away. Yes, at first you were my assignment, but I...."

Nicole turns on her with a fierce expression. The first honest emotion since she read the prophecy. "You should have told me, Alex. I fucking trusted you!"

When my brother steps in front of Alexandria, as if to shield her from Nicole's wrath, my eyebrows arch in astonishment.

"Get out of my way, vampire." The silver returns to Alexandria's eyes, her delivery rough and menacing for such a small creature.

Bastian blinks and peers over his shoulder at her. He appears confused by his move to defend her.

"Brother, lock down whatever shit is going through your head." What is wrong with him? When he does not move, I seize the rigid shoulders and draw him away from the valkyrie. "We could be walking to our deaths in a few minutes."

"Of course, you... you are right." With a shake, Bastian glances at Alex staring at him with hatred, and something more. Fear?

"You have until tomorrow to get packed," I warn Nicole, and thrust aside my apprehension over her complete about-face. I will do what I always do—put her safety first. "Tomorrow night, we leave Newport."

When she glares at me, I attempt to soften my command with a caress on her cheek, but she recoils and takes a step back. My insides flame with dismay. Nicole must come to grips with it and get on board or we are all dead. The time to make her see reason has ended.

"Nicole. So much was thrown at you tonight, but you must understand, everything was done to protect you. Not because we had to, but because we all care about *you*. Obey me or you will not like the consequences."

Her only response, a slight nod of agreement. Frustration pounds in my skull. I'd prefer nothing more than to haul her over my shoulder, smack that delectable ass, and transport her some place secure, but time has run out.

With a nod at Sebastian, we dematerialize to the castle. Neither one of us is in a rush to greet what is coming.

Chapter 28

Nicole

I blink as if waking from a dream, a new coldness rushing through my veins. My friends lied. For years. They weren't my friends because they wanted to be. They were my friends because they were commanded to. To spy. By their rulers. By Jimmy. Because of the fucking prophecy.

My breathing hiccups repeatedly. They all messed with me. Weaseling their way into my life in one capacity or another, watching my every move. Pretending to be a friend, mentor, father figure... dream lover.

A cold tear trickles down my icy cheek. The inner bitch is arctic and silent for the first time in my life. Hurt and betrayal freeze my heart.

Breathless, I shake my head, letting it fall back on the threadbare pillow. The moment dawn hit the next morning, I watched Alex pack, hardening my heart to the silent tears tracking down her cheeks. The second the red glow of her taillights disappeared down the drive, I grabbed my bug-out bag and hit the road.

Being on the road is familiar. Easy. It fits my skin like a glove. It's been a month since I vanished, and no one has found me or followed me. There've been no attempts on my life. Of course, I never stay in one place for more than a few days at a time. With the cash I stashed in my bag over the years, I could stay on the run indefinitely. If I'm careful. And I am. Always.

If there is one thing I do well, it's flee. According to Logan, all that needs to happen until the transition is to stay hidden. Don't need anyone for that. Nor do I want their interference in my life anymore. When this change hits, according to the prophecy, I will be powerful enough to take down the bastard, Dimitri. That's precisely what I plan to do. I don't give a shit about the rest. I have no clue if they plan to imprison him, banish him, or what. That's up to Logan.

This taught me a crucial lesson—if you let people in, they hurt you. In fact, in my case, it's what I grew up believing was a natural consequence of loving someone.

My father. My mother. Logan. And now my friends.

They failed me by pretending to be something they were not. By lying. Logan failed by not protecting me when it mattered most. When I could not defend myself. He claims he had no knowledge of what Dimitri did, but how can that be true? If this group of individuals was watching over me my whole life, then, where were they? They screwed up ten times? Not likely. Someone betrayed me.

Every one of them were under the assumption their actions were justified. For the greater good. Were they? Doesn't matter. It still doesn't negate the fact I no longer trust them. Trust isn't a one- way street.

For the first couple of weeks after my disappearance, Logan attempted to enter my dreams, frantic to find me. It took great effort and concentration to expand my mental barriers and protect my mind even in sleep. Not that I've slept much over the last month.

I shake my head hard. A cold shudder racks my body as I turn on my side and stare at the paint peeling from the walls. Canada is as cold as my heart. We are a perfect match.

With a frustrated sigh, I give up on sleep, and slip out of the hard, lumpy bed. Cautious, I lift the corner of the drape over the window, and peer out at the dark parking lot and the still-bustling streets of Vancouver beyond.

During my years of running, I believed the best places to fade into the shadows were small towns. Places only the population of the town, and maybe the surrounding farms, knew about. But I've discovered anonymity is found in the big city. Here, no one knows who the hell you are, or even cares.

This run-down motel has been home for the past two days, but the itch to move on is crawling up my neck like a thousand spider legs. My ever-expanding bag and boots sit by the bed. Annie is at the ready on the nightstand. My new norm is sleeping in jeans and a t-shirt, in case I need to make a quick escape. The decision to head east to Alberta flared early this morning. Let's see where this butt- ass-cold wind blows me.

Fuck. Logan is a vampire. Jimmy is a damn werewolf, which means Liam is too. Kurtis is a shapeshifter, and Alex is a valkyrie, whatever the hell that is. My brain hurts from trying to wrap around it all. Not to mention, I'm a... Halfling.

Shit.

During this transition, I will need to drink blood to stay alive. Not just anyone's blood, according to the prophecy, only the blood of my mated male. Logan.

"Logan." With a sigh, I turn from the window. If I plan to hit the road at first light, I should probably get some damn sleep. My time on the run is coming to an end. The episodes are hitting at regular intervals now. Two or three times a day. The constant ache hammering my body unbearable, even though my senses continue to improve, and my strength has doubled.

What should I expect once the transition hits? What *powers* will pop to the forefront, and will I be able to handle them? Like it or not, I will need Logan. At least his knowledge and blood.

The ice in my veins melts a bit at the remembered pain etched on Logan's features when I told him to leave. And, not for the first time, I wonder what happened when he and Sebastian went back to Dimitri's side.

If I had real emotions left, I'd be concerned. I know he's still alive. I sense it in my soul. A fresh batch of freezing tears well in my eyes, and I whisper on the barest breath to the lonely motel room, "Love is a bitch. All it brings is emptiness."

A familiar awareness creeps along my spine. Speak of the devil. Guess a business doesn't need to conform to the vampire- invite-only rule. The only reason Bastian popped in and out of my house willy-nilly was because he owns it. That little tidbit still pisses me off. Causally, I reach for Annie on the nightstand as the deep, sexy voice washes over me.

"Have you ever loved, Nicole?"

I point her at Logan's chest for the second time. My features harden into stone.

"No," I lie.

"Then how do you know if it brings emptiness?" The calm in his voice doesn't deceive me. Logan's pissed. The clenching of his jaw and the glow in those incredible eyes give him away, not to mention the deadly fangs on full display.

He looks fantastic, those lean hips and thighs wrapped in black jeans, and the silk of the garnet red shirt emphasizes his wide, muscular chest and arms.

"Why did you leave?" The deep rumble of anger ripples along my skin. "If you care so little about your own life, so be it, but can you so easily disregard the thousands of lives lost if you fail?"

"How did you find me?" Lowering Annie, I ignore his questions. I'm so numb inside, the sight of Logan's anger doesn't even faze me. This day had to come, he just saved me the trouble of hunting him down.

"It was not easy, I will give you that, but if I found you, so can Dimitri, or his enemies who want him dead."

"What makes you think you can hide me any better?" The ice thickens around my heart. "I've been on the run most of my life. It's what I do." With care, I shove Annie into the waistband at my back, and reach for my bag, but his words halt me.

"I am not here to bring you back, Nicole." His delivery is cold, hard. "You've made it abundantly clear you do not want or need my help. I am here to educate you on what to expect during the transition and offer you this." Logan throws a small cooler I hadn't noticed before on the bed.

My gaze darts to it with trepidation, though having a pretty good idea what's inside, I ask anyway. "What's that?"

"My blood." My eyes shoot to his and his lip lifts in contempt. "Bagged for your convenience. Jimmy or Alexandria are on standby to help with your training. Once your transition is complete, and you have mastered your powers, Bastian will come to collect you for the final meet-and-greet with your father."

"And where will you be?" I can't help but ask, the ice cracking at the hatred in Logan's gaze.

"I will fulfill my end of the prophecy. An army stands at the ready to back you up."

"I see," I whisper. "Once my father is captured, I will relinquish the throne to you, Logan. I have no desire to be the first vampire queen." His lip curls in anger and disgust at my decision. "And, since we are over, there will be no vampire heir to walk in the sun."

"As you wish, Your Highness." Logan bows, the tension in his body belying his words. "I am sure I will have no problem finding a wife to give me an heir when the time comes." Standing to his full height, he stares down his nose with such hatred and disdain. I allow the ice to surround me, relying on it to keep me from losing control.

An inner part of me growls with jealousy at the mere image of him with another woman. Thankfully, the frozen tundra insulating my emotions keeps it buried.

When I don't respond, Logan's eyes flare to life for a split second, but quickly dim to a frigid green. "My blood is the catalyst to complete your transition. Drink one bag a day. From this moment on, Nicole, whether you continue the road alone, or you go home, you will be watched over. You may not care about your future, but thousands of others are depending on you."

He takes a step toward me and my heart jumps in my chest.

If he touches me, I'll lose it.

"I warned you if you ran there would be consequences. You do not wish to be mine, so be it. I will not seek you out again, Nicole. If your heart changes, you know how to reach me. Good luck with your transition. I will be there on the other side. If you survive."

He vanishes. The green glow of his eyes lingers in the air for a split second before it is gone as well. It hits me, Logan gave me his blood, told me how much to drink, but he forgot to instruct me on what to expect during and after the transition.

"Well, shit. This should be fun."

Chapter 29

Nicole

Okay, I'm calling it. It's official. Logan's not coming back. And who could blame him after the way I treated him in Canada. As soon as his form evaporated from the room, I'd grabbed my go-bag, and the stupid cooler, and hit the road again, but instead of heading to Alberta, I went home.

The second I saw the cooler, I understood there was no way in hell to undertake this on my own. Freaky shit was gonna go down, and I had no concept of how to handle it. If I wished to survive this, I needed to swallow my resentment and pride, and surround myself with the individuals who are familiar with what the hell to do.

Back in my house for a month, and my body is being ripped in two. I fucking hurt. Everywhere. This metamorphosis is taking its damn sweet time. Childbirth must be better than this, not that I even fathom what that's like, but at least it's over in a matter of hours, not dragging on for weeks.

To top it off, the minute I stepped through the front door, the icy wall around my heart shattered into a million fragments. In the kitchen, I recall the heat of his body behind mine. The supple leather of the couch causes physical pain, reminding me of the hard press of his erection against my core, the fiery green power of his eyes.

And in my bedroom; it's the worst. A glance at the chair, and my mouth waters with the savor of Logan's silky hardness. When I collapse in an exhausted heap onto the mattress late at night, visions of his tongue—licking me, stroking me—overtake my brain. The sharp sting of fangs sinking into my flesh bombard every nerve, like darts being fired at a dart board, and I'm the fucking board.

Every day the inclination to crawl into a ball on the floor and howl my lungs out until I can't speak tries to overtake me. How can I move on when the absence of him is everywhere?

Being betrayed by the people I hoped I could trust overrode my common sense. This will go down in the history of fuck-ups, but I refuse to accept all the blame. Logan's the one who lied. And not just about what he is, the council or the prophecy. How many times did he proclaim I was his everything, his mate? Whatever the hell that means.

Apparently, Logan's a man... male of his word. Hell, he hasn't even attempted to visit me in my dreams since those barriers crumbled into dust the minute I stepped foot in Newport. He declared I would know how to reach him if I changed my mind. Well, I have no clue how to go about doing that. It's not like I can send him a text or call him on the phone, even if I had his number.

A myriad of chaotic emotions is spiraling me into a dark pit again, and every muscle is wound so tightly, my skin itches for release. Even my music doesn't mollify me. I perch at the baby grand, glare at the ivory for hours, but never hit a key, night after night.

Kurtis banned me from the dojo until I get my shit together. This after a red haze of rage consumed me and I lost control and beat the crap out of my opponents. The pre-transition causes every emotion to become hyper-aggressive, and I took all my failures, hatred, and fear out on whoever was in front of me. On a few occasions, I just surrendered. Allowed them to beat me to a bloody pulp. I was counting on the pain to be enough to expunge the ache in my heart, or kick-start this damn move into immortality.

It hasn't.

The episodes are pretty much every hour on the hour, and they're freaking Jimmy out. He's called or come by every night since I returned, only leaving my side when he's had no choice, even though Alex moved back in.

They're all stumped with the delay in completing this shift, afraid I'm ready to off myself from the chronic torment. Am I weak enough to require the club, and the release it provides to bring me through this? Yes, but I would never take it beyond that.

Not as long as Logan lives. I may wander through life as a pain-crazed zombie, but I would never end myself if there's a slim chance Logan could come back.

Pathetic. How will I ever be the next queen of vampires when I can't even handle my own stupid life? My heart? These emotions?

The most pitiful part? For some unexplained reason, my body is rejecting Logan's blood. It tastes awful. Violent cramps twist and knot my stomach until the blood hurls back up. My clothes hang off me from the amount of weight I've dropped, but the thirst is a continuous burn in the back of my throat. It craves the blood I can't contain.

"I don't understand why you can't keep his blood down," Jimmy growled in frustration one evening.

"Because it's fucking disgusting, that's why," Kurtis mutters with a curl of his lip.

"Kurtis, if you hate vampires so much, why are you helping them?" Now that I know who they all are, Kurtis's hatred for "bloodsuckers" as he calls them, is blatant. "I'm half vampire, remember?"

He sighs, running his hands through his hair. "Nicki, you could be a centaur and I wouldn't care. You will always be human to me."

"There are centaurs?"

TONIGHT, THE COLD, hard piano bench presses into my bones. The shorts and tank top offer no protection against the chill in the house since I haven't bothered turning on the heat, even though it's October. The beautiful colors of fall have arrived.

Lightning flashes on the smooth, black surface of the lid as I stare at the keys. Lost. Thunder rumbles through my exhausted body and I rack my brain for a song, one which will encompass the turmoil raging inside.

Weakness invades my spirit, and I shudder. It will be a miracle if I make it through this transition. Even human food holds no appeal anymore. The only thing keeping me going: coffee. I'm so screwed.

Why did I run away? I hurt him. I saw it in those beautiful eyes, behind the turbulent anger. Why do I always jump to condemn him? For everything: my past, my father, the suffering, the prophecy. In truth, I've hurt myself by hurting him. Logan's not to blame. Dimitri is. Everything revolves around that bastard. Everything wrong in my life is his fault. Not Logan's.

The song slams into my brain. It couldn't be more perfect.

Thank you, Christina Aguilera.

With a gentleness I am far from experiencing, I lay frigid fingers on the cool keys. A sudden tingle of awareness whooshes through my veins, and every instinct comes alive with his presence. Relief floods through me. I want to weep in delight and run into the warmth of his embrace. I don't. Instead, I keep my head bowed and let the shroud of my hair conceal the turmoil in my expression.

Logan needs to understand me through this song because the song *Hurt* will convey every emotion bottled up inside so much stronger than my fumbling attempts ever could.

The soft huskiness of my voice fills the living room. It conveys the sorrow and anguish, and declares through the words the misery I've been through without him. As I sing, Logan's presence descends into my soul, soothing me.

The last note of the song fades, and tears burn behind my eyes, but I blink them away. My stubborn ass refuses to let them fall. The warmth of Logan's presence has me panting like I just ran a mile at full speed. Goose bumps pebble over my body, and the fine hairs on the nape of my neck stand in awareness.

It takes everything not to glance up. I can't. My insides and my hands shake so badly I clutch the edge of the bench to steady them. I'm hanging on by a thread here. And it's fraying; stretched so taut, it could snap at any moment.

He needs to say something. Too much is happening inside me. Emotions gut me. I want to scream. I want to rage. I want... him.

"Baby."

At the sound of Logan's deep voice, I snap. Whirling on the bench, I launch myself at him. I mean, I literally fly, catapulting my body into his. Logan doesn't even stagger as I slam into him.

Relief floods through me the second those powerful arms wrap around my waist, enshrouding me in the warmth and scent I've been craving. The string inside me loosens. This is home. He is home, my heart, my life.

I lift my legs and wrap them tight around his waistline. My frigid arms encircle his neck. I grip the vampire hard as he holds me and submerge my face in the silky softness of his hair.

"God, Logan." My voice breaks with so many emotions. Lips next to his ear I whisper, "I'm sorry for leaving. Sorry for the hideous things I said. Please, don't leave me again."

His arms tighten for a brief moment before he eases back. He pulls me away with a hand at my nape. Logan gazes deep into my eyes while holding me with little effort. Not that I'd slip, the death grip of my thighs won't allow it.

"Nicole, no more running." The voice is a low command, and my fingers sink deeper into the silky strands, craving to be even closer.

"No more running." With no doubt or hesitation in my answer, I inhale a deep breath as I struggle to control this overwhelming need for him. "I should've stuck around." I blow out a noisy breath at my own stubbornness.

Lips curl into the sexy, lopsided grin I've missed, revealing a quick flash of a fang. The strangest urge to lick it darts through my mind, but before I can act on it, Logan's sliding me down his body and striding away.

What the hell?

"We need to talk, Nicole. I sense your transition is close, so I brought more blood, but I have limited time." Tension edges his voice. Hell, his whole body is ridged with it.

My instincts emerge after two months of nothing. Warning bells resound in my ears. Guilt radiates from Logan in waves. Oh God, he didn't show up to be with me. Did he return to say he was done with me?

Jesus.

To keep from crying out, I clamp my teeth down on the inside of my lip. Should I beg him to stay? No. I am not that pathetic. This Halfling is a warrior. A warrior. I'm a goddamn warrior. If I chant it enough, I might believe it. Or better yet, act like one.

"Oh?" I work to hold my panic behind a perfect shield of indifference even though my heart is beating a mile a minute. Which he hears, of course.

Logan's eyes narrow as he takes in my rigid stance and closed off expression. Tiny nudges push against my barriers, trying to delve into my thoughts. I slam another layer into place.

An angry growl rumbles between us. "No more hiding your emotions from me, Nicole."

For the first time since Logan appeared, I take notice of what he's wearing. Instead of the jeans and button-down from Canada, tonight he's dressed like the night of the shootout: black leather pants and combat boots with a snug black t-shirt. Two deadly swords sheathed in a harness lean against the potbelly stove. I note with a grimace the cooler next to it, this one much larger than before, and a black leather duster drapes over the La-Z-Boy.

"Where've you been, Logan?" My gaze swings back to his.

Don't let your emotions rule you, Nicki. Keep your cool.

Logan's hard-as-granite jaw clenches in frustration. "I was trying to keep my distance, as per your wish." When he steps closer, my greedy lungs inhale his tantalizing scent. "But you are not making it easy." Logan's gaze travels my body with a slow, sensual caress.

Alaric Logan Moretti ignites every cell in my body. It's as though I'm made of gasoline, one spark away from being engulfed in flames. And he knows it.

I push the lust away and concentrate on the guilt radiating from him in waves. He's hiding something. If Logan lies again...

"What have you done, Logan?"

For the longest time, he stares into my eyes with an indecipherable expression. Fear he won't respond cascades down my spine. But when he finally does, I so wish he hadn't.

"I got married."

Chapter 30

Logan

The past couple months have been a perpetual hell. I have fed and slept little, and it has taken a toll on my mind and body. I am risking brain injury from Icarus's spell to be here tonight, but I needed to be with Nicole. I needed to assure myself she was okay, and to inform her she was safe, for now.

Not knowing what my reception would be this evening, after the hurtful things we said to each other, it would not have surprised me if I had faced the barrel of her gun. Again.

As I listened to her sing, Nicole's song revealed much. It eased the fear in my heart. The second she launched herself into my arms and clung for all she was worth had exposed so much more. That unguarded moment gave me a glimpse of Nicole's real emotions, and it cut me like a double-edged sword. Her sorrow and despair gutted me.

I wince, recalling Sebastian and I's arrival back at the castle.

We materialized in the midst of a mating ceremony. Mine.

"As head of my Guardians, Logan, I've decided you need a companion," Dimitri declared the minute I walked into the throne room.

At first, shock seized my tongue. I had not seen that coming. What was Dimitri's end game? Had he discovered Nicole was my one true mate? Was this the first step of many to divide us, to break the prophecy of Nicole and I producing a vampire who could walk in the sun and hold claim to the throne?

Once my shock had worn off, I argued with Dimitri. Tried to state my case against such an arrangement. "As commander of the

Guardians there is no time for a mate. My sole focus needs to be on my responsibilities and assignments."

When those had not worked, I attempted to appeal to Dimitri's ego, "My lord, I want nothing to draw my attention away from the needs of my king."

It had not taken long before he flew into a rage. "Enough!" he bellowed. "You either take the mate of my choosing or I will execute Sebastian." Not me. Sebastian.

With no choice, I married.

It surprised me when Dimitri's companion of choice was none other than the only female Guardian in our group, and one of my most trusted allies, Lucretia Bramen.

If Nicole were not my destined mate, Lu would be my first choice for a companion. She is tall for a female, at five eleven, with the slim, athletic body of a warrior. Long black hair she keeps secured in a tight braid down the middle of her back. Amber eyes glow like molten lava. Clear, porcelain skin, and full lips. Her beauty is beyond measure, as is her loyalty.

A hundred years ago, when she first enlisted to be a Guardian, I almost dismissed her out of hand. There had never been a female Guardian in our history, but the results of her psychological evaluation had been off the charts. Wanting to witness firsthand her fighting skills, I pitted Lu against a few of the king's finest warriors and was amazed by her abilities and technique.

She is proud but stoic, and quietly assesses everything. Always takes time to process before offering an opinion. Lu is quiet and withdrawn most of the time, but when she speaks, I listen. Her sharp intellect and combat strategies rival my own. And she has never once tried to overshadow my authority. I trust her with my life.

She is not my mate. No female will ever take the place of Nicole in my mind, heart, and soul. Nicole possesses all three, whether she accepts it or not. For all eternity.

Nicole's sharp inhale bounces me back to my present dilemma. Shame flows through me that I led with that, but when another barrier slammed over her mind, anger got the better of me. Like a petulant child, I went with the shock factor, hoping it would drop her guard.

"Are you fucking kidding me?" Nicole blinks with surprise.

"No." Resentment and fury at the situation wash over me again as I recall the shock and dismay on Lu's face at Dimitri's announcement.

The ceremony had gone on for days, as was vampire custom, ending in the exchange of blood... and sex. It was witnessed by all, with the fucking king front and center.

Guilt twists my insides at my greatest betrayal. I did everything to make the deed as quick as possible, for Lu's sake and my own. Sickened with remorse and anger, I blocked out the actual act as I performed my duty.

No matter what, I must remember the vow. Do whatever is necessary to keep my mate safe and away from Dimitri. But this betrayal? This crossed a line. One Nicole can never discover.

Once I explain the situation, she might forgive the necessity of the marriage, but she would never forgive the act of having sex with another woman. No matter the reason. Who could blame her? I would rip the heart out of any man who dared to touch what is mine.

Tonight, instead of sinking my aching cock deep into her body, and quenching this raging thirst on the blood that nourishes above all others, I must draw back once more.

Nicole's transition is not yet complete, and by her haggard appearance, it is taking a toll. More than anything, I wish to be here, to help guide her through this, but after the king's insistence of a shadow, it has been nigh impossible to shake him.

Only through the quick intervention of Bastian tonight, I ditched Sedric, but I do not possess much time before he questions my absence.

"Are you saying that since I saw you in Canada a month ago, you've met someone else, fell in love and got married?" Nicole's voice is halting, shaking with disbelief.

"No." Why does she always believe the worst of me? *Mayhap, you gave her plenty of reasons to?* "Let me explain."

"Oh, I can't wait to hear it. This should be entertaining. Should I pop some popcorn?"

The sarcasm causes my jaw to clench in anger. With one menacing step, I reach down, grab hold of her thighs, and haul her over my shoulder.

"What the hell," she yelps in surprise, slapping her palms on my lower back.

With my mate struggling in one hand, I clutch the cooler before teleporting to her studio in the garage. Alexandria's scent was in the house, and this conversation requires complete privacy.

A hard punch lands on my kidney, and I drop the cooler to the floor. My palm comes down with a resounding smack on her beautiful ass.

Fuck, that felt great.

Her breath catches, her body tensing. Expecting Nicole to fight in earnest, my grip tightens, and I wait for her small fists to pummel my back. But her body relaxes. Her hands clench my shirt. Lavender and spring fill the studio.

Christ. Nicole enjoyed that as much as I did?

A vision of bending her over my knee, stripping off the black shorts, and pinking her backside while she moans and grinds against me causes my cock to swell in the stiff leathers.

Again, my hand comes down with a loud smack on the other cheek, the brief shorts not much of a barrier. Her heart rate increases along with her breathing.

"Are you going to be a good girl and listen?" I demand in a low controlled tone. The voice I use in my playroom. Nicole hesitates, so I smack her a third and fourth time. Hard.

"Yes."

Nicole's breathy moan stiffens me further. The zipper a delicious bite of pain.

My mate is perfect.

Chapter 31

Logan just spanked me. My insides quiver with instantaneous lust. *Please, don't stop*, whimpers through my brain. The need to have his big palm against my bare flesh consumes me, and the urge to grind my hips against his muscular shoulder pounds through my skull. For years I've fantasized about this. Well, not in this position, and not fully clothed, but still.

After the first smack, a red haze of desire overtook my brain, so the question didn't penetrate until Logan smacked me a couple more times. The sexual submissive took control, answering as commanded.

With excruciating slowness, Logan slides me down his rock-hard body, and my core clenches as his massive erection glides over my pelvic bone and stomach. My muscles twitch with the need to climb back up this tower of a vampire and let him have his wicked way with my body.

Instead, I lower my head and squeeze my burning eyes shut. After a deep, cleansing breath, I attempt to get control over this raging hunger by pressing my quivering thighs together to ease the throbbing ache at my center.

"Look at me, baby." The deep command wets my panties. Internal muscles clench as my gaze lifts. The green fire makes me swallow.

"You never cease to surprise, or please me." Logan's voice fills with wonder as both hands grip my face. A callused thumb slides over my trembling lips. "As much as I would love to explore this further, I cannot. You need blood, and we need to talk."

"Logan. I can't drink your blood. It won't stay down."

"What?" His hands drop in shock.

See, knew I wasn't normal.

"Have you not been consuming my blood this whole time?" At the shake of my head, Logan erupts. "Goddammit. Why did no one say anything? No wonder you have lost so much weight."

"Jimmy thinks it's part of being a Halfling. That I need to drink blood..." my face heats with embarrassment and I stare at his gigantic boots, "straight from the vein."

A deep sigh fans across my bent head, followed by a gentle kiss, before Logan turns and walks to the couch in the corner. He lowers his powerful body in the center and spreads those massive thighs. My mind flashes to the last time, and I lick my dry, cracked lips.

"Come here."

Those two words have my legs shaking with lust, but I do as commanded, never taking my gaze from the simmering green glow. When I'm standing between his open thighs, Logan reaches for my hand.

"Straddle me, Nicole. Let me nourish you."

The deep, husky voice washes over me like warm rain. Holy crap. I'm so turned on by the mere idea of drinking Logan's blood, I'm dizzy with it. The thirst—shredding and burning my throat for weeks—shoots straight to my gums. Lust clenches my core, my skin ignites with fire, and hunger cramps my gut.

His nostrils flare as he scents the air. "Hmmm. The transition is upon you, baby." When Logan smiles, a groan vibrates up my throat at the display of sexy fangs. "My blood will help relieve the symptoms and complete the change. Get on, and I will show you how to take directly from the vein."

Anxious but eager, I do as I'm told, and grip his hips with tense thighs. I ogle his smooth, tan throat and salivate. A frown mars my forehead when my tongue runs along the surface of my teeth, and only feel the flat ridges of normal teeth. No fangs.

"Logan?"

"Hush." With a shift forward, Logan reaches down into a boot and pulls out a small dagger. I eye the thing with curiosity, having complete trust in him. When he slices open the vein in his neck, I gasp in horror.

"Drink, Nicole. Before it heals."

Ah, okay. That makes sense. I lean in, ready to lay hungry lips against the wound. When the scent of Logan's blood hits my nostrils, all thoughts except one leave my brain—feed. With a speed and violence which should shock and dismay, I strike.

Logan's body tenses at the attack, but at the first deep pull on his vein, he moans, and wraps warm arms around my back. Long sensual strokes up and down encourage as I suck hard on the wound.

Sweet baby Jesus. Logan's blood is like ambrosia, sweeter and yummier than anything I've ever experienced before. Better than coffee. Holy shit, I can't believe my mind uttered that betrayal.

The bagged blood had gone down like sawdust, and curdled the second it hit my stomach. This is pure power. And fucking addictive. Like cocaine times one hundred. The more the sweet, spicy nectar flows down my throat, the stronger my desire ramps up. A sudden pain shoots through my gums, and the long- awaited fangs descend in an instant. A good thing too because the wound in Logan's throat just sealed up. On pure instinct, I plunge my new fangs deep into his smooth neck, hitting the artery on the first try.

"Yes. Baby!"

At Logan's shout of pleasure, I pull harder, needing more. A warm hand clasps the back of my head, holding me tighter to his neck. His other hand on my ass grinds me along his massive erection.

I moan in ecstasy and grip fistfuls of his silken hair. I rear back and strike again, sinking deep. The best thing ever created flows down my throat, cooling the flames. The intense power of Logan's blood electrifies my body. With each swallow, my hips move faster, matching the heat pulsing through my clit as it ignites on fire. My nipples tighten into painful points as Logan's sweet, spicy blood quenches the raging thirst. The need for his cock pounding into me while drinking this powerful essence is a driving force consuming me.

After several minutes, the burning thirst ebbs and I ease my new fangs from his neck. On pure instinct, I lick the wound closed. I lean up and drop my head back with a moan, rubbing my drenched, aching clit along his leather-clad length with a frenzied need. "Logan. Need you inside me. Now." Did that demanding growl just come from me?

"Look at me."

With Logan's command, and his blood fueling my desire, I stare into the extraordinary green glow while he examines me, his palms cradling my face. "Christ, you were beautiful as a human, but as a vampire, you are incredible."

A sharp inhale fills my lungs at the reminder, and my eyes widen. "The transition's finally over?" The quiet question comes out husky from the desire still raging inside. "I'm a vampire?"

"Yes." In quiet awe, his lids heavy with need, he watches me.

"I assumed there would be more... pain," I confess. In the movies the newly turned writhe in pain and then die, before being brought back to life.

"You have been living with the pain of transition for months, Nicole. Normally it only lasts for a day or so."

Figures I'd draw out the pain and suffering.

"Does that mean what I think it means?" I ask, hovering my lips over his. "You can fuck me now?"

"Baby,"—man I love it when he calls me that—"If you want to fuck, I will fuck you until you cannot remember your damn name, and you never forget mine." Like that would ever happen. Logan is imprinted on my psyche.

In the next breath, my back hits the couch and the sexy vampire leans over me. Teeth bared, eyes glowing with lust.

"Ahem... sorry to interrupt. Again."

"Fuck, Bastian. Your timing sucks," Logan growls.

No, no, no. Dammit. Peeking under Logan's arm, I glare daggers at Sebastian, hating him. This is the second time that ass has kept Logan and I from being together.

"Hey, Nicki." Sebastian gives an embarrassed wave. "Sorry, but Logan needs to come with me." His blue eyes rake down my form. "Welcome to the club, my lady."

I growl and bare my fangs. Bastian cocks an eyebrow, smirking.

Logan's sigh is filled with regret, and for a moment, long, dark lashes close over the beautiful glow and his forehead leans against mine. "Wait outside, Bastian. I will be right there." In a blink, Logan's standing, holding his hand out and Bastian is gone.

Away from his delicious heat, my brows draw together in frustration and disappointment. *So* not what I want, dammit. My body still vibrates with the nourishing power of Logan's blood pumping through every vein, but as the red haze of lust dissipates, his revelation from before bounces to the forefront.

Logan is fucking married. I almost had sex with a married man. How could this happen? What about being his damn everything? Anger and jealousy boil to the surface, but I tap it down with a sledgehammer. Could there be a rational explanation? Not sure what the fuck it would be, but I'm gonna at least hear him out. Then I'll punch him in the nose. With my newfound strength, I just might break it.

With pain-free movements for the first time in months, I stand. "Logan. Thanks for... for... finally completing this god- awful transition," I whisper. I self-consciously wipe the corner of my mouth, before lifting my gaze. "But you want to tell me how it is you're married?"

After a long sigh, Logan spews out all the details of the whole crazy, convoluted story. Not only what's been going on for the last month, but the ultimate end game regarding my father. Plans he's put in place the previous twelve years. The secret army he's built. The witches he's secretly recruited to perform the needed spells to capture Dimitri. The small victories—and larger defeats.

He doesn't pace or fidget. There is no wild gesturing with his hands. Logan stands in front of me in all his glory, arms relaxed at his sides, body military-straight, as if he's debriefing a commanding officer on the progress of a war strategy.

Although it's a brilliant plan, and years in the making, there's just one small flaw: how is he planning to draw Dimitri out of the castle?

How will we do that? Me. As bait. I am Dimitri's Achilles' heel after all. Per the prophecy, don't I lead this operation? To be the one to end my father's reign and capture him? It must be me.

With patience I'm far from feeling, I listen to everything he reports, loving the sound of his voice as it washes over me. With my newly enhanced senses, I examine him closely. His skin is pale, and dark circles ring the underside of his eyes like he hasn't slept in weeks. The leather pants, while still hugging his hips, are looser. He's lost weight too, and his heart rate sounds slow, irregular.

It hits me—Logan is starving. And he just let me practically drink him dry. Damn it. There's a part of me, the insane, jealous part, that's ecstatic he hasn't drunk from the new ball and chain.

Wife. Just the word, and the image it evokes is enough to make my blood boil. If the bitch dares to come near me, I will not regret removing her head from her body.

Then there's the other part, the one worried about my man. How long can he go without nourishment? If we're going to battle Dimitri together, he needs to be at his best. Well-fed and rested, but I don't want him drinking from anyone but me.

"I want in. Who better to draw him out, than me?"

"No. Have you not heard a fucking word I just said?" With speed, he reaches out and grabs my upper arms, bringing me against him. "I need you safe, and worrying about you is a distraction I cannot stand."

My palms rest on hard pecs. "I'm in this whether you want me to be or not, Logan. It's my destiny. Don't protect me, shield me, as if I can't handle it, as if I can't fight too. Lead me into battle, and I will follow you. I'm a powerful vampire. Remember?"

"Thinking about you involved in this... I have tried to protect you from him your whole life. Unsuccessfully, it would seem. Now you are asking me to let you face him? To put you in a situation that could get you hurt? Killed? I understand it is prophecy, but it goes against everything I am." Logan rests his forehead against mine. "So many things you still need to learn, Nicole. All your powers are not yet upon you. They will be immense. In the next few weeks, you will be bombarded with abilities and powers that took Dimitri centuries to gain and control. It will require time to get a handle on them all."

"But how will I learn to do that? Who will teach me?"

"Nicole." Sorrow fills Logan's gaze when his head lifts, and a sigh of breath fans my checks. "As much as I want it to be me, to train you myself, I cannot. Dimitri assigned me a shadow who reports back to him my every move. That and the binding spell linking me to him allows him to know where I am at all times." His hands leave my shoulders, and Logan starts pacing. His agitation throws needles of pain into my skin. "Sebastian and Icarus bought us time tonight, but I cannot come back for some time."

What the... he's leaving me? Again? Panic flutters in the pit of my stomach.

"Your transition is complete so my bagged blood should be sufficient." He nods to the dreaded cooler. "I am also assigning one of my most trusted warriors to train you." Logan stops pacing and comes to stand in front of me. "She is a fierce fighter and she will guide you. Help you control your powers."

My eyebrow lifts. "She?" Logan's holding something back, so I probe further. "Who is she?"

"Lucretia, a female Guardian and one of my best warriors." Truth, but there's more. "And?"

"And my..." Logan hesitates, swallowing. "my pseudo-wife."

Oh, hell no. My head rears back as if he slapped me. "You can't be fucking serious? We just made out, I fed from you, and you're sending your *wife* to train me?" My laugh holds no humor. "No. Fucking. Way." Fangs shoot through my gums in an instant. "If she comes near me, Logan, I will eviscerate her."

"Nicole..." With a sigh, Logan runs a hand through his hair.

"Wait... back up the bus. Pseudo-wife?" My voice vibrates with a low intensity. Logan's eyes to snap to mine. "Does that mean you haven't had sex with her?"

Please say yes, please say yes.

"Yes."

Lie.

Pain pierces my temple. I absorb the blow without an outward sign, but a part of me withers and dies. Logan had sex with her. The pain is unbearable. My hopes and dreams are being ripped to shreds, but I'll never allow him to see me flinch. Ice, my newfound savior, builds and thickens around my heart.

"Jimmy or Kurtis will train me."

"Jimmy yes, Kurtis no."

Oh no he didn't! He has a damn wife he's fucked, and he's pissed because I want Kurtis to train me? Hypocrite.

Bastian emerges in the studio again, angry and agitated.

"I must go, Nicole."

I don't hear him. It's like I'm seventeen again and he's dropping me off at the school. My mind shuts down. All I can manage is a slight nod.

"Obey me in this. I agree to no Lucretia, but it is either Alexandria or Jimmy." Logan presses his lips to mine, but I don't feel it. Don't respond. "Make me a promise." Lifting my chin with a finger, Logan frowns at my expression. "Promise me, if he finds you, before you are ready, do not fight him. Dimitri will take you alive. Submit. Do whatever you need to do to stay alive. I will come for you. Always. Until my last breath." The truth of his vow eases the pain of his lie somewhat, and I blink at the glowing green embers. "Promise me, baby."

Nausea grips my insides and I don't dare open my mouth. I nod and lower my gaze before Logan and Bastian fade away. I'm too numb to be shocked by it. How could he have sex with another woman? And the worst part, he lied about it. That's what cuts the deepest. The lie. He fucking lied.

The reasons why the whole marriage thing had to take place, I understand. Logan had no choice. Sebastian's life was at stake. I get it. And someday, years and years down the road, I *might* be able to get over the fact he slept with the bitch. Again, perhaps he had no choice.

What I can't forgive, what's eating me from the inside out, is the fact he lied right to my face. Trust is not one of my strong suits, and with one little word, he'd taken a flamethrower to the shredded tatters of mine and burned it to ash.

Chapter 32

Nicole

It's been over a month since I drank from Logan. Six weeks without any blood at all. His bagged blood had the same damn effect. One, it tasted like shit, and two, it curdled in my stomach and within minutes, back up it came.

I've kept that little secret to myself though. Every day, I select a pouch out of the cooler and dump it down the toilet. Why? Because Jimmy checks the cooler to make certain I'm drinking it.

Thank God I can still eat regular food, but with my heightened sense of taste, I'm particular about what goes in my mouth. I've been surviving on Ding Dongs, which are amazing, and my drug of choice, the elixir of the gods: coffee.

I'm supposed to save the vampire race, but I can't even get through my day without coffee; I'm a vampire but can't even drink blood.

The healthy glow and strength from Logan's powerful essence is wearing off, and my apprehension grows every day that Kurtis or Jimmy will notice.

One of them would go tattling to Logan. One guess on which one. Then Logan would drag himself away from his "pseudo-wife" to show up to feed the other woman. So not going to happen. I don't care if I'm cutting my nose off to spite my face.

In the initial week of vampire training, the pyrokinesis ability swept through me like a damn fire tornado, and I feared the tremendous power would blow Kurtis or myself up. In fact, I set the forest ablaze. Twice. Thank goodness the fire chief was a member of Jimmy's pack. He and the crew camped out in the vast clearing on my property we designated for practice.

The first time I set myself on fire, I freaked out, screaming my damn head off while doing a drop and roll across the field. Kurtis and the sexy firemen howled with laughter while I burned to a crisp. Okay, I didn't burn to a crisp, but Kurtis failed to tell me the only way to quench the inferno on a person was with the same pyrokinesis ability I used to start it. It took everything within me not to throw a fireball in his grinning face.

Yup, I disobeyed Logan's orders. All of them—Jimmy, Alex, Liam, and Kurtis—tackle training me on one or more of my abilities. What my mate doesn't know won't hurt him. Besides, he's off doing God-knows-what with fucking Lucretia.

The new presence inside my mind and body shifts with anger. It replaced my inner bitch. This manifestation ramps up my instincts to a whole other level. It's animalistic. Carnal. Survives on my baser emotions. I think I will love it and squeeze it and call her Georgie. Important things must be named. It's written in law somewhere.

During the second week of instruction, we tested my telepathic capabilities, which are sweet. According to Jimmy, if a species possesses telepathic abilities, it only extends to bonded mates or blood relations. Vampires, fae, and Icarus are the only races he knows of with the ability. I, however, communicate with every species. Distance doesn't matter. So during battle, I can talk to Logan and my friends, but only my mate or a blood relation can respond back. I *could* reach out to Logan right now, but I refuse.

With a grimace, I recall how my telekinesis ability arrived without warning. Poor Joe took the brunt of that one. One morning I woke wishing he was on my nightstand with a mug of heaven brewed and ready. When Joe came sailing through the bedroom door straight for my head, I screamed like a girl.

Sad to report, Joe was damaged beyond repair. If the demand for coffee weren't so extreme, I would've performed a goodbye ceremony and buried him out back. But, since Ding Dongs and caffeine are my only sustenance these days, I employed my other newfound talent, mind control. I ordered Liam to rush out and purchase a new Keurig. Still haven't selected a name for it yet. It will come to me.

Two days ago, I attempted to trace. This is the one ability that scares the shit out of me and I've been unable to master. The goal was to teleport from the house to the clearing, but instead, I materialized in Jimmy's office at the LeLoo, and scared the crap out of both of us.

What happens if I transport to Siberia or something? That would suck ass. Normal vampires only trace to places they've been. There is nothing normal about me. So, for now it's just a few feet at a time, which has worked to gain the drop on Kurtis several times during training.

Woo hoo!

Alex and I also discovered I have no sensitivity to silver when one of her blades passed through my shoulder. Can't lie, it hurt like a motherfucker, but repaired in an instant with no weakness or side effects.

"You're not weakened by silver," Jimmy exclaimed in a stunned whisper as he inspected my healing wound.

"No. Which means neither is my father, right?"

"I can only assume so."

"Well that shoots plan A to shit, doesn't it? The silver darts will have no effect."

"We still have the mystical shackles, and you," he said with confidence.

"Since we don't have any restraints to test yet, let's hope the mystical shackles work then," I retorted.

Throughout my training, I discovered Alex is a badass little fighter, with an agility and speed rivaling a vampire, and is deadly accurate with those silver daggers as several more body parts can contend.

"Jump, spin, and then kick," she instructs for the hundredth time.

"I thought that's what I was doing?" I yell in frustration. All these years, I tried to encourage Alex to take self-defense classes. She must have laughed her damn head off. I'm still uncertain if I've forgiven her for lying for so long, but we've reached an understanding—just don't mention it.

Alex is the youngest of the group. At only a hundred years old, she's considered the baby. Wow. What must they think of me; I'm an embryo?

Liam is next at a hundred and fifty. My training sessions with him are the ultimate. His easy, laid-back attitude makes training fun, and his jokes make me forget the seriousness of my situation.

During one of our sessions, after I threw him into the trees, he came waltzing back in his wolf form. Liam transformed into a massive white creature, weighing in at 250 pounds of beautiful sleek muscles and glistening alabaster fur. I grasped in an instant it was him. The intelligence and humor in those blue eyes gave him away.

Speaking to a wolf telepathically was the coolest thing I'd ever experienced. Granted he couldn't communicate back, but it didn't matter. After he kicked my butt, pinning me to the ground with his massive weight, his teeth *gently* clamped around my throat, we relaxed in the grass. Him on his side with my head resting on his enormous chest. It was peaceful listening to his huffing breath and pounding heart, and my love for Liam grew.

Kurtis is over two hundred years old. He's never shifted during our training, and I never asked him to. Even though curiosity burned to know what kind of animal he was.

Out of all my trainers, he was the most ruthless, pushing the limits of my endurance, and his. He always knows what I need—the pain in my body, even if it was momentary. The extreme concentration of my mind, until I can't process anything else. Kurtis's training was once again my lifeline. An outlet from the ball of suffering in the center of my chest.

In all these weeks, I haven't sensed or seen hide nor hair of Logan. Oh, I've detected his *wife* lurking around at night, although she never materializes. Is the bitch too much of a coward to show her face?

What would happen if she did?

The green demon thrashing around inside would rip her goddamn heart out and devour it while she watched, not giving a flying fuck if she's innocent in all this. All I visualize is Logan having sex with her.

Ugh.

When will this torment end? My dark need is stabbing at my brain with sharp jabs, desperate to climb to the surface. It demands its due. I'd hoped once I became a vampire, I wouldn't require it anymore. I haven't borne the demand for a reboot since Logan popped back in my life.

Until now.

Sweat pours off my body even though it's forty degrees outside. I duck and weave, spin and kick, strike and retreat, driving myself harder and harder. In my mind, the goal is Dimitri, and since he's the most powerful vampire in existence, I'd better up my fucking game.

The short dagger tucked in my palm is my weapon of choice today. The blade is like a part of my body. It lays along the outside of my right forearm, ready for defense or a quick flick of the wrist to strike. For training, the blade is wooden. As a shifter, Kurtis can regenerate, but I don't want to kill him.

That would suck.

I'm in complete awe of Kurtis's abilities. For a big guy, he moves with the velocity and grace of a panther. Or should I say shapeshifter? Now that I'm no longer a fragile human, he's attacking with the speed and power of an immortal. He's fake-killed or injured me multiple times, but I continue pressing forward, anticipating and praying for a hint of vulnerability. A specific moment when I can strike a death blow.

His sleek muscles glisten with sweat, which provides me a small measure of satisfaction. For the first time, the immortal is exerting himself. The gray muscle shirt clings to his torso. Instead of the usual cargo pants, he's wearing black workout shorts that just brush his knee.

"Concentrate, Nicki," he growls at me. "Push harder. Move faster."

I duck and weave away from his relentless advances, tracing behind him in an instant, but he expects the action. His vivid blue stare pins me when I reemerge. Sweat soaks my sports bra, chafing the underside of my breasts. The black shorts stick to my backside, and for the first time, the prospect of an ice bath is appealing.

"Do the unexpected," he grates out with impatience.

What the fuck does he think I'm doing? I block and evade Kurtis's barrage of kicks and punches and jab out a rapid series in response.

Around the perimeter of the clearing, a small crowd of firefighters gathers, along with Alex, Jimmy, and Liam, their gazes wide with apprehension.

Afraid the big man will kill the inept Halfling?

No doubt that's what it looks like. Kurtis is attacking with a ferocity I've never experienced before. Intense blue eyes calculate my every step. His punches, jabs, and kicks are fast and full of power. To the spectators, he's hitting with everything he's got.

If Kurtis really wanted to hurt me, he could knock me across this clearing with ease. At three times my size and over two centuries of experience, with muscular arms bigger than my thighs, he could seriously injure me. I'd heal, but it would hurt.

He's checking his blows at the last second and it's pissing me off. Is it because he still regards me as a fragile human? Or is it because I'm a woman? Would he check them if I were Liam or Jimmy?

"Stop pulling your damn punches," I whisper in annoyance. His eyes take on a feral glow. When I block his next punch with my forearm, it contains way more power than any of the others. I wince against the pain and stagger. A concerned frown mars his forehead. He hesitates and steps back.

Faster than the human eye can track, I flip the dagger into an offensive position and jump into a spinning flying kick. My foot smashes into the side of his head with a loud, satisfying whack that has everyone gasping.

A second of regret passes through me when he stumbles, but I drop low and sweep those powerful legs out from under him while he's still unstable. The resounding thud the big man produces when his back slams into the ground has me grinning with savage intent. I leap on him before he recovers and straddle his hips. I lift the blade for the final death blow, but Kurtis expects the advance, and reaches for my wrist. I'm not naïve. This immortal is powerful. If those strong fingers latch onto me, it's over.

With extraordinary speed, the wooden blade flies to my other hand and a savage battle cry permeates the sky. When it strikes into the center of Kurtis's chest, an image of it plunging into Dimitri's cold, black heart fills my vision.

Loud applause snaps me from the glowing haze of vengeance, and I refocus on Kurtis squeezed between my thighs. A sexy, proud smile lifts his lips, showcasing his pearly whites. An impulse to bend and press my lips to his flashes through me.

What if I did? Logan's married. Yeah, okay it's a bogus marriage, but it sure as hell wasn't in name only. He'd had sex with another woman... correction, vampire. Looked me right in the eye and lied about it. A small spark exists between Kurtis and me. Nothing like the raging inferno that ignites with Logan, but a spark, nonetheless. Should I test the waters?

Kurtis desires me, and based on our last interaction, he holds the potential to be a legitimate sexual dominant. If Logan would get out of my head and heart, we'd be golden.

Kurtis grabs me around the waist, and fluidly pushes up from the ground. The heated blue eyes never leave mine. Several moments pass before I gather the only thing keeping me attached to him are my thighs wrapped around his waist. Embarrassed, I release the tight grip and hop down.

"Those are some bright gray peepers. I'd love to know what or who you were thinking about toward the end." A grin plays at the corners of his lips. "It brought out the side of you I've been waiting to see."

"You don't want to know." The burn in my lungs eases with each sweet inhale. Sweat drips down my neck, and travels in small rivulets between my breasts. Kurtis's stare follows the salty flow, and the smile evaporates. Blue eyes darken with hunger, and a muscle ticks in his jaw.

"Show's over folks," Kurtis announces to the crowd, ending the training session.

In the sea of faces surrounding us, Alex beams, and she offers a fist pump, her grin as proud as a mother lion acknowledging her cub's first kill. I shake my head, but a small smile lifts my lips.

As the firefighters head off to their trucks, Kurtis reaches for my hands, starting the process of removing the tape wrapped tightly around them. No gloves for immortal training, and I don't require the tape either, but Kurtis insisted. Still trying to look after me?

"Take a few days off. You've been pushing hard, and you're about ready to crash."

"I don't need—"

Kurtis cuts me off with a stern glance and a raised eyebrow. "It's not a request, Nicki." I glower at him. "Teleport to my office after you hit the showers." Kurtis notes my apprehension and smirks. "You can do it. Learn to control it."

Chapter 33

Nicole

An hour later, after a soothing hot shower, the burn and ache in my abused muscles has faded. Dressed in snug black yoga pants, a purple tunic sweater, and—of course—boots, I attempt to teleport to Kurtis's office, but instead make it as far as the parking lot.

Oh well, I shrug. Close enough.

Entering Kurtis's masculine realm, I plop my backside in one of the high back chairs just as he's wrapping up a call.

His hair is still damp from his own shower, and the darker strands enhance the blueness of his eyes, eyes that haven't moved away from me since I strolled in. A slight tingle of awareness crawls across my skin.

"How far did you make it?" He asks with a knowing grin as he hangs up the phone.

I shrug and roll my eyes. "The parking lot."

He snickers and brings up the schedule on the computer. We quickly figure out dates and times for next week's training.

Once that's done, Kurtis comes to settle in front of my chair, leaning against the desk.

My God, he's so good looking and tall. My gaze travels the length of his imposing body, savoring the view. The tight, dark green t-shirt accentuates the trim waistline, the bulge and dip of his pec muscles, and the massive girth of his shoulders and biceps. The light-colored camo pants hug his hips, flaring out to accommodate those massive thighs. Sand-colored military boots complete the whole badass soldier look.

I finish the delightful little excursion all the way down and back up again, pass the provocative curve of full lips, before stalling on the oceanic, passion-filled eyes.

"You like what you see, Nicki?"

The low intensity of his voice snags my attention, and my eyes drop to follow his lips as they move. Instead of answering, I ask a question. "Why do you want me, Kurtis? You know what my fate is." The magnetic intensity in those vivid baby blues has me swallowing.

"Nicki." Strong hands pull me from the chair to rest between his spread legs. My trembling palms land on his powerful chest as Kurtis wraps one arm around my waist. He drags me closer to his scorching heat. Long fingers tangle into the depths of my damp hair, and I shiver. Not with cold, but with anticipation of what is coming. Anxiety churns in my belly as well.

What the fuck are you doing, Nicole?

As incredible as Kurtis is, he's still not Logan. As a woman, I'm aware of him. There has always been a small measure of interest there, but it's not the all-consuming lust and demanding need I endure for Logan. Every waking thought isn't of Kurtis. The erotic dreams at night are not of Kurtis.

'But they could be,' my inner voice hisses.

Logan had no problems having sex with another woman. Should I? Not with a woman of course. With Kurtis. Could this small attraction with him grow if cultivated? Will it eclipse my unnatural obsession with Logan? Free me from needing him?

"You're the most incredible woman I've ever met," Kurtis rumbles before lowering his face to mine. "Strong." A light kiss on the corner of my lips. "Beautiful." The other corner is graced with a similar, feather-light caress of sensuous lips. "Sexy as hell." His mouth hovers just above mine. "And I crave to watch you come apart under my touch."

His lips devour mine with a ferocity that startles me, and I don't react at first, so overwhelmed with the skill of Kurtis's mouth. His hunger and need burns through my frame, kindling a response.

The rich, masculine scent of his arousal surrounds me. The citrus and pine, all Kurtis, overwhelm my taste buds. Large heavy hands grip my ass as they tug me tighter. I push everything else out and give my all into the kiss.

A rough growl rumbles through his chest. It causes a ripple of sensation to dance over my skin. Need more. Need my body to melt, to release the juices quick to wet my panties by just looking at Logan. But they're absent. I want to want Kurtis. I do. The expertise of those lips and tongue are a strong indication he'd be a generous but dominant lover.

He's not Logan.

Logan lights a fire in every molecule of my body, which spreads with ease to my nipples and core. I desire to be dominated by him and only him. To run my tongue along every inch of his flesh. And since consuming his blood, and my transition, the hunger for him has only strengthened tenfold.

An image of Logan sinking those sexy fangs into my neck at the same moment his cock spreads my pussy forces me to unconsciously rub against Kurtis. He reacts to my perceived need for him by hoisting me up with both palms under my butt, draping my legs around his waist. He plants my ass on the desk and grinds the impressive erection against my core. The cloth of my black yoga pants is so meager, it's as if the sole barrier between us is the stiff material of his cargo pants.

Soft, sensuous lips trail hot kisses to the hollow of my throat with a pleased growl. "You smell so fucking good. I could devour every bit of you."

See. That right there should make me swoon. It doesn't. Guilt assaults my senses. And Georgie, my inner vampire now duly named, recoils at my actions. Angry. This is wrong. It's a betrayal to Logan. The vampire who owns my heart.

Yes, I'm furious and hurt because he lied, but no matter how mad or upset I am, this is not the way to deal with it—using Kurtis to get back at him. It's not fair. All I'm doing is offering him false hope. As long as Logan breathes, his hope is misplaced.

Palms on his chest, I give a gentle nudge. "Kurtis, stop." Instantly, he freezes, before removing his lips from my neck.

The half-mast stare locks with mine. He evaluates my expression, the rigidity of my body, the hands pressing at his chest. Does he see the heartache and regret in my eyes too? Whatever he observes causes him to step back, eyes closing as if in torment.

"I'm sorry... this... we...." I can't deliver the words that will break his heart.

"Logan."

I blanch at the hurt and anger breaking through in the deep, controlled manner of his tone. "Yes."

"I see." Kurtis's voice is gruff and tight with emotion. He strides around the desk, placing the barrier between us.

With a deep, fortifying breath, I hop off the desk and shift to face him. "Have I completely screwed this up? Can... can we still be friends?" I don't want to lose Kurtis. Not just as my mentor and trainer, but as my closest friend.

When his eyes bore into mine without saying a word, I fear I've lost him. Remorse consumes me and I sigh at my foolishness. Shoulders hunched, I turn for the door. My fingers grip the knob as sadness echoes through me. "I'm sorry, Kurtis."

"Nicki." The growl spins me around. "No matter what my feelings are, or what transpires in your life, I will always be your friend."

Tremendous relief washes over me. Stubborn tears threaten, but I blink them away. "Thank you, Kurtis. Your friendship means more than you realize."

As I focus on tracing to the cottage and not bum-fuck Egypt, the dark need rises to the surface. The time has come to change into my submissive costume and hit the club. There's no resisting any longer. Every square inch of my skin crawls with the demand for release, and if it's not fed, it'll consume me. Music isn't working, training isn't cutting it, and I don't even have Logan to help me through it.

Damn you, Logan.

Chapter 34

"**W**here are you going dressed like that?"

The deep rumble causes my heart to skip, and I spin around to face Logan standing at my bedroom door, dressed for battle again, minus the leather duster.

Fuck. Four weeks of nothing and he shows up tonight. Why did he pick this exact moment to come back?

Every day has been hell, imagining Logan at that damn castle, sleeping the daylight hours away with the little wife. His lie. The cluster in Kurtis's office. My inability to keep down Logan's blood, and my utter failure to control these stupid powers.

After teleporting to the end of my drive—not the cottage, just the driveway—and with no sense of Lu or Bastian around, I'd stomped up the lane and headed straight for my room. I needed to take full advantage of no babysitter and hit the club.

"Nicole?" Logan's confused glower narrows on mine.

What the hell do I say? *"Oh, by the way, I like to get spanked and whipped by total strangers while being tied up. Hope that's okay with you."* Logan would lose his mind.

Although it would be infinitely better to hear it from me than for him to track me down one night and discover me with a random man... in restraints... being flogged. Shit, just the visual makes me shudder. Logan would rip the man's throat out in a heartbeat and we... we would be finished.

With a deep, fortifying inhale, Logan's scent washes over me. And Georgie stirs. Do I take the most significant risk ever?

I can get over the fact Dimitri forced him to wed Lucretia to save Sebastian. In time, the need to eviscerate the bitch for having his cock buried deep within her will fade. I might wrap my brain around the reasons he lied. But this, my dirty little secret, will either make or break us.

"Logan, I need this."

He freezes, shoulders tensing. "Need what, Nicole?"

My fists clench in uncertainty. Wait... shit. I can't do it. The feeling of being suffocated by my breath hits hard. Will Logan understand? Or regard me with disgust, walk away and never come back?

I'm unraveling. Every dirty part of me will be on display in front of the one man I've loved my whole life. My Guardian. I'm... gutted. Weak and vulnerable and I *hate* it. Logan's abandonment led to this point. This is *his* doing.

"Dammit, Logan. Do you know how long I waited for you to come back to my dreams?" I shout. "Two fucking years you abandoned me. Every damn night I went to bed hoping and praying you would be there. But you weren't. You never came, Logan." My voice breaks because I don't know how to explain. I don't get it myself. "So... I found the escape I needed by other means."

For a second, shock widens his eyes and his mouth drops open, then everything changes. Eyes glow and narrow. Jaw clenches as he takes in the leather outfit.

"What means, Nicole?"

"Pain." The honesty pierces the tension in the room and my eyes drop to the carpet. I wanted to lie. My instinct is screaming to run for the door, or jump out the damn window, but he'd catch me before I even took a step.

"With fucking Kurtis?"

My gaze jerks back to his. With the way his hands are clenching and unclenching, his fangs bared, eyes hard and glowing green; it is apparent that Logan is holding on by a thread.

I shake my head. "No. Strangers."

"Strangers? You find some random guy and..." he stops. The green glow intensifies. My eyes water just to look at him, but I don't lower them. A deep, animalistic growl emerges from Logan's throat, and his fangs lengthen. "Tell me they did not give you those scars."

Oh boy.

"Tell me!" This is the vampire out of control. This is a side of Logan I never wanted to see. A Logan I imagine no one would want to encounter—every muscle in that powerful body is tense, hands clenched into fists. Jaw hard as granite and lips raised in a snarl, putting those deadly fangs on full display. The heat of his fury pulses into me like a raging wildfire.

"Things got out of control once. But... it makes the pain of my past go away, Logan." I whisper brokenly.

"No. It does not. You keep it alive and relive it every time with total strangers because that is safe." Logan strides toward me and grabs my arms in a bruising grip that I welcome. "Look at me."

He's right dammit. I am holding on to the pain of my past, with the pain strangers can give, so I never forget. I used those men to release all the pent-up emotions built up over the years. My subconscious was aware of the guilt, the shame for being unable to stop the abuse, the anger and the hatred for Dimitri. Even if my conscious mind didn't remember, it drove every notion. In my nightmares. It manifested in my physical and emotional turmoil.

Logan's fingers tighten even more. He stares at me for several seconds before whispering, "Your body, your blood, your life... are mine. I can give you what you need, Nicole."

My breath hitches.

The green glow softens, its harsh light subsiding to an intense, mesmerizing pulse. "Baby, I can give you what you truly need. Stop blocking, stop hiding your deepest needs and desires. Trust me."

The temptation to trust him is not insignificant. Shit, this all-consuming need to surrender to Logan frightens the hell out of me. But, if I were to open my mind, let him in on my innermost desires the way he requires, there would be no going back. I would give him all that I am.

"You don't know what you're asking?"

"I am asking you to trust me," he growls. "Why is that so difficult for you? You would trust a total stranger to give you what you need, but not me?"

Wow, when he puts it like that, it does sound stupid. Why wouldn't I trust Logan? Why can't I? I've trusted this vampire so readily with my life, but not with my heart. Not with my deepest, darkest needs.

"The way you trusted me?" I accuse. "You lied, Logan. You fucked Lucretia."

Green eyes widen before his jaw hardens. "I had no choice, Nicole," he whispers, admitting the truth, but not apologizing for it.

"Maybe not, but you had a choice in telling the truth. But that's not the only reason I don't trust you." My voice is quiet, resigned. "I can't trust you with this because you... you *are* my past." My breath exhales, the words tumbling from trembling lips.

Logan's head jerks back as if I'd slapped him. His lips open, eyes wide with shock and pain. "You still blame me." The whisper is rough and low. His wide shoulders slump in defeat. The punishing grip on my arms releases, and his hands drop as if weighted.

He takes several steps back. The distance is a deep chasm of torment between us. The pain and anguish displayed on that beautiful face hurts worse than anything I've ever experienced, and that's saying a lot. Nothing compares to this agony. It's too big for my body. I want to grab back the words, shove them down my throat like they were never uttered.

I can't. The damage is done. I see it the minute Logan's face shuts down, goes devoid of emotion. My throat convulses as I try to swallow back the bile rising. How do I salvage this? I can't lose him.

"Logan, I..."

"Do not." The coldness in that sexy voice causes goose bumps to spread along my skin. "I think you have said more than enough." He takes a menacing step toward me and my eyes widen. For the first time, fear streaks through me as he advances. He growls, grabs my wrist in a punishing grip, and spins me around.

The heat of him presses close at my back. Logan's anger invades my senses and I tremble. "All this time, I have been gentle, thinking that was what you needed. That you could not handle what I wanted to do because of your past." The growl of his voice in my ear makes me tingle all over. Logan's lust wars with his anger, his hurt. It rolls into me, wave after wave, and my center melts, wetting my panties.

Holy fuck. He's been holding back.

"No one touches you. This body belongs to me. Do you hear me?"

With a swallow, I respond with a nod. There's no way I could utter a coherent word if I tried. I've had years of buildup. Fantasy after fantasy of Logan as my sexual dominant. In my heart and mind, he's been the one since I was old enough to know what that meant. A dream I never expected to happen.

And to add fuel to the fire, Logan's blood calls to me. I'm starved for it. Crave it with desperation. Need cramps my stomach.

"Say you are mine, Nicole," Logan rumbles, and presses his erection into the crease of my ass over the leather of the skirt.

I bite back the words he wants to hear. They terrify me. These emotions terrify me. I want to tell him he is mine, but that fact didn't stop him from touching another female. This bond between us didn't keep him from lying to me. Instead, I allow the lust to override reasonable thought. I arch back and grind my ass harder into his cock.

"I will take that as a yes. But know this, my true nature is not tender, Nicole. I demand control." At his words, my insides tremble and clench. Georgie stretches. He continues in a gruff timbre. "But, always pleasure, yours and mine, as the goal. I will never give you more than you can handle. Will never physically hurt you beyond what you desire. I will know your limits because your mind will be open to me, and I will experience your pleasure as my own. That's what I need from you."

Oh, I'm so screwed.

"What do you mean, my mind will be open to you?" Apprehension seeps into my bones. The control Logan's demanding over my mind petrifies me. My body is one thing, but too much darkness lives there. It wouldn't bring us closer, just the opposite.

"You know exactly what I mean," he says in a low growl before spinning me around to face him. "We need to lay down ground rules before we begin."

Oh, hell. We're beginning?

"First, you need to feed." Logan nods toward a new cooler. I eye the fucker. Oh boy.

How will Logan react when he finds out I haven't been drinking his bagged blood again? By the look of him, not well. The glow in his eyes may have subsided, but they are cold, hard, emotionless, and that terrifies me more than his anger of moments ago.

Where is the vampire who claims to be my mate? The man who tried to protect and take care of me my whole life? When I peer into his face, none of those things are evident. The beautiful lips purse, his massive body is held erect and tense. A stranger stands before me. Granted, a full-blown dominant, but a stranger, nonetheless.

Okay. This situation calls for the big guns. One of my favorite new abilities. Mind control. It's worked on everyone else, why shouldn't it work on Logan? If I calm him down enough, maybe he won't go on a rampage when I reveal I haven't fed in a month.

"Logan," I whisper and push my vampire power into his mind. "You need to remain calm."

Silent for several long seconds, he stares deep into my eyes before finally answering. "I do?"

"Yes. You must remain calm, Logan. No matter what I say." I push harder, and when his shoulders relax, I try not to reveal my triumphant smile. Holy fuck, it's working.

"Yes. Calm," he responds.

"Okay. Good. So, I still can't drink your blood from the bag."

"Goddammit!" He erupts.

Shit. I so suck at this.

"Mind control does not work on mates. Just like mine didn't work on you, yours will not work on me. Nice try though." The snarl showcases the fangs I crave. "I will beat Scott to a bloody pulp. How can you be strong enough to face Dimitri if you are weak from starvation?"

"He..." Oh boy, it's about to get worse. "He doesn't know." I lift my chin and refuse to lower my gaze. "I take a bag out every day and flush it down the toilet. Jimmy thinks I've been drinking it."

Fury lights up his eyes. "Nicole..." Instead of finishing, he clamps down on his anger, and brings forth the controlled Dom of moments ago. "This is way overdue." With the lithe grace of a lion, Logan strolls over to the chair where I devoured that big beautiful cock for the first time, and eases into it with controlled elegance. He beckons me. "Come."

Helpless but to obey, my fangs descend with anticipation of Logan's spicy nectar. The cramps intensify, and every muscle vibrates with need. I approach him with eagerness, disregarding the strange light in his eyes as he watches me. When I reach him, I go to lift a leg to straddle him like before, but he shakes his head, and I lower it with a frown.

Strong fingers grab my wrist and pull down with a hard jerk. My stomach hits his rock-hard thighs and I lose my breath. My palms thud onto the carpet to keep from toppling over. One of his heavy legs comes up and across the back of mine, and I know in an instant what's about to happen. I don't know why, but I'm shocked by it.

And... turned on.

Logan lifts the hem of my leather skirt with agonizing slowness, revealing my bare ass. A low growl vibrates his body and mine. "Tell me you did not have sex with these strangers at the club, Nicole." Logan's demand is low, guttural, his body tense with fury.

"Never." His tension eases at my whispered vow.

"You disobeyed me. Kept things from me for the last time, Nicole. This is for starving yourself for no good reason. Keeping your needs from me. And defying me by training with Kurtis."

Oh, shit. Someone had a big mouth.

Before I can contemplate who the traitor might be, Logan's palm comes down on my ass cheek with a resounding smack. I jerk upright at the pain, but he slams my chest back down with his other hand, holding me in place. My insides quiver and my ass cheek burns. I can't help the moan that escapes as heat spreads straight to my core. He doesn't give me time to recover before he smacks the other side with such force, I grip the carpet to keep from crying out. Shit it hurts, but it hurts so damn good. This is exactly what I needed.

A sense of rightness and peace spreads with the heat as he continues to spank me, alternating cheeks. By the tenth strike of his palm, I'm moaning and grinding my hips into his thigh. I'm so close to exploding, my body trembles with need.

"Logan," I moan breathlessly.

"Hush." Fingers run through the juices at my opening and flowing down my thighs. Logan groans low, swirls them around my center, and I want to combust.

"Do not come until I tell you, Nicole."

The brusque order squeezes my insides to obey, but when the pad of his thumb rubs at my anus, sparks of electricity shoot straight to my core. I can't help the deep guttural moan. Strong fingers reach for my clit and start a slow, circular motion that has me pumping my hips in time with the thumb that is now moving with ease in and out of my ass.

Just as his other hand smacks my already burning bottom and his fingers pinch my clit, he commands. "Come, Nicole."

I explode, crying out as fireworks spark straight from my throbbing center, and shoot throughout my body in wave after wave of heat and pleasure. I've never experienced this intensity before, and I'm not sure if it's because of my newly heightened senses, but the pleasure rippling through me goes on and on. My whole body tingles with sensation, my nipples painful, hard points of ecstasy I rub against the side of the chair, seeking relief.

All I can do is go with it as my fingers grip the soft carpet. I push my ass harder against Logan's fingers, moaning and whimpering for more. He doesn't disappoint. Three more resounding smacks on my burning ass and the trembling eases.

In the next instant, Logan grips my waist, flips me over, and guides my quivering legs to straddle his hips

I stare into the eyes of the vampire I love *and* the Dom I desire.

"There are always consequences for disobeying me, Nicole."

If this is the consequence, hold on to your hat, buddy, because I will push your buttons every chance I get.

"Now, feed while I fuck you."

<h1 style="text-align:center">Chapter 35</h1>

Nicole

Undoing his belt and zipper, he pulls out his massive erection and guides me over it. I grip his shoulders for support and try to help, but my body is a mass of quivering goo. Logan handles me with ease, directs the head of his cock into my opening. His immense size stretches me to the point of pain. Damn he's big.

"Fuck, you are so tight," he moans deeply before ripping my leather top in half and clamping his lips onto a nipple. He sucks hard as he pushes deeper into my core.

I've never been so full, so complete. I want to ram myself onto the rest of his length, but his strong hands hold me steady. Inch by agonizing inch, he invades my heat as his mouth devours my nipple.

"You okay, baby?" he asks in a guttural tone like he's barely holding on to his control, his breathing as erratic as my own.

"More," I demand breathlessly.

"Christ," he moans as he slips more of himself into me. "Your tight warmth encasing me is better than anything I ever imagined."

When he's fully seated inside me, he pauses. Giving me the chance to get accustomed to his size. I peer into the green depths, wrap my arms around his neck, and bury my fingers in his hair.

I crave to touch his magnificent body, so I reach down and lift his shirt over his head. Immediately his muscular, tattooed arm wraps around my waist, holding me in place, while his other hand clutches my ass. My hands explore the absolute perfection of his pecs, the hard dips and ridges of his abdomen.

A soft caress of those strong fingers skitters dangerously close to my anus once again. Holy shit. An image of his finger in my ass, alongside the fullness of his cock, has my juices flowing around him. Then another vision flashes through my brain. In addition to all that, I envision those fangs sinking into my nipple, and my insides clench hard around him.

As if he can read my mind, his finger runs past my entrance, dipping into the juices oozing around his cock buried deep. A slow sensual slide back up and he begins to gently probe my opening. I can't help the moan that escapes my lips. I lay my head on his shoulder and start to move along his length.

The stretching of both my openings is almost too much, but I revel in it. Wanting more, I move my hips in earnest. Every downward thrust impales me on his hardness and slides his finger deeper. When I retreat along his length, to the very tip of his head, his finger slides out.

Fucking bliss.

Logan lets me set the pace, and at first, I move with slow, precise movements, but as the ecstasy builds, my hips grind on him faster and harder. I've never experienced anything like this. He surrounds me, inside and out. I grip the thick shoulders tighter and ride him harder and faster. Loving how his cock and finger move and stretch me.

"Feed, Nicole." The command is a low growl, his eyes an intense green glow. Yeah, he doesn't need to ask me twice. I strike his throat with sudden violence. My fangs sink deep just as he slams his cock balls deep. An orgasm claws through me with a suddenness that startles me as his blood gushes down my parched throat. The power in Logan's blood fills me, nourishes me. His cock pounding into me energizes me, and I come alive for the first time.

"Yes, baby. Drink," he groans. "You are mine."

Yes, I acknowledge silently, still afraid to say the words out loud. Technically he's not mine. By law he belongs to another woman.

I shove those thoughts away in my little mental box and concentrate on the intense pleasure of the here and now. Logan's cock stretching me, filling me, driving me toward another explosion. His blood replenishing me.

Withdrawing my fangs, I lean back to peer into the eyes of my Guardian, stopping the friction with new strength.

Logan's head lifts from the back of the chair, the heavy- lidded green gaze locks with mine. An eyebrow lifts in question, and his panting breath matches my own.

"I want to nourish you, Logan."

"As much as I would love that, Dimitri would smell you on me. I cannot risk it," he growls.

I grab hold of his face with both hands. "You've risked so much for your people," I whisper against his lips, once again moving my hips up and down, the slow, tight resistance incredible.

"No, Nicole." With a firm hold of my waist, Logan sets the pace. "For you, baby. Only for you," he whispers as he pounds into me with desperation.

I'm on the edge, waiting to jump into bubbling fire, but I can't topple over. The intense ache just keeps building and building within me, and I'm unable to let go. To release the pressure.

"Logan..." I whimper in frustration. He looks me square in the eyes and commands me to come. I finally explode, breaking into a million pieces. I throw my head back and scream out his name.

"Fuck, Nicole!" he shouts the second before his hot seed shoots deep within me. I grip his shoulders as he brings me to the brink once again, and sink my fangs deep into his throat, loving how he fills me so completely.

"I'M... I'M JUST NOT sure I can open my mind the way you're asking."

Dressed in regular street clothes, thoroughly satiated, we continue our talk. The power of Logan's blood courses through me, making me strong once more. The tingle and burn in my ass center me.

That was *the* most intensely satisfying sex I've ever had. My muscles feel like they do when I walk out of one of the clubs. Or I've just worked out for two hours straight. Jell-O.

I've just had a significant reboot. With Logan. I've never been so relaxed and at peace in my entire life as I am right now. This is my new drug. My new addiction. Sex with Logan.

Until he brought up the subject of opening my mind to him again.

What if this is a deal breaker for him, what will I do? Can I walk away from him, from us, because I am unwilling to trust the one man who means so much? The one who risked his whole life for me? Who just gave me what I craved and needed. If I open my mind... will he be able to handle the deepest, darkest parts of me? Parts even I'm too ashamed to examine?

"If you cannot trust me enough to even try, then this," he indicates by waving his hand back and forth between us, "can never be. I will always make sure you are protected, kept safe, and fed. I will fulfill my end of the prophecy, but beyond that..."

He doesn't need to finish. I understand exactly what he means, and inside I'm breaking. Tears well in my eyes and I look away.

What the hell?

I turn from him and stumble to my window on shaking legs. The dark shadows of tree limbs swaying in the breezing does nothing to soothe me.

How could we go from the best fucking sex in my life to the possibility of it ending in a matter of minutes? My hands clench into fists, and I dig nails into my palms, praying the pain centers me. It's an illusion. Nothing will center me except Logan.

What the hell are you doing, Nicole? Your fear and trust issues are screwing everything up.

"I've lived my whole life learning never to trust anyone, to guard my mind and secrets. Now you expect me to just open myself up because you said so? I need more time, Logan."

"You are the most stubborn woman I have ever met." His anger pushes at me. It tries to penetrate my skin. Amidst the anger is something more... pain. "I would like nothing more than to force you to submit to my will, but I will not do that. Not with you." His frustrated sigh brushes my neck. "You are my mate, Nicole. Since the day I discovered your existence, everything I have done was to keep you safe. I am unsure what else I can say or do to convince you to trust me, and frankly, I am tired of trying. Until you can open yourself, submit, and trust me, I will once again keep to the shadows."

No, wait! The plea echoes through my mind but is never uttered. I can't... I can't go back to my life like he never existed. If he leaves me, I won't survive. It galls me to admit that, but I can't ignore the trembles in my body at the truth. What if opening my mind pushes him away? I don't care. I have to try.

On a broken whisper, I concede. "Okay. I'll do it." I turn to tell him I will do whatever he asks, but he's gone.

"Logan!" The scream circles the empty room and I frantically search every dark corner, hoping beyond hope, he will be there.

"Oh, God, what have I done?" The tears spill readily from my eyes as I fall to my knees. "I'm sorry... I'm so sorry. Please come back."

Great, wailing sobs shake my body as I fall over on my side, burying my face in the carpet. My arms grip my stomach as I let go for the first time in my life. Crying for all the years I never dared, for fear I would never stop. I've lost the one thing that means more to me than my own life.

Logan.

I am breaking.

Chapter 36

"**M**y Guardians," the king bellows, cleaving through the chatter around the table as effectively as a hot knife through butter. He waits until all eyes turn before continuing. "I have wonderful news."

I spare a glance at Bastian across the table but keep my worries to myself. Over the past few months, my brother and I squelched every possible inquiry or lead into Nicole's whereabouts, even planting false intelligence, sending Dimitri's spies on wild goose chases across the globe.

Our plans are complete. There is just one last detail to hash out, an aspect that forced us to an impasse. Years of planning and strategy relies on using Nicole as bait.

Not fucking happening.

Their solution is to allow Dimitri to locate her. Or for her to call him out to a meeting place of our choosing: the clearing on Nicole's property. Our army will remain in waiting, ready to attack, since Dimitri would never be so foolish as to show up alone.

King Scott confirmed Nicole is ready, and at maximum strength. Her abilities are under control, which makes her the one powerful enough to take on Dimitri.

There are so many loopholes in that plan that it is ludicrous. The most meaningful one—using Nicole as bait. I loathe it. I appreciate it is the prophecy, but it goes against every vampire instinct within to protect my mate.

Sebastian and Lucretia report back on a regular basis regarding Nicole's training. And I dutifully go back once a week to offer my wrist. It takes everything to suppress my base urges when she drinks from me. I want to force her over the bed and thrash into her so hard, spank some sense into her. Why can she not trust me?

When I allow myself to reflect on that night months ago, I recognize I had to take off. Not just because Nicole cannot let go of the past and trust me, but more for her sake than mine. I had already risked so much by being with her. It had been selfish, but I had been unable to resist.

Even now, the desire to stare into those luminescent gray eyes, to caress the silky-smooth skin, or hell, just breathe in her essence, is driving me mad. There is a war being waged inside my body, and it is ripping me to shreds. A male could be torn in half by the relentless need.

Part of me is furious, and hurt, from her lack of faith. I am enraged at her for pursuing other males to soothe the pain of her past; scared that they offered her more than just pain for release. I am frustrated as hell with the hurdles between us.

The other part is obsessed with the demand to take that luscious body and defend what is mine with every ounce of my strength. Which is why staying away has been essential, only going back to nourish her, make certain she is strong, and support what is mine.

All the desires kept banked the last few months roar over me in full, raging force, hounded by the images of her glistening pussy, and ass reddened by my palm. The remembered sounds of her moans and screams as she climaxed. Her tight hole clenching my thumb then finger as she came. That tight, wet sheath as it contracted around my cock.

Fuck.

To be the one to give Nicole what she needs, and desires is my ultimate fantasy. Hell, I am a Dom. That is my nature. To unleash my inner self with Nicole, to learn it is also what she covets, is too unbelievable to assimilate.

My mind drifts to my playroom and all the varied stations throughout, envisioning her in every one of them. Or naked, secured to my bed as I take her to heights of ecstasy with my hands, tongue, cock, and toys. Nothing would grant me greater pleasure than for her to submit. Both in the bedroom and out of it, but I would be content with just the bedroom. For now.

"All our endeavors finally paid off," Dimitri states with exuberance, clapping his hands together like a child who has been allowed a lollipop. I shove the erotic images away and concentrate on what Dimitri is saying. "Soon, the fruit from my loin will be here, gracing us all with her beauty and many talents."

What the fuck?

How can that be? My inner beast rages. It claws to defend what is mine. Protect my mate. Dizziness fogs my brain. It has been weeks since I fed. I was so concerned with making sure Nicole was nourished and strong, I overlooked my own sustenance.

'Brother, if this is true, we have no alternative.' Sebastian whispers into my mind.

I cannot answer. My mind is swirling with so many emotions, and I am weak from lack of blood. We have time to warn her, I remind myself. Dimitri is as impotent as any of us until sundown. If he aims to abduct her during the day, using humans, I hold every confidence in my mate's ability to defend herself.

"Logan." Dimitri turns the full force of his dark glower upon me. It takes everything to keep from revealing my hatred.

"Yes, my lord?"

"You, Sebastian, and Lucretia will accompany me at dusk to fetch my rebellious daughter."

Shock widens my eyes. "You go yourself, my king?" He is falling right into the plan without even realizing it.

"Yeeeessss," he hisses with pleasure. "Nicole sought me out, calling for a meet-and-greet with her papa." The evil grin makes my insides burn. "My sources assure me she has not completed the transition yet, so this should be a walk in the park. She will be mine in a matter of hours. With much to plan and discuss before dusk, I am afraid there will be no sleep for you."

'*Well, damn*,' Sebastian swears in my mind.

Goddamn her. Nicole escalated the timeline and set events in motion against my wishes. When I get her alone, granting we both survive this, I will tan her backside beet red.

'*Make sure everyone is ready, Bastian. Nicole established the time-frame whether we like it or not.*'

Dimitri points at Lu and motions her to his side. What is he up to?

"You have not been feeding your husband properly, my dear." Slowly he runs his long fingers down the side of Lu's breast. Her jaw clenches in reaction, but she does not move. "Straddle him and present your neck. I require my best warrior nourished and strong for what is about to come."

What does that mean? With an inward growl, I offer Lu my hand, and scoot my chair back to allow her room. She hesitates for a moment before swinging her long leather-clad leg over my hips. Once settled she displays a tight smile, but it is the fire in her amber eyes that reinforces my resolve to do whatever is necessary to crush our king.

Dimitri pulls her braid away from her neck, wrapping it around his fist. "I find that I am parched as well, Logan. Shall we partake together? Like old times?" The blackness of his insanity leaches out, engulfs the whites of his eyes. The king is on the brink of a full-on rage.

Expecting my objection?

"By all means, my lord." The lifted brow is the sole indication I have surprised him. He yanks Lu's head back with a snap of his wrist and strikes her neck with a viciousness that causes her to cry out.

I grit my teeth against her pain and vow vengeance as I ease closer. Mindful not to rip Dimitri's fangs from her throat, I slip mine into the other side of her neck. Lu's potent blood surges through my body. The thick richness restores my strength and grants me the much-needed surge of power I will require for the coming war.

Her blood is heavy with vampire strength, but it is not Nicole's. Nicole's blood is like a full-bodied wine. Lush, and as exotic as the woman herself. It satisfies the thirst like no other.

It dawns on me; I have not fed from Nicole since she became a vampire. And not just any vampire, a queen, with all of Dimitri's tremendous power. No doubt her blood is potent. Addictive.

I am unsure who the king's source is, but thank God he is misinformed. It is not Nicole who will receive a great surprise, but Dimitri himself.

I withdraw my fangs, not bothering to close the wounds. They mend in a matter of seconds.

When I lean back, I notice Dimitri's blackened nails are slicing into the nipple of Lu's breast, through the tank top. Blood darkens the gray fabric as the sharpened points pierce the skin. My fists clench around the arms of the chair to keep from flinging him away. Her amber eyes stare into mine and I read her need for justice loud and clear.

I shift my focus to the king, and revulsion curls my lip at the erection straining the zipper of his designer jeans. His hips buck against the hand Lu clamped around the back of the chair.

And just as swiftly as he struck, he rips his fangs from her throat, seizes my hand in a brutal grip, and slaps it over his erection. With his head thrown back he bellows his climax while rubbing against my palm.

A red haze of madness obscures my vision at being forced to bring him to climax, but it is the name he bellows to the rafters while he ejaculates that is my undoing.

Nicole.

Chapter 37

Nicole

Despite my best efforts, my life developed a routine. Eat, train, sing, drink, pass out. Usually in that order. The eating is due to Alex. She tries to cram food down my throat at every given opportunity, and demands I give up my Ding Dong obsession. I about took her head off one day when she tried to take my fourth cup of coffee.

"Don't ever touch my coffee," I barked at her.

"Too much caffeine and no food are not good for you."

Wow. She's braver than I thought.

"You know what? I don't give a dead moose's last shit." That snapped her mouth shut.

My precious Ding Dongs are the only food that hold my interest. The constant hunger in my belly is for Logan's blood.

Kurtis drags my ass out of the house kicking and screaming to train practically every day. On my dirt drive, the clearing in the woods, or even on the beach. But krav maga lost its appeal.

The only reason singing survives this numbness is because either Jimmy or Liam abduct me from the cocoon of my house and force me on stage. They're hoping it will snap me out of this temporary funk that's taken over my mind and body.

One day, unexpectedly, Jimmy grabs me by the shoulders, compels me with those warm, comforting eyes, and offers his fatherly advice in a gruff voice.

"Kid, if there is one thing I've learned in my four hundred years, it's this. To get over the past, first you must accept the past is over. No matter how many times you revisit it, analyze it, or regret it, it's over. It can't hurt you anymore. You are one of the most powerful immortals in existence now. It will not be Dimitri who hurts you. It will be your stubborn ass pride and mistrust that will be your downfall." His dark eyes soften. "To find true happiness, you have to take a risk."

If only it were that easy.

Every week, right on time, Logan materializes to *feed* me. I want to bawl and wail at the indifferent expression in his beautiful green eyes. But I don't. As Jimmy said, my stubbornness won't allow it.

If he'd just given me a moment more that night, he would have witnessed my submission to his request. But no, he was hurt and angry and didn't give me the chance to overcome a lifetime of resistance. That alone angers me more than anything.

He's had six hundred years to come to terms with what he wants and needs. All I'd required was just a few goddamn minutes.

It's comical really, and if I had any humor left, I'd laugh. We stand in the middle of my living room with Alex and Jimmy as chaperones as I politely pierce the flesh of his offered wrist. Inside, my heart is breaking, but I'm too damn stupid to make the first move to salvage things. I'm not even sure where to start.

The alcohol consumption is voluntary. It's the one thing I want. I'm not talking about a cute little glass of wine with dinner either. Nope. Go big or go home is what I always say. Well, it's what I say now, while drinking myself into oblivion. Which unfortunately takes vast quantities of alcohol now that I'm immortal.

"What's your damn plan, Nicki?" Liam asks one night at the bar. Reluctantly, he's been serving me whiskey after whiskey with the threat of beheading if he stops.

"I plan on sitting here and drinking until I come up with a better plan."

And the next day, the cycle starts all over again.

My friends are worried about me, but I can't muster the oomph to care. 'Cause hey, I don't think anymore. I'm just a zombie going through life at the insistence of others.

Thank God I've gotten beyond the point of crying every five minutes. I view that as a success. My heart is numb, all dried up. Nothing left to give. Even Georgie went dormant. If I could burn to a crisp at the kiss of the sun, she wouldn't even object if I walked into its blazing heat at full noon. Because no matter how I look at it, that's what he does. Logan ruins me. For other men. For a life without him. I hate him, fear him, desire him, need him, and love him.

I fell for Logan the moment he slipped into my dreams. It's taken me a long time to recognize that. Too long. Being with him in the flesh is like breathing in so fast you become lightheaded. All he wanted was for me to be who I am. Desired all I had to give and more. And I couldn't give it to him. Even after he pulled me from a place within myself where I'd been dying. Without him, I'm right back there again.

Three agonizing months have passed. This needs to be over. Dimitri needs to suffer for what he did to me, and I'm tired of waiting. On a rash impulse, I contacted Liam.

"Hey, Bro. I need a favor."

"If it's more alcohol, forget it. I'm done being your pimp for whiskey."

"Not sure pimp is the right word. Although in this case I could see your point. I do lust after the dark creamy yumminess. But that's not why I called."

I secretly recruited Liam to help get a message to my father. It wasn't easy either. He went through several channels before he was able to contact King Grayflame, the dark fae king, directly. Who in turn, got my message to Dimitri.

When Jimmy and Logan find out, they'll be livid. Good. Besides, I'm ready. More than ready. I've mastered all the abilities. I trace to Canada and back in the blink of an eye. I control the minds of everyone in the bar with complete success, commanding them to do my bidding. Which kinda freaks me out.

I'm a virtual flamethrower too, able to conjure and direct fire with a command from my mind with pinpoint accuracy. I can even affect the weather to a certain degree. Just rain, thunder or lightning in small areas.

It makes me question if the fierce storms every time Dimitri visited were his doing. If I possess the ability, he sure as shit does. Just one more layer he added to scare a child.

While fighting with Kurtis, I've lifted the entire group of firefighters in the air and held them with little effort, much to the macho men's chagrin. These powers are so beyond black belt, Kurtis gave up on training me last week because I kick his ass every time.

Liam, my secret double spy, convinced King Grayflame that when he takes over as pack leader, the werewolves would back Dimitri. Hinted that my transition was not complete but warned him time was running out and if King Giordano wanted to strike, he should do so now. Gave instructions on the where and when. The vast clearing I've been training in for months. It gives Dimitri my location, but at this point, what does it matter? It's perfect. Wide open with no places for Dimitri or his allies to hide. It's set for tomorrow night.

I've no doubt, Dimitri won't come alone, but I hold complete faith in my friends. Even with the short notice I'm forcing on them.

It should be fine. What could go wrong?

Standing in the middle of my closet in bra and underwear, I scan my clothes with dispassion. What does one wear to wage battle against their own father? Something loose and comfortable that will give me ease of movement but with pockets to hide my various weapons? Or something grand and queenly?

I settle on black tactical pants, a dark, purple long-sleeved shirt, and my ever-present boots: black shitkickers that will give more oomph to my kicks and provide a perfect place to stash my silver daggers.

As I'm sliding Annie, loaded with iron bullets—the sure-fire way to kill a fae I'm told—into the holster at my back, Jimmy strides right into the closet. I eye him with indifference, not caring that his fear and agitation swirl around him like water draining in the bathtub.

"Kid, have you lost your damn mind?" Jimmy runs a shaking hand through his short-cropped hair. "The shit is about to hit the fan, and you need to get the hell out of here."

"No."

"He's found you, Nicki," he breathes with a huge sigh. "I'm instructed to get you out of town, ASAP. So, grab a bag and let's go."

Jimmy's voice takes on a drill sergeant authority, and I want to snap to attention and salute him. This is Logan's doing. Still trying to protect me. But the cards, and fate, are stacked against him.

Once I'm locked and loaded with extra magazines in my pockets, I stare into Jimmy's worried eyes.

"Who do you think orchestrated this, Jimmy? I want this to end. I want him out of my life."

"Ah hell, kid," Jimmy sighs. "What did you do?"

"Only set in motion what's been in the works for years, Jimmy." The first sparks of anger ignite in my gut. "You know I am more than ready to face Dimitri. To do what needs to be done."

"Nicki." Striding over, he places his palms on my stiff shoulders with a gentleness I don't want. "This will be your greatest challenge. You may enjoy the same powers as him, but Dimitri's had centuries to perfect and hone them." He pauses, his dark chocolate regard intensifying. "Your father will show tonight with a full regiment of fae and vampire to take you. He will not go down without a fight."

I stare into Jimmy's familiar, warm contemplation for a full minute, and let his words sink into my brain. The end has finally come.

With a feral smile, I respond. "Yes. I'm counting on it."

Jimmy's eyes widen with surprise. Was he expecting me to scream and pull my hair out with fear? I'm not afraid anymore. When Dimitri comes for me, let him surround himself with whomever he needs. It will not be enough.

For the first time in months, I'm alive with purpose. Because where the king goes, Logan is sure to follow. The mere notion of seeing him again makes my insides quiver with butterflies, desperate to gaze into his beautiful face, be in his commanding presence one more time, before I either fulfill my destiny or perish. I want the opportunity to tell him how much I love him. That I'm sorry for letting my pride and stubbornness get in the way of our happiness.

"I'm going to the clearing, Jimmy. With or without you."

At my words Jimmy's wolf growls low. "With. I'll always have your back, kid."

The vow vibrates through my heart.

Chapter 38

Nicole

Three hours we've sat in the field waiting. Dimitri and company are still a no-show. The good news, it's given my allies time to get their troops assembled. My scrutiny swings to my friends on either side of me. Jimmy, Liam, Kurtis, and Alex's presence bolsters my courage. They intensely scan the clearing and forest beyond; remaining vigilant, just as I've done for the last three hours.

Behind me is King Cipher Ruse, Kurtis's powerful and gorgeous-as-hell father. Queen Arra Svaldana, Alex's small but impressive mother, stands next to him. The extraordinary energy these two give off sinks deep into my back, fortifying my strength.

I shake my head, and peek at Kurtis. It still boggles my mind he's a shapeshifter.

Each ruler brought a few friends. A small contingent of shapeshifters and valkyrie hide among the trees, waiting. In the limited time I gave him, Jimmy gathered his entire Northwest territory, wrangling over fifty werewolves from numerous packs. They stand at the ready near the edge of the clearing at my six. All prepared to fight to the death.

Compared to a human army, our numbers are paltry, but with their power and strength, one Other equals ten humans, easy.

It's a potent thing to carry the fate of so many in your hands. My actions tonight could lead to the death of dozens. With the fulfillment of my own powers, the immense abilities Dimitri shares, many will perish. Husbands, fathers, mothers, and wives. The burden weighs heavy on my shoulders.

Then it happens. Every part of my body reacts to his presence, lighting it on fire. My eyes close as I savor it, maybe for the last time.

Logan.

"Why are you still here?" His angry growl races over my skin, and a firm hand grips my arm in a punishing hold. "Just once, I would love it if you did what you were fucking told to do."

Logan's anger seeps into my bones and my head lifts to those brilliant green eyes. Damn, he's a sight. Eyes glowing like emerald fire in his anger, fangs hanging low. Immense swords are fastened to his bare back, the straps crossing over his muscled chest, glistening in the moonlight. The beautiful black tattoo gives him a sinister, exotic appeal. His lean hips and muscular legs are covered in supple black leather. Every single part of me wants nothing more than to melt into him and lick every delectable inch. Remove those leather pants, free his impressive cock, and have it sink deep into me. I need the sharp bite of his fangs sinking into my flesh, to have him claim me.

"Hello, Logan." The low huskiness of my voice reveals my passion. "Are you here to join the party?"

His nostrils flare as he scents my desire, but it does nothing to diminish his anger. "Yes." The low growl liquifies my insides and when he steps closer, the solid body brushes mine, and I swallow back a moan.

'When this is over, I will spank that pretty ass of yours until it is bright red.'

The angry promise growled in my mind does nothing to alleviate the instant pulsing between my thighs at the sight of him.

"Promise?" The breathy taunt causes Logan's eyes to darken with hunger, but instead of a direct response, he announces to the group.

"I have brought a plus-one. Hundred."

In the blink of an eye, the dynamic presence of a hundred vampires fills the clearing. All dressed like Logan. Their beauty and power are a spectacular element to behold.

My people. In awe and reverence, the concept floats through my head. These compelling and potent beings are my clan. They fight tonight because they believe in me. No. Not me. In a prophesied promise. One they expect me to deliver.

No pressure.

With the arrival of the Guardians, my friends crowd in closer. The anxious stares of the Other species eye the mighty warriors with unease. They fidget or clutch their weapons tighter. With so many vampires assembled in one place, an uneasy tension emanates around the field. These are the fierce vampire warriors of legend. The hushed fables parents tell their children to keep them in line. Their viciousness and renowned skills on the battlefield are illustrious. And the most feared one of them all is mine. Logan.

An immediate peace invades my system. This is what I was born for. To lead this battle. To assume command of the vampire race and spearhead these factions into peace. I close my eyes, draw a deep breath, and allow their extraordinary powers to sweep through me, to strengthen me even further.

In turn, I project an outward sense of calm and tranquility into the imposing army surrounding me. Logan inhales at the display of influence, even as I sense it easing the tension and anger in his body.

I open my eyes and the gray bloom reflects from Logan's pupils. "Thank you for all you've achieved in preparing for this moment, Logan, but now it's my turn." At his nod, I inquire, "How much time before Darth Vader shows?"

"A few minutes."

"That will do," I whisper. "Mind if I borrow your sword?" At Logan's nod, I slide one from the harness at his back with my mind and place the hilt in my palm with little effort. At Logan's raised eyebrow and proud grin, I throw him a saucy wink before slipping past the heat of his body and tracing into the center of the clearing.

The vast army of various species moves in, surrounding me on all sides without so much as a rustle of sound. I expected to be nervous or anxious speaking in front of all these powerful beings, but I'm not. There's a certainty in my mission; a simple understanding of my purpose settled deep in my soul the minute I stepped on the field tonight. Georgie came alive once again, and I'm ready to stand and fight for them. For Logan. For my friends, and for myself. My whole existence has been evolving to this juncture in time, whether I was aware of it or not. I won't let them down. I refuse to fail.

Standing tall and proud atop a tree stump in the midst of the field, I rotate and encompass them all in my glowing regard. So many species of every shape and size stand before me, ready to attack. The force of their hope seeps deep into my bones.

"Tonight, is a turning point for all factions, all species, and humankind." With a proud, strong voice full of conviction, I begin my battle speech. "You have been manipulated for centuries by a tyrant, King Dimitri Tobias Giordano. My father. Behind your backs, he instigated, financed, and planned out your many wars. Created chaos by undermining our one and only governing body, hoping to divide us, diminish our ranks, and cripple our resistance. Tonight, it ends. Tonight, we put aside our differences, our strife, and band together in this place to stop the oppression of one vampire and his followers. This is not just a field of a few acres of ground, but a cause we are defending. A place where we will destroy our common enemy in battle."

Shouts of agreement fill the space. Many are nodding their heads or stomping their feet. I pour out more of my power into them, but this time it's saturated with aggression.

"I stand before you, humbled by your presence, saddened it has come to this, but resolved to finish it. My father is an ancient, powerful vampire, and even though I have acquired his extraordinary abilities, my strength comes from you, in the trust and faith you place at my feet.

The purpose of my life is to defeat King Giordano. It is my destiny. Mine and mine alone. Your destiny is defeating his allies. No one is to kill the king. He must be captured, and only by me." I give them a moment to let that sink in. "Let us go forward in this battle, fortified in our convictions that we fight for our freedoms. For peace. Now is the time to act." I raise Logan's large, silver sword high above my head and shout. "Now is the time for victory!"

A deafening roar fills the air as hundreds of warriors throw their heads back in a fierce battle cry and lift their weapons to the sky.

They are ready.

Chapter 39

The weight of hundreds of eyes follow my every move as I step off the stump and walk to the cluster of individuals I trust with my life, hoping I don't stumble and fall flat on my face. Yes, I could have traced, but I needed them to understand my alliance is with them all, not just the vampires.

I hand Logan his sword, our fingers brush and electricity shoots up my arm. I stare into eyes as vivid and lush as the rain forest. This is the man I love above all else. The pride and adoration radiating from the green depths eases the burden crushing my shoulders. With this vampire by my side, I can accomplish anything.

So many things need to be said and apologized for. Like allowing my stubborn ass pride and fear to come between us, and for not trusting him with my heart sooner. The desire to say the words Logan's been waiting to hear burns in my throat. This extraordinary vampire is my mate. Mine. Just as I am his.

'You are already a fierce leader and queen, my love.' The sexy baritone rumbles through my head.

'Logan, I—' The words cut off as my eyes widen in astonishment when a stunningly beautiful woman materializes at Logan's left. Her long black hair cascades in loose, glossy curls to her midriff. She boasts flawless skin, lush red lips, and exotic amber eyes. For a woman she's tall, with a slim, athletic body.

Rage ignites in my gut and my heart pounds in my chest. This is none other than Lucretia. Logan's wife. Figures she'd look like a damn movie star. As the green demon of jealousy fills my vision, my eyes heat and brighten with hostility.

A pleasant image of drawing Annie and emptying the clip into her head bursts through my mind. Her amber stare flicks to mine in apprehension. I curl my lip, brandish a fang, and eye her up and down with disdain before dismissing her altogether. First order of business as queen—dissolve their stupid marriage.

"Fuck me."

At Kurtis's whispered curse, Logan and I turn in his direction, searching for a threat, but he's only gawking at Lu. Blue eyes wide, mouth hanging open, and nostrils flaring as if breathing her in.

Does Kurtis know this vampire? When I glance to Logan in question, he shrugs and shakes his head, perplexed as well. Lu gives Kurtis a stunned glance before dragging her focus back to the clearing.

With a slight push, I probe Kurtis's mind as he continues to gape at Lu. Shock and confusion bounce around in there, but also an underlying combination of anger and... lust? Oh, hell no. Fury boils in my abdomen. First Logan, now Kurtis? God, I despise that bitch.

'Get your fucking head in the game, Kurtis.' The mental shout causes him to jerk in surprise and he rotates his gaze to mine. Dazed eyes blink several times as he attempts to recover from whatever the hell just transpired. Guilt flows from him, his eyes lower, and he offers a brief nod.

Of course, the last to arrive? Sebastian. He materializes on Logan's other side. Is it taboo to ogle Logan's brother? Those sky- blue eyes flash to mine with humor, and a sexy grin lifts full lips.

'For once your timing is impeccable, Sebastian.'

The baby blues widen in amazement with the mental push into his brain. "Yes, my lady." With a smirk Sebastian bows, but his regard settles on Alex with a frown before drawing his sword and standing at the ready.

"Who has the shackles, Bastian?" I ask in confusion. They are an integral part of this plan. Without them we are S.O.L.

"Icarus. He said he would arrive at the precise moment of need. Whatever the hell that means." Bastian rolls his eyes.

Figures. The little blue priest is so weird.

Since it's crunch time, I stride over to Kurtis's father and Alex's mother. "King Ruse, Queen Svaldana, thank you both for your support, not just for tonight, but for the role you played in protecting me throughout my life."

King Ruse steps forward into my space and I swallow at the magic power leashed beneath the surface of those fabulous muscles. Cipher Ruse is one sexy beast. His dark, sinful good looks are the stuff of historical romance novels involving pirates. More appropriately, if anyone ever produces a movie about the devil, they should cast Ruse as Lucifer.

One glance from those sexy blue eyes and he could make you do or say anything he desired. And his body? Sweet baby Jesus. He's what Alex calls 'sex on a stick.' With only a pair of cargo shorts—I'm assuming for easier shifting abilities—the impressive bulging muscles on his upper body are on full display. Yikes. Can you say eight pack?

"There are many reasons we are here tonight, Queen Giordano," Ruse says in a deep timbre.

Good God, he just called me queen. I get it's my destiny and the reason all these beings are gathered in this place tonight, to support me, but just hearing someone speak the title out loud, startles me. I can't think about the big picture. It will blow my mind. So, I do what I do and tuck it in the little box in my mind to delve into at a later date.

"And even though Arra and I have not been as intimately involved in your life as Scott, Logan, and our children, we trust their judgment. They have faith in you, therefore we do as well."

I shift my scrutiny away from the masculine beauty of Cipher to Arra, and she nods in agreement. The blonde queen is so petite, but poised and beautiful. I perceive Alex in the shape of her mouth and nose. How can something so tiny contain such power?

"We all want peace for our people," Ruse continues and my focus turns back to the enthralling beauty of his blue eyes. "Kurtis, Alexandria, Liam, and you, my young Queen, are the future leaders of the Council of Unity. We have survived for centuries, waiting for this day. The tremendous power surging within you is staggering. A power rivaling your father's. Only you can defeat him, my lady, and for that alone, we would follow you to the ends of the earth."

Wow. Just wow. The words ring true. I am humbled by the faith and conviction he deposits in me, that all of them placed in me. Glancing over to Queen Arra, I see her smile warmly, agreeing with Cipher. A special harmony and trust surges between these two, one extending back more years than I can contemplate. My gaze bounces between them, and I perceive the secret love they possess for one another. What would it be like to experience a love like that, one which spanned centuries? Survived through the required mating with their own species because their love is against the law.

It took weeks to read through all the scrolls the weird little Oracle brought me. And according to council law, it's forbidden for members of different species to mate.

Geez, I thought Logan and I had huge obstacles to conquer. These two win the contest, hands down. There is a story there, and one day I would love to hear it, but now's not the time.

"Thank you both. There is no doubt I will need your council and wisdom down the road." Shit, I even sound like a queen.

With a brief nod at the couple, my regard travels beyond them to the many vampires, werewolves, shifters, and valkyrie lined up in a remarkable display of solidarity. Although they shift about— uneasy having to remain so close to species they don't usually encounter, unless in a battle or skirmish—they hold firm.

For a brief minute, my senses open to their magic and strength. It pours into me, and I soak it up. With a sharp inhale, my eyes warm as power surges through my veins.

"Remarkable," Arra whispers in admiration. "You draw strength from us."

"Yes. Every individual here contributes to this conflict. As a whole, their power strengthens me. That will be my father's downfall. Our combined power and resilience."

At Arra's small, wicked grin, I wink and turn to face the clearing once again. Logan and Sebastian move with me, flanking me on either side. Jimmy and Kurtis step in behind, boxing me in.

I peek over at Alex, standing next to Kurtis, and she blows me a kiss. She bounces on the balls of her feet in readiness, her silver swords loose in both hands. When Sebastian plants himself right in front of her, I grin when she scowls at his back.

Why does Sebastian always want to shield her? Interesting.

A familiar black presence from my past creeps along my skin. It seeps hard into my bones, and my smile evaporates. Raw, malevolent power permeates the vast space, and draws the oxygen from my lungs.

The imposing, evil entity emerges from the shadows a football field length straight in front of me. His piercing blue leer pins mine in an instant. I freeze and stare into the eyes of my worst nightmare.

The beast I call Father.

Chapter 40

My gut twists as over one hundred vampire warriors materialize behind my father, all dressed in their battle uniforms of black leather pants, black t-shirts, combat boots, and long leather dusters.

Well, this makes it obvious. My vampires are the skins, and Dimitri's are the shirts. Thank God. I would hate to slaughter one of Logan's just because I had no indication which team he was on.

On one side of Dimitri is the most beautiful, exotic looking woman I've ever encountered. Her waist-length, shimmering red hair is the same hue as her full, pouty lips. Light blue eyes are outlined with thick, black liner and lengthy black lashes make the blueness of her eyes even more startling.

Her narrow waist is cinched tight in a black leather corset with glistening silver daggers strapped to the front. Charcoal- colored lace hugs a shiny silver bra, displaying her generous breasts, stretching to an off-the-shoulder style that falls down her arms to just past her wrists. Curvy hips flare, then taper to long legs wrapped in black leather. Thigh high black boots finish out the erotic, porn- like outfit.

'*Who the hell is the woman?*' I ask Logan.

'*Jilaya Oresha, Queen of the Succubi.*'

Ah yes. I've read about Queen Oresha. Her beauty and sex appeal are her most potent weapons. And I understand why. She is alluring, even to me. Jimmy informed me that while she's highly skilled with short daggers, having sex with her could literally kill you.

'*And the... being next to him?*'

I say being because this guy could never pass as a normal human. He stands over six and a half feet tall with a slim muscular build decked out in full metal armor from medieval times. A massive broadsword strapped to his side completes the outfit.

He's strange and beautiful, with alabaster skin, broad pale lips, and a straight, thin nose that comes to a delicate point. Those are the only features about him that are remotely human.

Below the dark eyebrows, silver eyes glitter like diamonds. Thick, flowing snow-white hair with silver highlights twinkle in the moonlight. Large pointy ears peek through the white strands, and a braided silver crown adorns his head. The delicate crown falls to a sharp point mid-forehead. This creature is an imposing figure for sure, but what sets him apart, and leaves me staring in awe, are the blinding white wings unfurled behind him. They extend out six feet in both directions.

'Syn Grayflame, the Dark Fae King. He can put half of the werewolves and valkyrie to sleep in a matter of minutes and possesses telekinetic abilities. Those wings are not just for show. He can fly. All the fae fly, so check the sky during the battle.' Logan responds. *'Syn will be Cipher's initial target. Once he is taken out, the rest of his people could withdraw. The fifty fae flying in are here because they fear their king, and he gave them no alternative.'*

'Good to know.' It's an effort not to display shock as the substantial group of dark fae come in for a landing behind their fierce leader. It's almost too much. *"Ya know, if you'd told me a year ago winged men existed, or I'd be fighting them in open combat, I would have said you were fucking cray cray."*

Logan doesn't even crack a smile.

I shift my focus back to my father. Nothing about him has changed in nine years. Tall and slender, he's dressed like he's going to a nightclub instead of engaging in battle. Dark designer jeans, a blue striped, button-down with the sleeves rolled up, and black Doc Martens grace his feet.

Guess you don't need to bother with weapons and combat when you're an eleven hundred-year-old vampire. Instead of the usual braid down his back, the long, dark blonde hair flows about his face and shoulders.

A shiver of revulsion runs through me as my father's black- hearted gaze works to devour every inch of me. A barely discernible blonde mustache tops a thin upper lip and full bottom with a short blonde scruff covering his chin. They curve with feral intent and display two huge, savage-looking fangs.

They are monstrous. Why don't I ever remember Dimitri having fangs? I recall the blackened, sharp-as-hell nails in vivid detail, and all the pain they'd inflicted, but not the fangs.

On the outside, Dimitri is handsome. Masculine. But it's the evil eating away at his insides like a cancer that makes him ugly.

"At last, the prodigal daughter has been found." Dimitri's snarl is heavy with sarcasm. "And I was misinformed," he says with an angry growl. "You *have* completed your transition. That changes things, does it not?"

'*Time for our game to begin, sweetheart,*' his voice hisses through my mind. My jaw clenches to keep from hurling the bile in my stomach. An inky blackness swirls in the whites of his eyes. '*I waited for you for so long. It is time to play our game, my pet.*'

'*Never, you sick fuck.*' My teeth clench harder and I struggle to eliminate the images from my past. Images of his sick little games.

"I so missed you, my child. What a delectable female you have become." Dimitri's voice is all sweet and fatherly for the crowd.

Logan's eyes close and a muscle pulses in his jaw. The rage at Dimitri, his loathing and hatred for my father flows from him, unchecked. No longer does he need to suppress his emotions, play the double spy. Logan would love nothing better than to rip Dimitri limb from limb. As powerful as my mate is, he's no match for my father alone.

But I am.

"And look what we have here." The maddened glower shifts to Logan. He points a long finger in his direction, contempt showcased in the soulless eyes. "Surprise, surprise. My most trusted warrior betrayed me."

By the sarcasm, I take it he's not surprised.

Adrenaline and fear tingle along my scalp when Dimitri throws his head back and laughs. I must say, I've watched my fair share of scary movies, but the sound emanating from the depths of his throat sounds like the devil himself. It's evil personified, and a shiver runs down my spine.

"Alaric Logan Moretti, did you honestly believe I had no clue my daughter was your one true mate?" Dimitri ignores the collective gasp of the surrounding army. Most of them have no idea I am Logan's. "Or that you committed treason by conspiring behind my back with your little trusted band of allies to keep her away from me?" The growl in his voice expresses his building rage. "And what a piss-poor job you did of safeguarding what is yours, Logan. I have forgotten how many times I slipped past your guard detail and entertained myself with your mate."

A deep, all-vampire growl builds from Logan's chest. It fills the clearing. Tension arises from behind me at the sound, and the ranks shuffle with nervous anticipation. His head lowers, brilliant green flares to life in his eyes, and his shoulders hunch. The muscles in his arms bulge and his jaw clenches tight. Logan vibrates with the need to kill Dimitri, but it wrestles with the need to protect me.

Logan's reaction is expected. Lucretia's is not. Behind that cool mask of indifference, shock and guilt consumes her at Dimitri's comments. Why? Now what did that bitch do?

'*Easy, Logan. Do not let him bait you.*' Sebastian warns in Logan's mind.

'*He's right,*' I pipe in, provoking a raised eyebrow from Logan at my abilities once again. Hmmm. Is the ability to hear others' telepathic conversations not typical?

If I can do it, then so can my father.

Realization hits us both at the same time. It's how Dimitri gathered what was going on. How he found me as a youngster. He'd been listening in on Logan and Sebastian's internal dialog.

'*How did I not know he had that ability?*' Logan questions, more to himself than me.

Placing my palm in Logan's, I project calm into his mind, and call for the strategic, deadly warrior. Pure instinct tells me Dimitri can't hear Logan and I's discussions. Is it a mate thing, or the fact I'm his flesh and blood? I not sure which. Maybe both. I just know he can't.

'*Let nothing Dimitri or I say in the next few minutes rile you, Logan. I require the deadly calm of my warrior.*'

He needs to get it because I'm about to hurl things back at Dimitri that will anger and hurt him. Logan needs to find the strength to block it out and stay the course. His gaze flicks to mine with hypnotic intensity. Heated and impassioned, the green eyes gleam with the effort to contain his fury.

He bows his head and whispers. '*I understand why I put my whole existence at risk. Why you suffered so markedly. It was to get to this moment. I will stand firm. Always.*'

His words warm my heart and I squeeze his hand just as a powerful force slams against my mental barriers with a swiftness that paralyzes me. Good God, I've never experienced such immense strength before. It's all I can do to keep my walls from crumbling into dust while still managing an outward calm.

"You will fail tonight, Dimitri."

Logan's low, forceful voice booms around the clearing, producing a ripple of fear among the vampire and fae warriors behind my father. Logan's savagery and prowess on the battlefield are legendary. Their fear is justified. Dimitri ignores him, his scowling stare never leaving mine.

"Truly extraordinary, my dear. Your psychological shields are strong." Then, like a switch flipped, his frown vanishes, and he's back to enjoying his mind games, which, I recall from experience are where his talents lie. Never lifting his mischievous regard from mine, Dimitri points at Lucretia and panic flutters from her. "In case you were not aware, my child, this rare delicacy is Lucretia, Logan's new bride." The grin is pure evil.

Oh, my God. Now I want to throw my head back and do a Vincent Price laugh. The great and mighty vampire king has no fucking clue I already know? That just made my night.

When he doesn't get the reaction he was hoping for, he continues, "She is a vicious warrior that one, with so many secrets it boggles the mind, but I must admit, she tastes heavenly. As a matter of fact, Logan and I enjoyed her just last evening. Is that not right, Logan?"

Truth. Before I can stop it, a rough growl rumbles from my chest. Logan drank from her? Damn it. Guess I better take my own advice and not let Dimitri's remarks upset me. I picture Lu in an intimate embrace with my Logan, his fangs sunk deep into the flesh at her neck. It burns through me like acid. I want nothing more than to trace to my father, hack his heart from his rib cage and crush it beneath my boot.

I can't. I'm not in any hurry to die. Instead, I force the jealousy into a colorfully wrapped gift box in my mind, to open at another time. If I have to listen to him blathering on for one more second, I'll go psychotic. Let's bring this little game back full circle, shall we?

As much as it mortifies me to air my dirty secrets in front of my friends, and the hundreds of warriors surrounding this clearing, everyone here needs to learn what a sick, vile creature my father is.

If they understood the depths of his depravity, maybe they'll think twice before fighting to the death for him.

"Since it's slipped your mind, *father*," I sneer the repulsive title and step forward. My fingers slip from Logan's. "Let me remind you how many times you tortured and raped your own child." The shock and outrage from the crowd slam into me with such pressure I almost stumble as I edge forward even more. "Ten times you brutalized and molested me." The calm in my voice projects none of the turmoil within from the memories my words bring forward.

"Christ." Logan's painful whisper fills my ears, just as Kurtis's low, menacing growl vibrates the ground. And again, Lu's panic and guilt.

Finished with this reliving-the-past bullshit, I send Dimitri flying in the air with my mind, before slamming the bastard down with such force the ground trembles beneath my feet, and a small crater forms where he strikes. Before he can conceal it, shock fills his expression at my display of speed and strength. Dimitri's never come against anyone whose powers rival his own, and he's shaken by it.

And just like that, all hell breaks loose, and the battle of a lifetime ensues.

Chapter 41

Nicole

With a sharp flick of his wrist, the horde of vampire Guardians behind my father traces forward, engaging the warriors who surged to intercept them.

With my heart in my throat, I stare in sheer astonishment as Jimmy moves with lightning speed and fangs bared. The wolf within alters his build, making him taller, more muscular. Claws extend from his fingertips, slashing and ripping through his enemies with the fatal precision of a sword, but he doesn't fully shift; he remains in human form.

Next to him, King Ruse's body contorts and pops as he shifts into an enormous, deadly looking lion. The shifters around him absorb the impact of his transformation. He lunges with a mighty roar and engages the Dark Fae King who dive-bombs him from the sky. Arra does an impressive spin and leap, decapitates a winged fae midair, before rushing to protect Cipher's six while he battles Syn.

The rest of the werewolves, valkyrie, and shapeshifters surge forward when their leaders engage. Logan, Sebastian, and Lu battle the fae, and their own kind, as they advance to get to King Grayflame.

The eerie sounds of battle surround me on all sides— screams of pain, the clashing of swords, inhuman growls, and piercing shrieks. Lightning streaks across the sky with the unnatural absence of thunder.

The heady aroma of blood fills my nostrils as I hold my ground against vampire and fae. Where is dear old dad and why hasn't he attacked me yet? Knowing him, he's biding his time, watching for the precise moment to take me by surprise.

Not wishing to showcase all my abilities, I battle with my small sword and fists like never before. I cleave heads from bodies, rip wings from backs with just a thought. With swift agility, I let loose my rage and aggression on Dimitri's Guardians, killing dozens in a matter of minutes.

Fifty feet to my left, Logan battles four Guardians with his impressive swords. In no time, his chest is gleaming with vampire blood as he swings and twirls with lightning speed. He severs limbs with a flick of his wrist, cuts vampires in half with a swing of his arm and removes heads with a scissor-like motion of his swords. But as soon as he's killed one, two more emerge to take their place. The same is happening with Sebastian and Lu.

Alex, Kurtis, and Liam cover my back, attacking all who dare to sneak up on me.

Besides the initial surge, the fae are avoiding engaging in battle with the vampires directly. Instead, they target the werewolves and shifters.

The small but stealthy valkyries spin, duck and twirl into the fray with their daggers and swords with such speed, you don't even see them coming until it's too late.

I hunt through the chaos again for my father. He's just playing with us. He enjoys watching the battle, only allowing Guardians to enter the fight when one is slain. How many does he hold in the wings, just waiting their turn to kill everyone I care for?

"Nicki, look out!" Kurtis bellows as he body-slams a gigantic black Guardian creeping up behind me.

Kurtis is no match for a Guardian. "Kurtis don't!" But my warning chokes off. In total shock, not trusting my own eyes, I watch Kurtis change from the big, muscled soldier I know and love into... Loki?

Holy mother of God. Kurtis is Loki. I stand there in utter confusion and gawk as Loki/Kurtis sinks his massive canines into the vampire's neck and rip the head clean off with a deep guttural snarl.

Do you know how many times I've given that dog a belly rub?
Son of a bitch.

With a mental shake, I push my shock and dismay aside for the moment and plunge back into the fray. I give Georgie full reign. A fae head explodes all over me when I empty a magazine into it. Before I realize it, my tongue slides out and licks the blood from my lips.

Yum, magical blood. Of course, it does nothing to nourish or fortify my energy. Only Logan's blood does that.

With a swift flick, I eject the spent magazine and jam in a new one like Kurtis—the gigantic malamute —taught me. With a snort, I ascend to the sky to intercept three fae midair, before peering down. I take in the battle waging below and my heart plummets.

Logan's making quick work of the dark fae, while Sebastian and Lu fight numerous Guardians at once; they just keep popping up, even with Liam, Kurtis, and Alex helping to slow them down. Dread eats at my insides. We are severely outnumbered, and if I don't do something quick, the deaths of everyone I care about will be on my hands.

Just as the idea traipses through my head, my focus zeroes in on my father. Suspended high in the air, the last of the three fae spiral in a death roll to the ground. Dimitri strides over to Jimmy with a velocity that's hard to track. Before I can even shout a warning, Dimitri plunges his fist into Jimmy's chest and yanks out his heart. Shock fills Jimmy's expression as he stares at his pumping organ in Dimitri's blood-soaked hand.

"NOOOOO!" I wail.

Jimmy glances up, his eyes fill with sorrow before his body collapses on the grass with a dull thud. Blood flows from the gaping hole in his chest and soaks the ground around him.

In a massive explosion of white light, Liam shifts into his giant wolf and charges Dimitri with a deep, mournful howl. Four

Guardians intervene and batter him to the ground several feet away, but not before he tidily decapitates one. The echo of Liam's bones cracking reverberates throughout the clearing, but it's the sharp dog-like cry that pierces my heart.

In a blink, I've traced to Dimitri. Fire shoots from my fingertips, engulfing my father. I peer down at Jimmy's lifeless body, his warm brown eyes open wide, the shock forever frozen on his face. The large hole in his chest still oozes blood. Tears blur my vision and my heart cracks.

"You killed him! You fucking bastard." My cry is a mere whisper, saturated with anguish as I war against the hysteria threatening to engulf me.

Dimitri laughs, consumed in flames. "Ooohhhh, this is getting good." A quick flick of his wrist and the fire extinguishes.

Alex's gentle sobbing fills my ears as she covers Jimmy's body with her own, but I never take my eyes from the crazed scrutiny of my father.

Just as I'm about to leap at Dimitri, rip his head from his body and damn the consequences, the peculiar, blue-tattooed Oracle materializes before us. With a wave of his hand, he suspends the battle raging around us in an instant.

I gape around the clearing in disbelief. Icarus just froze in place dozens of warriors immersed in battle. Some in the air, mid- dive bomb, their features contorted in rage. Others with swords thrust in their enemy's bodies, or severed limbs hovering suspended in the air. Several shifters were caught mid-change in a grotesque display of magic. Half-human, half-altered into their animal of choice. It's like looking at a wax museum of every nightmare you could imagine.

Only Icarus, Logan and I move about freely. Logan traces to my side and we both inspect the priest with dread. I glance up at my father; his eyes blink. So he's aware but unable to move. He watches us with rage and hatred, and I have this insane urge to stick my tongue out at him.

"Where are the shackles, Icarus?" Logan demands, unfazed the little priest froze time.

Icarus eyes Jimmy's body with sorrow. Had he predicted Jimmy's death? Why didn't he say anything? I could have stopped it.

When he adds no more, I growl at him. "Spit it out, Icarus."

"Yes, my lady." He nods before the turquoise of his eyes take over the sockets completely, moving and swirling like a turbulent ocean. The cobalt tattoos on his face and body pulse and glow.

"The mystical shackles will fail."

"Goddammit!"

Logan's bellow mimics my sentiments as shock and anger ripple through me. This can't be. There must be a way to defeat him.

"Well, this just gets better and better." I peer at my father. His black eyes narrow in anger. "It appears we are at an impasse, father. I can't kill or capture you." Dimitri offers a slight lift of his eyebrow in response. "What the fuck do we do now, Icarus?"

"You must let him go."

My stunned gaze swings back to him. Is he serious? My left eye starts twitching. "Obviously, I'm not going to let him go. So how the hell do we imprison this ancient vampire?"

"I cannot say, my lady."

The non-answer ramps up my anger. My jaw aches from clenching it so tightly, and the harsh blaze from my eyes reflect in the deep blue of Icarus's. This little freak is pissing me off. He can't or won't say? Did he predict the outcome of this battle and refuses to tell us?

Icarus walks forward and lays an ice-cold palm on my cheek. In an instant my anger vanishes. The power flowing from him sinks deep into my bones. This dainty looking priest contains so much magic it's staggering. If he wanted to, he could kill me with a mere thought.

'You know what to do, my Queen,' he whispers sadly in my mind. *'Your destiny is to defeat him. Dimitri's destiny is to perish. Your mate's destiny will be revealed when yours is finished. You will know what to do, and I will be here to help implement it.'*

And with that, he disappears. But before Icarus's image dissipates completely, he imprints a vision of my future. I inhale sharply as I foresee my death.

I glance up into the eyes of my father's suspicious sneer as comprehension zings through me. I finally understand my role in this fucked up world, the conclusion to this battle, and final justice for all I've suffered.

If my destiny is to defeat Dimitri, and the only way to do that is by ending my life, it's what I must do. He will not walk away from this clearing. Will not live another day. But it won't be quick. I'll make him suffer.

"What did Icarus say to you, my love?" Logan asks.

Turning my back on my father, I step into the warmth of my mate. Icarus gave me a moment to say goodbye by keeping time frozen.

Logan sheaths his sword and encloses me in his embrace. I lower my lids and relax into him, not even caring we are both covered in blood.

Our lack of time together breaks my heart. My stubborn pride kept us apart. If I could go back in time, I would surrender to him that first night and every night thereafter.

"Baby, what did he say?" Logan asks, concern creeping into his voice.

"It does not matter." With a heavy sigh, I tilt my head and peer into the green depths of my mate. "We have but a few moments before... before the surrounding chaos begins again." I raise blood-soaked fingers and cradle his face. "I love you, Logan. Always have and I always will, for all eternity. No matter the outcome of this battle, I submit myself to you. Mind and body."

"Nicole," he whispers in awe before his lips claim mine, and lifts me from the ground, crushing me to his chest. He devours my mouth in a kiss that leaves me shaking and craving more, but the consequence of what I must do crushes my heart. Logan will suffer.

My death could destroy him.

Icarus said Logan's destiny will be revealed when mine is finished. That means Logan will become king of the vampires and lead his people to peace. As it should be.

With reluctance, I ease back and gaze into the magnificent eyes of my first and only love. I lick his flavor from my lips and savor it for the last time.

Chapter 42

"What is the plan, my love?" Logan asks.

Instead of answering, I step back, and time rushes forward with a swiftness that steals my breath, leaving me dizzy. Everything was at an absolute standstill, no breeze, no sounds, no movement. Then bam, we're back.

Before I can regain my equilibrium, Dimitri has Logan by the throat, and lifts him above his head as if he weighs nothing. When the other hand hovers near his heart, braced to snatch it, everything inside me freezes.

Dimitri whines with annoyance. "As much as I have enjoyed this little drama, it is starting to bore me. Come here, my dear. Step into my embrace or the deaths of everyone here will be on your conscience, starting with your mate, and you will be mine anyhow." Thin nostrils flare with his displeasure. The hand ready to end my mate's life, the one covered in Jimmy's blood, reaches out and beckons me to him.

"Nicki!" Kurtis bellows from my left. He's back in human form, naked and bleeding profusely from several nasty, gaping wounds slashed across his chest. A rib bone protrudes from his torso. His intent is written all over his face; in the severity of the blue eyes that meet mine. Kurtis will fight to the death. They will all fight to the death. Just like Jimmy. I can't allow that. I refuse to let anyone else die because of me.

"No more."

'Sebastian, you and Lu trace my friends to the safety of the castle when I give the signal. Logan will meet you there shortly.'

"No, my lady." Shock and anger cover his bloodstained face. With a gradual shift, I pin Bastian with a fierce glare. "Do as I command, Sebastian Roman Moretti."

With a sharp inhale, he lurches back a step as in a split second I hit him with all Icarus revealed. Understanding dawns, and he glances at Logan with hopelessness and apprehension.

'Get him through this, Bastian. Help him be the king I know he is.'

When his gaze lands on mine once more, they are filled with respect and sorrow. A solemn nod. "Yes, my lady."

'Nicole? What are you plotting?' Panic enters Logan's tone as he struggles in Dimitri's hold.

'The only card left in the deck, my love.'

I turn to Dimitri once more. "Face me in battle, father. Mano e mano. You enjoy hurting me? This is your one and only chance." With the strength of my mind, I pry Dimitri's fingers from Logan's throat. No sooner does he drop to the ground then four Guardians are upon him in a heartbeat, subduing him. "We fight until one of us can fight no more. We may not be able to slaughter each other, but I sure would love the opportunity to give you a taste of your own medicine. No one interferes. Just you, and me."

"I am intrigued." An evil smile lifts his lips before he licks Jimmy's blood from his fingers one by one. "What are the stakes?"

Okay Nicole. Time for your famous poker face. "If I'm the last one standing, you will surrender. Never set foot in the United States or Canada again. You will be stripped of your crown and excommunicated from the Council of Unity. You must sign over every share and holding you possess here. I will be crowned the queen of vampires and assume your seat at the council."

"Hmmm. And if I win?" Dimitri asks in a flat nasal tone.

"Nothing changes. You keep your crown, your holdings, and the seat for another three hundred years." I recognize what he's after, but

I'm hoping his continued reign will be incentive enough. Not that it matters, we will both be dead soon enough.

A gasp of shock and outrage thickens the surrounding air. Prophesied to be the long-awaited hope for these people, the destined child who destroys Dimitri and brings peace, is bargaining it all away.

"I agree on the stipulation that if I prevail, you submit to me, to do with as I please during my entire reign." The bastard counters back with what I figured he would.

'*Do not do this, Nicole. We will find another way, goddammit.*'

Dimitri's vampires struggle to hold Logan still as I step close. The blinding glower stays locked on his king, his growl so deafening the sound vibrates against my entire frame. I'm not one hundred percent certain how to deal with this situation, but I will not let Logan sacrifice his life for mine.

I lay a palm on his bloodstained cheek. His eyes blaze as he growls continuously, his predator showing through, the fangs bared. The bone structure of his face is even more sharply defined, appearing more beautiful, and savage, at the same time.

'*It's the only course, my love. I don't wish to be in a world where you don't exist. I can survive anything as long as I know you live.*' Logan's growl continues a moment longer and at a rougher quality before his focus shifts to mine. The madness eases its influence at the power of my caress. Pain and anguish take its place. In a gentle voice, one you reserve for people going off the deep end, I say, '*Trust me, Logan.*'

Logan growls so powerfully the sound vibrates the ground. The Guardians tighten their hold. '*Hit him with everything you have. I will come for you, no matter what it takes. Just stay alive.*' The anxiety and panic in his voice breaks my heart, because staying alive is the last thing I plan to do. '*Vow it!*' he shouts in my mind, his eyes a fierce, dazzling green.

'*So little faith in me.*' I whisper sadly before dropping my hand. '*But for you, I vow it,*' I lie before hitting him with a dose of soothing magic to try to ease his mind.

The suffering and despair stamped on Logan's face are too much. I turn my back and focus on my father once more to renegotiate. "If you win, I will go with you, Dimitri. Endure whatever your sick, fucked up mind has in store for me." *Not.* "But only if you give up your throne and seat on the council to Logan." I counter back with my last bargaining chip. Myself.

Dimitri tilts his head, scans me up and down with those malevolent eyes. Bile rises in the back of my throat. "Why would I yield my throne and allow these traitors to live?"

In response, I raise the silver dagger clasped in my palm, and plant the tip on my chest. A little push and it pierces the skin and bone—protecting my heart. Dimitri's eyes swell with shock and fear. A roar erupts from Logan.

"Even you aren't quick enough to stop this blade from piercing my heart," I taunt, my glower laser-focused with suicidal intent on Dimitri. "You want me? Agree to my demands, or we both die. Right here, right now." A silver dagger through the heart and beheading are the only two ways to kill Dimitri or myself.

'*Nicole, what the fuck?*' Logan's voice slams into my brain as he renews his attempts to be free. '*This is you staying alive?*'

My friends and the remaining allies stand shocked into immobility. It comes down to this. Will Dimitri see through my plan? Will I kill myself to save my friends? My people? My mate?

Abso-fucking-lutely.

Chapter 43

The deadly intent in Nicole's eyes stops my heart cold. Her dark side emerges, the one that terrifies me more than the blade piercing her chest. Nicole declared she could not live in a world where I did not exist. Does she imagine I could? That I could rule without my mate? Without Nicole, I would surely go insane. Just as the king did after the death of his mate.

Dimitri eases his hands in the air, tension radiating from him, wise enough to recognize the gravity of the situation and the determination in Nicole's stare. "Easy, child."

Her gray eyes harden. "Icarus, if you please." The blade still protrudes from her chest. Her fist clenches around it, ready to slam it home.

Christ.

Icarus materializes next to Dimitri.

"The Oracle has organized two sets of documents. You are nothing if not predictable, Dimitri."

Son of a bitch. She prepared all this without my knowledge, and without including me?

"We will sign them and no matter the outcome, they are binding."

"Deal." Dimitri signs the document Icarus holds out at the same time Nicole signs the one Sebastian holds for her.

Before the pen leaves the paper, Dimitri is in front of Nicole, snatching the dagger from her chest.

"You will not need this." Dropping it to the ground, he seizes her, and wrenches her against his body with a hard jerk. Bile rises in my throat, burning my insides.

Blood drains from my face as the realization hits me right between the eyes with more accuracy and pain than a bullet ever could. I must watch my mate battle with Dimitri and suffer agony at his hands without being able to intervene.

When Dimitri's fist connects with Nicole's jaw, I roar with fury. How could she do this? She is no match for his years of control and fighting abilities. Nicole has been on this earth a mere quarter of a century. Dimitri holds a millennium of experience and skill.

Those left alive in the clearing move out into a wide circle to give the two powerful beings plenty of room to maneuver. Pride spikes through me when Nicole spins Dimitri around and delivers a brutal punch to his kidneys. He grunts, bends from the pain, but immediately recovers.

He spins, and kicks out with a mighty force, snapping Nicole's left arm in two. My beast thrashes around inside me. The need to protect and defend consumes me.

With her arm dangling at an odd angle, she picks Dimitri up with brute force and hurls him across the clearing. Blood erupts from his mouth when he crashes into a massive tree, snapping it in half. Fear smothers my insides like thick tar as Dimitri leaps to his feet and plucks a heavy broadsword from the ground. His prowess with a sword rivals my own.

Nicole traces to Sebastian, the bone in her arm already mended as she steals his sword before he can even offer it. She gives him a hasty nod before tracing back to Dimitri and blocking his next blow. They twirl and move with such velocity it becomes hard to track. My heart lodges somewhere in my gut, but my stare never leaves the battle.

'I am sorry, brother.'

The pain and grief in Bastian's voice penetrate my rage, and my gaze flickers to his. He is forcing a reluctant Alex and Liam into his embrace just as Lu gathers the wounded and angry Kurtis. Disbelief and anger register at the same time.

Sebastian is deserting us?

Before I can question him, they trace away. This must be Nicole's doing. Was this her plan all along? Engage Dimitri and give Bastian and Lu time to escape with her friends? Why would she do that? We need them to get her out of here.

Unless Nicole intended to never leave this clearing alive. My insides congeal with disbelief. Goddamn her. Rage and fear build once more and my focus swings back to my mate. Even amidst the haze of fury, I am in awe of her grace and precision on the battlefield. Her natural skill with a sword is astonishing; it's like an extension of her arm.

Dimitri's eyes narrow in concentration. He has to focus and exert himself in battle for the first time. Each clang of metal vibrates down to my soul, tearing me apart.

Dimitri's clothes are ripped and smeared with blood from the various strikes from Nicole's blade. A deep slash down his cheek mars the perfect skin he so admires. A feral snarl lifts my lips as I bask in his torment.

'More my love. Hurt him more.' The mental command is low and guttural, virtually unrecognizable as my beast demands retribution. It's unnecessary. No one yearns for my king to suffer more than Nicole.

"There is no escape from me, and soon I will bring you down with my sword." Dimitri pants between striking blows and evading blocks. "You will pay a hefty price with your flesh for hiding from me."

"Never!" Nicole shouts and plunges her sword into Dimitri's shoulder with a violent thrust.

That's my girl. Pride unfurls in my chest as she wears him down, cutting him open piece by piece, and glorying in it. The pure elation of her emotions heats me from the inside out.

Dimitri bellows with fury and rushes, but dips and weaves right before reaching her, slashing downward with his broadsword. Nicole parries with her small blade; sparks fly into the air. With a swift uppercut, the tip of her silver blade catches Dimitri below the chin.

Before he can counter, Nicole punches him with both fists in the solar plexus, knocking the wind out of him, stunning him for a moment. The quick blow opened Dimitri up for another attack and Nicole obliges him. A simple sidekick into his stomach doubles him over. She follows up with a vigorous rising uppercut.

The warriors left around the clearing give a mighty shout of triumph. I had forgotten they were there; I am so engrossed in the survival of my mate. She could do it. Nicole could beat Dimitri. Amazing. I understand the prophecy said she would, but I never imagined it would be in a one-on-one battle. Dimitri rebounds, coming at her once again, but something in Nicole's demeanor changes. Resignation and sadness fill her expression.

Fear seizes my lungs. What is she doing?

An eerie stillness settles over her. She waits until he is mere feet from her before raising her sword. But instead of pointing it at her father, she shoves the tip into her own flesh at her heart. Dimitri slams to a halt in a millisecond.

"No!" I redouble my efforts to escape my captors. The vampire within surges to the forefront in panic, the fear of losing its mate unthinkable.

"We had a deal, sweetheart," Dimitri pants, more fatigued than I have ever seen.

She shrugs. "I lied." She pushes the blade an inch farther. "Did you actually believe I would let you live after everything you did to me?"

Nicole's bright glowing eyes peer over at the warriors struggling to detain me. "When Dimitri is dead, you will release Logan."

"Yes," they acknowledge in unison as they fall prey to her powerful mind control.

"No! Do not do this, Nicole. Please." Terror takes over my mind. I cannot lose her. "We will find another way."

With no fear in her expression, she stares into mine. "This is my path, Logan."

Panicked, Dimitri lunges for the blade just as Nicole plunges the silver sword right through her heart. Dimitri gurgles a startled gasp before collapsing in a heap at Nicole's feet.

Agony. It infuses every nerve in my body, and I roar with it. The Guardians release me and disappear. I trace to her side, and gently catch her body before it hits the ground. Cradling Nicole in my arms, I sink to my knees.

No. No. No. This cannot be happening. She cannot die. Nicole is the bringer of peace and sunlight to my people. To me. The light in my darkness. The purpose of my life. Without her, I am just an empty shell, as dead as Dimitri lying next to us.

"My love."

In shock, my heart constricts. She is still alive. Barely, but alive. "Baby, do not leave me." Unchecked tears slide down my face and land on her cheeks. "I am nothing without you."

"You will be a great and mighty king, my love." Nicole's voice is so feeble that even with my vampire hearing I must lean closer. "Icarus said that your..." she stops as she chokes up blood, wheezing in a breath.

"Do not talk, baby. Reserve your strength." Reserve it for what? There is no coming back from this.

"Icarus said," she continues with an effort, stubborn to a fault. "My destiny was to destroy Dimitri, and your destiny would reveal itself when mine is finished." She wheezes several more times, and my heart shatters into a thousand pieces. "I've finished my destiny, Logan. Yours has just begun."

"No, baby." My lips tremble against hers. "My destiny is with you." When her lids flicker closed, I shake her, pleading. "Nicole, stay with me."

"Kiss me. Need your lips." Her voice is hardly a sigh, but I hear her last wish even over the madness and grief waging its own battle inside me, ripping me to shreds.

"I love you, Nicole," I breathe against her cold, trembling lips before claiming them in a tender kiss. Her soft mouth moves against mine for a moment, then stills.

With shaking fingers, I brush the blood-soaked hair from the beautiful, brave face of my mate. The gray emptiness of her stare produces a paralyzing fear. It coats the back of my throat. I kiss each eye closed.

How will I go on without my Nicole? Pain lances through me, igniting a terrible anguish that threatens to devour. Sorrow chokes the air from my lungs, stops my heart, and I sink my face in the silky fragrance of her hair. With her clutched to my chest, I sway forward and back. My anguish overtakes every motor function and brainwave. Silent tears run unchecked, soaking her face and hair.

In all my centuries, never have I suffered such agony and torment. It is a roaring inferno inside me, building and building until I cannot bear it in any longer.

I throw my head back and roar my misery to the heavens while clutching my dead mate to my chest.

Chapter 44

I have no idea how long I lay there in that clearing with Nicole in my arms. Long enough for Bastian to come searching for me, just as the first golden rays of dawn kissed the sky.

The moment he sought to take her, rage ignited in my belly. A fierce, menacing growl erupted and my fangs descended. Sebastian did not say a word. Instead, gathered us both in strong arms and traced us to the castle.

In the dining hall, a complete funeral procession is set up around the grand table. Rose petals and candles are arranged around the center, awaiting Nicole. Hundreds of vampires, werewolves, and valkyrie line the vast hall, their heads bowed in reverence to their fallen queen.

Not caring if they are suffering or sad, I stare at them dispassionately. I have nothing to give them. The heart that once beat for the beauty in my arms is withered and dead. Empty. The one light in the darkness gone. Snuffed out by her own hand.

"Logan?" Icarus comes forward when I refuse to move from the exact spot where Bastian traced us. "You must arrange the queen on the table."

"No," I growl and clutch her body closer, the hilt of the blade I could not bear to remove stabbing my rib cage. My voice is so hoarse from roaring my anguish to the stars and I do not recognize it as my own.

"Brother," Bastian whispers with a squeeze on my shoulder. "You must allow Icarus to help Nicole into the afterlife."

Pain tears through my soul at his comments and I want to rip his goddamn head off. When a small, delicate hand lands on my bicep, I whip my head in the owner's direction, baring my fangs.

"Please, Logan." Tears spill down Alex's face. "It's what she would want."

Those words penetrate the gray haze of grief, and I waver. If that is true, I have no alternative. I must honor my mate. But the prospect of giving up the precious bundle in my arms almost forces me to my knees.

With a terse nod, I grit my teeth against the pain and plant one foot in front of the other. Every eye follows our progression. Each step is pure agony. The closer I get, the more the impulse to trace her to my chambers and bar anyone from entering becomes overpowering.

I cannot do this. Give her up? How can they ask me to lay her upon that cold, hard table? To say goodbye. I would sooner cut off my own limb.

When my steps falter, Bastian and Alex urge me forward with guiding hands. Across the table, with an irritatingly serene regard, Icarus stands, his strange eyes filled with curiosity. Next to him, Kurtis's sorrow is etched all over his face as he battles to keep the tears in check. Arra clutches Cipher's hand with head bent, weeping softly.

I peer down the lengthy table. Jimmy's body is spread out on the other end. The mighty Werewolf King looks so silly among all those colorful blossoms and candles, but also peaceful.

One day the loss of my friend will strike hard, but there is no place in my heart to grieve him. Every spare inch is shrouded with the loss of my mate.

The slight weight of Nicole's small form in my arms is all I have left. I brush a soft kiss on top of her head and lavender hits my nostrils. My teeth clamp down against wave after wave of agony. Her soft tresses brush my arm with every step.

I am shattering into a million pieces that will never be whole again. What will happen when her weight is absent? When my arms are empty? Panic sets in and my head shakes at Icarus, refusing to let her go.

"My lord, you must relinquish her," Icarus advises calmly. "Trust in me."

"Trust you?" Anger flares. At last an outlet for these emotions. "*You* told Nicole to kill herself." My heated green glow lights up his odd face.

"It was her destiny."

The little priest is not even apologetic. Rage clouds my vision. If Nicole was not in my arms, I would not hesitate to draw my sword and sever his head from his body.

"When this is over, priest, I will kill you." The words alone are punishable by death. Oracles are divine to all Others. Why should I care? My reason for living lies dead in my arms.

"I doubt that, my lord." Icarus's blue eyes start to swirl and shine with power. "Set her body on the table if you please."

The immense magical energy crawls over my skin, compelling me to obey. Pain shoots through every tendon as I resist the pull with every ounce of strength left, but I am no match for the elemental force of the priest. With lurching and erratic movements, I am forced to comply.

When Nicole's body is enveloped by fragrant flowers and softly glowing candles, my limbs can carry me no more. Before I slump to the floor, Bastian shoves a chair under my backside, and I drop into it with a heavy thud.

Needing to touch her, even if she no longer feels it, I scoot closer and clasp Nicole's frigid hand in mine. How many times did I fail my mate? It was a miracle she did not despise me.

Silent tears slip down my cheeks as I gaze into the pale perfection of her face. Even in the stillness of death, Nicole is the most beautiful creature I have ever encountered. My abused heart splinters with so much grief, breathing becomes painful. Drawing closer, I wrap an arm around the top of her head, inhale through the blockage in my lungs, and press light kisses on her forehead, her eyebrows, eyelids, and cheeks, before finally brushing her lips with mine.

"My lord, it is time to remove the dagger from her heart," Icarus urges.

My eyes squeeze shut against his words. It will mark the end. Once I draw it from her heart, there is no turning back. She will be gone forever. But it is what I must do. Nicole would be horrified to learn it was lodged there for this long already.

Drawing a deep breath, I gulp back the insanity threatening to consume me, and let go of her hand to grip the hilt. As I attempt to lift it from her chest, Icarus places both his hands on mine, gripping the sword. I glance at him in confusion. The blue gleam of his tattoos pulse to life.

"From where I was, take I to return. Please take this soul and return it to the body that was once Nicole Tianna Giordano." Icarus's chant rings out with strength and authority. His hand crushes mine in a painful grip that penetrates the haze of grief.

What the hell is he doing?

"I will for these words to set her free. With the power of the ancestors and elements intertwined, return to us what was once ours. With the whisper of the wind, the roar of the flames, the crash of the waves. Allow these words and powers of the room intertwine, return this soul to that which was hers."

The dark magic swirling around the table causes the hair on the back of my neck to stand on end. I rise, eyes glued to the Oracle as he continues to chant the words repeatedly. Is this some spiritual burial rite I was unaware of? A human religious thing Icarus researched for Nicole? The atmosphere changes. The dark magic blankets the room.

An unholy power surges through me in an instant, my eyes shoot back to my hand, and dizziness takes hold. My vampire power prowls inside my body. Sweat beads on my skin as Icarus grabs hold of the power within me.

I grunt as a whirlwind of magic rips down my arm into the blade in Nicole's heart and I endeavor to remain upright. With a violent jerk, Icarus forces us to wrench the blade from her skin, and the wet sucking sound makes me cringe. Before I can blink, he has pierced the flesh of my wrist, opening my vein.

"What the fuck, Icarus," Sebastian bellows.

But the Oracle ignores him, never taking his swirling blue gaze from mine.

"What is this, priest?" I growl in confusion.

"It is time to fulfill your destiny, Logan. *You* are her lifeblood. Pour it into her heart, and she will live."

Gasps fill the room. Shock and elation soar through my soul.

Could it be true?

Not taking a second to contemplate it further, I grab the blade from Icarus and slice deeper through my wrist, hissing against the pain when it hits the bone. A river of blood flows free, and I hold it over the open wound in Nicole's chest.

Sebastian steps next to me. He bares his fangs at Icarus. "You better be right about this, priest, or I will kill you myself."

Never taking my scrutiny from Nicole, I ignore them. My sole focus is keeping my wound open and my blood flowing into her. Power churns in the air around us, enough to toss the flowers on the table into the air, and the candles to snuff out. Icarus continues his eerie chant.

After several minutes, my reasoning blurs. I grind my teeth and dig deep for every ounce of vampire strength to stay standing. Sparkles form in my vision, but I lock my knees and reopen my wrist, not even hesitating to give every last drop to get her back.

When my vision blackens at the corners, and dizziness threatens to topple me, Kurtis shoves the chair back under my legs, my ass landing hard on the seat.

"Don't you dare stop, vampire," Kurtis growls in my ear.

"I do not plan on it." I keep my arm steady over her chest as Icarus continues chanting in a language I have never heard before.

Just as I am close to passing out, the Oracle shoves my hand away and replaces it with his own. I am vaguely aware of Bastian sealing my wound with his blood, but I do not look away from the white glowing power of Icarus's palms as they hover over Nicole's chest, somehow sealing the wound like it never was.

Lu places her wrist to my lips. "Drink, Logan. You might need to give her more blood, and you need to replenish."

A low, feral growl erupts from Kurtis, and Lu and I glance at him in mild surprise.

"Leave, shifter, if you cannot handle this," Sebastian barks.

"Do it, Lucretia."

"I wasn't seeking your permission, shifter." Lu brings her wrist to my lips again, but her gaze remains glued to Kurtis.

I do not hesitate. I strike. Starved beyond anything before in my life. I drink, my gaze fastened on Nicole, watching for any small sign of life.

After a moment, my power is restored. I detach from Lu's wrist and stand over Nicole once more. Icarus stops his chant. The glow in his hands dissipates, and he backs away.

When there is no evidence of life, panic sets in. "What now, priest?"

"We wait, my lord."

Chapter 45

Nicole

I'm in Hell. Cold. Suffocating. Helpless. Weak.

Panic claws at me as I fight to get through this hellish imprisonment. Can't give up. Need to escape. But pain and weakness invade every bone and muscle in my body. Darkness envelops me, dragging me deeper and deeper. It wraps around me in a strangling grip.

I open my mouth to scream, but no sound emerges. Agony and terror enshroud my mind and soul. Exhausted, the yearning to just give up, to let the darkness take me, is compelling. It pounds away at me like a heavyweight boxer that lands blow after bone- crushing blow.

For a split second, Logan's presence pierces the blackness. His heat warms the cold stiffness from my icy bones. He eases the suffocating darkness in my lungs and infuses every weakened muscle with strength.

My back arches, I fight against the dark shackles, and gulp in a lungful of blessed oxygen filled with Logan's masculine scent. I need to get to him. His suffering seeps deep into my chest, crushing my damaged heart. I can't stand the torment; I must ease his pain and anguish.

Logan's my lifeline. My escape. Hell contains no hold as long as my glorious vampire stays with me. I thrust forward with all my might, choke for air, attack with teeth and claws against the suffocating imprisonment of this dark abyss.

My one thought: Logan.

"Nicole," the familiar voice calls. "Baby, come back to me." I'm trying, dammit, but I can't move no matter how strongly

I fight to be free.

'*Logan,*' my mind cries, hoping he hears me.

'*I am here, baby,*' he responds brokenly. '*Fight, Nicole. Come back to me.*'

Something inside me breaks. It is a real, physical pain causing me to cry out. A roar fills my ears, the heat, and pressure of the sound heavenly on my skin. With tremendous effort, I force my lids to open, but they only flicker before sealing shut again.

Dammit. You can do this, Nicole. Push through. Get to Logan.

A mental image of my mate forces me to push harder. If I could just gaze into his brilliant green eyes, it would give me the strength to fight, to escape this eternal darkness.

At last, the weight on my lids dissolves, and my eyes open to the beautiful face of my Logan. The mere sight of him clears the last of the darkness from my soul, and the green glow of his gaze surrounds me, filling me with its light and warmth.

"Baby. I thought I lost you." Logan's groan is laced with pain, and tears well in those brilliant eyes before slipping down his cheeks. Soft lips rain gentle kisses on my forehead, my nose, and both sides of my face.

"Never."

I attempt to move or sit up, but my body is numb and unresponsive. Maybe I just need a few minutes to recover. I was dead, after all. I gawk at my mate, note his haggard appearance— the dark circles under his eyes, the torment of my death still lingering in the green depths. I want to reach up and caress his face, reassure him through touch that I'm here and that nothing will ever keep us apart again.

"Logan, there is a certainty in us I've never experienced before. The mere notion of you brought me back. Your voice gave me strength. I will never leave you again, just as you will never leave me. Nothing and no one will come between us. Ever. Not even death itself."

"Nicole, you are my everything and if you had not come back, I would have followed you into the afterlife." His fingers brush the hair from my forehead. "I love you more than I could ever express."

Icarus interrupts. "She will need to feed again soon, my lord."

I turn my head to regard the weird little Oracle, and elation sears through me. I moved my head. Progress. But when my eyes land on that strange blue stare, resentment and anger poke their heads to the surface. This was his plan all along? To bring me back?

"Sure wish you would've clued me in on the final outcome, Icarus."

"Only so much one can reveal, my queen."

A non-answer and so typical. "What happened to Dimitri? Please tell me he is dead, Icarus?"

"Yes, my lady," he answers with a slight bow. "His body burned with the dawn."

The priest's words ease the tight bundle of muscles that's been lodged between my shoulder blades since I was thirteen years old. It's finally over. My father is dead. It's a strange sensation when the sole focus of all your anger is no longer relevant. I'm... free, for the first time in my life.

"Were there ever any shackles, Icarus?"

A small grimace, or maybe it's a smile, lifts the corners of his lips. "No, my lady. The mere idea of them served their purpose."

"Purpose?" Logan asks.

"To give you the courage to fight your father."

"That's where you're wrong, Icarus." He tilts his head and examines me more closely. "The mystical shackles didn't give me the courage to face my father. You did." His eyebrow arches. "Logan did. Alex, Kurtis, Liam, Jimmy. The people I love and care about brought me to that field."

"Nicole Tiana Giordano. The prophecy chose wisely," Icarus mummers.

"Care to explain how you brought me back? Not that I'm complaining."

"Only so much one can reveal, my lady."

Why do I have the impression I'm going to really hate that phrase? "Get me off this table, Logan." With a tired sigh, I dismiss the Oracle from my mind.

Without a word, Logan lifts me in his powerful embrace. Pinpricks of pain dance along my arms as I force them around his neck, but I glory in the ability to move, even if it's with discomfort. Anything to have the hardness of my mate in my arms once again.

When that blade pierced through my heart, it was with the certainty I'd never see him again, let alone experience the warmth of his embrace. Being able to bury my fingers in his satiny hair forces my eyes to close in amazement. I inhale his rich aroma deep into my lungs. No longer able to deny my desire for the silky softness of my mate, my lips brush along the corded muscles of his neck. He brings me closer with a low growl, and slides his cheek along mine.

"Logan?"

"Yes, baby?"

"You big stud. Take me to bed or lose me forever." I always wanted to use that line, just never had the opportunity.

Alex snickers behind me, and Sebastian laughs outright.

"Why would you say that?" Logan asks.

Shocked, I lean back and note the confused frown. Clearly, my man's never seen the movie *Top Gun*. I press my lips together to keep the sarcastic remark from bubbling to the surface. Since Sarcasm is my middle name, restraint isn't easy. Then I catch a glimpse of Jimmy's body lying on the other end of the table, and the smile fades.

"Jimmy." My heart constricts with grief. Until this moment, I'd forgotten what Dimitri had done.

"Take me to him, Logan."

Nodding, he turns and walks the length of the table to Jimmy's flower-enshrouded body. Instead of placing my feet on the floor so I can pay my respects, Logan sits in a chair, keeping us linked together, like he can't bear to let go for even a second.

The feeling is mutual. The need to caress and be stroked by him is all-consuming.

I stretch forward and place a gentle kiss on Jimmy's forehead, brushing my fingers through his thick hair.

"Is there anything we can do, Icarus?" I ask the Oracle without taking my focus from the face of the man who protected me with his life. The man who had shown me what a real father was. Loving, caring, and protective. Willing to sacrifice himself for the ones he loves.

"No, my lady. If there is no heart, there is no power."

Sorrow flows through my now-beating heart and I close my eyes against the pain. What I wouldn't give to go back in time and stop Dimitri from taking this beautiful man from us.

"Thank you for always looking out for me, Jimmy. For showing me what it means to have a family. You will forever live in my heart."

When Logan squeezes my thigh in comfort, I lean back and nestle into his arms once again. I must do what Jimmy advised me to do—forget the past, let it go, and look toward the future. Across the table, Liam stands stoically by his father's body, his usual humor gone.

"Liam." When the warm chocolate gaze lands on mine, his pain envelops me, and I grip Logan's hand to keep from crumbling to the floor. "Let us honor him by being the leaders he wanted us to be. Together with Kurtis and Alex, we must strive to lead our people to peace." I watch him as my words sink in, and hope they penetrate the grief blanketing him.

He stares at me for several long minutes. When Liam's eyes soften and the corner of his lips lift, I fight the urge to cry with relief.

"You know I will be a better leader than you, *Halfling*." A spark of humor dances in the eyes so like his father's.

"We shall see, asshat."

It still boggles my mind I am the queen of vampires. Liam now the werewolf king, and soon, Cipher and Arra will step down and hand the reins over to Kurtis and Alex. Our foursome will lead the Council of Unity, and lead our people to peace. Undo all the damage Dimitri caused. It will not be easy. Much heartache and strife are ahead. But we have each other.

"What happened to Syn and Jilaya?" I ask Sebastian when it hits me the council will only be four members. Plus Icarus.

"Not sure. They took off back to their strongholds."

"We will need to find them and bring them to justice, but their seats at the council must be filled." With a tired sigh, my head falls back onto Logan's shoulder.

"Yes, my love, but not tonight," Logan commands. "You need to rest."

"And to feed," I whisper. I lean in and lick his neck, need cramping my stomach.

Logan stands with a growl, knocking over the chair in his eagerness to get to his—our room. This castle is now my home. Our home.

"Wait." Logan stops and I peer over his shoulder. "Alex?"

"Yeah?"

"The cottage is now yours. My home is with Logan." His arms tighten around me.

Her eyes widen in shock, before laughing softly. "Sweet."

"And my first order as queen cannot wait. Please put me down, my love." Logan frowns but does as I request. I walk on sure legs over to the bitch. "In front of all these witnesses, I absolve the marriage of Logan and Lucretia." With a growl, my glower brightens as I glare at her. "If you ever touch my mate or feed him again, I will rip your heart out and consume it for breakfast. Are we clear?"

Logan's lips twitch in amusement.

Lu bows at the waist and a relieved smile graces her face. "Thank you, my queen. I understand."

This queenly stuff is a piece of cake.

I glance at Kurtis and he sighs with sadness. "Kurtis," I whisper, and he steps to me. "Thank you for always being my friend. You helped me through some very difficult times in my life and I will never forget it. If you ever need anything, I will always be here for you. I vow it."

Kurtis bows his head. "You have my undying loyalty forever, Nicki. I vow it."

"Are you quite done, my love?" Logan mocks with humor, coming to stand at my side.

"Careful, Alaric Logan Moretti or I will have you thrown into the dungeon." Mock severity laces my command, and he laughs. Happiness fills my heart at the glorious sound of my mate's laughter. We've not had many opportunities to laugh.

Yes, there are many trials and tribulations ahead of us, according to the prophecy. But right now, I want to bask in the love and happiness of my mate. Explore every inch of his magnificent body and let him bring mine to heights of ecstasy. Queen I may be, but I'm more than happy to let Logan rule over me in the bedroom.

He scoops me up in his arms once again as his long strides gobble up the distance. I don't even gaze around the vast castle. There will be plenty of time to explore later. I only have eyes for Logan and my insides clench anticipating his blood, and sex.

Once in his room, he places me on the edge of his massive bed and kneels to remove my boots. Our minds are in sync. Open. He will know when I want a soft caress or a firm grip. How I crave the fine line between pleasure and pain. He senses what I need even before I know myself.

"Logan." His love-filled regard rises to mine. "I want you to know I didn't fall in love with you." The fingers untying my laces hesitate and his brow furrows. "I walked into love with you with my eyes wide open. I believe in fate and destiny. Hell, my whole life is an ancient prophecy, but I also believe we're fated to do what we'd choose anyway. I chose you. In a hundred lifetimes, in any form of reality, heaven or hell, I'd find you, and I'd choose you, Logan."

Green eyes glow with emotion as he rises to his feet. With the tenderest of touches, he clasps my face between warm palms. His scrutiny travels over me like he's still trying to reassure himself I'm here.

"Baby, I have endured your pain. Stroked your soul. Experienced your dark side. Seen the secrets you kept buried. I want the parts you tried to throw away. The ones you were convinced I would never want." He brushes his lips against mine, and I groan at the contact. "You are mine and I will love and cherish every delectable, dark, and sinister part of you."

There are no words to describe how amazing it is to be caressed by a man who understands my mind, acknowledges all my flaws, but loves my soul.

"Now strip," Logan commands in that panty-wetting Dom voice. "I need to feed and fuck my queen."

"Yes, Sir."

THE END

Don't miss out!

Visit the website below and you can sign up to receive emails whenever A.R. Vagnetti publishes a new book. There's no charge and no obligation.

https://books2read.com/r/B-A-QAPM-QEEKB

Connecting independent readers to independent writers.

Also by A.R. Vagnetti

Storm Series
Forgotten Storm

Watch for more at https://www.arvagnetti.com.

About the Author

A.R. Vagnetti is an American writer who grew up in the scalding Tucson desert. Her debut novel, Forgotten Storm, is the first book in her Storm Series and won the Top 20 Best Indie Books of 2019. Forbidden Storm, book 2, won the Readers Favorite Five Star Award in 2020. She does her best writing while camping, traveling, and on the beautiful shores of Lake Huron where she is now blessed to spend her summers away from the Arizona heat. A.R. loves to transport readers into a fantastical world of paranormal romance where bold Alpha males will sacrifice anything for the strong, deeply scared, kickass females they love.

Read more at https://www.arvagnetti.com.

About the Publisher